Leila C

M000095723

Charcoal and Chalk
John Ogilvie and the Beginnings
of
Black Education in Texas

A bit of history
important
for you. Enjoy!

Flora Beach Burlingame

Charcoal and Chalk
John Ogilvie and the Beginnings of Black Education in Texas

by

Flora Beach Burlingame

Fireship Press
www.FireshipPress.com

CHARCOAL AND CHALK: John Ogilvie and the Beginnings of Black Education in Texas - Copyright © 2011 by Flora Beach Burlingame

All rights reserved. No part of this book may be used or reproduced by any means without the written permission of the publisher except in the case of brief quotation embodied in critical articles and reviews.

ISBN:978-1-61179-187-7
eBook ISBN: 978-1-61179-188-4

BISAC Subject Headings:
FIC014000 FICTION / Historical
FIC049040 FICTION / African American / Historical
HIS036130HISTORY / United States / State & Local / Southwest (AZ, NM, OK, TX)

Address all correspondence to:
Fireship Press, LLC
P.O. Box 68412
Tucson, AZ 85737
Or visit our website at:
www.FireshipPress.com

1.0

Acknowledgments

Without the following people, this book would never have happened:

First and foremost, a huge thanks to my husband, Arvin, for all the afternoons and evenings he spent alone while I toiled away in my "office"—a converted storage room off the garage.

Much credit goes to the patience and wise assistance of the Wednesday afternoon critique group and especially to our mentor, Elnora King, who has an acute sense of knowing what is right and what is wrong. Thanks, too, for my special group of friends who write for children and continued to support me while I took "time out" to write this book. They patiently wait for me to return to my stories in progress for a younger audience. One member, Evelyne Holingue, was a valuable resource for French words.

I'm indebted to Jo Olmstead of Scotland who instructed me in the use of certain expressions unique to her homeland.

This book would have been dumped long ago if it weren't for my son Glen Burlingame who kept the computer running. His wife, Lisa, an exceptional daughter-in-law, patiently read through the impossibly long first draft in spite of her too busy schedule.

And what would I have done without the wonderful staff at the Mariposa County Library? They cheerfully located any resource I requested, especially the thesis by Professor Barbara Hayward on *Winning the race: education of Texas freedmen immediately after the civil war.*

Thanks goes to Barbara Hayward, whom I later met in person at a Texas State Historical Association meeting and who thereafter provided me with additional information, including the fact that John Ogilvie Stevenson taught the freedmen longer than any other bureau teacher in Texas.

I was fortunate to have connected with researchers and Librarians at the Rosenberg Library in Galveston, in particular Casey Edward Greene, Head of Special Collections; Carol Woods, Archivist; and Jane Chapin, a private research specialist.

Dora Guerra, Librarian at the DRT Library at the Alamo, San Antonio, Texas, welcomed me like an old friend, and her enthusiasm for my research spurred me on. Also, Sheron Barnes, Special Collections Librarian, Victoria Regional History Center, Victoria College, Victoria, Texas, directed me to many valuable resources. Thank you, Ladies.

James W. Hosking of Watertown, Connecticut, great grandson of Sarah Barnes, helped me sort through truth and fiction in my great grandfather's vignettes of his relationship with Sarah.

George Fred Rhodes of the Calhoun Historical Commission took an entire afternoon of his time, describing the fascinating history of Port Lavaca and Indianola, Texas.

Idella Conwell of Dodge County Historical Society, Mantorville, Minnesota, got caught up in the intrigue of research and sent me a huge packet of information on Sam [Carl] Cranston and the now non-existent town of Rice Lake.

I owe special thanks to my brothers and Stevenson cousins who entrusted me with the precious family documents that inspired this story, and to Lesley Payne for her professional edit and assistance in reducing a 700 page manuscript to a more logical size.

And lastly, deep gratitude to Jan Holmes Frost and Tom Grundner of Fireship Press, who believed enough in this story to say *Yes*, and welcome me aboard.

Contents

The white man is not God's special pet. God cares as much for American charcoal as for American chalk; as much for Booker T. Washington as for Benjamin F. Tillman; as much for the humblest swamp Negro who can neither read nor write, as for Rev. Dixon who can write *The Clansman,* or *The Leopard's Spots.*

John Ogilvie Stevenson
(1841-1912)

If I rise on the wings of the dawn,
if I settle on the far side of the sea, even there
your hand will guide me, and your
right hand will hold me fast.

Psalm 139: 9-10

Chapter 1

April, 1867, Lavaca, Texas

John Ogilvie flattened himself against the rough siding of the waterfront shed and willed his labored breath to hush. Coming to this small port town suddenly seemed a big mistake.

A voice, thick with whiskey, penetrated the darkness only feet away from his hiding place, calling out to an approaching figure. "You there! Ya'll seen that meddlin' Yankee teacher? We got a present for him." Muffled laughter followed.

A rope cracked in the crisp night air. John could almost feel it wrap around his neck, strangle his last breath. The words of his landlord, Pierre Duval, earlier that day throbbed in his head. *"Did you hear? A teacher of the freedmen in northern Texas was beaten near to death and his schoolhouse burned to ashes."*

John tried to swallow, but no spit came. His biceps flexed, and without thinking he raised his fists, ready to fight. For a moment he was a young lad in Scotland again—daring Cameron MacLeod to punch him one more time, blood running from his nose, seeping between his lips, tasting of copper and dirt, and praying to God Almighty the punch wouldn't come. "Hey, goody goody preacher's boy," MacLeod had mocked, "are ye scared?" John *had* been scared, and he had run.

But tonight he wasn't running. These weren't youngsters taunting him. They were grown men, angry and drunk, wanting to hang him. One sound and he was a dead man for sure. Fear coursed through him, centering his mind on one thought—he must leave Texas. All his Scots-Presbyterian upbringing and education wasn't worth a halfpenny if he ended up twisting in the wind from a tree branch. Tomorrow he would leave on the first lighter out of Lavaca and seek a safer missionary calling. One up north where the pay was more reliable and he could put some away for his own higher education, his American dream.

Laughter crackled through the darkness—hilarity, devoid of humor.

"Speak up, man. You seen that there Mr. Ogilvie?"

"Now you men don't mean no harm, do you?"

"Jest want to teach the teacher hisself a little lesson. We don't need no northern carpetbaggers here teachin' our niggers."

The laughter ripped into John like a serrated knife.

"Nope. Cain't say I seen him tonight, though he does often walk the shore in the evening."

John didn't recognize the voice, but he was learning an affable face often masked a contrary spirit. He preferred those who outright objected to his teaching the freedmen. Not that he cared much for them either, but at least he knew where they stood.

"Shucks. Guess there won't be no fun tonight."

Others mumbled in disappointment as the group disbanded and men moved off in different directions.

When only the soft lapping of the bay water against the shore met his ears, John eased away from the building and worked his way across the sand toward the house in town where he rented a room. He stopped now and then to look behind him. Gradually his pulse rate slowed.

Pale criss-cross patterns of light slanted outward from the windows of shacks along the water—homes where the colored folk lived. The flickering candles helped show John the way as he sought the path leading up the bluff toward town and to the safety of home.

Suddenly, a figure leaped into sight no more than six feet away. John's knees jellied and his breath caught in his throat.

"Is that you, teacha?"

John almost choked with relief. "Aye, Jeremy, 'tis me. You gave me a start."

"I knows you walk out here after class, and I come to tell you I kin do it." Excitement jangled in the boy's voice.

"Do it?" John's fright had clogged his mind.

"The letters, suh. I know I kin tell you next class time, but this heah is Friday, and I'd have to wait clear 'til Monday."

"Of course," John said, still sorting through the information.

2

To the rhythm of soft ripples of bay water, Jeremy recited the alphabet. "*A, B, C, D, E, F, G* ..." With each letter the pitch of his voice rose. By the time he reached K his toe was tapping. At Q his hands clapped to the beat, and the finale, *X,Y,Z*, segued into a dance. The moonless night could not hide the obvious joy he'd found in his newly acquired knowledge.

John clapped along with him. "Praise be to God! And this is just the beginning, laddie. There is so much more to learn."

"I be there, teacha. I be there on Monday."

John pulled out a handkerchief, blew his nose, and wiped away tears. A definite cadence rocked his steps as he concentrated on Monday's lesson for Jeremy and his classmates. Any notion of catching a boat in the morning was lost in the thrill of witnessing one youngster dance to the alphabet in the dark of night.

Chapter 2

On Monday, after prayers and soul searching, but mainly because of Jeremy's unbridled pride, school began as usual in the drafty upstairs room of the warehouse.

When John first arrived in Lavaca, up a bay from the Gulf of Mexico, he hadn't felt threatened. This wee port town with its wide, dusty main street and board walks held the friendly feel of similar towns in America. His French landlords, Pierre and Evelyne Duval and their two children, had opened their home to him. Braman and Company willingly rented a space for a school room in an empty warehouse below the bluff along the shore, and a Yankee merchant by the name of Johnson helped him put together benches from leftover planks and crates.

Aye, there had been some grumblings about his purpose here, and Lieutenant Mitchel, the agent he reported to for the Freedmen's Bureau in Indianola fifteen miles distant, had suggested he buy a gun for protection. John refused to do that. He had his faith in God to give him strength for whatever lay ahead, and he most certainly was not going to hide behind a revolver.

***

The wind blew constantly through a broken window pane in the old warehouse, the splintery floor slanted, and teaching supplies were nonexistent. During the first week after his arrival, and before the official commencement of classes, John had tacked the sides of packing crates to the walls in lieu of chalkboards, on which he printed, in charcoal, the alphabet and primary numbers. Twenty smaller boards served as slates. Another crate, to be John's temporary desk, sat at the front of the room. On it he placed pen and paper, for his own use to write the names of the pupils, and a brass bell with a wooden handle—a parting gift from the Cranstons, Lucy's idea.

Ah, sweet Lucy. Before John left Rice Lake, Minnesota and headed for Texas, he had had a discussion with Lucy's father.

"Have you ever even seen a Negro, John?" Carl Cranston had asked.

John was taken aback by this question from Cranston, a farmer for whom he pitched hay and otherwise helped out around the place. They stood in the shade of a large elm, the scent of mown hay hanging in the late summer air.

"Aye, sir, I have." John felt his cheeks grow warm, irritated that his recent decision was being challenged. He reached up, tugged a leaf from a low branch, and crumpled it in his fingers. "Several coloreds were employed at the hotel in Canada where I stayed when I first came from Scotland."

"Ah, and did you actually talk with them, become acquainted on a first-name basis?"

Lucy had crossed the yard from the farmhouse porch and stood listening to the conversation. "Father, John feels good about this. Don't ruin it." She was near John's own age of twenty-four, though she looked younger when she worked up a temper. Now she all but stomped her foot, and John wasn't sure whether it was the heat from the sun or her emotions that brought such high color to her cheeks.

"That's not my intention," her father said, "but he needs to think things through first. This is not only a serious decision, it could be dangerous."

"Dangerous?" Lucy's voice rose. "I can't imagine that freed slaves who want an education could possibly be dangerous." Her brown curls shook as she glanced at John, then back to her father.

John had heard these warnings before, and from a more reliable source. The words of the Reverend George Whipple of the American Missionary Association rang in his ears above the ongoing argument between father and daughter:

"It is a noble calling, son, yet you need to be on your guard. There are folks who won't want you there."

The Reverend hadn't minced words when he preached at the little church in town only days ago, recruiting teachers.

Drawn back into the immediate conversation, John turned to Lucy. "Aye, your father's right. There is a wee bit of danger, though not from the pupils. Some Southerners object strongly to the Freedmen's Bureau opening schools for former slaves."

"Everyone's entitled to an education. No one has a right to object to another's wish to learn." Lucy folded her arms in defiance, and a breeze rustled the elm as in agreement.

Her reaction didn't surprise John—Lucy had been scoffed at herself for studying to become a doctor. Like Lucy, John felt ready for a challenge. In the two years since his arrival in America he had not only farmed but taught at a one room school nearby. He found he had a knack and fondness for teaching, and there were folks in the south hungering to read and write. Defending his scholars would be part of his job, and as a God-fearing Scots Presbyterian, he could certainly stand up to a few southern dissidents.

***

On the day classes began, John arrived two hours early, hopeful that at least twenty pupils would come. A tight feeling in his stomach spread to every muscle until he felt like dry kindling ready to ignite.

Then footsteps sounded on the stairs, and a black curly head peered around the open door. "This heah be the school place?"

"Aye. Yes. Do come in and take a seat, lassie." John motioned to the planks.

A girl about twelve eased into the building. Two followed her, a young woman perhaps in her twenties holding the hand of a small boy, and then several more wide-eyed children. For the next half-hour they came, wedging together on the makeshift benches.

As John greeted each new face, his tension eased. The pupils, well scrubbed and dressed in what John guessed to be their best clothing, though patched and worn, ranged in age from a boy of about four to Mrs. Wallace, a middle-aged woman. They represented skin color from the blackest black to white and every hue in between, including the browns of Mexico. John had not expected this mixture, although it should not have surprised him. The Freedmen's Bureau, after all, was established to protect and provide for the needs of not only former slaves, but for any refugees of the war.

A hush filled the room, gazes settled upon John, and he addressed the class for the first time. Forty-five bodies crowded onto the benches. With hands clasped behind him, he struck a stance to appear scholarly and self-assured, trembling fingers concealed. The commitment to teach this unexpected throng

7

suddenly overwhelmed him. Still, there was nothing to do but forge ahead.

He picked up the bell and rang it for attention. After introducing himself and stating a few rules of deportment, the lessons began.

John pointed out the letters on the board nailed to the wall. "Words are made up of a combination of these symbols. By the end of the week each of you will know how to read and write your own name."

An immediate hum of excitement spread through the room as John pronounced each letter.

"Now comes the fun part," he said. "One at a time, I will ask your name and we will put together the letters that spell it." He motioned to a girl of about eight sitting in the front row. "You get to be first, lassie. What is your name?"

"Patsy Harper," she said with an embarrassed giggle.

John first wrote it on a sheet of paper to keep an account for himself, then lifted a board from his stack of twenty and inscribed *PATSY* across the surface. Holding it up for all to see, he said the name of each letter before handing it to the girl. "As soon as we get real slates, you can practice making the letters yourself."

Patsy fingered the board with awe, tracing the pieces of her name, dark eyes glowing. Classmates crowded around, touching her treasure.

"Let me see!"

"Me next!"

"No, me!"

The enthusiasm grew louder. John felt the excitement and reveled in it, almost forgetting it was his job to control the class. Once again he ran Lucy's bell. "Everyone will have a turn," he said. "But we must keep quiet."

Still, as the lettering was done for each pupil, the commotion erupted again. Finally, when no more boards remained, John dismissed the class, though it was only noon. "Tomorrow bring a lunch and plan to stay longer. Our regular hours will be nine until two."

He needed the extra time to make more name plates, both for the day class and the evening session—the latter arranged to accommodate pupils, mostly men, who labored all day. John lunched on a thick slice of bread and slab of cheese washed down by strong coffee as he worked. By the time he had cut thirty more name plates a blister throbbed on his right thumb and daylight had softened into dusk.

He flexed his hands and pulled a watch from his pocket to check the time—twenty-five to five. The evening pupils were due to arrive at five. He lit two lamps and waited. In spite of the successful daytime session, a feeling of inadequacy grew in him once again.

Standing at the top of the stairs, John breathed in large gulps of the cool night air. Shadowy figures moved through the street and gathered near the building. In single file they climbed the steps. John retreated into the room—his pulse beating double-time. Twelve men filed in and seated themselves on the benches. Homespun shirts bore stains of sweat and dirt, and though weariness etched each face, the glow of hope was unmistakable.

A tall, muscular man, who had given his name as Samuel, stood. "Teacha, Mr. Ogilvie, suh, we all have come for some learnin'."

"Yea, suh," another voice said. The same response echoed throughout the classroom.

Breathing easier, John smiled at this tough looking assembly, so childlike in their eagerness for an education. In spite of his earlier fears, he thought, *This might be my favorite class.* He did not need to ring the bell for attention with this group.

"Good," he said. "Very good. First you will each learn to spell your name."

***

By the end of the initial week, seventy-one enthusiastic day and evening scholars crowded onto the benches at the freedmen's school. A routine settled in, and as the days swept by, John tried to push the terrifying moments on the wharf that first Friday evening to the back of his thoughts. Classes continued without incident, yet he was ever mindful that a certain element in Lavaca objected to his presence.

He had other concerns, one being the lack of teaching supplies. He constantly wrote to both the missionary association and the bureau ... *please send slates and primers.* In the meantime, he continued to learn more and more about his peculiar mix of pupils. It wasn't long before certain ones wiggled their way into his heart. There was Jeremy, so eager to learn; and little Ezra, whose feet hardly touched the floor when he sat on the plank bench;

Pablo, a shy Mexican lad of about twelve years of age; and, surprisingly, two little white girls, twins, Ophelia and Melinda Houcks.

John felt especially drawn to black, woolly-haired Patsy Harper, who had announced the first day of school, "My mammy say if I get enough learnin' I can be a teacha, too."

He met such confidence with contradicting emotions: joy and terror. He was thrilled to have determined and motivated pupils, yet moments of inadequacy plagued him. *I mustn't fail, or it will mean failure for Patsy and her classmates, and their high and mighty dreams.*

But it wasn't just the younger ones that spurred him on. Each day Mrs. Wallace, his oldest daytime pupil, became more of an assistant, almost motherly in her attitude toward John. "Ah jes' don' see how come that bureau don' git you mo' hep," she would sputter. "Lawd knows one man cain't nevah teach seventy students by hisself." She'd click her tongue and huff in loyal dismay.

Certain men in the evening class stood out. Quiet Jeb walked several miles to class after wrangling all day on a cattle ranch; slow to catch on, his determination to learn at times seemed almost desperate. Samuel Canfield continued to be a leader. He worked as a blacksmith in town, arrived early and left late, helping John any way he could.

"You learn your lessons well, Samuel," John told him early on, "and you obviously knew your numbers and letters before coming to my school."

"Yes, suh. My master done taught me some so I could help with orderin' supplies and such."

"You are a lucky man for that."

"Yes, suh. And I'm lucky agin now that you come to teach."

As each school day ended, John felt a bond growing between himself and Samuel. It was a good feeling and not one he had anticipated. However, the stature of the big Negro sometimes intimidated him. Pitching hay on the Cranston farm had made John lean and muscular, but at five foot nine he was dwarfed next to Samuel, who stood at least six four. John had taken to growing a beard in an effort to appear older than his twenty-four years; though still not as thick as he hoped, he liked the look. He felt more mature, and this seemed to counter his insecurities around bigger and older men.

During school days John found hardly a moment of spare time from sun up to late at night. Weekends, however, were a different matter. The walls of the Duval home seemed to close in on him, and though he welcomed a break from the demands of teaching, these were the hours when loneliness cut into him—when he missed Mr. and Mrs. Cranston and Lucy; but mostly he missed Scotland and his father, stepmother, and brothers. He took to writing letters early on Saturday, then walking them to the post office before continuing on through town up the dusty road and out along the Chocolate Bayou. Here he could breathe easier. Rarely did he meet anyone, and thus he felt safer; and simply to walk helped ease his homesickness.

One Saturday in April John covered a greater distance than usual. He was so immersed in thought he neglected to notice the sun's disappearance behind dark clouds until raindrops plopped holes in the dust at his feet. He pulled up his coat collar to meet the crown of his hat and turned for home, picking up his pace as the shower increased.

Startled by the sound of pounding hoof beats, John tensed and peered through the downpour at the road stretching before him. Since the incident on the wharf, he had been wary of anyone he didn't know. A voice hollered through the windswept rain as horse and rider pulled up beside him, "Best get on behind me. Won't keep you dry, but you'll get to town faster."

John recognized the young man as one he had seen around Lavaca, though he didn't know him by name. The voice carried a friendly tone and, what's more, lacked a southern drawl. The rider removed his boot from the stirrup and offered a hand. John took it, placed his foot in the stirrup and swung up behind the saddle.

They took off at a gallop. The wind blew directly toward them, and though buffered by the man in front, John felt the rain soak through his coat and trousers. Minutes later they pulled into the livery on the edge of town, halting only once the barn roof covered their heads.

John slipped off, followed by his rescuer. "That was quite a ride. Much obliged. I'd be knee-deep in mud and even more drenched if you hadn't come along." He held out a hand. "Name's Ogilvie. John Ogilvie."

The young man returned the gesture with a wet but cordial clasp. "Neal Wright. Once I get the saddle off Barney here and wipe him down, how about joining me for a cup of coffee? I live right next door. We can't get much wetter than we already are by walking from here to there."

John brightened. "Aye, a hot drink would be fine."

His new acquaintance led the way from the stable in the rain into what appeared to be a business office, then through another door and into a larger area in back of the same building, obviously a combination kitchen, bedroom and sitting room. John removed his soaked coat while Neal stoked a fire in the wood stove. Enough heat remained from early morning that the pot on top still held warm coffee. Heavy rain snapped at the window panes.

At Neal's invitation, John pulled up a chair and took a few sips of coffee. "I can't quite place your accent, but I'm guessing you're a Yankee."

"Right. Home town is Walthum, Massachusetts. I'm a mustered out soldier. Was in Texas when the war ended. Liked the country and thought I'd stay around. Met up with Antonio Giovanni, and we decided to open an import business." He nodded toward the room they had passed through.

John studied his new friend. He appeared to be younger than himself, perhaps only twenty-one or -two. A scar slashing his left cheek did not detract from his handsome features. "Ye have no family in Massachusetts?" John asked. He couldn't imagine not wanting to go home after the war.

"A mother. She wants me to come home, of course. I was a boy when I left. If I go back she'll still treat me as a boy. I need to stay here awhile." He opened the door to the stove and poked at the log. "Had a sweetheart. We were to be married. I got shot up pretty bad." He touched the scar on his cheek and rubbed at his chest. "Figured I was going to die. I wrote to her from the field hospital and never heard back. Learned later she had already up and married somebody else." He paused a moment, gazing out the window at the storm, then shook his head. "I have no craving to return." Settling back in his chair, boots off and feet warming on the brick hearth, he looked at John and grinned. "Here I am spouting off about myself. You're that teacher opened the school for the coloreds in the warehouse, aren't you? Now there's a tough job."

They talked for two hours, until the rain had lightened to a fine mist. When John pulled on his coat to leave, the cloth felt almost dry. "Didn't mean to take so much of your time, but I'm much obliged for the rescue and the coffee."

John headed for the Duvals' with a light step. Saturdays suddenly looked brighter.

Chapter 3

On Sundays John attended the Methodist Church that shared a pastor with the town of Victoria, a larger community up the road a ways. Every other week the Reverend William T. Harris rode by horseback to preach in Lavaca. On the alternate Sundays, members gathered and a lay person spoke. John enjoyed the hymn singing, but the sermons were often downright dreary. He missed his father's stirring preaching in the kirk in Bannockburn. He scanned the congregants. Stylish hats and bonnets adorned the heads of the ladies. Men in suits and waistcoats, beards combed and boots polished, lined the pews. There was not one colored person in the room.

Part of his responsibility to the freedmen was to nurture their souls and familiarize them with the Bible. He opened each school day with a prayer and a hymn, as instructed by the AMA and demonstrated by Sarah Barnes, a comely missionary teacher whose classroom he had observed in Galveston. He hadn't yet asked his Negro pupils about their religion, just offered up what he had been taught his whole life.

One early Monday morning in the warehouse school room, as John and Mrs. Wallace prepared lessons, she hummed a tune he recognized as a spiritual.

"Do you attend a church?" he asked.

"Yes, suh, Mr. Ogilvie. I be good friends with de Lawd."

"Where do you worship Him?"

"Houses. We take turns."

John mulled this over. He knew some of his pupils had stayed on the land with former masters, working as sharecroppers. Those who had their own homes in town lived in shacks along the bay, any one of which would hardly hold more than a handful of parishioners.

"Do you have a preacher?"

"Different folk talk about God. Mr. Samuel he even own a Bible."

"You have no other place to meet?"

"No, suh. But the Lawd don't care."

"Aye. I'm sure you're right." Suddenly a seed that had been growing in his mind for days burst open. "How about meeting for church in the school room?"

Mrs. Wallace's eyes widened in surprise, and when she responded her words trembled with excitement. "Why, I think that would be mos' good. I will ask around and git back to you."

She had an answer first thing the next morning—a resounding "Yes!"

Praise the Lord. John could hardly keep his mind on the school lessons. The door to his missionary work had been flung open. He would worship with these people. *I'll teach Sunday school, offer prayers, sing hymns, and maybe even preach occasionally.* He had accompanied Miss Barnes and her associate, Miss Skinner, to a raucous service in a black Baptist church in Galveston that would have seemed sacrilege in the staid kirk of his boyhood. He wasn't certain he could deliver a message with the same force, but maybe that wouldn't matter as long as it was the word of God.

That evening in class Samuel greeted him with a wide grin. "I hear we going to have church in the schoolroom. That is a mighty fine idea, suh. A mighty fine idea."

"Mrs. Wallace says you own a Bible."

"Yes, suh, and I can read some parts. They like me to do that." He spoke with assurance and pride. "Someday when I can read better, I'm going to be a preacher."

John reached out and touched Samuel gently on the arm. "You will be a fine preacher, Samuel."

That night, in his room at the Duvals', John wrote two letters, one to Jacob Shipherd, his AMA contact in Chicago, and one to his father in Scotland. He asked Shipherd if it would be appropriate for him, a layperson, to preach should the opportunity avail itself. To his father he wrote of his pupils, his inch by inch achievements, and the possibility of leading a church in Lavaca. *And one of my scholars wants to be a preacher.* At the thought of Samuel, John stopped writing and just sat, pen in hand, grinning. Samuel. An extraordinary human being. Dipping his pen in ink once again, he told of his new friend, Neal Wright. He did not mention those members of the community who were unfriendly, nor the fear that huddled in the back of his mind.

Writing to his father was always bittersweet. It evoked scenes and scents of home so far away, causing an ache in his heart for his native land. Although his forbearers had been elders and preachers, his family had fallen into honest poverty and could not give John the education his soul craved. It was well known that he was studious. Teachers took an interest in him and gave him private lessons. Work in the coal mines, a woolen mill, and as a tanner simply didn't generate the funds required to attend nearby Stirling Academy.

"Go to America, lad," his barber in Bannockburn had urged. "There are jobs and schools aplenty in that land."

The notion had grown, and as soon as John could pay for his passage he set sail for Canada, the first step to America for many Scotsmen, and crossed into Minnesota, where he found Carl Cranston and a job.

And now here I am, two years later, teaching the freedmen in Texas and planning church services for my colored friends.

He shook his head, still not quite believing this radical change in his life.

His days were a mix of frustration, challenge, and reward, all of it often fatiguing. In addition, he struggled with an ever present fear of those nameless folks who wanted him gone. He no longer stayed late after school or strolled the shore. The moment the evening scholars left, he locked the warehouse door, thumped down the stairs and jogged up the bluff to the Duvals'. He had even set to letting class out a little early most nights.

***

During the gap of time between the day and night schools, John worked on lessons at his makeshift desk in the classroom and walked outside, it being daylight and, he presumed, safer. He sometimes went home for a bite to eat, and three times a week, when the mail arrived in town, he strolled to the post office— always looking for a letter from his father or Lucy Cranston, or perhaps even Sarah Barnes, the missionary teacher in Galveston. He would liked to have lingered a while longer in Galveston to get to know her better, and a note from her would be a joy. Yet most often the envelopes handed to him by the postal clerk came from the AMA or the bureau. The former lifted his spirits, and the latter became increasingly frustrating.

One afternoon, not long after his rescue by Neal Wright from the torrential rain, John stepped out the post office door, two letters in hand, when a familiar voice hailed him.

"Ogilvie!" Neal hurried over from across the street and fell in step beside him. "Apparently you didn't catch pneumonia from our thorough soaking."

"And you look hearty yourself," John said, grinning.

"It will take more than a little rain to get me down. Where you off to?"

"Back to the school room. I have an evening class to prepare for."

"I'll walk with you." Neal glanced at the envelopes in John's hand. "Ah, letters. From a sweetheart, maybe?" he said, his eyes teasing.

John felt his cheeks warm at the suggestion. "Afraid not. Missives from the bureau, most likely forms to fill out."

They reached the steps to the warehouse room. "Come on up and see our makeshift classroom."

"Another time. I have some business to finish before the week ends." Neal started to leave, then hesitated. "Do you like Italian food?"

It struck John as an odd question. "Don't know if I've ever had it."

"Then you must try some. Antonio cooks dishes from the old country that will make your mouth water. Tomorrow night—say eight o'clock? Come to the back door."

"I'll be there."

When his friend disappeared around the corner of the building John took the long flight of stairs two at a time, just like the younger boys. While organizing lessons for the evening class he hummed Jeremy's song: *A,B,C,D,E, F, G.*

By the end of the week he was sorely in need of a diversion. Fortunately, he had decided against teaching on Friday nights. Normally, it meant a long evening for him, but today would be different. He told Mrs. Duval not to expect him for supper, hurried to his room, washed up, clipped his beard neat and trim, and changed into a clean shirt before heading out. As he approached the door to Neal and Antonio's living quarters, an enticing aroma drew him along.

The door swung open at his first rap. Neal, coat off and wearing a checkered shirt, motioned him in. "Right on time. Come in, Ogilvie, and meet the best Italian chef this side of the Atlantic."

A dark-haired man, whom John guessed to be in his thirties, sleeves rolled up and a towel tied around his waist, stood over the stove stirring red sauce in a kettle. The air almost burst with the heavenly scent.

"This is Antonio," Neal said, sweeping his hand with a flourish toward the other man, "a good business partner, an excellent cook, but a lousy roommate." He whispered a loud aside to John, "He snores."

They all laughed. "My sauce covers any of my faults," Antonio said.

A table in the middle of the large room held plates on which Antonio piled servings of macaroni topped with generous portions of his sauce. Uncorking a bottle of wine, he waved a stemmed glass in the air. "Special for our guest. All the way from Italy. You will have some?"

"No, thank you. Coffee is fine." John had seen enough drunken coal miners in Scotland, to say nothing of dock workers in Lavaca. Alcoholic drinks were seldom served in his boyhood home and never at the Seventh Day Adventist farm house of the Cranstons in Minnesota.

Neal asked for coffee also, and John wondered if he did so out of deference to him. Undeterred by their refusals, Antonio poured a large glass of the burgundy liquid, took a swallow, and said, "Let's eat."

John's initial taste of Italian food was enough to make him want to change nationalities. Only as their plates gradually emptied did any conversation occur.

"So, how are you and your students getting along?" Neal asked.

"It's slow, but then I've been here only a short time. There is a wee bit of encouragement each day. It's the bureau I'm upset with at the moment."

Neal sipped at his coffee. "And why would that be?"

"Well, when they approved the contract for the rental of the warehouse school room, they demanded a change—that rent be paid at the end of every month rather than in advance. This didn't sit well with the agent, Mr. Oswald."

"He's damn well lucky to be getting the money," Antonio said, pouring himself another glass of wine. "That wreck of a building's been for sale for over a year."

"It's more than that; it's small things that get in the way of teaching." John had an uncontrollable urge to unload all his annoyances of the past weeks on these two men. "Every time I turn around I have to fill out a voucher, and if the Ts aren't crossed exactly right, back it comes. Nothing seems to get done because the paperwork is always being returned. Then there are all the reports and accountings that must be written in triplicate."

Antonio swallowed more wine and shook his head. Neal stirred his coffee, took another sip and commented, "That's the government for you, though it seems they are doing a good thing, setting up these schools."

John felt uncomfortable. He was turning an enjoyable evening into a grumbling session. These two businessmen had probably spent the day doing their own paperwork. Groping for something positive, he blurted, "I do have permission to hire a carpenter to make real benches. Would you know of somebody here who might do that?"

"I think we could help you there," Antonio said. "Mr. Slater in town does fine work with wood."

"Thank you. I'll look him up. But enough about me and my problems." He turned to Neal. "How's your mother?"

"Same as always. I hear from her once a week. 'Come home,' she says. I write back and tell her I will one of these days, but for now Antonio needs my help with the business."

When John left, Antonio was slumped over the table, having consumed most of the bottle of wine.

"He does that at the end of the week," Neal said, walking John to the street. "Sometimes because business is good, sometimes because it is bad, and sometimes just because."

John placed a hand on Neal's shoulder. "Tell him again how much I enjoyed the meal, and thanks for lending an ear. I promise next time I won't be full of complaints."

During the few short blocks to the Duvals' in the dark of night, John whistled a tune. He whistled for joy, and to keep his fear at bay.

Chapter 4

At breakfast the following morning, Pierre, who worked as a clerk keeping records of merchandise unloaded on the wharf, handed John a sheet of paper and said, "A crate bearing your name arrived on the boat last night and is waiting dockside. I took the liberty of signing the receipt. You can use my horse and wagon to fetch it, if you like."

John read the caption on the receipt and broke into a wide grin: Barnes and Burr, Booksellers, New York. *Thank you, Dear Lord. Books!* He could hardly wait to get the box to the school room and open it up. All he had to do was go down to the wharf and claim it. The thought sent a chill racing along his spine. He had avoided the port since those moments of terror, the memory of which still lay coiled tightly inside him.

Evelyne Duval stood to clear the table. "You're free this morning, Pierre. Why don't you drive the wagon to the dock and give John a hand?"

"May I come too?" Alexandre asked. Their nine year old, always eager for an adventure, jumped up from his chair.

Pierre wiped his mouth with a napkin and took one more sip of coffee. "Well, I suppose I could at that. And yes, you may come." He reached out and patted his son's head.

John sent Evelyne a warm smile for her suggestion, then turned to Pierre, hoping his face did not radiate great relief. "I'm much obliged, but first I need to see a man about benches. Could we meet at the warehouse in an hour?"

John walked the short distance to the address given him by Neal and Antonio. The smell of wood shavings greeted him as he entered the small shed. A man, wiry and white-haired, stooped over an unfinished table top, working on the surface.

John cleared his throat. "Mr. Slater?"

The man straightened with a start, dropping his plane. He peered toward the glare of the doorway. "Who are *you*?"

The challenge sent an uneasy feeling flickering through John, but he launched into his prepared speech before too many doubts overtook him. "Name's Ogilvie. I've opened a school for the freedmen, and we need benches. I understand you do good work and I would like to hire you."

Mr. Slater stepped toward John, studying him all the while. "Exactly how many do you need, and by when?"

The positive tone allowed John to relax. He left a half hour later with an agreement. The thought of sturdy new seating to accommodate each of his pupils propelled him on to his next mission for the day.

Even with a contract for benches in his pocket and Pierre and Alexandre seated next to him on the wagon, the distance to the precious box of books seemed to John like a trip to purgatory. He rode stiff with tension, wondering what he might encounter on the wharf.

It all came off without incident. They were totally ignored along the crowded dock by workers who busily tended to their own duties. John recognized none of them, but then how could he? The dark of night had protected the trouble-makers from identification. He noted many of the stevedores were colored. These men, he knew, would not have been among his would-be assailants.

Pierre helped carry the crate up the stairs to the second floor of the warehouse, though John could have easily handled it himself. Once alone, he pried open the lid to examine the contents. Inside lay twenty-four primers—just twenty-four to dispense to seventy-one eagerly waiting students. He picked up a book and leafed through it, imagining Patsy's eyes aglow at reading the words in her very own primer. *Well, Patsy, you and the others will simply have to share.* Still, with books, no matter how few, and real benches on order, things were looking up.

***

On Sunday he awoke to rain, but the damp air did not keep him nor a handful of colored residents from arriving at the warehouse for a different kind of lesson. John felt the same thrill on walking into the room as he had his first day of teaching the freedmen. Yesterday he had fashioned a cross from two pieces of wood salvaged from George Slater's workshop and placed it on the makeshift desk—now an altar—changing the atmosphere from school room to sanctuary. The congregants, many of them his pupils, took notice and sat in reverence, speaking in hushed tones. John envisioned his father appearing at the door, nodding in approval.

In spite of his desire to preach, John had no intention to immediately thrust himself on this little gathering. This was their church. He found a seat three rows from the front so as not to be too conspicuous. The thought prompted an inward chuckle—the only white skin in the group.

Samuel, dressed in a suit coat and tie and holding a well-worn Bible, approached him. "Mr. Ogilvie, suh, do you suppose you could start things off by praying like we do first thing in school?" *So much for simply being one of the crowd.*

John's opening prayer was the most subdued part of the entire service. Following his "Amen," Joe Wallace grabbed a fiddle and the group launched into a lively rendition of "Let the Church Roll On, My Lord," accompanied by clapping and sprinkled with hallelujahs. From there Samuel read a verse from the Gospel and, in lieu of a sermon, folks stood in turn and spoke of their love for Jesus. After more singing and Bible verses, Samuel asked John to close with a prayer. If it hadn't been for the loud "Amen!"s at the conclusion, his final contribution would have dulled the entire event. Even so, folks shook his hand with polite vigor.

"Thank you, suh. Thank you fo' the meetin' place."

"Thank you for your fine prayers. You are mos' truly a man of God."

Samuel invited him home for Sunday dinner, for what would be John's first glimpse into the daily world of his pupils.

When he entered the clapboard hut, his breath caught. Here was the home of which Samuel was so proud. "Our very own. Just like the white folk," he had said. It consisted of one room in which were crowded a small stove, a table with three mismatched chairs, a dry sink, and an iron frame bed. Shipping crates hung on the wall for cupboards and another sat beside the bed as a nightstand.

Samuel's wife, Ellie, a pleasant, quiet woman, had skipped church to prepare the meal waiting for them. "Set yourself down, gentlemen, afore it gets cold," she said. Her expression said it all: the teacher of the freedmen was her guest, and she was proud. John had never felt so humbled. There were times as a boy when he had been embarrassed by his modest home in Bannockburn, wanting it to be finer. But its several rooms would have seemed a castle to these folks.

Ellie spooned generous helpings of greens, grits, and chunks of pork onto plates. Samuel bowed his head. "Lord, thank you for providin' this here food. May it give us strength to do your work. And thank you, Lord, for sending us Mistah Ogilvie. He is a good man. Amen."

Ellie added, "Yes, suh. Amen."

The kind words both embarrassed John and pleased him. He managed a polite thank you, then realized his host and hostess were waiting for him to take the first bite, so he complied. While he chewed, Samuel talked.

"We are most thankful for the school room and your help, Mistah Ogilvie. The good Lord done us right by sendin' you here."

Samuel's statement opened the way for John to ask the question foremost in his mind. "Would your congregation like a Sabbath school class after the church service?" He thought he knew the answer but wanted to hear it confirmed.

Samuel grinned. "That would be extra nice. And you will teach it?"

"Aye, it would give me great pleasure. Shall we start next Sunday?"

Samuel's broad smile was answer enough. John made a mental note to write the missionary association for Sabbath school material. Surely there were northern churches willing to provide papers. And hymnaries. He enjoyed the emotional spirituals, but the congregants should learn some traditional music also.

"Have you ever preached a sermon, Samuel?"

A frown wrinkled the black man's brow. "Oh, no, suh. I don't expect I could do that. I just read from the Bible—words I know real well. Folks seem to like that."

"Maybe you could find a particular verse each Sunday from which to teach a lesson. I would help."

Samuel sent a quick look to his wife before answering in a low voice. "I cain't read them all, suh."

"You are a very good scholar, Samuel. You learn fast. We could decide the week before what verse to use, and I could go over it with you, teaching you to read the words."

"You would do that, suh?"

"Certainly. Between the two of us we could talk to the congregation about its meaning."

"That would be mighty fine. Mighty fine." His eyes lit up. Grabbing his Bible, he handed it to John. "You choose, suh."

It was late afternoon before John left Samuel's, and all the way home he walked with a lively gait. Not because he hurried; he simply couldn't get the tune and words "Let The Church Roll On, My Lord" out of his head. Though the rain had ceased, gray clouds still hovered in the sky, causing the end of day to be darker than usual. Strands of mist curled up from the bay, twisting through the empty streets. *You can put the Devil out, my Lord, Let the church roll on, my Lord. Just put the sinners out, my Lord, And let the church roll on.*

John jogged up the front walk to the Duvals', entered the house and closed the door behind him, safely away from any evil-minded people who might be hiding in the swirls of fog.

Chapter 5

"I must say, Mr. Ogilvie, you get the prize this week for receiving the most mail." The postmaster handed John a packet containing four envelopes.

He sorted through them quickly as he left the building, noting two from Lt. Mitchel in Indianola, one from Shiperd of the AMA in Chicago, and—his breath caught—one from Sarah Barnes.

It was Thursday, between classes, and he was on his way to the Duvals' for a quick bite to eat before the evening session. Tucking the letters in his coat pocket, he hurried to the privacy of his room. There he laid the envelopes on his desk and fanned them out. Carefully removing the seal, he unfolded the note written in a delicate feminine script, the scent of roses rising from the paper. His fingers trembled ever so slightly as he read.

> *Dear Mr. Ogilvie,*
>
> *Because we are two bureau schools in the southernmost part of Texas, I feel we should occasionally communicate as to circumstances in our respective situations.*
>
> *The attendance here increases monthly, and Miss Skinner and I have our hands full teaching the extreme range of abilities in our classes. As you know, we are encouraged by the AMA to allow our brightest scholars to assist us, and we have done so with good results. I'm sure you have discovered this to be true, also.*
>
> *I make a point to visit the family of each scholar when time allows. This enables me to gain their trust and also opens the way to introduce our Lord and Savior through the eyes of a Protestant. So many of these poor, uneducated folk know only a peculiar mix of Voodoo and Catholicism. I also visit Negro families who have no*

members attending the school and encourage them to do so. Although I am often greeted with suspicion and reserve, I find my welcome in their humble homes usually warmer than that I receive in the stately houses of white citizens here.

I trust all is going well with your teaching. We think of you often. Please write so we may keep in touch. With the help and guidance of our Lord, may we carry on in His name.

Most sincerely,
Sarah Barnes

He smiled broadly as he read, clinging to the phrases "Please write so we may keep in touch" and "We think of you often." Surely she really meant "*I* think of you often." He certainly thought of her. Yet she had been the one to correspond first. He had purposely waited until his message could be a positive one. Now with some text books in hand, new benches on the way, and a Sabbath school class about to commence, it was time to write. That would be his joyful project for later this evening.

Next he opened the envelope from the AMA, hoping for a response to his query about preaching. He wasn't disappointed. Shipherd had written:

You are sufficiently authorized to deliver such scriptural addresses as you may be able to make, provided they do not interfere with your school work.

We shall be pleased to hear of your entire success in the labor you have so heartily undertaken.

The other envelopes he left unopened. Undoubtedly forms to complete, they could wait until after class. For now he fairly burst to share the news in the first two. The go ahead from the AMA he would share with Samuel. *And maybe I'll just march over to Neal's after class and casually mention I have indeed received a note from a lady friend.* He stuck the two open letters in his shirt pocket and went downstairs for supper.

Evelyne Duval had formed the habit of setting out coffee, bread, cheese and fruit for him before his evening class. Today Suzette, the Duvals' eleven-year-old daughter, sat at the table pondering arithmetic problems on a slate. For a moment a stab of jealousy struck John. His students still had no slates.

"Adding and subtracting?" he asked, trying to shove his negative thoughts aside.

"No. That's baby stuff. This is fractions," she said, tossing her head of long curls. She chewed on the end of a stylus, frowning at the problem before her. "These are hard, and *Maman* says I can't play until I finish." Tears swam in her eyes.

"May I help?" John glanced at the girl's mother.

She nodded her approval. "*Oui*. I am no good at it."

John leaned toward Suzette and explained the principle of the problem she was trying to solve. By the third set of fractions, she was catching on and a smile dimpled her cheeks. "Thank you, Mr. Ogilvie. You are a good teacher. And you smell good, too."

"Suzette!" Evelyne threw a harsh look at her daughter.

"Well, he does. He smells like roses."

John felt himself flush, then laughed. "That's from the letter in my pocket."

Mrs. Duval raised her eyebrows and a soft "Oooh" escaped her lips. She and Suzette exchanged knowing glances. Without further explanation, John moved to his chair and commenced to eat his supper.

After the evening class John didn't actually read Shipherd's letter to Samuel. He paraphrased it, saying the missionary association authorized him to deliver "scriptural addresses."

"Yes, suh," Samuel beamed. "We is—are—on our way to having a real church." He hummed as they cleaned up the room following class, and John recognized the tune that had circled through his own mind since Sunday, "Let the Church Roll On."

With no more thoughts about stopping by Neal's, he headed straight for home to respond to the piece of mail that had perfumed his mind all evening. Of course, the message from Miss Barnes wasn't really a love letter, but the fact she took time out of her crowded day to write meant she thought of him. That was worth a lot.

Sitting at the desk, John pulled out paper and pen, then eyed the two envelopes from Lt. Mitchel, still unopened. Laying down his pen with a sigh he took the top one, thicker than usual, broke the seal and began reading. As he suspected, the packet included vouchers to be completed and returned: one for Oswald, the warehouse agent, to fill out and sign when requesting rent money; and one for whoever John had engaged to construct benches. Also included in this envelope was Circular No. 4 from General Griffin at Bureau Headquarters in Galveston. John read through the official printed document—a lengthy and confusing explanation of the government's rules and regulations regarding teachers and the establishing of facilities for freedmen schools. He noted Lt. Mitchel had underlined paragraph II which talked about the monthly reports required of the teachers—one to be sent to the sub-assistant and one to the superintendent of schools for the state. The circular ended with the statement:

> *Sub-Assistant Commissioners will take particular care to see that the signature to the Receipt of a certified account corresponds precisely with the name of the head of the account and with that on their Reports of Persons and Articles.—If the name reported is John Smith, and the receipt to his certified account is signed J. Smith, the account will not be paid.*

John ran his fingers through his hair and pursed his lips. Surely these rules couldn't be that important. He had little time after preparing lessons and teaching late into the night. He had done the best he could.

Stifling a sense of annoyance, he reached for the last piece of correspondence. Upon pulling out the contents, a check floated onto the table. "Well, what have we here?" he said aloud. Perhaps he had saved the best for last after all. The accompanying note was actually from a Lieutenant Garretson in Galveston forwarded by Mitchel. It read in part:

> *I enclose my check No. 32 on the National Bank of Texas at Galveston, Texas, for Thirty-Five dollars payable to the order of John Ogilvie being in payment of his account for services as a teacher of Freedmen school at Lavaca, for 1 to 31 March, 1867.*
>
> Chas. Garretson
> 2nd Lt. 17" Inf. 7

John picked up the check and smiled for several long minutes. Maybe working with the government would be tolerable after all. He vowed to start on the required reports with no further grumbling, but first there was another matter at hand. He dipped his pen into ink and began writing: *Dear Miss Barnes ...*

Chapter 6

By mid April, the storms blowing off the gulf lost some of their fury, and John found his Saturday walks more and more pleasurable. The uniqueness of his new surroundings began to take hold.

When first arriving in southern Texas, he saw little beauty in the sand-swept, grassy prairie, but now when he strolled away from town, spring flowers emerged beneath his feet. What he noticed most were the colors: the brilliant red of Indian Paintbrush, the orange and gold of Indian Blanket, and a purple carpet of Texas Bluebonnets, all the more striking because of the contrast with the otherwise austere terrain.

And there were birds, some as colorful as the flowers. Warblers and Purple Martins delighted him. Ruby-throated humming birds often whirred busily by, dipping their beaks into bright blossoms. Many unfamiliar varieties of birds appeared for a few days, then disappeared, to be replaced by others.

"They comes flying through heah on they way to somewhere. Like presents from Heaven singin' us songs," Mrs. Wallace said, after John commented on the birds one day in class. The fact that the gulf lay along a migratory route fascinated him. And as he became increasingly appreciative of the beauty of the region his longing for Scotland lessened.

The success of the church service and Sabbath school class helped too. He had preached his first sermon and felt it went well, though he struggled to accept the continuous interruptions of "amens" and to understand it was a good sign when these spontaneous responses became louder and more frequent. A couple of times he had lost his train of thought due to the spirited congregational reaction.

One Sunday afternoon as he strolled toward home following services, John met Pastor Harris from the Methodist Church. The preacher smiled broadly, removed his hat, and extended his hand, warmly clasping John's in his own as though he were a shepherd finding a lost lamb.

"We've missed you, Mr. Ogilvie, missed you indeed." A more somber expression replaced his smile. "Is there anything to the rumor that you've started your own church?"

"Not really, Pastor. I'm assisting the freedmen in setting up their services in the warehouse where we hold school during the week."

"Well, now, that is a fine thing." His grasp remained firm. "They should have their own church. And we look forward to seeing you back in our congregation when you have them all settled. We miss your presence and your hearty singing of the hymns." With those few remarks, he released John's hand, placed his hat back on his head and continued on down the street, his pastoral duty seemingly accomplished for the moment.

John pondered the man's remark, "They should have their own church." Though he felt a certain kinship to Pastor Harris, he wasn't certain he approved of the man's tone. The seal on John's commission from the AMA stated *"Go ye into all the world and preach the gospel to every living creature."* Did that mean all living creatures should be separated out in order to hear the gospel? He didn't think so. Yet he knew for a fact the coloreds *wanted* their own church where they could worship as they pleased without being subservient to the wishes of their white brethren. So for now, separate was the way it was. And as for returning to the Methodist congregation, so long as Samuel and the others wanted him, he planned to stay with his Negro friends.

John was acutely aware that the more he mingled with his pupils after school hours, including Sundays, the more he alienated himself from the white community. Though his mission here was to assist the coloreds in their new role as freedmen, every step in that direction honed his isolation from the white town folk.

Mrs. Wallace seemed particularly aware of the estrangement he suffered from his own kind. More than his assistant, she had become the self-proclaimed matriarch of the day class, and her mothering in no way excluded the teacher. Like everyone else, John respectfully referred to her as Mrs. Wallace. She always stayed after lessons to help him tidy up the room. One day when she and John walked toward home from school together before going their separate ways, two women hurriedly crossed to the other side of the street, obviously avoiding them. "They be afeared," Mrs. Wallace remarked.

A tiny wave of alarm rippled through John. Afraid? To be unhappy or even angry with him for raising the level of the freedmen and refugees in society, he could remotely fathom, but afraid? Fear did strange things to people, and their actions could become unpredictable.

Like Lt. Mitchel's encouragement to buy a gun, Mrs. Wallace's comment wedged into the back of John's mind and lodged there. Yet he refused to allow it to interfere with his task of teaching. Wee rewards wove in and out through the days and weeks of instruction.

"Patsy, how do you spell *home*?"

"Home. H-O-M-E. Home."

"Ezra, what is the sum of 8 and 12?"

"Twenty, suh."

Such moments as these carried the triumphant smiles of the pupils directly into John's heart. Each success overrode the sterner times so necessary to maintain order in the large class. The constant prodding to keep some at their studies ate away at him, and often at the end of the day he felt almost drowned in fatigue.

Then there were the times when excitement energized and linked them all together. Such a day occurred in late April. The new benches arrived at last.

"Oh, Teacha," Patsy squealed as she walked through the door and spied the new seating. She fluffed her skirts and plopped in the middle of the first row. The brilliant smile across her face as she sat there swinging her legs made John wonder if she ever planned to leave.

Jeremy took center front row, arms crossed and chin up, a look of importance etched across his face. John chuckled and thought, *King Jeremy*.

The scent of freshly planed and sanded wood perfumed the room to the point of intoxication. The width of the benches accommodated posteriors of all sizes far better than the makeshift plank seating. John had ordered an extra row and for the first time since school opened, pupils could sit without crowding their neighbor. Joyful comments echoed through the room.

"I ain't so squeezed now!"

"Lawd Jesus, thank you."

"Jus' lak a real school room in pitures."

The chatter continued for the first hour before subsiding, but the communal sigh of relief seemed to spur the pupils on to their best scholarly efforts for the entire day. Even the tired and more serious evening class perked up at the sight of the new furniture.

Upon delivery of the benches George Slater had presented a signed voucher for the sum of fourteen dollars. That very afternoon, between classes, John sent it on its way to Lt. Mitchel, accompanied by a note ... *The addition of proper seating has created a vast improvement in the overall attitude from the scholars.*

John hummed all the way home that evening, his step lively, to the tune of "Onward Christian Soldiers." After washing up, he joined Pierre and Evelyne for their late supper in the family dining room, their normal routine. Alexandre and Suzette took their evening meal earlier and were usually in their rooms preparing for bed. As soon as he was seated, John sensed the mood of the Duvals was very different from his own.

"Is everything all right?" he asked, as a solemn-faced Evelyne passed him a platter of buttered potatoes.

She glanced at her husband, then lowered her eyes to her plate, pushing together a small mound of food with her fork, then separating it, never putting any to her lips.

"What is it?" John asked, a dryness growing in his mouth.

Pierre cleared his throat. "It's about the school, John. You know we approve of teaching the coloreds, and commend you for doing so. Not being from here and never having been slave owners, it seemed only right to help out, but—"

"It's the children," Evelyne said quickly.

"Their classmates make it difficult," Pierre continued. "We've encouraged them to stand up for what is right, but it is not easy when you are young."

The muscles in John's jaw tightened. "My pupils aren't only Negroes," he said. "Some are as white as you and I, and there is a Mexican lad and others of varied skin color. They all have a right to an education." He knew he needn't explain this to the Duvals, but he couldn't contain himself.

"Today a boy spit on Suzette." A tear slid down Evelyne's cheek as she spoke.

"We are sorry, but we think it best that you move to other living quarters," Pierre said. "We will give you time, of course, to find something suitable."

John felt sick. Sick that sweet, spunky Suzette had to suffer, sick that so many others thought so differently than he. The words of Mrs. Wallace pounded in his ears. *"They be afeared."*

As though Pierre could read John's thoughts, he spoke again. "Groups are organizing throughout the South, making trouble for those who encourage the freedmen to read. We worry for you, too, John."

"I'll be fine, and I don't want to cause problems here. You've been good to me." He could think of nothing else to say. The remainder of the meal continued in awkward silence. Upon finishing, John excused himself and trod heavily up the stairs to his room. He stood at the window for a long time looking out at the prairie.

Suddenly a fit of rage tore at him. He would seek out Suzette's narrow-minded classmate and shake some sense into him. And he wouldn't stop there; he'd find the hoodlums who terrorized him on the wharf and make them listen to his anger until they understood the good he and Miss Barnes and all the teachers of the freedmen were doing. He slumped onto the bed, resting his head in his hands. *You fool. Maybe you can teach the oppressed their ABCs, but you can't force people overnight to think differently than they have for as long as they can remember.*

He reached for his Bible.

***

John slept fitfully that night and awoke on Saturday morning while the sliver of a moon still hung in a dark sky. He dressed without benefit of lamplight. Creeping down the stairs, shoes in hand, he stopped in the kitchen for a slice of bread, then slipped out the door. Once in the cool morning air, he sat on the stoop and put on his shoes. He ate his meager breakfast and, in the first flush of dawn, strolled away from town. The sun rose as he walked, warming his back and illuminating the Texas primroses as he passed. By midmorning he had walked further than he had ventured since arriving in Lavaca—sometimes deep in thought, sometimes simply trying not to think at all. It was time to head back to town.

The sound of hoofbeats caused John to turn. He squinted into the early morning sun. Three riders galloped toward him, kicking up dust as they approached. When they were almost abreast of him, they reined in their horses and circled around, so close the boot of one man grazed John's arm. Triangles of bandanas concealed their faces, and slivers of eyes glowered below the brim of their hats. John froze in place, his heart drumming in his ears.

"Well, look at what we got here," one of the riders sneered. "That northern fellow who figures he's so uppity he can come down here and teach our niggers to be uppity too."

"He don't look so almighty important at the moment. I'd say he's even trembling a little."

All three men laughed and moved their horses in closer. John felt smothered, the sweat of the animals invading his nostrils. Swallowing hard, he looked steadily in the eyes of one of the men. "I'd be much obliged if you would give me a little breathing room."

"Ha ha! Hear that? He'd be *much obliged*. That ain't northern talk. This guy's a real foreigner. We don't even got an American teaching our slaves. Now that's downright pathetic." The man pulled the reins to one side, causing his horse to turn. Its rump hit John, knocking him to the ground—face down into the dusty earth. He attempted to sit up only to be pushed back down by a hard boot in his side.

"We'd be *much obliged* if you'd jest wallow there awhile, an maybe think about changing jobs. Come on boys. We got our own work to do."

By the time John had wiped the dust from his eyes and pulled himself to his feet, his aggressors were far down the road. During the walk home, his side ached where the boot had struck him, and by the time he reached the Duvals' his fear had turned to anger. He now had a greater understanding of why he must leave the home of the French family. Spitting at Suzette was one thing, but what if the children were to be injured because of their association with him? He couldn't bear the thought. These men were certainly capable of more than threats.

John made no mention of his encounter with the horsemen. There was no point in alarming the Duvals. The decision to leave their home, and the reasons why, had been made.

Suzette's absence during the day was glaringly apparent. She didn't join the family for lunch and quickly disappeared if John entered a room where she was present. Her avoidance of him weighed like a stone in his chest, yet he could not help but understand. The burden she carried—that of his dismissal from her home—was far heavier for a young girl than those he had willingly taken on himself. Late in the afternoon he found her on a bench in the yard.

"Suzette, we must talk."

She would not let their gazes meet. "*Je suis désolé.* I am sorry."

"Do not be. This problem is not of your making. I am the one who should be apologizing to you, lassie."

She kept her head turned away from him and her shoulders shook as she tried to control her sobs. John bit his lip and cleared his throat. "It will be all right."

He talked of his pupils and their progress, how so many were learning to read and write and do arithmetic. He told her of the men in his evening class who somehow managed to find the strength to concentrate on lessons after working hard all day.

"Because you and your brother and mother and father are brave and good people, I was able to start this school, but now it is time for me to find another place to live. Everything will turn out for the best. Aye, you will see."

He left her sitting there, entered the house and climbed the stairs to his room, his heart heavy. He wanted desperately to believe the words he had used to console her. Still, if there were other white folk in the community who were willing to jeopardize their own lives for the sake of the "nigger teacher" and accept him as a boarder, he didn't know of them.

John remembered his father saying, "Every burden is sent us for a reason and in the end we are stronger because of it." Well, if this was to toughen him up, it wasn't working. He would stay in Lavaca, of course, and put up a brave front. Somewhere he would find a place to bed down, but as long as there were people who didn't want him here, he knew there might be more unpleasant encounters.

Chapter 7

Dependable Mrs. Wallace came up with the solution.

"Y'all come move in with Mr. Wallace and me 'til you can git yourself a house," she said. "We got room, and I ain't afeared of nobody."

John admired her bravado and said a silent prayer that he wasn't endangering another family. He packed his things and, after a cordial goodbye to the Duvals, headed for the bay. Mrs. Wallace stood waiting for him at the top of the bluff, as prearranged. Beside her danced a very excited Ezra, his eyes glowing. "You goin' live nex' to us now," he said, and insisted on carrying John's satchel.

The Wallace home, a simple structure of unpainted board and batten, sat not far from the warehouse and close to the water. The main living area was of the same mold as Samuel's, but with a slight upgrade. In addition to a dry sink and table with benches, Mrs. Wallace had a real cook stove and a pie safe. This little dwelling also boasted two sleeping quarters separated by a curtained doorway. One, an eight by ten cubicle, was to be John's. A wooden peg on the wall provided a place to hang his coat. Beneath it on a packing crate sat a pitcher of water and a basin. There was no need to ask where to stow his belongings. Setting the satchel on the floor, he pushed it under the bed next to the chamber pot. On another crate, close to the bed, he placed his Bible.

"This heah room is Jacob's, "Mrs. Wallace said. "He won't bother you none. He comes and goes and don't say much."

She gave no explanation as to who Jacob might be, or where he would sleep now that a stranger had taken his space, but John let his questions ride for the moment.

Mrs. Wallace always carried with her the subtle scent of fried pork rind, and from the minute John stepped into her house the smell of cooked food typical of poor Southern folk overwhelmed him. With a stab of dismay, he suspected in due time this same aroma would cling to his own clothing.

When he first applied to teach the freedmen, the indoctrination he received from the American Missionary Association made it clear that living arrangements would not be lavish. Rooming with the families of students was commonplace among the teachers. This included partaking of the meager meals provided. As grateful as he was to Mrs. Wallace and her kind offer, it also struck John how fortunate he had been the first few months of his tenure in Lavaca.

As he sat in the windowless bedroom with no place to prepare his lessons, realization moved slowly across his mind like a dark cloak. The more deeply he became immersed in his obligations to the AMA and the bureau, the more demanding would be his sacrifices. Things were going to be different from now on. Head bowed, he repeated words from Psalm 18: *"The Lord is my rock and my fortress, and my deliverer; my God, my strength, in whom I will trust; my buckler, and the horn of my salvation and my high tower."* He sat on the edge of the narrow bed for a long while—waiting. Waiting for a calmness and acceptance of this new chapter of the challenges he had so readily accepted months ago and far away in Minnesota. Whether the tranquility he sought had actually occurred or whether he had begun to doze, he wasn't quite certain, because the stillness suddenly broke with the voice of Mrs. Wallace.

"Mistah Ogilvie, you can wash up an' join us for suppa' now."

After a filling meal of collard greens and corn cakes, John and Joe Wallace continued sitting at the table while his wife rattled dishes and busied herself by the stove.

In spite of the humble surroundings, John couldn't help but be impressed by the independence of his hosts and the obvious luxury of certain possessions in the house, such as the cast iron cook stove.

"You've done well in a short time," he said.

"No suh. It's been a long time. I built this heah place with my own hands." He began telling his life history. The flame in the lamp flickered shadows and light on the older man's features, adding a dramatic touch to the fascinating story.

Joe Wallace, whom John guessed to be in his late fifties, was born free long before President Lincoln's Emancipation Proclamation. His father, a slave boy in the state of Maryland during the Revolution, had been promised freedom by the British if he joined their ranks as a soldier. After the war he fled familiar land, out of reach of his irate former owner. Settling in Kentucky, he worked as a laborer for a Methodist farmer who practiced "what the Good Book taught."

Joe's father took up with the daughter of another farm worker, a relationship that resulted in several children, the youngest being Joe. "One day when I was 'bout sixteen, I jest left," Joe said. He told how he kept pushing west and eventually found his way to Lavaca, where he hired out as a handyman.

"I don' cause no trouble and I works hard." He paused, gazing at the lamplight. John waited for more.

Joe ran his hand across his forehead as if to pull out memories, then started up again. "I saved up and bought land and built this here house on part of it. They is still a piece I own, waitin' to do somethin' with. Not many niggers got land like I do." The pride in his voice was strong and clear.

John smiled right along with him. "And Mrs. Wallace?" he asked. "Where did you find her?"

"Well now, she's the bes' part." Joe stood, strode across the small room, and leaned against the frame of the open door before continuing. He told how he met his wife while he made deliveries to a plantation near Green Lake. She worked in the kitchen and often helped carry in the produce and other supplies he brought.

"She always smiled real purdy at me. Then one day when no one was lookin' I up and grabbed her and kissed her." He said from that moment on he saved every extra cent, paid for her freedom and brought her to Lavaca to live in his house. "We wuz married right and proper by a preacha."

It was his idea to send her to the freedmen's school when it opened. "She's mos' smart and can learn letters quicker'n me," he said. "She be my teacha." Joe walked to the wood bin, took a piece of charred wood between his thumb and forefinger and with great deliberation spelled out J O E on a flat piece of firewood.

As a ragged-toothed grin emerged on the man's face, John was overcome with the feeling that the accomplishment had been in part his own, and suddenly the small dark cabin seemed much less confining.

Adjustments still had to be made. Now each morning John arrived at the school room several hours early to prepare lessons rather than working at home into the night as he had done at the Duvals. The Wallaces were early risers, so this arrangement accommodated them all.

John learned quickly in whose bed he slept. The Wallaces' nineteen-year-old son, Jacob, worked for the Victoria railroad, repairing and laying track. He would be gone for days at a time, then suddenly appear for home-cooked food and a night's rest. Where he would sleep was a mystery to no one but John—in his own bed, of course. The fact that John was there seemed of no concern to Jacob. He slept just fine, while John felt smothered and unable to move, and when the late spring air turned heavy, the sharing became almost unbearable. This test of his Christianity was stretched to the point he often awoke out-of-sorts following the bed-sharing.

On one such morning, groggy from lack of sleep, John arose earlier than usual, scribbled a note for Mrs. Wallace explaining he had extra work to do, and quietly left the house. He made his way in the dimness of pre-dawn toward the dark outline of the warehouse. To his right the rhythmic chuffing of a tug boat leaving dockside joined the cry of a gull and the gentle lapping of wake-water against the shore. Though early May, a cool breeze belied the promise of a warm day to come. John inhaled deeply and acknowledged to himself that after only a few short weeks here, his senses now stirred to these sensations unique to port towns. They were becoming a part of him.

Climbing the steps to the classroom, he paused a moment on the landing to observe the first light of day glow pink across the bay waters. Inside he lit a lamp, sat at the teacher's table and contemplated the stack of slates, first primers, readers, and copy books before him. These he had received not long ago from bureau superintendent of education, E. W. Wheelock, at the Galveston Bureau headquarters, after many frustrating requests to the agent in Indianola. Though these recent supplies represented a big step forward, he still needed additional first primers and arithmetic books. Now, in spite of a sleepless night, he felt a buzz of sweet anticipation that his requests would be fulfilled.

Over the past weeks he had made the acquaintance of Herbert Martin, a local businessman who seemed willing to stop by and chat now and then, apparently not bothered by John's work with the freedmen.

"I make trips to Galveston on occasion, in fact may relocate there. I'd be willing to deliver messages to the Freedmen's Bureau, for a small fee of course," he'd often say.

John always politely refused, somewhat put off by the obvious mercenary motivations of the man. Then when this most recent delivery of books arrived, with a personal note from Wheelock, he got an idea. He would bypass Lt. Mitchel in Indianola and request supplies of the bureau in Galveston directly. It would be worth the expense of Martin's *small fee* if he could finally teach with the proper tools.

So Martin had left a week before with a note to Superintendent Wheelock requesting the much-needed books. The man pocketed the list and a few dollars of John's hard-earned money, tipped his hat, and assured him he would make contact with the bureau shortly after landing.

Fatigued from his sleepless night, John relaxed and dozed at his desk. A soft knock on the door awoke him with a start. This couldn't be one of the scholars. Classes weren't scheduled to begin for another two hours.

"Come," he said, rubbing his eyes awake.

With a squeak of hinges, the door swung open revealing the small figure of Alexandre Duval. The boy carried three pieces of mail and a basket covered by a cloth of blue calico.

"*Bonjour, Monsieur* Ogilvie."

"Alexandre. What a wonderful surprise." John stood, motioning the boy in with a broad smile. "What brings you here?"

"Letters, sir, for you. The Postman sometime forgets you no longer live at our address. And *Maman* sent bread and cheese." He laid the envelopes on the desk and set the basket beside them.

The aroma of fresh-baked bread suddenly reminded John he had eaten nothing since the night before. "Ah, Alexandre. You mother is so thoughtful. Now, tell me, how is school?"

"Good."

"And Suzette? She is good, too?"

"*Oui,*" the boy said.

John tried to read his face and tone of voice, hoping things really were better for the children now that the stigma of the Yankee teacher was gone from their household. Visions of the sinister horsemen and the ugly incident on the waterfront always hovered in the back of his mind. Yet, if Alexandre said all was good, surely he could be believed.

Smiling, John wrote a quick thank you note from his dwindling stack of precious paper. He lifted the still warm loaf and quarter-round of cheese from the basket and laid the message in their place.

"Tell your mother thank you very much." He reached out and shook the boy's hand. Alexandre grinned, picked up the basket and left, thumping down the wooden stairs, his departure much less stealthy than his arrival.

John returned to the bench, pulled off a chunk of bread and stuffed it into his mouth. He chewed with his eyes closed, savoring every swallow. With taste buds and hunger appeased, his attention turned to the mail lying before him. Two bore the familiar lettering of the Bureau of Refugees, Freedmen and Abandoned Lands, one from Indianola and the other from Galveston. A third was from Lucy Cranston. In spite of her tight schedule at seminar, she found time to write. He opened it first, a one page account of her studies, obviously written in haste. He chuckled as he read the few words...

> *Miss you, John. Hope you don't love Texas so much that you never return to Minnesota. More later.*
> *Regards, Lucy.*

Not much, yet enough. Lucy and he had similar goals, and on the farm she always brightened his day. For now, words from her would have to suffice for her presence.

Still smiling, he picked up the piece of correspondence from Galveston, surely a response from Superintendent Wheelock regarding his book order. Tearing open the seal with eager fingers, he began reading:

> *Dear Sir,*
> *Herbert Martin, late from Lavaca, informed me that you wish me to forward you 75 Slates, and 30 Second Readers, together with Primers, 1st Readers and Copy Book.*
> *... Mr. Martin informed me that he has lost the list of books you gave him but that he is positive as to the accuracy of the number of Slates and Second readers wished for. Of course I cannot judge the reliability of his memory, but have concluded to send the articles, thinking you may be in immediate need of them.*
> *Let me know if Martin's statement is correct, and if you need anything else.*
> *Very Respectfully,*
> *W. Wheelock*

The glow from Lucy's letter vanished. Martin lost the list? John stood and paced the school room floor, grasping the letter so tightly its corner crumpled in his hand. The numbers and specific books remembered by Martin, and therefore understood by Wheelock, were all wrong.

"That irresponsible scoundrel!" John dropped on the bench, shaking his head. "Forgive me, Lord. I am angry too much of the time lately." In spite of the penitence, his fingers tightly clutched the bureau letter. He took a deep breath and his grip gradually loosened. Wheelock's note fluttered to the desk. Holding his head in his hands John remained in a prayerful state, knowing his intemperate reaction was due in part to his lack of sleep, though still inexcusable. *Perhaps this is my punishment for the pomposity I displayed by-passing the correct chain of command.*

After a period of deep thought, John pulled a piece of paper from his desk, picked up the pen, dipped it in ink and scratched a note to the bureau superintendent. With any luck, an immediate response might reach Galveston and a correct order put in place before the erroneous shipment of books was sent.

With his carefully worded message placed in an envelope and sealed, he focused on the second letter delivered by Alexandre— the one from the agent in Indianola. Upon opening it, he couldn't help but emit a wry chuckle. Here was a twenty-five dollar draft in his favor for services rendered—a timely counter-balance to his frustrations. However, he noted one peculiarity. The accompanying letter bore the signature of an A. B. Bonnaffon, not that of sub-assistant Mitchel.

Chapter 8

John didn't have time to puzzle out this new twist in the higher command of the freedmen's schools. Already voices and footfalls rounded the building and came up the stairs. The door opened to the first group of his pupils who scattered to their respective seats.

"Mawnin', teacha."

"Good morning," John said. He searched the group for an appropriate courier and settled on Pablo. He motioned the boy over and handed him the letter he had just written to Wheelock.

"Would you please deliver this to the post office, laddie? It's important that it go out with today's mail boat."

"*Sí, Señor.*" Pablo was not a particularly good student, and John sensed his enthusiasm stemmed more from having a legitimate escape from class than a willingness to please.

Ezra stood close by, observing the out-of-school assignment. "I don' think it be good for him to go by hisself."

John pondered the comment. This canny youngster deserved a reward for his eagerness to help John move to the Wallaces'.

"Aye, you are right, Ezra. Both of you scoot. Don't take too long."

Loud voices brought his attention back to the class. A tug of war raged between Patsy and Ophelia, the object of dissension a first primer being destroyed by the struggle. John rapped his desk sternly with a ruler, to no avail.

"Give me that," Ophelia hollered, "It's mine!"

"No. It be mine. Teacha, she got my book." A tearful Patsy grabbed at the book tightly clutched to the other girl's chest.

John scowled at the two youngsters. "Enough. Bring the book here."

A blustery Mrs. Wallace strode over to the children, grabbed each by an arm and led them to where John stood. "Now y'all mind the teacha. Y'all heah?" Her eyes were dark as smoke.

Patsy bowed her head, causing a steady stream of tears to drop directly to the floor. In her hand she held the book, the pages ripped loose from their binding.

Someone in the back of the room snickered. John glared, his sweeping gaze connecting with each face in the overcrowded class. Quiet settled like a cold fog, broken only by Patsy's sniffling. John gently pulled the damaged primer from her hand, and addressed the class. "I know it is difficult to learn with not enough books. There will be more, I promise. Until they arrive, we must share. Now, I want everyone to work on the spelling lesson."

With attention focused on the slates, few pupils noticed when the door opened and Pablo quietly eased inside. John, reading distress in the boy's face, motioned to Mrs. Wallace to take over the class and, placing a hand on Pablo's shoulder, whispered, "Where's Ezra?"

"Come quick, *señor. Es muy malo.*" A solemn Pablo backed out onto the landing. John followed, closing the door behind them. The boy led the way down the stairs and around to the side of the building. There, huddled on the ground, sat Ezra, elbows on his knees and head cradled in his hands. Blood oozed between his fingers.

"*Piedras,*" said Pablo. "It was rocks throwed at us." He pulled a folded note, grimy and torn, from his pants pocket and handed it to John.

John opened it, his fingers shaking as he read:

Close your school and git out of town

"Who gave this to you?"
"A man."
"Do you know his name?"
Pablo shrugged.

John thrust the crumpled message into his waistcoat pocket, then knelt beside Ezra. "Let's see your wound, laddie." He lifted the boy's hand away from his head. The blood came from a small nick in the skin above his eye. Although a slight swelling and bruise appeared to be developing around it, the injury did not seem serious. Tears on young Ezra's face, however, spoke silently of a hurt throbbing far more deeply.

"He say to give you that note. He say bad things an' I kicks him hard. Then we run and he throwed rocks. I turns back to look an' that's when I got hit."

"Looks like the bleeding stopped," John said. "If you are ready to come to class you can wash up in the basin there."

John dismissed school early. A restlessness had undercut all he tried to accomplish until it seemed futile to continue for the day. He stood on the landing and watched the last pupil disappear from sight, the day half-spent and his enthusiasm with it.

"Hey. You there!" A shout from below brought him to quick attention. A stranger dressed in the garb of a stevedore approached from the direction of the dock. He stopped at the foot of the stairs, looking up at John. Strong, ruddy hands rested on his hips and the sleeves of his shirt bulged over muscular arms. "You Mr. Ogilvie, the freedmen teacher?"

John tensed, half-expecting the man to stoop, grab a rock and hurl it in his direction.

"Aye. How can I help you?" His preacher's voice, loud and sure, belied the fear in his belly.

"There's a heavy crate from Galveston with your name on it. Jus' been unloaded from the steamer. You need to make plans to fetch it." With that simple announcement, the man turned and departed.

"Thank you. I'll see to it," John called after him, releasing a huge breath of relief.

Two hours later, and minus a quarter each for the two men John hired to bring the shipment by ox cart and then push and pull it up the stairs, the crate lay open in the classroom. Seventy-five slates and thirty second readers. No first primers or arithmetic books among them—those which he most desperately lacked. The extra slates would be good to put aside in the event a student mislaid or somehow destroyed what he already had, but the more advanced books in lieu of first primers would not do.

For the second time that day, John dipped his pen into ink and composed a message to E. W. Wheelock.

> *Dear sir,*
> *The books and slates have arrived, and although I greatly appreciate your expediency in sending the order, Mr. Martin's memory served him wrongly in that my most immediate and urgent need is for additional first primers*

and arithmetic books. Of these I need forty each. Please send as soon as possible.

The heavy May air hinted of approaching summer, and John began to perspire as he struggled to put down the appropriate words. He couldn't shake the incident involving Ezra from his mind. Dipping his pen again into the ink, he continued:

I believe you should be aware that I have been threatened, as have some of my pupils. Of course, I have no intention of being intimidated by those who do not agree with our endeavors...

As he wrote he felt a surge of renewed strength. On completion of the letter he sealed it, hurried down the stairs, and marched to the post office. The walk helped his mood, and by the time he returned to the classroom a welcome breeze stirred, cutting through the thick humidity. His midday meal prepared by Mrs. Wallace—corn bread and a tin of cold beans—tasted better than usual, or perhaps he was simply adjusting to food once alien to his customary fare.

By the time John had prepared lessons for the evening class, his spirits were back to normal. As soon as Wheelock received his most recent note, the books he needed would be on their way and here in a couple of weeks. He pulled a few second primers from the box. Perhaps Samuel or even Jeb could use one. Samuel was ready for the challenge, and one would serve as a reward for Jeb's perseverance—a tangible goal to be reached. Aye, John liked that idea. But when all the regulars were in their seats, Jeb had not appeared. Night scholars often skipped class. Most were grown men, some with families, and they worked long hard hours. But Jeb, like Samuel, never missed.

"Where is Jeb?" he asked Samuel as class began.

"Don't know, suh," Samuel shrugged his shoulders, concern registering in his dark eyes.

John looked to the other pupils for a response. None came. He pushed down a feeling of alarm. If the younger scholars were targets of bigotry, surely the older ones were, too, and the consequences likely more serious. *Please, God, let him be safe.*

Chapter 9

Jeb never arrived, and his absence cast a somber mood over the night class. John closed up the classroom and trudged to his shared quarters with anxiety coiled inside him like an old bedspring ready to snap.

Joe Wallace sat in a rocking chair out front of the shanty, plucking at the strings of his fiddle. Lately, the warm evenings pushed him from inside the house and onto the porch.

On seeing John approach, he lifted his head and smiled. "Evenin'."

"Good evening," John said. He paused long enough to shake the hand of his host before continuing into the house. A quick glance around told him Jacob had left, and the stress of his troubling day eased a little at the thought of a night's sleep alone in bed.

"I kept your suppa' warm." Mrs. Wallace motioned for him to sit, as she ladled oyster stew into a bowl and set it, and a plate of biscuits, on the table.

Lowering herself onto the opposite chair, she let out a huge sigh. "That poor young 'un. He's learnin' 'bout some of life's troubles for us colored folk." She looked steadily into John's eyes as she continued speaking. "You is learnin', too."

"Aye. That I am."

They sat in silence while John ate. Afterwards, he washed his bowl and spoon in the pan of water left steaming on the stove for that purpose, and bidding the Wallaces goodnight, entered his tiny room. He lit the lamp, pulled off his shoes, and lay back on the pillow. His arm rubbed against his waistcoat pocket, reminding him of the note tucked inside. Pulling it out, he smoothed the crumpled paper then reread the message—now cast in eerie shadows from the glow of the burning wick.

Charcoal and Chalk

Close your school and git out of town

It wasn't so much the threats to him alone. What bothered John most was how danger spilled over to others—the Duvals, Ezra and Pablo, perhaps Jeb, and what about the Wallaces? As he pondered the magnitude of this domino effect, weariness stilled his burdensome thoughts, and he fell asleep.

***

The crow of a rooster in the cool predawn awoke John. He met the day rested and determined to fight the battles that lay ahead. Later, as the pupils arrived for class, at least one of his concerns was minimized. Ezra gloried in the attention he received from his classmates. His swollen eye had blackened enough to show against his dark skin, and he seemed the envy of all the other boys, plus the object of much sympathy from the girls.

"I kicked that whitey till his leg be purple. I showed him," Ezra exaggerated, demonstrating with a swift thrust of his left foot while he held his fists up ready to punch an imaginary foe.

John rang the bell on his desk for class to come to order. "The best way for each of you to show your superiority is by getting an education." He opened with the customary prayer, asking for forgiveness for all of them, and help in learning to love their enemies, suspecting the latter thought was lost to bad timing. Clearing his throat, he moved on to something more tangible.

"Who will read from today's lesson?" Four eager hands shot up, and class began.

The morning went well. John breathed more easily and shoved yesterday's ominous note to the back of his mind. *I must learn that most threats lead to nothing. They are simply words—folks letting off steam as they continue to adjust to the new status of the freed slaves.* Rumors of an organization forming to keep "niggers" in their place perhaps were true elsewhere, but not here in southern Texas. The fact that there had not been a repeat of his scare on the wharf proved that.

He stayed at school between classes, having brought along extra biscuits from last night's supper, washing each bite down with sips of cold coffee. Thoughts of Jeb drifted in and out of his head while he worked on a lesson plan for the evening class.

Footsteps on the stairs snapped John's attention to his surroundings. Mrs. Wallace was the only one who knew he was still here, but these were not her feet coming up the steps. He stood quickly, facing the door, the hair on the back of his neck prickling. He grasped the metal bell in his right hand, ready to throw it, as a diversion if nothing else. The door swung open and in walked Neal.

John let out a whoop of laughter, dropped the bell with a clatter, and strode forward to embrace his friend. "You are a welcome sight!"

"Well, I must say, I didn't expect such a greeting. If I were a woman, I would have slapped you." Neal flashed John a playful smile. "Then again, maybe not. How is your love life, anyway?"

"Same as yours, I suspect. This wee hamlet doesn't seem the best place to meet bonnie lassies."

Neal straddled one of the benches and sat. "I've missed you, John. You've made yourself scarce since you left the French family. Uptown too good for you now?"

"Nay. Not at all. How've you been? And Antonio?"

They talked for over an hour about whatever came to mind, and they laughed. John couldn't remember when he last had a good laugh. *Dear God, it felt good.* There were serious moments, too. He told his friend of the threatening note, Ezra's injury, and his concern about Jeb.

"I wouldn't worry about Jeb," Neal said. "I've seen that black cowboy. He can take care of himself. Now, how about supper Saturday night? I'll hide the wine so Antonio stays sober."

John laughed. "Don't be too harsh—how about a half bottle. We wouldn't want to make the cook mad."

At a quarter to five, the evening scholars climbed the stairs and entered the room two and three at a time, voices low in conversation. Hats came off, and each pupil greeted John with a smile. As they paraded to their respective spaces on the benches, John looked for Jeb's tall, strong figure to come sauntering through the door. By five fifteen he began to worry about Samuel's whereabouts, too. Thumps on the wood steps quickened his pulse.

In walked Samuel. "Sorry, I'm late, Teacha', but I have this for you." He held out a folded paper.

John's eyebrows lifted and Samuel responded to the unasked question. "From Jeb."

John took the note and opened it.

I be gone for sum days. Jeb

Relief tumbled through him as he re-folded the paper and focused on Samuel, who still stood quietly by.

"Did Jeb give you this note personally?"

"Yes, suh."

"Did he tell you why he can't be here?"

"No, suh."

"Did he seem ill?"

"No, suh. He said he had something to do more important than school."

Something more important than school? John couldn't imagine what that might be. The phrase locked into his mind, and he couldn't shake it all evening. School meant a lot to Jeb. He worked at it harder than most of the pupils. Whatever the man's reason for being gone, John had to believe it had nothing to do with threats against the freedmen's school. Nevertheless, he was glad he had written to Wheelock about the harassments. After all, one of the bureau's responsibilities to the teachers was protection. There were troops in Indianola to defend him, and his pupils, if necessary.

***

On May 25, two letters arrived from the bureau, though neither from Wheelock. One from Lt. Mitchel, dated May 11, which seemed to have strayed before it reached its destination, and one dated May 24 from the as yet unexplained Lieutenant Bonnaffon of Indianola. The messages were similar and equally maddening.

Mitchel wrote, from Indianola:

...the papers in this office show that the building was rented from C.W. Oswald, and must be so signed, not A. W. Oswald.

The letter from Bonnaffon dealt with the benches:

Mr. J. Ogilvie,

I enclose herewith new copies of Form 11 as the former were not made out on the proper form. I call your attention to the fact that, to obtain payment, the name of "Slater" must be signed Geo. W. Slater, not G. W. Slater. Please return the papers with the correct signature at as early a date as possible.

John took a deep breath, closed his eyes and counted to ten, recalling his thoughts weeks ago upon reading the printed circular from Major General Charles Griffin, reciting strict bureau rules for turning in reports. When the money owed for rent and benches was not immediately forthcoming, John had paid the two bills from his own meager funds. If it was just a matter of signing new vouchers, surely payment would arrive shortly. Rent was due and John could ill afford to rob his own funds to pay it again. He snatched up the new forms, marched downstairs and rounded the corner of the building to Oswald's office.

Upon hearing the explanation, Oswald shook his head in disbelief, signed the paper and pushed it toward John. "The government don't make anything easy," he said. "Just so I get paid. How much longer you figure on needing that room—don't school close up for the hot weather?"

"I haven't heard yet if I'm expected to work through summer," John said. "I'll let you know as soon as I get word. Anyway, the room here is supposed to be temporary. We'll be building a real school soon."

The words spilled from his mouth before he thought, but as he left the warehouse office heading toward George Slater's workshop, he had no regrets about what he had said. After all, he had been charged by the bureau, and the AMA, with establishing a permanent schoolhouse. Not only had he done nothing about it, he didn't even have a place to build one. Getting acquainted with his students, learning how to do lesson plans, frustration over the lack of books, plus problems with his living arrangements had taken all his energy. And he wouldn't allow himself to admit that at times fear for his own life might have kept him from moving forward with the building of a real school. But now it was time to focus on the future. As he walked through the streets of Lavaca, an idea began to grow.

That evening after supper, John leaned against the post on the porch where Joe Wallace sat in a rocker. Twilight breezes stirred across the bay waters, bringing a sigh of relief from the warm day. A mosquito buzzed near John's ear and he swatted at it unsuccessfully.

"I've been wondering," he said, clearing his throat, "how big a piece is that extra land you own?"

The rocking chair stilled. "Why you askin'?"

"We need a school and a church. I'm looking for a piece of land where we can put a building to serve those purposes." John swatted at another mosquito.

Joe chortled—the first semblance of a laugh John had heard from this quiet man. "You think I be a king or something? I ain't got *that* much land."

John gazed toward the bay. Except for a couple of straggly trees and some low brush there were no houses, no fences, nothing, just empty land—plenty of space for the building he had in mind.

"That's not all yours?"

Joe laughed again. "What would I do with all that?"

"Sell it to the Freedmen's Bureau."

Joe shook his head. "They don' want the little piece I got. See that there tree?" He pointed to a small oak struggling to stay upright against the constant wind. "Up to there be mine."

John's heart sank. A small shack might fit in the few yards between the Wallace's house and the tree, certainly not a school to hold seventy pupils or a congregation of exuberant worshipers.

"A house jest for yo'self there might work."

But John wasn't thinking about that, it was the larger piece he had his eye on. "Who owns all the rest?"

"Cain't say."

Their conversation ended, though John stayed on the porch a while longer listening to the rhythmic creak of Joe's chair and the rustle of leaves in the nearby trees as the dark of evening settled in. *Surely a piece of property below the bluff, skirted by shacks of the colored folks, is affordable. I will find the owner and make an offer.*

Chapter 10

Long after settling into bed that night, John stared at nothing in the dark. His plan to build a school, and all the attendant probabilities, drove out any suggestion of sleep. Sometime, the exact hour unknown, Jacob crawled into bed beside him. As John lay shoved against the wall, his body damp with sweat, his thoughts shifted. If he planned to stay in Lavaca and be true to his commitment in spite of threats, a place of his own, for the sake of his sanity, suddenly seemed more important than the school.

He didn't know when sleep finally caught up with him, but he gradually became conscious of daylight squeezing through cracks in the roughly hewn wall. The other half of the narrow bed lay empty, and voices drifted in from the main living area. The thin fabric drape serving as a door to the room provided no sound barrier, nor did it stop the scent of sizzling pork fat from wafting through.

"If that Mistah Ogilvie sleep too much longer this Saturday mawnin', he ain't gonna have no hoecakes," Mrs. Wallace's teasing voice rang deliberately loud.

John quickly dressed and pulled back the curtain.

Mrs. Wallace stood by the stove flipping the cakes. Jacob sat at the table working on a half-eaten stack, dabbing each forkful in a pool of molasses. Strains of fiddle music outside meant Joe was already done with breakfast.

John found his place at the table, and Mrs. Wallace set a full plate before him. As he took the first bite, the realization hit that he had grown accustomed to this unrefined Southern food—actually liked it. There were times when he sorely missed the food from his youth—even that poor man's fare, haggis, a mixture of minced sheep's heart, lungs, liver, oatmeal and seasonings. And what he wouldn't give for a mutton pie. But that was then, and now he was in Texas. If he dwelled on it, homesickness would sneak into his thoughts and he mustn't allow it. Mimicking Jacob, he spooned a generous serving of molasses on each cake before putting it into his mouth, savoring the warm sweetness. After his first few bites, he turned to his young bed mate.

"So, how's the railroad?"

"Fine, jus' fine, thanks to me and the other coloreds what keep on fixin' and layin' track. We the ones who keep that there railroad runnin'."

Mrs. Wallace said her son was a man of few words. John found this generally to be true, yet Jacob always seemed willing to talk of his work—work that was obviously hard and the reason the young man slept so soundly whenever he arrived home. Firm muscles bulging from beneath the rolled up sleeves of his coarsely woven shirt offered proof of heavy labor.

Once breakfast was over, John had plans for the day. The letter from Sarah Barnes had renewed his determination to visit pupils in their homes. *I will start with Ezra,* he thought, *I owe the boy's parents an explanation for the unpleasantness at the dock and subsequent injury.* He headed toward a shack farther down the bay. As he approached, a voice called out.

"Teacha!" Ezra came running, a big grin stretched across his face. The swelling around his eye was gone, the bruise faded. In a day or so the visual remnants of his injury would completely disappear, transforming him from hero status back to ordinary boy.

"I've come to visit and meet your folks," John said.

Ezra scampered away and vanished into the cabin. Moments later he reappeared holding the hand of a tiny woman, stooped and wrinkled and leaning on a hand-hewn wooden cane.

"This be my gran'mammy."

The old woman studied John for a long moment. She had no teeth, but her eyes snapped with a strength not manifested in the frail-looking body draped in a cotton dress several sizes too big. She pointed the cane at a bench along side the house.

"Set yo'sef down."

John sat, amused at his instant inclination to obey this tiny black woman. The gran'mammy eased herself down beside him. Ezra stood before them, suddenly shy, drawing circles in the dust with a toe.

"You come to tell me my gran'baby doin' bad in school?"

The toe stopped in mid-circle.

"No, not at all. Ezra is doing good work. He tries very hard." John flashed the boy a smile, and Ezra stood a little taller, abandoning his artistry in the dirt.

"What you heah fo, then?" the woman said.

"I plan to visit all my students at home during the school term. Does Ezra have other family?"

"Nope. I be it." She stomped her cane on the ground to emphasize the statement.

"I also wanted to check on his injury. Did he tell you what caused the cut over his eye?"

"He say a man throwed a rock at him cuz he be a nigger. An he say he kick dat man. An I say good. De Bible say to do dat. One eye for de udder."

John winced at her comment, but saw an opening for his favorite subject. "You are a Bible reader?"

"Cain't read."

"You can come to school with Ezra and learn to read."

"Nope. Too old."

"Maybe you would enjoy coming to the church service on Sunday. We read from the Bible and sing songs."

"Cain't git up them stairs."

"Aye, that is a problem. One of these days we will build a church easier to get to, then you can come."

"Might."

Between comments, she made sucking noises with her toothless mouth and never took her gaze off her grandson. After this initial verbal exchange, they sat in silence and Ezra took up toe-drawing again. John felt he had covered all the subjects pertinent to his visit. He supposed he could talk about the weather, but it seemed beside the point.

Rising from the bench, he faced the woman. "It's been a pleasure meeting you. And it's also a pleasure having Ezra in class. I hope we can talk again sometime."

The expression on the old woman's face remained solemn, but she nodded. A serious-looking Ezra scooted immediately to his grandmother and helped her to her feet.

John smiled at the boy. "I'll see you Monday, Ezra."

"Yes, suh." Ezra's grin reappeared as he turned to assist his gran'mammy into the shanty.

As John continued toward his next destination, he marveled at the insight he had gained into the life of one pupil by this short visit. *I wonder who really takes care of whom in that household.*

Jeremy Jackson's house was next. John had told the energetic twelve-year-old he would be coming, and the door sprang open before John had a chance to knock. He stepped across the threshold into pandemonium. The crowded, two-room shanty smelled of a peculiar mix of sweat, urine, and freshly baked biscuits. A thin woman, her hair covered with a bandana, her brown eyes dull, held a crying baby on her hip. Two toddlers clung to her soiled skirt, and a girl of about five sat at a table, shyly eyeing John.

Jeremy made introductions, indicating each family member with a broad sweep of his hand. In spite of the adverse conditions, he glowed with pride. "This be my Momma, my sister Josie, my sisters Rose and Lily, and my baby brother Theodore."

"Pleased to meet you, Mistah Ogilvie," Mrs. Jackson greeted him in a voice matching the tired eyes. "Have yo'self a chair."

John removed his hat and took the chair nearest him and opposite little Josie. Mrs. Jackson made no effort to sit herself, but continued to bounce the crying baby. With her free hand, she picked up a platter of still-warm biscuits from the stove top and plunked it in the center of the table. "Hep yo'self. They be fresh baked."

Josie reached for one and the woman slapped her hand. "Mind yo' manners. Those is for the teacha." The little girl's face twisted up tight in a stifled cry and she began to sniffle.

John cringed at the slap, trying to control his discomfort at the situation. "Thank you for the biscuits, Ma'am. I appreciate your labors, but I couldn't possibly eat them all. One will be plenty, and it would be fine to have the children join me." Though not hungry, he took a biscuit and bit into it, pushing the plate closer to Josie, who cautiously reached for one. Jeremy took the only remaining chair, grabbed a biscuit and stuffed half into his mouth. His mother cast John a weary look. He was obviously expected to do the talking. Swallowing his bit of biscuit, he cleared his throat. "Jeremy is a fine lad and very enthusiastic about his studies. Has he told you of his accomplishments?"

"I done tole her I know all my ABCs, and numbers clear to a hundred." Jeremy flashed John a big grin.

"I knowed he be smart," Mrs. Jackson said, her eyes showing the first glimmer of shine John had seen. She shifted the baby to her other hip and tucked a stray curl on her forehead under her kerchief. "I hope he learn to read real good real fast cuz soon he gonna be helping his pappy bring in the fish."

This was news John hadn't considered. "He's doing well, but the longer he stays in school the better. And what about Josie? Will she be starting soon?" He looked over at the little girl who had not yet said a word. John's comment coaxed a smile onto her pretty face. One of the toddlers had crawled up into Josie's lap then put her head on her sister's chest, thumb in mouth.

Mrs. Jackson shook her head. "It'd be good if all the chilluns could get some learnin', but I need Josie here to hep."

John could see this was true, and what was more, if he guessed correctly, the mother was expecting another baby in a few months. The importance of education simply couldn't override other immediate needs. He rose to go. "It was nice to meet you, Mrs. Jackson, and thank you for the biscuits."

John called on three more pupils, and though each home proved unique, a common thread tied all the families together—the desire to have the children learn.

The day of visiting ended with another satisfying meal at Neal and Antonio's. Even before his first glass of wine, Antonio seemed extra jovial, singing while he prepared another Italian specialty. The tune was familiar and John burst into song, his tenor voice blending with Antonio's deep bass notes. Neal, who didn't sing, raised his arms and, waving a fork in place of a baton, pretended to direct the duo.

The high-spirited mood continued throughout the meal. Once stomachs were full, the evening tapered off with the three of them moving chairs outside. Antonio drank from his third glass of wine. Neal and John held mugs of steaming coffee. A breeze carried the scent of the bay waters. John looked up at the quarter moon flanked by the first star of the evening and reflected on the past twelve hours. It had been a good day.

"Things going okay at the school?" Neal asked.

"Aye, well enough." John told of the visits to the homes of his pupils. How he had learned so much by simply entering their private lives.

Neal seemed to study the content of his cup a moment. "Too bad you have to teach in that run-down warehouse," he said, "I suspect the roof leaks whenever a squall passes through."

John chuckled. "Aye, that it does. I keep buckets to catch the drips. But it's temporary. The bureau wants a new one to be built."

Surprise registered on Neal's face. "The bureau's got land around here for that?"

"Well, not exactly. Not yet." The conversation the night before with Joe about his extra land had circled in John's mind all day. He took another swallow of coffee and looked at Neal. "Say, you wouldn't happen to know who owns the empty lot next to the Wallaces', would you?"

Neal shrugged. "Not off hand. I suppose we could ask around, or you might go to the court house in Indianola and check out the deeds."

Later, after they had said their goodbyes and John strolled toward home, he thought about Neal's suggestion. Aye, a trip to the courthouse in Indianola would be good. He needed to see Lieutenant Mitchel about several things as well. He picked up his pace and began to hum. Maybe by fall his pupils would have a new school. For the moment, thoughts of who might be waiting in the dark shadows to waylay the Yankee school teacher were pushed aside his enthusiasm.

***

During lessons the following Monday John could scarcely keep his mind off the plans for the new school. He envisioned a level floor of smooth wood and solid windows that kept the blustery bay winds out, allowing plenty of sunshine to stream in. He whistled a happy tune as he strode to get the mail after the day classes had been dismissed.

The one letter handed to him shifted his focus. The response from Wheelock regarding the book shipment had finally arrived:

OFFICE SUPERINTENDENT OF EDUCATION,
Refugees and Freedmen, State of Texas
Galveston, May 25, 1867

John Ogilvie, Esq.
Dear Sir,
Your two letters bearing the date of May 13 have reached me though delayed. I am sorry that Martin has succeeded in causing both of us some annoyance, but for the future I have him earmarked; he has left Galveston in some haste.

You can have whatever time is necessary to dispose of the books and slates sent by deception on the part of that precious scamp. At present I am entirely out of primers and arithmetic books. Did you receive the illustrated papers I sent you care of Lt. Mitchel?

When the discontented in your town do aught "out of the common," I will be obliged for the particulars, as I keep a record.

Let me hear from you soon, believe me always ready to assist you.

Very respectfully,
E.W. Wheelock

John chuckled at Wheelock's use of the word "scamp" to describe Martin, yet he felt let down by the lack of primers and arithmetic books. And he knew nothing about illustrated papers or why Mitchel hadn't sent them.

At least Wheelock acknowledged John's account of the threatening note and the attack on Ezra and Pablo. If records were being kept, it was important to report any further incidents. *With God's help,* he prayed, *may there be none.*

The evening session went well, though John missed Jeb and had trouble shaking the thought from his mind that something was amiss.

After class Samuel turned to him, as though reading his mind. "Suh, I think mebbe Jeb is gone looking for his family. Evah since freedom come, he jest goes off sometimes lookin' for his wife and chilluns what was sold away from him. I expects he be back. Learnin' is mighty important to him."

John knew families were torn apart during slavery—members sold to different masters—still, the thought dumbfounded him. He sorely missed his father and stepbrothers left behind in Scotland, but they had not been ripped from him against his wishes. He knew of their whereabouts and could communicate with them.

He shook his head in dismay. "Thank you, Samuel, for sharing that. We must pray for Jeb's safe return and that he finds his wife and children."

"I do that, suh. I pray every day for all my brethren and their struggles."

John smiled at his helper. He had always pictured angels as female, white, and golden-haired, but now he wondered if God had sent this remarkable black man from Heaven to keep his Scots teacher humble and teach him a thing or two about loving mankind.

They closed up the schoolroom, climbed down the stairs, shook hands and parted.

"I'll see you tomorrow evening," John said with a wave.

"I'll be there," Samuel said, then disappeared into the dark of the night.

As John approached the Wallaces' shanty, he observed Joe on the porch in the rocker as usual, but tonight, beside him in a straight-backed chair, sat Mrs. Wallace. Neither seemed to be doing anything in particular, just sitting and waiting. Even in the twilight John could tell their gazes were on him.

"Good evening," John said.

"Evenin'," Mrs. Wallace answered.

"Set a spell." Joe motioned to a stool next to the door.

The seriousness in the man's tone caused a flutter of alarm deep inside John.

"You ain't paid us no rent lately, Mistah Ogilvie."

So that's it. They need money, and I haven't come through. A friendship only accounted for so much, and for all practical purposes his living here was a business arrangement. "No sir. I'm waiting for a paycheck from the bureau. It should come any day now. I apologize for the delay."

"We got us a idea," Joe continued.

John glanced at each of them. A smile flickered across Mrs. Wallace's face. Something other than an eviction was afoot.

"How's about puttin' up a house next to here—on my land. It be yours to live in, but mine to keep, an' you don't pay no rent."

At first the idea was too wonderful to fully grasp. A place to come and go as he pleased, do what he wanted, when he wanted, and best of all, never having to share his bed. Then reality took over.

"I like that idea just fine, but it takes money to build a house. Right now I have none."

"Joe and the night scholars could hep build it," Mrs. Wallace said. "That part won't cost none."

"Think on it," Joe said, and he and his wife got up and walked into the house.

In spite of the bothersome mosquitoes, John remained in quiet solitude on the porch for another half hour before heading for bed. There must be some way to make it work.

He did have a little cash: fifty dollars, held aside for emergencies. A man shouldn't be without reserves. Still, maybe he could use that for lumber for a house. It wouldn't require much. One room would do. There was his monthly allotment from the missionary association, but it was put directly into his college fund account, and he shouldn't start dipping into that. Surely his May pay check from the bureau would arrive any day now.

John pondered the pros and cons of the tempting offer throughout the night during a fitful sleep and into the next day during class. At four o'clock that afternoon, as he sat at his desk trying to prepare the evening lessons, the sound of a knock on the schoolhouse door interrupted his thoughts. He stood and strode to the door, opened it and found a heavy-set man in a fancy checkered suit standing at the top of the stairs.

"Are you the teacher of the freedmen?" The man's voice boomed with self-assurance in an accent similar to Neal's.

"Aye," John replied. This stranger did not frighten him like others who asked that same question. His eyes snapped with intelligence and smile lines creased his face.

"I hear you've been inquiring about the empty lot down by the bay," the man said.

"Aye, yes. Please come in."

"Name's Ware. George Ware." The man entered and shook John's hand. He scanned the temporary classroom, taking it all in —the cracked window, slanted floor, and John's desk made from planks set on packing crates.

"We need the lot to build a real school for the freedmen," John said. "The pupils deserve better than this. Do you own that property?"

"No, but I know who does, an acquaintance of mine in Victoria. I think he'd be glad to unload it. I know it's not worth much, and teaching the little colored children is a worthy cause. I think you could get it for a good price. How much are you willing to pay?"

John had no idea what property cost—here or anywhere. The bureau wanted him to build; however, they hadn't gone into any details with him. Without thinking further he blurted, "I have fifty dollars I can give you now, and more later from the bureau, but I can't say how much."

63

To John's astonishment, that satisfied Mr. Ware. "I'll be back in a few days with a deed and will collect the fifty dollars at that time," he said. There seemed to be no doubt in the man's mind that his friend in Victoria would go along with the arrangement.

After the man left, John chastised himself for not asking more questions. Mr. Ware seemed sincere and at least no money had changed hands, but who was he and how did he learn John was interested in that particular piece of property? Not many folks knew of his plans—Oswald, the Wallaces, and Neil and Antonio. He pulled his watch from his waistcoat pocket. Twenty-five past four. If he hurried, he could talk to Neil before the evening class.

In the office of Giovanni Imports, Neil admitted he had sent the man to John. "He's a widower who lived in Lavaca before the war, but left when Texas seceded," Neil said. "He moved in with family in my home town in Massachusetts; that's where I met him. Now he comes and goes between the two places. A strong abolitionist, he tries to help out where he can. You can trust him. His heart's in the right place."

John returned to the classroom in good spirits and tried not to dwell on the fact that once his fifty dollars was gone, so was the hope of a place of his own. Instead, his thoughts danced with the idea of a new school building becoming reality.

That night he wrote to the bureau, enthusiasm flowing through his pen with every stroke. He told of the property to be theirs in a few days and of the money he had promised. *As soon as you forward a check to me I will pay the balance for the property, purchase lumber and begin building.* Recent correspondence from Bonnaffon in Indianola concerned and confused him. But until he received official word otherwise, John assumed Lt. Mitchel was the bureau agent still in charge there, and so his letter to Indianola was addressed accordingly. And to make certain his request reached headquarters, he wrote a duplicate copy to Superintendent Wheelock in Galveston.

Upon sealing the two envelopes, John sat at his desk thinking how construction of a schoolhouse would impact the community. He needed an architect and carpenters, and possibly more money than the bureau could offer. *Surely, some of the businessmen of Lavaca would be willing to help,* he thought. He massaged his forehead with his fingers to ease a mounting tension; then dropping his hands he folded them together, bowed his head, and prayed for tolerance in the community, for continued patience on his part, and for the mysterious Mr. Ware. *Dear Lord, impart to him the willingness to offer us a fair deal, and bless him. Amen.*

The days following John's posting of the letters to Mitchel and Wheelock seemed to drag. Early June foretold a hot, muggy summer. The heavy air that drifted across the shoreline of the Gulf of Mexico seemed to have a body of its own, and it wrapped everyone in the cloying moisture, barely allowing one to take a breath before very late at night. But John tried to accept it as a warm, caring friend, and he felt a part of the quiet land. Nevertheless, his anxious mind made the wait for a reply to his request that much more difficult.

Finally, on June 13th, an envelope arrived from Lieutenant Mitchel. John held it a full minute, whispering a silent prayer, before ripping the seal and casting his eyes on the contents. After a quick read through, he didn't know whether to laugh out loud or curse.

Refugio, Texas
June 11, 1867

> *Mr. Ogilvie,*
> *I regret to have to enclose herewith vouchers of C.W. Oswald. He must sign C. W. Oswald, and not Charles W. Oswald, as he is so reported on form No. 22...Very respectfully yours,*
>
> > *J.R.Mitchel*
> > *Lt. 35th Infy*

John slumped on the bench and slowly exhaled. *Unbelievable.* The Refugio return address, too, frustrated and perplexed him. If Mitchel had been sent elsewhere, there was a chance he never received a copy of the request for funds for the new school.

John sighed and shuffled through a stack of papers, looking for the blank forms. He pulled two from the pile, picked up the newly received letter and headed out the door for the warehouse office. *I might as well get this unpleasant task over.*

Oswald looked up from paperwork when the door opened.

"Yes, Mr. Ogilvie. What can I do for you?"

Closing the door firmly behind him, John crossed the room and, standing before the agent for J. D. Braman & Co., got straight to the point.

"I've come for a couple of reasons. First to let you know we have plans to begin building a school soon. Of course it will be a matter of months before it can be occupied." He felt a little uncomfortable speaking prematurely of this venture, but perhaps it would minimize the irritation of the next subject.

"That so? And where will this new school be at?"

"The bureau is purchasing a piece of property down the bay."

"Hm, that so? Seems like a big expense and bother, but I suppose that's your business." Leaning back in his chair, he placed his hands behind his head, elbows out, revealing perspiration stains on the underside of the sleeves of his white dress shirt. "You said you had something else on your mind. I trust you have brought the overdue rent money."

"I wish it were so," John said, and handed him Mitchel's letter and the blank voucher. "I received this today."

Oswald leaned forward to take the papers, the front chair legs thumping soundly as they settled down on the wooden floor. He began to read. John watched as a muscle in the man's jaw twitched and his eyes narrowed.

"Why in tarnation does the government give a damn how I sign a piece of paper? It all has to do with not wanting to shell out their precious money." Oswald stabbed his pen into the inkwell and scrawled *C. W. Oswald* across the bottom of the voucher and thrust it at John. "There. That had better satisfy the high and mighty bureau, or you'll be finding a new place to teach them coloreds before you get that school built."

"I apologize for the delays. This should take care of the situation. I will bring the rent money as soon as I receive it."

Oswald grunted. John left the building without further comment. He understood the man's frustration. He still waited for his own overdue pay for May.

So he was surprised but hopeful when the next mail boat brought yet another piece of correspondence from Mitchel—with a return address once again from Indianola, not Refugio.

This had to be his delinquent paycheck. John tore open the seal and with a stab of disappointment found no check inside, yet when he unfolded the one sheet of bureau stationery, the single sentence scribbled there brought a cry of joy to his lips.

Ogilvie, Proceed to begin building the new schoolhouse. The bureau will help with expenses up to $1,000.
J.R. Mitchel

Chapter 11

On Monday, June 17, John still glowed from Mitchel's go-ahead for the school. At breakfast Mrs. Wallace plopped down on the chair opposite him. "We have a 'portant matter to discuss," she said with great formality.

John swallowed his bite of grits and set his spoon down.

"Do you know 'bout Juneteenth?" she asked.

"Juneteenth?"

"Yes, suh, Juneteenth."

"I don't believe I do." He put his elbows on the table, rested his chin on his hands, and smiled. "Tell me about Juneteenth."

"Well, Mistah Ogilvie, it's 'portant that you know. On June 19, two year ago, freedom come to the slaves in Texas. I think we should have us a party at school. Iffen we don't, nobody goin' to show up on a counta they all be having they own celebration."

It hit John with a jolt. Only two years since these folk had been released from bondage. The struggles and accomplishments of his pupils in that short period of time were remarkable. Through his AMA training, he'd learned the Emancipation Proclamation was officially announced on January 1, 1863, but slaves in Texas didn't get the word for two and a half more years, and even then it took months to filter through the plantations. Many times John's anger rose at the injustice of it all. Juneteenth, as the freedmen here apparently called it, was indeed an important date.

"Aye, that would be a grand idea. How do you suggest we celebrate?"

"Music and food. I'll start cookin' tomorrow. You tell about it today at school so the mammies of all those chillun can start cookin' too. Joe, he can bring his fiddle, so's we can dance." She stood and started clearing the table with a frenzy. "I kin hardly wait."

"Will they do that? Cook, I mean? It's only two days away. And will the parents come?"

A look of incredulity shot across her face. "Mistah Ogilvie, don' you know nothin'? Of course they'll come. This is a very 'portant day."

Chagrined at her admonishment, John leaped up. "Thank you. It's a fine idea, and I want them to help. I just need to know how to plan."

During the short walk to the school for the day class, he mulled over the celebration. There must be more to it than music and food —some kind of introduction.

Among his papers was a copy of the Emancipation Proclamation.

I'll read that aloud, or at least part of it, to begin the festivities. Perhaps some of the students could tell where they were when they first learned of their freedom—about their initial reactions. Aye, that would be good.

An eagerness for the event began to rise within him.

He decided to wait until the end of class time to tell of the plan so as to keep order. Mrs. Wallace eyed him anxiously throughout the morning, obviously anticipating his announcement at any moment. Finally, after lunch recess she huffed, "If you don't talk 'bout it, I will."

But John had been wise to wait. Cheers erupted as soon as the words were out of his mouth, and all the next day excitement buzzed through the room. Pupils concentrated poorly on lessons, and he had to ring the bell for attention so often the place sounded like a discordant music class. Their thoughts were all focused on the coming celebration.

That evening, John discussed his plan with Mrs. Wallace. "I'll read President Lincoln's proclamation first," he said.

She looked at him a minute, pursing her lips. "I don' know. I suspect presidents talk long and fancy. Them words could get mighty tiresome."

He wasn't about to give on this. "It is very important—you said so yourself. And maybe one or two scholars can tell about their feelings on receiving the news."

She didn't like that idea either. "Nobody will want to talk. The dancin' and singin' will tell how they feel."

John smiled and shook his head. "We'll see."

He had announced there would be no lessons on Wednesday the nineteenth. All pupils, including the evening class and any additional family members who could come, were to appear at eleven o'clock bearing food. John, Joe and Mrs. Wallace arrived at the classroom early to prepare for the event. They arranged benches along the walls, leaving a big space in the middle for dancing, and then positioned two planks on crates to form tables for the food.

And parents came, as did most of the night scholars, all carrying generous portions of something to eat. Even Jeremy's mother appeared with little ones in tow. Josie followed with a plate full of biscuits. Dishes crowded the long tables until the planks sagged under the weight. John had never seen such a banquet: ham, roast chicken, chitlins, corn bread, pickled pigs' feet, greens, dried figs, persimmons, and the ever-present oysters dug from the beach close by. And desserts: cakes, pecan and sweet potato pies.

Excitement crackled through the crowd.

John began the festivities by welcoming everyone, and then, contrary to his original plan, chose not to read Lincoln's speech. Instead, he recited the first sentence of the order read by General Gordon Granger in Galveston on June 19, 1865:

"The people are informed that in accordance with a Proclamation from the Executive of the United States, all slaves are free."

When that phrase had been spoken, Joe Wallace pulled the bow across his fiddle, cheers erupted from the throng and the dancing and singing began. For the remainder of the event John stood back and watched the freedmen celebrate. This was their jubilation. Their life change. And try as he might, he knew he could never experience the deep stirring they felt within their souls.

Happy melodies rang through the building, but occasionally a wail erupted from someone in the crowd, and heart-rending words from a song of bondage ripped forth. A mournful version of "Go Down, Moses" sent chills through John: *"Oppress'ed so hard they could not stand, Let my people go."*

Things quieted down a bit when folks dug into the piles of food. Later, sitting around with appetites satisfied, recollections of June 19, 1865 came forth with no prodding from their teacher.

"I remember that day two year ago—plain as if it were yesterday," Samuel said. "Massa called us all to the big house to tell us we be free. At first no one talked—like they didn't hear right. Then everyone whooped and hollered and carried on like they seen the Lord coming."

Others shared, too, stories quite similar. The afternoon ended with another song: "*I am free, I am free, my Lord, I'm washed by the blood of the Lamb.*" The dual significance of the words drove into John's very core.

That night he walked. The days were longer now and darkness, veiling all its unknowns, came late. He would be home before the sun slid behind the horizon. Wavelets lapped at his feet as he trod along the bay shore. A breeze ruffled his hair and whispered around his ears. A restlessness invaded his being like a clock that wouldn't wind down. The Juneteenth celebration was a grand success. Mrs. Wallace had come through once again. He owed her much.

The emotion and significance of the event seemed reflected in the sunset glow rippling across the water. Today, for the first time since becoming their teacher, John's pupils had shared their pain and their joy. He felt privileged and awed at the experience and began to sense the real impact of his role in their future.

Now June would soon be done and maybe classes too, until fall anyway. That he didn't yet know. One thing he knew for sure, whether classes continued during the summer or not, he would stay here and build a school.

Chapter 12

By late afternoon the following Sunday, rain began to fall. John had stayed in the classroom after Sabbath school to prepare lessons for the next day. Perspiration trickled down his forehead, dripping onto the primer he held in his hand. He wiped at his face with the palm of his hand and sighed. When the storm clouds gathered he had hoped the air would cool as a result, but a warm wind accompanied the downpour. The upstairs room sucked in the heat and held it like a coal-burning furnace.

Maybe I'll conduct class at the foot of the steps under the trees during the summer months, when it's not raining. There would be distractions, of course, but it couldn't be worse than suffering from the heat. Then again, he hadn't heard if he was expected to continue classes in July and August. Regardless, by fall they would be in a new building. That knowledge gave him a shiver of joy whenever he thought of it.

On Monday between classes, John picked up two pieces of mail, both from Galveston. He hurried back to the schoolroom to read their contents. The first held a standard printed circular from Major General Charles Griffin spelling out the bureau's policies for the summer. The first few sentences told John what he had been waiting to hear:

The Schools for Freedmen in Texas will close, for the customary summer vacation, on the 30th inst., to resume on the 1st of October. Teachers desiring to continue their schools through the vacation can do so, on a self-sustaining basis, prescribing and collecting such fees as they think proper...

A letter from Wheelock, in the second envelope, elaborated further on the summer schedule, and added an intriguing paragraph.

Charcoal and Chalk

Galveston, June 15, 1867

John Ogilvie, Esq.

Dear Sir,

Whether you close school soon depends entirely on yourself; if you choose to teach through the summer the Bureau will be well pleased.... It is our policy to keep open every school that we can.

Have you heard aught of the missing books? Can't you take a run down to Indianola some Saturday and look them up? They must be there. Lt. Mitchel seems to have been neglectful.

Very respectfully, E.W. Wheelock

Whether to teach or not was thrown right back into John's own lap. He stood, walked to the window and gazed out at the bay. In spite of the heat, he hated to take a break from teaching. A gap in lessons could set back those who had difficulty learning. And now the long-awaited books might be only a few miles away.

Yet, to continue through the summer presented another problem—the matter of money. John couldn't survive doing this for free. He owed room and board to the Wallaces, and though teaching the freedmen was a missionary outreach, it was also his livelihood, and a means to put aside money for the college education he intended to have. He wasn't sure pupils could afford a higher tuition through the summer weeks. There was only one way to find out.

At five o'clock, he paced the length of the benches as the night time scholars took their places. When all were settled in, he stood tall before them, hands behind his back.

"Before we begin our lessons, Gentlemen, I have an important question to ask."

Feet shuffled and someone coughed, but no one spoke, and all eyes were upon him.

"Normally, school would be out in June and not start again until October. However, I will keep on teaching during the summer if you are willing to come."

"Yes, suh!" The immediate reply echoed throughout the room.

"There is one problem," John continued. "The government will not pay me during that time, so I would have to collect a dollar from each of you per month in order to keep the school open."

72

The room filled with silence, and John's heart sank. This was too much to ask. He watched and waited, clutching his fingers so tightly behind him they felt numb.

Samuel spoke up first. "I can pay a dollah," he said.

"Me too," another quickly replied.

Then others joined in until the room rattled with their voices, sounding almost as chaotic as the day class. A contented smile tugged on John's face. "Thank you, gentlemen. We will all benefit from your decision."

The reaction the following morning from the day class was totally different, as John had anticipated it would be. The adults seemed split on the idea of paying the dollar, some of the older children wanted a break, and they and the youngest pupils needed to consult with parents. Sending home notes was out of the question. Even if there was enough paper to do so, the parents couldn't read. John would have to visit them personally for an answer. However, in the meantime, he had already decided to continue with the school. It would be easier with fewer students, and those who chose to take a break would simply have to pick up in the fall where they left off and do the best they could.

In the midst of the other decisions, John could not shake loose the thought of having his own living quarters. His bureau pay for May and June might be enough money to build a small house. Unfortunately, the time to do it was now, and he had not received those checks.

During one of his evenings with Neal and Antonio, John mentioned the Wallaces' offer. "I wish I could do it," he sighed, "but I don't know how."

"You won't need much," Antonio said, "unless you plan on putting up a castle."

John laughed, thinking of Stirling Castle high on the hill not far from his home in Scotland. "Aye, that would be grand, but I'll settle for one wee room for now."

Neal stood and paced the floor with enthusiasm as though he were planning a house for himself. "A few two-by-fours, some nails, and lumber for the floor and sides is all it should take."

"A window would be nice. And a roof," John said.

"Now you're getting picky," Neal teased.

"Hey, if that's all, we'll advance you some," Antonio said.

John smiled and shook his head. "That's not why I brought it up."

"That's what friends are for," Neal said. "And besides, with a place of your own, you could have us over for Scottish food."

"We'll order the lumber tomorrow, put it on our account," Antonio said.

"I won't take charity," John said. "I'll pay you as soon as my paychecks come in. And I think I can scrape up a wee bit more from another source."

He had decided to ask the missionary association to send some of his savings. Borrowing from his college account just this once wouldn't matter, and he refused to be indebted to his friends.

The following day, as he sat at his schoolroom desk to compose the letter, the unexpected Mr. Ware appeared again at the door. The man bustled into the room, stood before John and pulled a paper from his coat pocket. "I've good news, Mr. Ogilvie." He laid the long, manila document on the desk.

John caught his breath when he read the title: *Deed of Trust.* He scanned the document top to bottom, his heart racing. The property by the bay had been deeded to the bureau, just as Mr. Ware had promised.

"Mr. Wilkins is asking one hundred fifty dollars and will take your fifty as a deposit, the remainder to be paid by the end of the year."

John sprang to his feet, a smile spreading across his face. "Thank you, sir. I am much obliged. The remainder should not be a problem. There is money guaranteed by the bureau for this project."

Mr. Ware left with John's money—every cent. Yet the future shone in his mind. There was lumber on order for his own house to be built, his pay checks from the bureau would surely arrive any day, and he had a promise of one thousand dollars to build a school. Now all he needed was patience.

But, there was plenty to do. The next evening at the supper table, after sharing the good news about the deed, John told the Wallaces he planned on traveling to Indianola in the morning.

"There should be a box of books to be picked up, and I need to talk to the bureau agent there about getting the money for the school as soon as possible."

Joe looked at him steadily for a moment. "Might be a bad idea."

"Why is that?"

"I heah they got the fevah down that way."

"Fever?"

"Yes, suh. Yella fevah. It ain't nothin' to mess with."

"Surely the entire town isn't tainted."

"I don' know, suh. I hear tell some folks got it who come by boat from Mexico. They been spreadin' it around."

John pondered this unexpected information. His trip to Indianola to pick up books and receive funding for building the school was important. *Surely the bureau agency isn't in contact with Mexican immigrants. I'll go.*

Chapter 13

By the next morning, in spite of Joe's misgivings, John walked to the livery on the edge of town. He hadn't been here since his wild ride with Neal in the pounding rain. The place was bigger than he had remembered. Wagons of various sizes stood in a neat row the length of the building, as though waiting for a parade to begin. A number of stalls lined one side, occupied by variously colored horses who gazed at John with large, dark eyes. A not unpleasant odor of hay and manure filled the air. The owner, a short, muscular German by the name of Malcolm Frank, was cleaning out a stable as John approached.

The man set the pitchfork aside and, pulling a handkerchief from his trouser pocket, wiped his brow already wet with perspiration. "Morning," he said.

"Good morning. I'm in need of a horse and wagon to fetch a load of books from Indianola. Would you have something to serve that purpose?"

Mr. Frank replaced the hemmed rag in his pocket. "When do you need to go?"

"As soon as possible."

"If you can wait an hour or so, I'm heading that way this morning to deliver some hides. You're welcome to come along. Wagon will be empty on the return."

The fifteen-mile trip in the hot sun seemed much longer than the ride on the steam lighter John had taken up the bay in the cool of March. The wagon wheels creaked slowly along the road of crushed oyster shells, and in spite of Mr. Frank's expert handling of the mule team, the wagon lurched and bumped, making an uncomfortable ride. The closer they traveled to their destination, the more barren the landscape. John hung onto his hat as the wind picked up.

During the ride, Mr. Frank talked of his home town in Germany and how he had come twenty years earlier with others from his country to find a new life in Texas. He told of entire German communities established inland from the gulf.

"Some of us chose to stay in Indianola and other towns nearby," he said. During the conversation he spoke of differences between the German settlers and the Americans, the German's opposition to slavery among them. This pleased John, and he made a mental note to approach this amiable man when he began seeking local support for the building of the schoolhouse.

When Indianola came into view, John felt the same sensation he had upon seeing the place when he first arrived by steamer. He wouldn't want to live there. Though bigger than Lavaca, the carefully laid out town was treeless and stark. It seemed to sit directly on the water. Two long piers stretched far into the bay, like boardwalks leading to nowhere.

Mr. Frank veered the wagon to the left, and the mules clopped along the water front. They halted at the doorway to the military headquarters. "I'll deliver these hides, then swing back by and get you in an hour or so," he said.

"I'll try not to cause you any delay," John said as he climbed down from the wagon seat.

John brushed dust from his sleeves and slipped his arms into the coat he'd removed while traveling in the heat. The door to the agency stood open, and he stepped inside. Mitchel appeared to be out, his chair empty against the back wall. A stack of papers lay piled on the desk weighted down with a beach stone smoothed by time. Disappointment gripped John.

He scanned the room until his gaze settled on two crates pushed into a corner. A board pried from the top of one revealed text books. His heart somersaulted, and in three strides he reached the boxes and lifted out a book. Letters imprinted in the cover of the blue binding read *First Primer.* "Praise the Lord!"

"Can I be of help?" An unfamiliar voice spoke from behind.

John turned to see a tall, lanky soldier leaning casually against the door frame, his blue Yankee uniform loose and rumpled.

"Ogilvie, John Ogilvie from Lavaca." John strode toward the man and extended his hand in greeting.

"Ah, yes. The teacher. Lieutenant Bonnaffon at your service." He shook John's hand, then motioned toward the books. "I guess those are yours. Mitchel didn't leave any instructions."

"I've been waiting a long time for these books," John said. "I plan to take them back with me, and I have another matter to discuss with you."

The two sat. John pulled the deed from a pocket and handed it over. "We have the land, and Mitchel has promised a thousand dollars from the bureau for a building. I would like to get started so we can move into the school this fall. I need that money as soon as possible. I'm also hoping to get some of the businessmen of Lavaca to help financially."

"Sounds okay to me," Bonnaffon said. "The bureau money will have to come from headquarters. I don't have complete authority to act on that until I have been given this post permanently, though it looks like that will happen. I'll forward a message to Mitchel and also to Galveston. In the meantime, if you have funds from other sources, I'd say get started. I'll make a trip to Lavaca to check on any progress as soon as my position here is official. Folks giving you any trouble up there?"

John hesitated a moment before answering. He didn't want to be a complainer and he had already advised Wheelock of the few incidents involving those opposed to his teaching the freedmen. "Nothing new," he said.

"Perhaps things are quieting down. Let me know if problems arise."

John thought back on Mitchel's comment about troops for his protection, which were in reality too far away to help in an emergency. He arose and extended a hand to the Lieutenant. "Aye, sir. I will keep you advised, and I'll look forward to your visit. Please keep me posted on the promised funds."

Bonnaffon returned the handshake and motioned to the boxes. "The books are yours."

John walked toward the crates. "I'll need some help loading these. A wagon will be picking me up shortly."

"Be glad to assist. And by the way, don't know if you have other business while you're here, but most of the stores are closing on account of the fever. I'd high-tail it out of here if I were you."

***

John should have been ecstatic during the ride home. The long-awaited books were in the wagon bed, he was about to get a place of his own, and soon he'd be building a new school. Instead, the farther they traveled, the more upset he became with himself.

He had no money from the bureau for the project, just a promise from a disappearing agent. He should have had the good sense to insist on something in writing from Bonnaffon. And another matter had slipped his mind entirely while there, that of his long overdue May check for services rendered. It was almost time to receive payment for June.

Still one more worry inched its way into his thoughts—that of the yellow fever. It seemed to him the lieutenant looked exceptionally pale and fatigued. John didn't know what the early symptoms of the fever were. It troubled him, and his head began to throb with each rotation of the wagon's wheels. Few words had been exchanged between him and the German since they began the homeward trek, Mr. Frank himself seeming equally preoccupied. Finally, after several miles, the man spoke.

"There's trouble in Indianola. Yellow fever's hitting that town bad. Think I'll not make anymore deliveries for a while. Folks die from that sickness, and we don't need it sweeping through Lavaca."

A wave of guilt struck John. He had been forewarned but realized now he had been blinded by the possibility of getting the books and money for the school. Surely, a quick trip in and out of that town wouldn't spread the disease. He had to admit, he didn't really know.

Mr. Frank drove the wagon to the warehouse and helped John carry the boxes of books up the stairs to the schoolroom. "I'm much obliged," John said, and handed the man more money than he had originally been quoted.

"I'm glad to have made your acquaintance, Ogilvie," Frank said. "It's always good to have company on those trips." He glanced around at the splintered floor and cracked windows. "And good luck with getting that new school built."

John walked into the shanty just as Mrs. Wallace dished up supper.

"Well, there you is. Sit and tell us 'bout your day."

Joe was already seated at the table. He didn't speak or look at John. *He knows*, John thought. *He knows he was right and I was wrong about the fever*. After saying grace, John buttered a biscuit and took a bite—a little fortification before admitting his serious error.

"Well?" Mrs Wallace's dark eyes sparked with curiosity. "How about them books? And did you git money for the new school?"

"Yes and no. But first..." He put down his knife and faced Joe, "You were right, Joe, about the yellow fever. The stores in Indianola are closing and Mr. Frank says he won't be going back until things look better." John hesitated a moment. "I should have listened to you. My mind was too set on getting those books." The impact of what he might have done—brought the illness to Lavaca —caused him to shudder. *Dear God.*

"Well, we ain't sick yet, but time will tell," Joe mumbled the words through a bite of supper.

"That don' mean we goin' to catch it, Mr. Ogilvie. Don't fret 'bout it. Besides, all sorts of folks is always coming and going to Indianola, not just you." Mrs. Wallace moved from the table to the stove, busying herself there for a few moments. When she returned, she set second helpings down on the table, plunked her heavy frame onto the bench, and looked at John. "Now, 'bout those books."

She couldn't wait until morning, so John led her to the warehouse where they lit several lamps and unloaded the box. Mrs. Wallace picked up one of the books, her dark, work-worn hands caressing the cover. She tenderly leafed through several pages. "I kin read these words."

John felt tears spring to his eyes as he observed her passion, and for a short time his worries about yellow fever took flight.

On Monday morning Mrs. Wallace could hardly contain herself. "We need to tell the chilluns about the books right off."

Her excitement slipped into John like warm rays of sunlight. "We'll bring out the books as soon as opening prayers are said," he promised.

When all were seated and Patsy had read a verse from the Bible, Mrs. Wallace looked at John and mouthed, "Now?" Her grin about split her face open.

He chuckled, cleared his throat and scanned the room. Everyone turned to Mrs. Wallace and then to John, eyes wide, sensing something good was about to happen.

"I have a surprise," John said. "How many still need books?" Hands shot up. John reached into the box beside him and pulled out several primers. "Jeremy, come help."

As books were placed in waiting hands, any semblance of order and quiet dissolved into cries of jubilation.

"Kin I take it home to read?" Melinda asked.

"I don' haf to look on with nobody no more!" Patsy exclaimed.

Even Pablo got caught up in the excitement, leafing through the pages of his book and stopping to sound out a word here and there.

When all primers were distributed, John stood at the head of the class, his back against the wall. His smiled turned to laughter at the joyful pandemonium. Everyone wanted to read at once. Tomorrow he would demand silence, but today was a day of celebration.

At the evening session, delight over the books manifested itself in a much more subdued manner, yet it was there. John could feel effervescence in the room. Those who often struggled with lessons eagerly sounded out words in the new texts. The entire day proved to be rewarding and satisfying for scholars and teacher alike, a glow eclipsed only partially by the possibility of yellow fever creeping into the community.

***

The threat of the fever seemed to diminish as time passed. John heard of no cases coming to Lavaca. Other good news prevailed. Both the lumber for his house and the check from John's college fund arrived the following week. Everyone was excited about the prospect of his new living quarters.

"Let's get it built," Joe said, his eyes shining.

Neal, Antonio, Samuel, and two other men from the night class arrived early on a Saturday morning with hammers and saws. By the time mosquitoes buzzed at dusk, a one-room shanty stood on the little piece of land between the Wallace's house and the oak tree. John could hardly believe it. Stepping inside the twelve by twelve space, he suddenly felt a strong kinship with the others living along the bay. He remembered Samuel's proud comment about his own home: "Just like the white folk."

"And now I have one just like the colored folk," John whispered—his own wee castle. He thought of his home in Bannockburn—three rooms and a thatched roof—and how during his teen years he had dreamed of something grander. He laughed. "One room of my own in Lavaca, Texas, is grand enough."

It was bare inside, but not for long. Soon a pitcher and wash basin, donated by Neal, sat on one of two shipping crates hauled in by Samuel. John nailed the other crate to the wall to serve as a cupboard in which he placed a cooking pot, utensils, a plate and a cup offered by Antonio. He didn't have a stove, but he would get by until cooler weather when he had the money. Mrs. Wallace had promised he could continue taking his meals with them. He would reimburse her once he received his pay.

The Duvals loaned John the brass bed he slept on while a tenant there. During all the months since he left their home, that friendship had remained quietly intact. Alexandre and Pierre delivered the bed, along with a small chest of drawers and straight-back chair, in a horse-drawn wagon.

Mrs. Wallace carried over the quilt from Jacob's bed. "It's a extra," she said, always the mother. For a moment John was afraid she would reach over and pinch his cheek like she did Jacob's.

Joe nodded his head solemnly. "You been a fine boarder."

John felt a glow in his heart, but even though a bond had formed among them, he suspected the Wallaces were as relieved as he over the new arrangements. They had their privacy back and another house that could be Jacob's someday, one that didn't cost them a cent. John smiled at the thought. Joe Wallace was a shrewd businessman.

The first night alone felt strange and John had to admit, even a little frightening. He seemed more vulnerable to those in the community who didn't want him teaching the coloreds. *I could be murdered in my sleep and no one would ever know.* When that thought popped into his head, he scolded himself, then laughed aloud. He wasn't much farther away from the Wallaces than when he slept in Jacob's bed. He could yell if need be. Still, it would take some getting used to—the good and the different of it.

Chapter 14

On a muggy Sunday early in July, John again delivered a passionate sermon on the need for building a new school to double as a church. When the offering plate was passed, members of the colored community, who had little to spare financially but had a huge desire for learning and their own meeting place, added extra coins. The fire of John's determination stoked even farther, he set out after Sunday school class to visit the Duvals.

Alexandre responded to his knock. "*Maman*, it's Mr. Ogilvie," the boy shouted.

Evelyne appeared at the open door. "Why *monsieur, bon jour.* Do come in."

John followed her into the parlor and for a few moments it seemed like he had never left this warm, homey place. "Is Pierre in? I need to talk to him."

"*Oui*, please have a seat. I'll bring some coffee and let Pierre know you are here."

The three talked of John's new house, the progress of his pupils, and of his frustrations with the bureau. Then he broached the subject that had brought him to their door.

"I have purchased a lot for the purpose of building a school. The bureau will put up a thousand dollars toward construction, and the colored people have already made a generous contribution. We will need financial backing from the white community as well. I am hoping you can provide me with the names of folks who might be willing to support such a cause. I don't mean for you to do the asking—that's my job—but I need to know who you think I could safely approach."

John presented the entire statement in one breath, his gaze steady on Pierre, attempting to gauge the Frenchman's reaction. Pierre listened politely, his expression thoughtful.

Evelyne anxiously looked to her husband. "It is for the good of all the people," she said, her voice soft.

Pierre placed his empty cup on the table beside him. He leaned forward in his chair, elbows on his knees. "I think I could come up with a list. Give me a few days. I'll see what I can do for you."

As John walked away from the Duvals', the boardwalk bounced under his step. The prospects of the new building seemed on a downhill roll, with each phase falling smoothly into place. He whistled "Onward Christian Soldiers" right up to the entrance of the Wallaces' shanty where Sunday supper waited. Busting to share the good news, he stopped short when Mrs. Wallace barreled out the door, her arm tucked through the handle of a cloth-draped basket.

"Might bettah change that happy tune to a prayer. I is taken this heah soup to my frien' Marlou. 'Peers she got the fevah."

John felt his face go slack. So it had come to Lavaca after all.

"Don' worry 'bout me bringin' that sickness home. I ain't goin' to touch nothin'. Jes' goin' to set this jah on the stoop and be outa theah. Suppa' for you and Joe is settin' on the stove." She continued up the path away from him as she spoke, rounded a corner and disappeared from view.

John stood stunned. Word of the illness here obviously had not gone far or there would have been talk of it at church and at the Duvals'. Folks got awfully excited at the suggestion of yellow fever. John never remembered hearing about it in Scotland. He wasn't sure how folks knew it was the fever or some other ailment.

He confronted Joe with this question as they ate the soup left simmering on the stove.

"Black vomit," Joe said, solemn-faced.

John placed his spoonful of soup back in the bowl, suddenly unable to bring it to his mouth.

"Fevah and black vomit," Joe repeated. "An white folk turn yella. Ain't no mistakin' what it is. Some die, some don't. Ain't no good reason why. If God say it time for to go, ain't nothin goin' to stop Him."

John ignored the statement blaming God, and resolved to remain calm. "Surely doctors can do something."

"Mebbe. Mebbe not."

John managed to choke down a bite of cornbread. His soup, now cold, no longer seemed palatable.

His resolve to stay calm weakened on Monday morning when only a few pupils appeared for class. It was not unusual for there to be absences, especially now that summer was upon them and a new fee involved. Some pupils attended inconsistently regardless. Today, however, each vacant spot seemed a big hole, and one in particular concerned John.

"Does anyone know of Ezra's whereabouts?" he asked.

"His gran'mammy be sick," Pablo answered.

Dear God, no. John pictured the old woman thumping her walking stick to emphasize a point during his visit there—so strong in spirit but frail in body. John no longer carried the guilt of having brought the illness to town, too many days had passed; but the thought of the fever creeping through Lavaca, taking lives, was sobering and frightening.

At two o'clock, as soon as the scholars scampered down the stairs for home, John closed up and set off on his own. One thought had nagged at him during class: Ezra never showed up.

John hurried along the shoreline until he stood before the shanty Ezra called home. Taking a deep breath, he rapped on the warped, wooden door.

"Who be there?" A muffled voice, not Ezra's, spoke.

"Mr. Ogilvie, teacher from the freedmen's school."

The door opened a crack and a woman John did not recognize peered out. "What you want?"

"Ezra. Is he all right? I heard his grandmother has taken ill."

"Ezra gone away. His gran'mammy very sick."

"Where is Ezra?" John stepped back a few paces, trying not to breathe the foul air released from within the cabin.

"He be with friends."

"Do you need help?"

"No suh, an you bes' be on your way." The woman shut the door in John's face.

And so he left, the trickle of anxiety from that morning no longer tucked in the back of his mind and no longer a mere trickle. And it hurt to be turned away. If this monster illness was going to sweep through town, he wanted to help where he could.

***

Two days later, during the early morning hours while John prepared for class in the warehouse, Pierre Duval opened the school room door.

John rose immediately and motioned him in. A question caught in his throat. "Is everyone well at your home?"

"*Oui*, they are fine, and I've done as you asked, at least the best I could." He handed John a piece of paper containing a list of names. "These are men I think will be willing to contribute toward the building of a school. I haven't talked to them, though, so I can't say for sure. James Browning listed first is an architect with carpentry skills. He might manage and supervise the work. You'll have to ask. And another thing ...." Pierre paused a moment as though figuring how to say what was on his mind. "These are businessmen. They'll want something in return for their help. What do you have to offer?"

Relieved that Pierre's visit was business, not another scare regarding the fever, John stood and walked the length of the room, hands in his pockets. He had given some thought as to what to offer those from the community who courageously agreed to help, and had come to one conclusion, a plan not yet approved by the bureau, but it seemed the only answer. "What if I make them trustees of the school and quitclaim the property to them?"

"It might work, if they're not afraid to go on record as part of the project."

John realized that could be the case. "There is nothing else to offer. I'll simply have to try."

Pierre rose to leave. "I must get to work. I hope this helps." He extended a hand to John. "You know I believe in what you are doing, Ogilvie. If it weren't for Suzette and Alexandre..."

John shook his hand. "I understand. I'm much obliged for all you have done."

When Pierre was gone, John picked up the list and studied it more closely. After James Browning, there were ten more names, some unfamiliar. Those would be hardest to approach. At others, John smiled and nodded his approval: Robert Johnson, the Yankee grocer, Malcolm Frank from the livery, and Giovanni Imports among them. At the bottom of the list he added George Ware, who had made it all happen.

John decided to start at the top and approach Browning first. This man would benefit the most from the project—if he agreed to do the plans and oversee the construction. With the knowledge that Browning was at the helm, it shouldn't be as difficult to convince the others to pitch in financially.

All morning, between lessons and questions from the scholars, John mentally prepared a persuasive speech to present to the architect. At two o'clock, when the classroom emptied, he pulled on his coat and marched to town. He was primed and dared not wait until courage escaped him.

A bell jangled when he opened the door to Browning's office. A dark-haired, bearded man sat hunched over a drafting table. He didn't look up, intent on the sketches before him. "Just set the box in the corner, Hiram."

John cleared his throat, suddenly dry, and for a moment he feared the words he had rehearsed all day wouldn't come. He cleared his throat again. "Mr. Browning?"

The man turned around and removed his wire-rimmed spectacles. "Oh, I beg your pardon. I thought you were the delivery boy. How can I help you?"

"My name is John Ogilvie, teacher of the freedmen. We are in desperate need of a new school building, and I understand you are the right man to see about such an undertaking."

"I see." Browning rose and approached a pair of worn leather chairs. "Have a seat, Mr. Ogilvie, and we'll discuss your proposal."

John sat and, glancing around, relaxed a little. Like the soft chair, the architect's office held an air of comfort. Long paper rolls of what John presumed to be plans stood upright in a corner. Sketches of buildings lined the walls. A half-finished drawing lay on the drafting table alongside several containers of ink and a cup crowded with pencils and pens. An orange tabby cat slept curled on a rug beneath the table.

Mr. Browning sat in the opposite chair and lit a pipe, filling the room with the scent of sweet-smelling tobacco. "First off," he said, "how do you expect to pay for this school?"

"Well, sir..."

They talked for an hour, or rather John talked. Mr. Browning listened, asking questions here and there. John about preached a sermon, feeling the same fervor as when he attempted to sway a congregation to seek the Lord. In the end, James Browning was convinced to take on the project. When John left the architect's office, he was ready to tackle the rest of the names on the list. Maybe this task he had dreaded—asking for money for an unpopular cause—wouldn't be so difficult after all.

But there wasn't time for that today. He had to prepare for the evening class. He returned to the warehouse in a euphoric state. Walking into Browning's office had been difficult, not knowing where the man stood in regard to educating the freed slaves. Yet this was John's mission and he was determined. Today's result bore promise. *Thank you Lord. You put the right words in my mouth.* He hummed as he wrote arithmetic problems on the blackboard.

The sound of footsteps caused him to turn. It was still early for night scholars to be arriving. In the doorway stood a solemn-faced Ezra. A tall black man stood next to him. John's cheerful mood plummeted and a chill gripped his heart.

The youngster spoke first. "My gran'mammy be dead."

John reached out and grasped the boy's hands. "I am so sorry, Ezra." John had the urge to hug the boy, but, not sure how that would be received, he said instead, "Your grandmother was a very special lady."

At John's touch and expression of sympathy, the boy's stoicism broke and he hiccupped a sob.

"Do you have a place to go now?" John asked softly. "Some place to stay?"

"He be living with us," the man said. "We be long-time frens of his gran'mammy." He stood a moment before continuing, fidgeting with the brim of a tattered hat held in his hands. "Ezra say you can preach some words at the funeral."

John motioned the man to sit. "Tell me what I need to do," he said. While they made plans for the burial of the old woman, Ezra sat silently, his eyes dark and blank. At the close of the discussion, the man took the boy by the hand, and after thanking John, they descended the stairs.

"God be with you, laddie," John whispered.

The following day, according to custom, friends carried the box bearing the tiny woman to a graveyard on the outskirts of town. There the Negro community, in their Sunday best, joined together to mourn the loss of their sister. Afterward, the crowd gathered in the stifling upstairs warehouse room.

Having never conducted a funeral service before, John was acutely aware of his lack of training. For the first few moments, he felt like a charlatan, but with a silent prayer for guidance, he drew in a deep breath, reached into his personal experience, and spoke the words of assurance he remembered hearing his father say upon the death of a parishioner. The congregation peppered his sermon with amens and hallelujahs, beginning softly, increasing in pitch to moans and shouts. At the end John found himself trembling, his own voice rising in accord with the others, as they all lifted the soul of Ezra's grandmother to heaven, an experience, to be sure, never observed at the staid Saint Ninian's kirk in Bannockburn, Scotland.

Through Ezra's loss, John had been shown the way he could help his Negro friends as this affliction crept through the community. The gift was there all along, the real reason why he was here, but it took a crisis to make it apparent. He would offer the balm of his faith in the Lord, a deepened compassion as shown to him by others, and a belief in a life hereafter.

Striving to build the school also had to continue, despite the undercurrent of anxiety caused by the fever. John contacted two potential donors a day, and by the end of a week he had a board of trustees for the school, including Neal Wright, Malcolm Frank, and George Ware. The amount of money from each varied, but the total equaled enough to start building while they waited for funding from the bureau.

Only two men on Pierre's list declined to help.

One said, "Sorry, Mr. Ogilvie, it's not that I don't approve of what you're doing, but not everyone does, you know, including some of my friends. If word got out, well, I've got a family to think of."

The other refusal was a flat out "No." All in all, however, John's quest had been successful. With the initial challenges behind him, he suddenly felt he could accomplish anything. A song erupted from deep within him and he marched all the way to Browning's office to share the good news. Together they drew up plans and compiled a list of necessary supplies to begin the project.

"The lumber will have to be shipped in," Browning said. "I'll get it ordered right away. In the meantime we can begin preparing the foundation. I'll meet you there tomorrow afternoon to get a general lay of the land."

Impressed with Browning's eagerness to forge ahead, John felt confident there would indeed be a new building by fall. Not only a place to teach the freedmen, but a place where Negro churchgoers could easily congregate.

On Saturday morning they met at the vacant lot as agreed. Browning unrolled an impressive looking set of plans, and they walked off the desired footage. Within the week the area had been leveled and corner stakes driven, leaving only the wait for lumber.

But John had few moments to dwell on this delay. During the interim his attention, and that of the entire community, turned elsewhere out of desperate necessity. Yellow fever continued to spread. Businesses shut down, and with absenteeism on the rise and the possibility of contagion, John felt compelled to close the school. This meant no income for July. He couldn't ask the pupils to pay for an entire month when only a few days had passed. That, plus the missing salary from the bureau for the months of May and June, meant he was unable to give the Wallaces past rent or money for the meals he still took with them. They didn't ask, but John felt the burden of this debt.

As the fever crawled through town claiming more victims, people took to mingling less. Doors remained closed in spite of the oppressive summer heat. A gnawing fear grew in John for this community, for both its colored and white folk who had become so much a part of him.

Chapter 15

The sickness manifested itself in a number of ways—high fever, delirium, and black vomit being the most prevalent. Those who could afford a doctor received quinine and tincture of iron, when available. Some of the colored folks resorted to Voodoo for healing, a practice that greatly disturbed John.

Doctoring had not been included in his ambitions, yet here he was thrust right into the middle of it, and he couldn't help feeling the Lord meant him to be here—to console and pray with the afflicted. The white people in the community seemed to suffer from the fever more than the coloreds, and those who didn't object to John's association with the freedmen respected him as a teacher and preacher. He often found himself beside a sickbed, sponging a patient with cold water and reading from the Bible, finding the words soothing to both himself and the patient. Everyone knew personally someone who had been stricken. A pall hovered over the town like the gray fog that so often crawled in from the bay.

One afternoon John encountered Evelyne Duval hurrying along Main Street, her lips set in a firm line, her brow creased. She would have marched right by if he hadn't called out to her.

"Mrs. Duval, is everything all right at your house?" From the looks of her, he feared the answer even as he waited for her reply.

She stopped short and looked at him blankly for a moment as though not recognizing him. "Oh, *Monsieur* Ogilvie, please forgive me. I have so much on my mind."

"And your family?" he asked again, his anxiety mounting.

"Oh, they are fine. I make them stay indoors, but so many others are sick ... or worse. I just lost a fine friend, and now I hear Pastor Harris succumbed this morning to that horrible malady."

"Pastor Harris of the Methodist church?"

"*Oui*, he's the one."

John shook his head, recalling his last conversation with the man.

The overload of losses was becoming too much, yet John knew he had to keep on going. Those who were sick depended on those who were not. Seeing Mrs. Duval, worn and frazzled, he suddenly felt protective of this woman who had provided a room for him during those first long weeks in Lavaca. "You should go home and rest before you get sick, too. Your family needs you to stay well."

"*Oui,* I am tired. Perhaps a little sleep will help."

She hurried away, and John trudged to the schoolroom, the knowledge of the Reverend Harris's death weighing on him. The man may have preferred that Negroes have their own church, but he was a man of God and had spent many hours caring for the sick.

Though folks were dying, there was still business to tend to, and before the day ended John had letters to write. His monthly report to the AMA included a request for funds, explaining the reason for his lack of money and telling of the yellow fever epidemic.

He then wrote to Superintendent Wheelock in Galveston:

> *I have not yet received financial assistance from the bureau for the building of the school, nor my pay for May and June ...*

Sealing the two envelopes, he closed up the building and hiked to the post office before heading to the Wallaces' for supper.

He and Mrs. Wallace met at the front door and entered the dark interior of the shanty together. John lit a lamp then dropped onto the bench at the kitchen table, his energy drained.

In spite of being almost twice his age and caring for others all day, Mrs. Wallace's strength seemed constant. She bustled about preparing supper. "Who you been to see?" She asked, stoking cinders in the cook stove as she talked.

"I read the Bible to an elderly woman first thing this morning. I don't think she'll make it. Her husband asked me to come." John turned up the lamp wick to brighten the room.

Mrs. Wallace talked about her day as she stirred leftover grits and beans in a skillet. "I been lookin' afta' Sally Potter, and she be bettah." She placed two bowls of the hot meal on the table and eased her heavy frame onto the bench opposite John. As they ate, he sensed her studying his face in the shadowy glow of the kerosene lamp. "You lookin' mighty down."

John shook his head. "Aye. that I am. This afternoon I learned the Reverend Harris died of the fever."

Mrs. Wallace said nothing, but made a little clicking noise with her tongue, something she often did, John noted, when dismay overtook her.

They finished their meal silently in the subdued light. Finally, he spoke, changing the subject. "Where's Joe?"

"I sent him up the tracks to find Jacob and tell him to stay away til the fevah passes on by."

***

As the first week of August waned, so did the cases of yellow fever. John spent fewer hours at bedside vigils, and his thoughts shifted once more to the building of the schoolhouse. Like everything else during the epidemic, progress had come to a standstill. Finally, on the fifth day of the month, a response from Wheelock to his latest letter arrived in the mail.

Office Superintendent of Education
Refugees and Freedmen
Galveston, August 1, 1867

Dear Sir,

In answer to yours of June 29ᵗʰ which has been strangely mislaid, I have to say that the Bureau agent at your place has been ordered to assist in the building of the schoolhouse. And I hope therefore that the work will be pressed forward rapidly to completion.

If new difficulties arise let me know at once. It seems that Lt. Mitchel, the former agent, did not report the matter, as he should, to headquarters, hence this delay and trouble.

John would have given a whoop of joy had it not been for the remaining two sentences:

Have you much fever at Lavaca? It is rumored here that there is much panic on the subject.

95

Charcoal and Chalk

Everybody that can run away is leaving Galveston and the prospects are not good.

Very Respectfully,
Wheelock,
Superintendent of Schools, BRF&AL

So, the fever had traveled that far. He read the last sentence again: *"Everybody that can run away is leaving Galveston."* His thoughts immediately turned to Miss Barnes and Miss Skinner. He pictured the two determined teachers. If any of their scholars fell ill, those ladies would be right by their bedside. *Dear, God, please protect them. They are doing your work.* But that hadn't saved the Reverend Harris. John ran his fingers through his hair, paced the schoolroom a dozen times, then sat at his desk. He pulled out pen and paper...

Dear Miss Barnes,
There is much fever in Lavaca and I have just learned Galveston is hard hit with it. Please let me know as soon as possible if you are well.

***

The early morning hour was still dark when something woke John from a sound sleep. He opened his eyes and listened and heard someone calling his name. A violent pounding began on his door, pulling him from bed. Groping his way through the room, he fumbled for the latch and threw open the door. There stood Antonio, lantern in hand, a coat flung over his nightclothes.

"Ogilvie. You must come. It's Neal." His voice broke as he spoke his partner's name. "He...he's in a bad way. He's asking for you."

"I'll be right there." John hurriedly pulled on his trousers and coat, his heart throbbing. He grabbed his Bible and strode out the door, catching up with Antonio who had already headed up the bluff.

The Italian rambled on about Neal as they hurried along. "He only took sick a day ago and didn't seem so bad at first, then tonight he all of a sudden got worse." The man choked and snuffled. The pale lantern light exposed the glint of tears sliding down his cheeks. "He's about dead, Ogilvie. We may be too late."

A numbness shrouded John, as though he were gliding through a bad dream. It seemed forever before they reached their destination. The bold, white letters on the building stood out even in the dark of pre-dawn: *GIOVANNI IMPORTS*. They entered through the business door and went on into the adjoining room. The stench of the disease, which had become so familiar in the past few weeks, struck John like a blow.

At first look he feared Antonio was right—that his friend had already passed on. The form on the bed lay still, the yellow pallor of the fever destroying the once handsome young face. John dropped to his knees and grasped a limp hand. "Neal," he whispered. When no response came, he raised his voice, "Neal, it's John."

Eyelids snapped open and Neal's head slowly turned. "Water."

Antonio fetched a cup and John poured a spoonful between the cracked lips. Neal's eyes closed again. "Pray for me."

The voice wavered so weakly John had to lean close to catch the words. Blinking back tears, he began reciting, "The Lord is my shepherd, I shall not want. He leadeth me beside still waters ..."

Neal's lips moved in tandem with his, and as they recited the Twenty-third Psalm together it occurred to John he had never talked religion with his friend. Never invited him to church, never asked him about his relationship with God or what his creed might be. This friend had been the nurturer, had given to John what he needed so desperately—companionship. Rescue from a storm, Friday evening meals, laughter, friendship. And John had taken of it greedily.

"What can I do for you, my friend?" John swallowed a lump in his throat, wishing he had asked such a question weeks ago.

"The answer came slow and raspy, "Write to my mother."

"Aye. That I will do."

Daylight took over the gloom of night. John got off his knees and pulled a chair up to the bed. As he had done with others, he wiped Neal's perspiring brow with a cool damp cloth and offered sips of water until it seemed useless, his friend's breathing now so shallow.

Antonio sat at the table behind him, blowing his nose and taking frequent swigs from a bottle. He blubbered on. "He was a soldier, you know. Fought in that hellish war. Got shot up and lived to boast about it. And now this damn fever..." His voice trailed off as he lifted the bottle to his lips again and again. Every now and then he would ask with little sound of hope, "Is he dead?"

At nine o'clock, John released Neal's hand, laid it across his friend's chest and in a broken voice, answered, "Aye, he has gone to be with the Lord."

Chapter 16

A scattering of the business community showed up for the graveside service. Under other circumstances more would have appeared. Neal was well liked, but people were afraid to mingle for fear of getting the fever. Wearing his best suit, Antonio stood beside the open grave, sober and stoic. Mr. Slater, who had hurriedly hammered together a coffin, stood next to him. Pierre and Evelyne were there, and Joe and Mrs. Wallace were hanging back on the edge of the small crowd of white folk.

Borrowing some of Antonio's words, John took a moment to tell of Neal's short life, including his injuries and survival in the great war. Then he read from the scriptures. "For all flesh is as grass, and all the glory of man as the flower of grass. The grass withereth, and the flower thereof falleth away, but the word of the Lord endureth for ever." As those present stood with heads bowed, the lone song of a mockingbird trilled—an impromptu taps for a faithful friend. As the August heat swelled, the mourners turned and retraced their steps to town.

John hadn't slept since Antonio awakened him so abruptly two days before. He knew he should go home and crawl into bed, but it was early afternoon and the heat stifling. He climbed the stairs to the warehouse. Now was the time to write to Neal's mother. It must be done. Maybe while he was at it, he would reply to Wheelock's query regarding yellow fever cases in Lavaca.

He labored over the simple note to Mrs. Wright, spoiling several pieces of paper before his words seemed a proper mix of sympathy for her and uplifting remarks about Neal—the joy of knowing him. Sweat dripped from his every pore until his shirt clung to him and two linen handkerchiefs became drenched from the continuous wiping of his brow. He desperately needed sleep. *Aye, sleep will surely refresh and clear my mind. First, a few words to Wheelock.*

Dear Sir,

...The fever still rages. I am tired—trying to get around to read to and comfort the sick and dying.

I have just returned from the solemn task of burying a young man who had been through all the war and now died of this foul infectious fever. It is sorrowful, it is pitiful to see such as he die...

John added another sentence then dropped the pen. His head pulsed like the constant throbbing of a ship's engine, and prickly chills crawled along his clammy skin. Sealing the envelopes, he walked the short distance to the post office before turning toward home. Each step accentuated the pounding pain in his skull. The act of pulling off his clothes and lying down on the bed drained what little strength he had left. He was on fire, and his stomach—he had never before felt such torment.

John remembered very little of the next five days except an awareness of hands tenderly soothing his forehead and forcing sips of water between his parched lips. He could not eat. Visions of angels passed before him, one wearing the serene face of a portrait he remembered from his childhood—that of his mother whom he scarcely knew, dead before he turned four.

Familiar voices ebbed in and out of his wee hut. Joe and Mrs. Wallace, to be sure, but others, too. Evelyne Duval and maybe Samuel? That in itself a powerful tonic. Words from the Bible sounded out with great difficulty by someone still learning to read drifted through John's consciousness. But every prayer penetrated his fevered mind, digging into the very core of his being. And finally, on the sixth day, his sleep became less fitful, his breathing easier.

"He be bettah," he heard Mrs. Wallace say. "Surely he be saved by the Lawd."

***

Each day John gained strength. Though recovery seemed tortuously slow, he often knelt to pray, thanking the Lord for friends who had watched over him. The experience deepened his faith and the conviction that he was meant to be in this place, working with these people.

His first outings were no further than to the front porch of the Wallace home, where Joe generously allowed him to sit in the rocking chair. It felt good to gently rock and breathe deeply of the bay breezes, watching the gulls glide above the water, their squawks blending with the creak of the chair. For the first few days he stayed out for an hour or so before he crept back to his own home to sleep, but slowly his strength increased. Soon he could walk to the schoolroom without feeling exhausted.

A full week after his recovery, he hiked to the post office. The clerk handed him a bundle tied up with string. "These kept piling up. I wondered if you might be dead and thought about sending them back. Then Mrs. Duval said you'd been sick with the fever but were getting better." He shook his head and peered at John's eyes. "Must say you still look rather puny and somewhat yella'. Sure glad it didn't catch up with me." He stopped his chatter a moment, fiddling with a pencil in his fingers. "Then I suppose it ain't done yet."

John thanked him for his kind words, though he wasn't certain that was what he had received. His joy at seeing the return address on the top envelope made up for the clerk's lack of diplomacy. *Sarah Barnes.*

Sitting at his desk in the school room, he tore open the seal and quickly scanned the short note.

> *Dear Mr. Ogilvie,*
>
> *Your letter was forwarded to me here at home. Miss Skinner and I left Galveston for the summer, thus we escaped that horrible affliction.*

Praise the Lord! A sense of relief flowed through John like a soft spring rain. The thought of this lovely lady suffering as he had would be more than he could bear. He continued reading:

> *I do not know when we will return to reopen the school —possibly not until the first of the year—because of the fever. When I learn more, I will advise you.*
>
> *I hope this finds you well. I have been greatly concerned about your health.*
>
> *May the Lord protect you.*
>
> > *Sincerely,*
> >
> > *Sarah Barnes*

John sat for several long minutes holding the letter, his head bowed in silent prayer, then picked up the envelope from

Superintendent Wheelock. In extreme contrast to that of Sarah
Barnes, this message was all business, posted shortly before John
took sick.

August 13, 1867

Dear Sir,

*I have sent you some blanks for reports. I have seen Lt.
Garretson with reference to your salary for May & June.*

*The clerk promises to send the June money to you <u>at
once</u>, but says the <u>May</u> vouchers were never sent him by the
sub assistant comm. You had better see that the omission is
rectified at once. In case the money for June is not received
in a week or ten days, write to Lt. Garretson or myself.*

*...If you desire it, I will endeavor to have your name
placed on the rolls again of teachers receiving pay from the
bureau. Let me hear from you on the subject.*

Very truly,
E. Wheelock

John laughed aloud at the irony. Here he was still trying to get
that owed him from last school term, and the envelope contained
no report forms. Tugging at his beard, he sighed, the frustrations
so familiar, and yet, he would write a note saying yes to his name
being placed on the rolls for another year. The thought of leaving
his pupils so soon after the start of their educational journey—
well, he simply couldn't.

An envelope from the AMA felt bulkier than usual. Perhaps it
contained letters from some of the sponsoring churches. Upon
opening it, John caught his breath. Five National Bank notes lay
folded inside.

Dear Bro:

*I send you herewith $25 on account, in answer to your
recent note. Please return vouchers.*

*...You have our sincerest prayers that you may be
shielded from danger and prosper in the work you so very
acceptably prosecute.*

Fraternally,
J.R. Shipherd, Sec.

Bless the missionary association. He counted the bills again,
feeling a wee bit light headed. The first thing he planned to do was

pay the Wallaces for back rent and meals. Now if the bureau would just come through, he might be able to survive until the beginning of the school year when he would once again be "receiving pay" from that fine military organization.

Another envelope held the missing forms, and the next simply acknowledged a letter from John sent weeks ago. The last envelope brought an instant smile to his lips. The sweeping, self-assured penmanship was unmistakably that of Lucy Cranston. Sweet, spunky Lucy. Unfolding the fine paper, he began reading. *Dear John*—she always used his given name, one of the things about her bold personality he so admired. The letter contained no news out of the ordinary, but it was good to hear from her. He could hardly wait to tell Neal he had received letters from two ladies. What would his friend say to that!

The notion had scarcely passed through his mind before he pulled tightly on the reins of the runaway thought and a sob caught in his throat. The fun and banter of sharing his love-life, or lack thereof, with Neal was gone forever.

Chapter 17

Though the plague continued to spread into other Texas communities, by the end of August the worst seemed to have passed through Lavaca. Mercifully, the intense summer heat and energy-draining humidity slowly released its grip. Each day John felt stronger. Sometimes when a steamer arrived in port he hiked down to the wharf, leaned against a piling, and watched the bustle of activity. Over the months his fear of the waterfront and who might be there had diminished. The cool breezes against his face lifted his spirits. *How precious it is to be alive.*

On one such afternoon he heard someone call his name. "Ogilvie! Look here." James Browning hurriedly approached from the end of the pier, waving a paper in his hand. Catching up to John, the architect stopped to regain his breath. "I see you are up and about. Well, I've got news to help speed your recovery. The lumber has arrived." He motioned to the ship docked at the end of the wharf.

For the first time in weeks, John felt a surge of energy. He clapped Browning on the shoulder, then shook his hand. "Aye, that is indeed good news. Does it mean we can start building?"

"Right away. With any luck the school might be ready for your students before winter."

John filled with hope. "I think the trustees should know about this, so they can go over the particulars. After all, it is their school. I'll call a meeting at the warehouse."

The group congregated three nights later, and it seemed to have the affect John hoped for. He marveled once again at the courage these men showed by taking part in the unpopular school.

***

Construction began immediately. With the help of Joe Wallace, a crew of colored carpenters was hired, and under the supervision of Browning the building began to take shape. John spent most of his waking hours at the site, assisting with as much of the actual work as his limited energy allowed. Each week he was able to do a little more.

Late one morning, while John pounded yet another nail, a horse and rider trotted up. A man in a blue military uniform dismounted, tied the reins to a floor joist, and sauntered around the construction site with all the bearing of an inspector.

"Lieutenant Bonnaffon," John called. He jumped down from where he had been working and approached the bureau agent. "How good of you to come." He hoped the man had brought a check.

The lieutenant shook John's hand. "I heard you had died. Decided I had better come see if we needed to find a new teacher for the school here. You look plenty alive to me, and I see the building is progressing. Glad on both accounts."

"There were days when I was about dead, but the good Lord saw fit to save me, with the help of some fine people here in Lavaca." The thought still choked him up, and he quickly changed the subject. "I'll show you around."

They walked the site together, John telling of the businessmen who donated funds. "The lumber you see here has been paid for, but we'll need much more." He couldn't hold back the question any longer. "Do you have a check from the bureau?"

Bonnaffon shook his head, and John's hopes collapsed as he listened to the lieutenant's words.

"I haven't heard much at all from Galveston, except the bureau has been hit hard with the fever. There's been some death—don't know exactly who yet. Nobody's writing."

"I got a letter from Wheelock in early August," John said, "I was told you had been ordered to assist in the building and that the work should be pressed forward. Surely, the money will be coming soon."

"They're not writing checks if they're in bed sick—or dead, Ogilvie. You should know that as well as anyone." His answer held a tinge of annoyance.

John had to admit the man was right, and the possibility of any bureau personnel having died was sobering. "I guess we'll do what we can for now," he said. "I'm much obliged that you came by."

They shook hands with the understanding that as soon as Bonnaffon heard from Galveston he would let John know.

And so, the building continued with the supplies on hand. Because of the proximity to the bay, the sills were laid on an underpinning of cedar blocks four feet in height to keep the structure above the water in the wet season. By the end of September, the frame was completed and a portion of the siding in place.

"It sure do look good," Joe said, as he and John surveyed the project one evening. "Won't be no time at all 'fore it be done."

"Aye, that will be a great day."

Yet it was the first of October and there had been no word from Galveston about anything—the promised funding, or the commencement of the schools for the new term. John had held off starting classes in anticipation of the completion of the school. Now it was obvious they would continue to meet in the warehouse, for awhile anyway.

On October third, all those worries were temporarily forgotten. John awoke during the night to howling winds and rain pounding so violently against the roof it sounded like rocks were being hurled at his hut. He sprang from bed and looked out the window. Through the sheets of rain he saw trees bent over like ancient creatures whose bones had shattered. Debris whirled in the wind and shingles tore from the Wallaces' roof. John pulled on his trousers and boots, flung a coat over his head, and unlatched the door. Once he got it open, it took all his strength to push it shut and secure the lock. Fighting his way against the gale, he staggered the few feet to the Wallaces' shanty where a light flickered through the front window.

"Joe, let me in," he shouted, hoping his voice could be heard against the storm.

The door cracked open and he slid in while Joe held onto the knob to keep them both from being yanked out.

"Your roof is coming apart," John yelled, though his announcement was hardly necessary. Rain gushed through a gaping hole in one corner.

Mrs. Wallace sat at the table clutching her night clothes around her. The woman whose strength John so often admired seemed frozen in fear. "It be like times before when the water and wind jest don't quit comin'." Her voice shook and the words turned to a wail when a fierce gust tore more shingles from the corner of the roof. Joe dragged a wash tub to the spot to catch the torrent cascading into the room.

"I'll see if I can patch it," John shouted. He opened the front door, only to have it flung from his grasp. Stepping off the porch, he struggled to stay upright, the rain driving at him like needles. Realizing how impossible his plan was, he stepped back into the shack, tugged the door shut and latched it securely.

Joe attempted several times to start a fire in the cook stove, but rain down the stack continually sizzled it out. John and the Wallaces huddled silently at the kitchen table in the dim lantern light. Sleep was out of the question, talk next to impossible over the roar of the cyclone. Twice more shingles flew away in wind surges. Somewhere nearby a prolonged crash surely meant the uprooting of a tree. John saw Joe's lips move but couldn't make out the words. Finally, the explosive wind gusts calmed to a moaning gale, and the rain, though steady, drummed the roof less violently. Still sitting at the table, the three of them dozed fitfully during the pre-dawn hours.

In the first morning light John rose stiffly and stretched, his soaked clothing clinging to him. The rain that had threatened to thrust everyone out to sea only hours earlier now pat-patted on the roof like an innocent autumn shower. Pings and plops into the buckets and kettles, placed beneath holes, added a subdued rhythm to the new day.

"I'll try that fire again and git us some mush goin'," Mrs. Wallace said in her regular voice, acting like the night's terror was of no consequence.

Joe and John pushed open the door and surveyed the storm's damage. Tree limbs lay fallen and twisted about, mixed in with shingles and other debris, as though a giant had stomped through the town in a fit of anger. Still, amazingly, buildings seemed to be mostly intact, though some closer to the bay stood a foot deep in water. John's own hut, being new, suffered no damage. The schoolhouse under construction next door had faired well, too. The recently nailed lumber held secure, and due to the elevated design of the foundation, flooding was not an issue.

"That was mighty scary," Joe said. "But not so bad as sometime."

John had felt other strong winds and rain during his short stay in Lavaca. If they got worse than this, he wasn't eager to experience it. "Let's see what we can do to fix those holes," he said to Joe.

Together they gathered up shingles, propped a ladder against the house and hammered pieces of roofing back in place.

"That'll keep us dry 'til the next one blow in," Joe said.

Inside the cabin a fire blazed in the stove. Mrs. Wallace dished up bowls of hot cornmeal mush along with cups of steaming coffee. With each swallow, the warmth and nourishment eased John's weariness.

Following the meal, he took off at a trot along the bay to check for damage at the warehouse. Water lapped at his feet, and when he reached the building it was evident Oswald's office on the lower level had suffered some flooding. John mounted the steps to the schoolroom. Opening the door, he found glass scattered across the floor from a blown-out window pane. A corner of a wall map had torn loose and hung wet and limp. Other than that, things were in good order. The text books and John's papers had escaped damage. Joe's remark about it being *not so bad as sometime* suddenly hit home. *Aye, it could have been far worse.*

***

Work on the new school continued, and one warm fall day as John rested at the building site after a morning of carpentry, George Ware strolled up, a gold-handled cane crooked over his arm. John scrambled to his feet and held out his hand. "It's good to see you, sir."

They shook hands. "It's good to be here, Ogilvie. I've been to Massachusetts and just returned yesterday. Thought I'd stop by and check on the progress." He stepped back and studied the construction. "It looks like things are coming along."

They walked the premises while John told of his pupils, their willingness to learn, and their excitement about having a building of their own for school and church. John motioned to a plank spanning two sawhorses, and they sat. For a few moments neither spoke. Hammers pounded, saws rasped, and the workers called to one another as little by little a meeting house grew.

"It's a sight to warm the soul," Mr. Ware said.

"Aye, it is. We've had support from some forward thinking businessmen," John said, "Though I am still waiting for money from the bureau." He turned to Ware, looking the man steadily in the eyes. "You know, sir, this would not be happening if you had not come along. You are the answer to many prayers."

"Yours and mine, son. I wasn't fit to be a soldier, so I set to praying about how to help the cause. I got my answer after the war, as plain as if the Lord was standing beside me. He told me to help educate these people and bring them proper religion, and he led me to you and your little flock of black children."

John felt a current of joy surge through him. *I must never doubt the power of prayer—even in moments of despair.*

Ware sat a few more minutes watching the progress on the building, then stood and dusted specks of sawdust from his coat. "I must be on my way, but one more thing, Ogilvie; could you use a bell? It seems to me your plans should include a cupola with a bell to announce the beginning of school and church services. What do you think?"

John grinned. "Aye, sir, a bell would be grand—just grand."

"Then you shall have one." Mr. Ware said, and sauntered off, swinging his cane, its gold handle glinting in the sun.

Every day John walked to the post office to check for mail. He made up his mind if he didn't hear from the bureau by the end of October, he would start school whether he had official word or not. Then, on October 29th, an envelope arrived from Lieutenant Bonnaffon. John's pulse quickened. Finally. He tore open the seal. What he read stunned him:

> *Mr. John Ogilvie,*
>
> *I have no blank service vouchers. I do not know whether the Bureau has opened schools in Texas or not.*
>
> *I have written to the headquarters of R.F & A. L. for the District of Texas for the proper form on which to get the contract for the completion of the schoolhouse at Lavaca and have received no answer. They have all died over at Galveston.*
>
> *Headquarters of the District of Texas is now at Austin, Texas.*
>
> *I am, Sir, most respectfully,*
> *Your obedient servant, A.B. Bonnaffon*

Chapter 18

An article in a Galveston newspaper, days old and handed him by the grocer that afternoon, gave John all the somber facts.

"You seen this, Ogilvie?"

John set his few purchases down on the counter, took the paper and gasped as he read:

GENERAL GRIFFIN OF FREEDMEN'S BUREAU DEAD.

Assistant Commissioner General Griffin succumbed to Yellow Fever on September 15. Members of the Freedmen's Bureau headquartered here in Galveston have been hard hit by that foul disease. Other fatalities among its ranks include two medical officers, eight sub-assistant commissioners, one inspector, three clerks, and three teachers...

Setting the newspaper back on the counter, John shook his head. "I knew some were sick, but I didn't know all this." He turned and plodded toward the door.

"Mr. Ogilvie," the grocer called. "You forgot your purchases."

At the warehouse, John methodically readied the room for school, stopping now and then to stare out the window at the bay. He had never met Griffin, but felt the blow of his death as if he had known the man personally. And what of others in the bureau he'd corresponded with regularly, Wheelock and Garrettson especially, were they among the dead? The one relief was knowing Miss Barnes and Miss Skinner had escaped.

John paced the room, wishing he had started classes days ago. No telling when he would get an official word from the bureau to open. The scholars were certainly ready. Every time he saw one of them during the past few weeks, the same question always popped out. "When we begin again, Mistah Ogilvie?"

Though he had yet to receive his June salary from the bureau, the missionary association had recently sent another fifty dollars. That, plus the promised one dollar each from most of the scholars, would allow him to begin the belated fall session. *That's what I must do—concentrate on the school—not on the deaths in Galveston.* He knew grief would have its own way and come upon him in waves. But for the rest of the time, he would do what he could to continue serving these folks who had held him aloft through the darkest of his own days.

Thus school convened the following Monday, in the warehouse, not in a new building as John had hoped. Most of his pupils from the earlier sessions appeared for the daytime classes, textbooks in hand, some of which already appeared dog-eared from use. The twins wore new calico dresses. Ophelia could hardly contain herself as she ran up the stairs and thrust what at first appeared to be a piece of her dress toward John.

"Look, teacher. Look what Ma fixed up."

At second glance John recognized the primer, smartly covered in the same calico fabric the girls wore. Taken with the idea, John addressed the twins as soon as roll call was completed.

"Ophelia and Melinda, would you please come forward and show the class your books?"

With wide grins, the girls flounced to the head of the room, swished their skirts, and held the colorful books up high so all could see.

"These girls have come up with a clever way to tell their books from others. I suggest you all find a similar plan for easy identification of your own books. This is a good way to start the school year."

Giggles and chatter seemed difficult to suppress the first day, but the excitement was contagious and spread a good feeling. John sensed it as keenly as his pupils. Mrs. Wallace slipped into her role of class mother, fussing with one scholar and scolding another, and Jeremy and Pablo started right off tussling. Patsy made a point to show everyone how she had been practicing her reading during the summer. Still, there were vacancies that caught John's attention. In particular, he missed Ezra, saddened that the boy might not return now that he lived with friends away from town.

Samuel arrived a half hour early for the evening class. John's heart soared when his assistant stepped through the doorway.

"I figured you could use some good help afore the others came," Samuel grinned.

John clasped his friend's hand. "Thank you, Samuel. I can always use extra help."

"An I got a surprise," Samuel said.

John raised his eyebrows. "A surprise?"

"Yes, suh. Look who I brought."

On cue, Jeb stepped into the room from where he had been waiting two stairs down. John reached for the man's hand. "This is a splendid surprise. Jeb, how are you?"

"I be fine, Mistah Ogilvie." His grip felt firm and his smile matched John's.

"And your family, did you find your family?" The words came before John thought.

"No, suh. But I guess I didn't really expects to. Somebody said they saw my wife working way over at Tyler, so I had to go see. It weren't her, and I 'bout got myself hanged. They don' much like free niggers in that part of Texas."

Before John could think what to say, Jeb spoke again. "I wants to come back to school, suh, iffin I ain't too far behind."

"Aye, Jeb, you can come. It won't take you long to catch up."

The week ended on another high note with a letter from Sarah Barnes. John had written to her at her home address, telling of his illness, the storm in early October, and rumors of bureau deaths in Galveston, not knowing at the time of writing who had been affected. He tore open the envelope, his fingers trembling ever so slightly, eager to read her response.

Dear Mr. Ogilvie,

By now you must know General Griffin and four of his assistants are all dead of the yellow fever. Such a tragedy. Miss Skinner and I are humbled to have been spared.

In the midst of the death and dying, the same devastating storm of which you wrote also struck Galveston Island. I'm told the church where we meet suffered some water damage, though apparently minor compared to other buildings in the city.

I thank the Almighty God that you were spared death from that vile fever. Surely, the Lord has more work for you to do yet on this earth.

Most sincerely,
Sarah Barnes

John spent all the next day reflecting on the final statement in the letter. This lovely woman, always strong in her faith, had a way of putting things in the right perspective.

He used her words as a theme for his Sabbath school lesson, with an emphasis on *"doing the work of the Lord."* He felt good about it, believed in it, and sensed the message got across and was well received.

Strolling home that Sunday afternoon, he looked forward to the new school year. The crisp autumn air held a sense of anticipation. A stiff breeze played with the trees, plucking leaves and tossing them helter-skelter. A paper skittered along the pathway in front of him. He reached to grab it, only to have it dance away from him. Quickening his step, he snatched at it again, this time successfully grasping the corner between his thumb and forefinger. Pausing to read the bold letters, his heart momentarily stopped.

ATTENTION!!!

Brethern of the Klan, and friends of the South! When the banner under which our heroes fought and bled was lowered from her proud position by overpowering numbers, we took the hands of our enemies once more in friendship, and listened to their promises, seemingly fair and honest. We resolved to let "the past be buried in the eternal past;" yea, shut out from sight our barren fields and desolate homes, and to forget whose guns contained the bullets that sent our brave and fair to their last resting places. Look around you now! See how their promises have been fulfilled! See upon what quicksand our hopes were built! Time has rolled around and finds us under the worst tyranny in the world. To Southern and working men, there is no fear. To "Carpet Baggers," enemies to our blood and country, we say, beware! You are clogs on the wheels of our prosperity. To you we may have smiling faces and extended hands, but our hearts are envenomed and we will act accordingly.

The 15th Legion of Lone Star are commanded to meet again. New members to be initiated. Personal business of great importance to be transacted. By order of
GRAND CYCLOPS

John glanced around and saw no one. He stuffed the notice in his pocket and picked up his pace. Of course he had heard rumors of these groups organizing, but not this far south in Texas. Yet here it was in bold print, including a threat obviously directed toward him and other Northerners living here since the war.

His pulse pounded with each step as he raced the rest of the way home. Upon entering, he shut the door firmly behind him and stood for a moment while he caught his breath. Some folks had always avoided him, others were simply rude, but he believed his presence in the community had gradually been accepted. Now he wondered which of his friendly acquaintances were charlatans. An icy chill crawled down his spine, and his thoughts raced back to the terrifying night on the wharf months ago and the intimidating horsemen not long thereafter.

***

School days settled into a normal routine. John kept a wary look-out for signs of unrest among the townsfolk that might affect his teaching or the safety of his pupils. Outwardly things appeared calm. People he dealt with on a daily basis still seemed pleasant, yet he couldn't shake that one horrible sentence. *To you we may have smiling faces and extended hands, but our hearts are envenomed and we will act accordingly.*

A week after the warning blew into his hands, John walked over to the site of the new school to check on the progress. To his surprise, no pounding hammers welcomed him, nor the hum of saws. No workmen milled about calling to each other. No one was there. John had not been able to lend a hand since the start-up of class, but others were to continue working. Alarmed and puzzled, he made his way to Main Street and entered the office of Mr. Browning.

The man looked up from his desk at the sound of the door closing. "Ogilvie, good afternoon. I hope you are here with good news."

"Good news?" The remark perplexed him.

"Money from the bureau so we can proceed with the project."

A sinking feeling swept through John. "No, sir, I'm afraid not. I've come to see why there is no activity at the building site."

"All the funds on hand are gone. Can't pay workers without money."

"What if I got volunteer labor for the remaining work?" John thought of the men in his evening class. Surely they would give him a week or two.

"The materials have all been used up, Ogilvie. Buildings like that don't come for free."

Chapter 19

John tore off the page on his daily calendar, December 1, 1867. The incomplete building stood along the bay like a wound that wouldn't heal. At least in the month since the poisonous notice from the Grand Cyclops whirled in on that devilish wind, there had been no more threats.

He paced the room. Surely there had been time for the bureau to reorganize since the yellow fever deaths. He tugged at his beard, now an impressive mass on his chin, heaved a big sigh, and sank down in his chair. At his desk he scribbled one more note to Lt. Bonnaffon in Indianola, again asking the whereabouts of the promised funds.

On December 3*rd*, an envelope from a J.P. Richardson of bureau headquarters in Austin arrived. John tore open the seal and a check fluttered to his desk. Picking it up, he stared at the amount: $25.00. The letter explained: ... *in payment of your account certified by Lieutenant Bonnaffon for services as teacher of F. S. at Lavaca, for 1 to 30 June, 1867.*

John let loose a long laugh. Here was one of his long awaited paychecks. It certainly wasn't construction money, and he was still missing his pay for May, but perhaps things were starting to get back on track with the bureau.

The daytime scholars seemed content with classes continuing at the warehouse, but some of the men in the evening class had worked on the new school and asked about its completion.

"We can help on Saturday and even the Lord's day because it's for His glory—you know, a church and all," Samuel said.

"It's not the labor that's holding us up. It's the money for materials." John said. "It should be arriving soon."

It was December, and Mrs. Wallace hummed Christmas carols as she prepared meals in the little shanty, but John had trouble shifting into the spirit of the season. All the pressures of the previous months held him down, and the balmy gulf air in lieu of chilly winter days stole the excitement he had always known during advent. He scolded himself for his despair and prayed for help to rise above it.

On his walk to school one morning, strains of the song Mrs. Wallace had sung at daybreak circled through his mind and an inspiration began to take hold. His step lightened the closer he got to the warehouse.

"We're going to have a party," he announced to his day class. "A Christmas party."

The idea received a jubilant response. Food and music would be part of it, of course, but the big event was to be a pageant of the birth of Christ involving everyone who wanted to participate. Rehearsals for the production took up a lot of class time, but it was well spent. On the afternoon of the performance, "curtains" rose to a well-prepared and unique cast of characters. Melinda, a white girl, draped in a ragged length of blue cloth sat demurely on a stool next to a makeshift manger. In her arms wriggled a black baby Jesus, and brown skinned Pablo struck a serious but fatherly pose beside her while multi-hued angels, shepherds, and wise men gathered around. Jeremy, who had initially wanted the part of Joseph, switched to narrator when he learned it was the dominant role. With a voice loud and clear accompanied by considerable theatrics, he read the story of the nativity from a script written by various class members. In conclusion everyone present sang "Mary Had a Baby...Yes She Did."

Throughout the performance John, finally filled with the spirit of the season, grinned broadly. *Lord, I hope you are watching. I know you would approve.*

School closed for the week between Christmas and the New Year. John took long walks across the prairie, and on mail days he stopped by the post office, still hoping for the promised check from the bureau. If construction on the school could start again, it wouldn't take long for completion.

During the break, he received only one piece of correspondence, a printed notice from the missionary association, dated December 12, 1867, obviously sent to all their teachers with a blank line filled in for the appropriate party:

> *Your attention is respectfully invited to the fact that your support for the current school year is furnished by:*

Flora Beach Burlingame

Friends in Winnebago & Muskegon.

One of the conditions upon which this support is furnished is an agreement made on your behalf for a monthly letter from the field...these letters will be read in the prayer meetings, Sabbath School, or monthly concerts, and if prepared with judgment and regularly forwarded, they will powerfully aid both you and us... Write out fresh and cheerful facts, anecdotes, narratives, such as you would confide to a personal friend. First say whatever is to be said concerning your own school, and then add any accounts of neighboring or larger interests which may be at your command.

John felt a swell of hope. He wanted to sit down and immediately write letters to the churches but restrained himself, understanding that a well thought out message would gain him more than a hastily scribbled account of his activities. He paced the warehouse room composing and re-composing until the right words came. Sitting at his desk, he dipped a pen in ink and began his plea.

Dear Friends,

It is with deep gratitude that I accept your support and it comes at a crucial time. A new school-church building stands half-completed and promised funds from the government have not been forthcoming.

With that important set of facts said, John painted a verbal picture of the small gulf community and told of the progress of his students, the mix of colors in his classroom, and their eagerness to learn.

I commend you for maintaining the higher ground and not descending to the same level as those who think themselves better than others; reach out a helping hand. We are in great need of help at present.

John lowered his pen, sealed the envelope, and prayed long and hard that the good Christian people in Winnebago and Muskegon would take his message to heart.

Charcoal and Chalk

Classes reconvened on January 6, 1868, and lessons once more fell into a pattern. It had been almost a year since John first began teaching here, and though there had been interruptions, progress by every scholar put all the struggles into the right perspective.

Rumblings from certain townsfolk about the school occasionally reached his ears, but nothing seemed out of control or particularly threatening. Then one Monday, when John returned from a walk to prepare for his evening class, a note tacked to the schoolroom door beckoned him. He slowly climbed the stairs to the landing, stopped, and read the words written in bold handwriting.

Mr. Ogilvie,

The warehouse has been sold. You must vacate the upstairs room in two weeks. See me to settle up your rent.

A.W. Oswald.

Chapter 20

John whispered a silent prayer, then turned back down the stairs. He strode around the corner of the building, rapped on the office door, and entered at a muffled response.

Oswald sat facing the entry, his feet propped on his desk. He made no effort to rise as John approached. "I see you got my note."

"Two weeks isn't much time," John said, trying to keep his composure.

"That's the way it is," Oswald said. He removed his feet from their casual position, leaned forward and rustled through some papers. "Let's see. You owe me some rent money." He picked up an invoice, squinted at it and pursed his lips. "That'd be twenty-five dollars for all of January. You owe me that right now. Then there'd be twelve-fifty for the first two weeks of February, and you're out."

"The new school isn't finished yet," John said. "Perhaps the buyer will allow us to continue using the room for a few months longer."

"Doubt that," Oswald said. "I don't think he'll take to renting space for teaching colored folk."

The words hit John as though he had been punched. His jaw tightened as he fought to keep his response controlled. "You'll have the January rent money by the end of this week and the rest on the day we vacate, as you wish." He left the warehouse office in haste, lest his demeanor dissolve into something other than Christian.

For the next hour, usually reserved for preparing lessons, he sat in the classroom contemplating this unexpected turn of events and praying for direction. When the heavy footfalls of his evening students sounded on the stairs, he sighed and rose. He would discuss it with these men. Most had good heads on their shoulders. Perhaps a solution was waiting to reveal itself with the help of others. When all were seated, he told of the mandate from the warehouse owners.

"We got us a new school just waitin'," Samuel said.

"I'm afraid it's not ready," John said.

"It's got a roof, ain't it?"

"An mos' of its sides is on," Jeb said.

"There's no floor, windows or doors," John countered.

"It's bettah than my house," another pupil added.

As the men argued their case, John began to see their point. Ideas crept into his mind as to how to make the new building habitable, even though not complete. "Aye, gentlemen, perhaps you are right. It just might work."

John wrote a note to Agent Bonnaffon in Indianola, explaining the situation and requesting the final rent money. At the same time, he made up his mind to pay it out of his own pocket if necessary, so as not to create any agitation from Oswald against the freedmen. A letter to the bureau superintendent of schools in Austin also flowed from his pen, explaining the need to occupy the half-finished building. Surely this would generate the long sought after government money to complete the school.

His last communication from Bonnaffon was the one dated October 28. *They have all died over at Galveston.* John's one piece of correspondence from anyone in the bureau since then was the form letter from the disbursing officer in Austin dated December 3, containing his June pay.

When he posted his letters, to his surprise, he was handed one bearing an Austin return address. His heart skipped a beat. "I'll take my envelope addressed to the Freedmen's Bureau back," he told the clerk.

The man shrugged his shoulders and complied. "Mail for there leaves on the train this afternoon and won't go again for a couple more days."

"I know," John said. "I may not need to send it."

When he opened the envelope just received, an involuntary sigh of relief escaped his lips. It *was* a letter from Wheelock.

> *My Dear sir,*
> *After a variety of strange adventures by flood and field, illustrative of Texas mails, your letter of Dec. 7 has reached me!*

I am stationed at Austin, working in the same position as before.

Enclosed find blanks for school reports.

I remained in Galveston with my family until a few weeks since, all of us had the fever but all recovered. Saw the account of your death but conclude now that it was a slight mistake.

Direct simply to me here (nobody's care) and it will reach me promptly.

Truly your friend,
Edw. Wheelock

John couldn't even quite remember what he said in his December letter. Certainly he must have asked the whereabouts of the funds for the building, yet that was not mentioned here. In spite of his disappointment, he had to chuckle at the account of his own death. At least he knew for sure that Wheelock was still alive, and perhaps this latest letter would reach him in time.

***

On a chilly Saturday in February, a handful of the evening scholars showed up to help make the move from the warehouse to the unfinished school building, and in spite of the wind and occasional sprinkles, the mood was jovial.

"Maybe it ain't done, but it be our own place," Jeb said as he balanced a crate of books on his shoulders and carried it down the warehouse stairs.

Everyone took a load, and they congregated at the building site.

Jeb set down his box and looked in the doorless entry. A look of concern creased his forehead. "I forgot it ain't got no floor. How we going to sit?"

"I think we can fix that," John said. "Help me with these." He picked up one end of a plank originally used as benches at the warehouse. Jeb grabbed the other end and they laid the board across the joists of the elevated floor.

"There," John said, "Instant seating."

"Well, I'll be," Jeb said, "That jes' might work."

They set to work hauling more planks, positioning them across the joists, and adding the remainder close together at the front of the room to support John's desk and hold supplies. The men sang as they worked. John joined in, his spirits soaring.

Several hours later, when the maps and large blackboard were nailed to the wall, they sat on one of the planks, legs dangling, and admired the results of their labor.

"Sure do look like a school, Mistah Ogilvie," Samuel said with a wide grin.

"Aye, it does at that," John said. "It does at that."

When school commenced in this unusual classroom the following Monday, John discovered most of his pupils considered it to be a great adventure. There were definitely some advantages: no banging of a door, no shuffling of feet, and perfect ventilation through the windowless frames and open spaces underneath. There were chilly days, of course, when squalls gusted in the open windows. Sometimes he simply had to let school out early. But usually the mild, southern Texas weather accommodated them, and teaching progressed on schedule.

Unexpected disruptions did, however, occur. Swallows darted in and out through the openings, and the younger scholars enjoyed swinging their legs as they sat on the planks.

"Oh, Teacha'," Patsy cried one day. "Jim done fall through. He swang his legs too hard."

And on another occasion, a neighbor's rooster strutted beneath the joists, crowing during a spelling bee. Then it grew quiet until Jeremy hollered, "Ow! Dat chicken done bit my toe!"

This disrupted the entire class, and until someone shooed the creature away John had no control. At recess, the children conveniently vanished through the floor, and when the break was over they popped up in their places. John found it all quite amusing and, though not ideal, the novelty of the situation helped to reduce the stress.

But he still anxiously awaited an envelope from Austin bearing the promised thousand dollar check. Finally, late in February, a letter from Austin arrived. He held his breath, ripped open the seal, and scanned the few short words:

> *Dear Mr. Ogilvie,*
> *The check you keep requesting for completing the school was long ago sent to the bureau agent in Indianola. You should have received it in ample time to finish the project before fall classes convened...*

The words blurred before his eyes, and John crumpled the letter in his fist, trembling with anger and disbelief. A cold dread washed over him. There was little doubt the money was gone—absconded by a dishonest agent who never had any intention of handing it over for a school in Lavaca. *And now I have seventy scholars taking lessons in a half-built schoolhouse who believe in me, a teacher who can't make good on a promise.* He opened his fist, letting the crushed letter, a small deflated ball, drop to his desk.

Holding his head in his hands, he whispered, "Dear God, help us."

He couldn't bring himself to tell the men in the evening class the bad news. Nor did he mention it to Joe and Mrs. Wallace that night during supper, or the class the following day. He needed to sort through the dilemma and calm himself first. He didn't even go to the post office to check for mail.

Several days after receipt of the devastating missive from Austin, Mrs. Wallace commented, "I met Mrs. Duval at the grocer's today. She said to tell you the postal clerk done wonder where you at, cuz you ain't come to get your mail." Mrs. Wallace clicked her tongue. "Seem to me it ain't nobody's business." She looked hard at John as she handed him a second helping of corn bread, her eyes bursting with curiosity. "Jes' why ain't you gone to get the mail? Don' you do that whenever it come in?"

The next afternoon between classes, he walked to town and picked up a larger than usual packet from the American Missionary Association. Placing it under his coat, he clutched it tightly against his chest. The bulk of it tantalized him, and rather than return to the school he hurried home. Once inside his hut, he slit open the large envelope and watched the contents tumble onto his bed. Notes in many scripts mingled with the more familiar printed letter head of the AMA. But what caught his eye were the checks.

He picked them up one by one, adding the amounts, until the tidy pile in his hand totaled $550 dollars. Slipping to his knees, John bowed his head and wept.

Chapter 21

After long fervent prayers of thanksgiving, John spent an hour reading the letters accompanying the checks. These messages came from men and women, boys and girls; strangers, yet from their pens flowed an unmistakable passion, a sense of family and caring. They each expressed an eagerness to assist in the education of the freedmen.

John carefully tucked the checks into his waistcoat pocket. Returning the letters to the large envelope, he placed it under his bed and left to call on James Browning.

The bell above the door jingled when he entered the architect's office. John's buoyant mood obviously showed, for when Browning looked up from his paperwork he smiled. "It appears you have good news."

"Aye, that I have." John handed him the fistful of checks. "Five hundred and fifty dollars. Will it complete the job? And are you willing to continue heading it up?"

Browning thumbed through the checks, an intent expression on his face as he mentally calculated the figures. When he had studied each one, he gave a low whistle, nodding his head.

"Looks promising, but are you certain these checks are valid?"

"These are good Christian people wanting to do their part to help the downtrodden."

Browning rubbed his jaw, thinking over the situation before responding. "I say let's wait until they clear, then order the rest of the materials needed. This should at least come close. I'm willing to oversee the project again."

John wanted to argue against waiting, but the missing bureau funds had taught him a lesson. Though anxious to get on with the construction of the building, he understood the caution.

The architect pulled a file from a drawer. "I still have a list of supplies required to complete the project. I'll go over them and get an order ready."

"Thank you," John said. He extended his hand and the two men shook on the agreement. The bell on the door jangled again as John left the building—a leading note to a cheerful melody he hummed all the way home.

John brought the packet of letters to the next class session. "I have a surprise. The school will be finished because of some generous folks in the states of Illinois and Michigan."

Cheers erupted. To John's ears it was a chaos as sweet as a symphony. He let it continue for several minutes before holding up the large envelope from the American Missionary Association. "I want to read some of these letters to you."

It ended up being a lesson in geography—John pointing on the map to the states of Illinois and Michigan.

Patsy's hand shot up. "Kin I write a letter to them nice people so's they know how happy we is about the money?" Her dark eyes radiated enthusiasm and the idea caught like sparks of fire throughout the room.

"Me, too." Jeremy stood and danced a little jig in his excitement. "On real paper cuz we cain't send slates in the mail."

John chuckled. Jeremy had often asked when he could write with pen and paper. Well, as scarce as those supplies were, this was the time.

The following day John mailed a packet to the AMA, as hefty as the one he had received.

"That's quite a load you got there," the clerk said. "In return you get this." He handed John one slim, white envelope post marked from Austin.

Wheelock's letter, written on March 3, still quibbled over his pay for the preceding spring:

> ...Now about your salary for May...no vouchers for that month from you are on file here; in some way they must have miscarried. I therefore enclose blanks which you will please sign and ask Captain Bailey to certify.... The teachers' salaries were discontinued by Gen. Reynolds simply because of lack of funds, and I am informed the same reason still continues.

...Let me hear from you soon, for any further delay will increase the difficulty that always attends the collection of overdue accounts...

John snorted at the last remark. *As if I didn't know the truth of it.* He had also learned that letters from the bureau often contained surprises and conundrums. This one included two. Not that vouchers were lost and teachers' salaries discontinued—he had come to expect that—but who in heaven's name were Bailey and Reynolds? A breeze wafted through the pane-less window, tugging at the note in his hand. He had half a notion to release the paper and let it fly off with the gulls. Puzzling out each twist and turn of the bureau hierarchy had grown tiresome.

Common sense told him Bailey must be yet another military agent in Indianola, Reynolds the replacement for the deceased General Griffin. Still, it would be nice to have been officially informed of these appointments. Sometimes he felt too removed from the more populated areas in Texas. Not only was he unaware of the goings on in the bureau, but the higher-ups seemed to forget about him.

Nevertheless, he complied with Wheelock's instructions and sent the vouchers requesting the delinquent payment, plus everything owed him to date, to this Captain Bailey. *Who it is doesn't really matter, as long as I get my pay.*

A reply was received just two days later. He opened the envelope and found, to his dismay, not checks but the very vouchers he had filled out and forwarded to Bailey. Wrestling with frustration and confusion, John unfolded the enclosed letter and read:

> *Office of Assist. Comm. B.R.F.and A.L*
> *Indianola Texas, March 11, 1868*
>
> *Mr. John Ogilvie,*
> *Sir:*
> *I enclosed herewith the vouchers for services rendered as teacher in the B.R.F. & A.L* <u>without</u> *approval as I have no means of knowing that you are employed with confident certainty.*
> *Mr. E. M. Wheelock who you quote so freely in your communication is entirely unknown to this office.*
> *I am, Sir, your obed. Servant*

Charcoal and Chalk

Jud W. Bailey, Captain 35 U.S. Infantry

Obedient servant my sin. The statement regarding Wheelock astounded John. Reaching under the bed, he brought out his file of correspondence received from the bureau over the past year. Sorting through the papers, he found the recent letter from Wheelock dated February 7... *I am stationed at Austin working in the same position as before.*

All John could think to do was copy Wheelock's letter, word for word, and send it to Captain Bailey, which he set to doing immediately. He also penned a letter to Wheelock telling him of the confusing message from this new agent in Indianola. That done, he lay on his bed, staring at the ceiling, teased by the subtle lamplight dancing with the shadows. He rolled over and sighed. Somehow, this too would be resolved.

At least everything else seemed to be moving in the right direction. The building of the school progressed, and with the addition of a solid floor and real glass windows a sense of respect for the new surroundings settled through the class. It felt like a place to learn. Discipline seemed much less necessary, and for the most part the skills of the scholars continued to improve. That, coupled with the AMA's consistent mailings of its portion of his salary, kept John's spirits on an even keel.

***

Sarah Barnes was back in Galveston, her school having opened in January. John wrote her of the money from the churches, how the school was finally nearing completion, and of the progress of his scholars. *Things are going well enough now I sometimes wonder when the other shoe will drop.*

It happened that very afternoon when he went to post his letter to her.

While in town, he stopped at the dry goods store to purchase new collars and cuffs. There he encountered Pierre Duval. At their greeting, the Frenchman's face appeared somber. "Have you seen the signs?"

John gave him a quizzical look.

"Come. Let me show you," Pierre motioned him out the door. They walked a few paces to a community bulletin board. There various notices were tacked announcing activities and comments of interest to the general public. Pierre pointed to one in the center. "I have seen these at several locations."

K.K.K.S.
The Moon is low
The Bull is rampant.
St. Mark: the Hour
S.X.
By order of the
KHENGIS KHAN

"Have you been threatened?" Pierre asked.

John shook his head. "Not directly. Not lately. There are always those who don't like what I'm doing, but I don't feel my safety is at stake." Though needles of anxiety stabbed inside him, he pretended nonchalance, and said, "These notices seem more set on simply scaring folks than anything serious."

"Don't be too sure, John. This K.K.K. is a powerful organization. They have killed in other parts of Texas." Concern darkened Pierre's eyes.

John removed the notice from its tacks and slid it into his coat pocket. He tried to appear casual, but fear for his school and all connected to it resurfaced like bitter bile.

That evening Jacob returned after a long absence. John had a stove now, and prepared many of his own meals, but Mrs. Wallace insisted he eat with them on this special night. Conversation hummed at the supper table.

"Where you been?" Mrs. Wallace questioned her son, as she ladled up steaming bowls of gumbo.

"Up to Victoria, fixin' track."

"They givin' you much money for all that work?" Joe asked.

Talk between parents and son see-sawed while John listened. It was a family conversation, so when he finished his meal, he stood to excuse himself.

"I'm much obliged for supper, and it is good to see you, Jacob, but I believe I'll head on home."

"So soon?" Mrs. Wallace's ability to look hurt and astonished always made him feel a wee bit ashamed. Still, he didn't want to stay. Pulling his watch from his waistcoat, he snapped open the cover and studied the face. "A quarter to eight, and I've lessons to prepare."

John received no more arguments and headed for his own shack. Ten or fifteen minutes passed, enough time for him to settle at his table with a book, when a rap sounded on the door. He figured it to be Mrs. Wallace with an extra biscuit for his breakfast. She often did that.

"Come in."

The door opened and in walked Jacob. Even the dim lamplight couldn't hide the glint of fear in his eyes. With trembling fingers, he thrust a piece of wrinkled paper at John—the K.K.K. notice. "Where you git this?"

John stared at the paper. It must have fallen out of his pocket at the Wallaces' when he checked his watch for the time. "They're tacked up around town," he said, "It's gibberish."

"No," Jacob said. "This heah be bad. I knowed a colored what be killed by the Ku Kluxes. An' I hear tell of a teacha' up nawth in Texas made to git out." He dropped the paper on the table as though it had burned his hand.

"I won't let them scare me off, Jacob. My work here is too important." John motioned for his visitor to take a seat.

Jacob shook his head and turned to leave. "Don't tell Ma about them words. It will skeer her to death, and if you is smart, you bettah be skeered, too." He pushed the door open and left, shutting it behind him with a hard thud.

John let the offensive message lay and returned to his studies. An hour later he closed the book. He had read twenty pages and not one word had registered. His mind was filled with Jacob's frightened face and the fearsome words laying face up inches away.

At dawn John awoke from a restless night. He dressed and made a pot of coffee, and as he poured himself a cup he heard Mrs. Wallace's voice next door. "You be keerful, now, an' come along home sooner next time."

Jacob must be leaving. These goodbyes were always tearful for his mother. John sighed. He was glad to no longer be a part of those difficult nights and awkward farewells. It was amazing how a few short feet and a wall could separate their lives. He took a sip of coffee and about dropped the cup when a face appeared in the window on the side of the house away from the Wallaces'. The early morning light gave it an eerie quality as a low voice penetrated the thin glass. "Mistah Ogilvie." The shadowy figure put a finger to his lips and motioned John to come closer. Bewildered, John obeyed, pushing up the lower sash. A gust of cool air blew in and he found himself face to face with Jacob.

"You be right," the young man whispered. "We mus' preten' not to be afeered, but you still got to be keerful." His agitated breathing and pungent body scent belied his bravado. He thrust a brown paper package at John. "Here, this be for you." And before John could answer, Jacob turned and hurried away.

John closed the window and carried the bundle to the table. It was heavy and wound tightly with string. Curious, he reached for the kitchen knife and sawed away until the loops of twine came loose. Lifting a corner of the paper, he sucked in a sharp, sudden breath. A revolver.

Chapter 22

John felt his heart constrict then pump wildly as he cautiously picked up the weapon. He had never before held a gun. He thought back on Lieutenant Mitchel's recommendation to buy one, an idea that had repulsed and angered him at the time.

The K.K.K. bulletin stared up at him from the table. Suddenly, its message seemed more menacing. Some folks in this community wanted him gone. He didn't know who or how far they would go to force him to leave. Carefully, he replaced the gun in its brown wrapping, not quite sure what to do with it. He slumped onto the bed, sitting with his head in his hands. The weapon represented a sacrifice—his safety for Jacob's own. John had never known more loyal friends—anywhere—than the Negro members of this little town.

Early on, the bureau had asked for reports regarding threats against the teachers of the freedmen or their schools. Now, with the Ku Klux Klan obviously gaining strength in the area, John felt compelled to write to the superintendent and advise him of the latest developments.

Sometime in March, a Reverend Joseph Welch had taken over the bureau's Texas school program. It didn't explain why Bailey in Indianola knew nothing of Welch's predecessor, Edwin Wheelock, yet John was only too familiar with inadequate communication between the different bureau posts. He wrote to both Bailey and the Rev. Welch, informing each of them of the recent notices posted about town. He concluded his messages by saying, *I am taking precautions toward my own safety which I heretofore felt unnecessary.* He did not explain further.

John tried not to dwell on the weapon which he had carefully tucked under his bed. Instead, when he wasn't teaching and preparing lessons, he worked on the new school. He was back to hammering nails himself. This time around he had more strength, having fully recovered from his bout of yellow fever.

One Saturday morning, while sweeping sawdust from the front steps of the building, he spied a familiar figure approaching. Setting the broom aside, he hurried forward, his hand extended. "Mr. Ware. What a pleasure. As you can see, we are finally on our way to having a real school and church."

The man shook John's hand with hearty enthusiasm. "Very good, Mr. Ogilvie."

"Let me show you what has been done since you were last here." John motioned Mr. Ware to follow. Entering the building, they walked on solid floor and beside glassed-in windows. "And here is our special treasure," John said. He opened a small door behind his desk at the front of the classroom. "We put the bell in last week. Would you like to ring it?"

Mr. Ware's face lit up with a broad smile. "May I?"

They stepped into the small, dim room of the tower. A rope dangled in the center, illuminated by sunlight beaming through slated vents from above. Mr. Ware reached for it with both hands and pulled. Bongs reverberated, loud, strong, and melodious. "Ah, how beautiful. And what a glorious message it sends to the community. Here is a place of worship and learning for the colored folks and their children—so deserving."

He gave the rope another hefty tug before they exited the tiny space. Back in the meeting room, bright with light from the big windows, John noticed tears on his visitor's cheeks.

Mr. Ware pulled a handkerchief from his pocket, wiped his face and blew his nose. "Thank you Mr. Ogilvie, and if you need anything at all for your little flock, please don't hesitate to ask. I live in Indianola now, but you can always send a messenger or a note by mail. I still make a trip to the north several times a year and can get books or papers for you. Just let me know what you need."

The man made his way to where a driver with a horse and wagon waited. As John watched the wagon roll away, his feet felt two inches off the ground. One George Ware made up for a dozen scare notices tacked around town.

Samuel climbed down off the roof where he had been fastening the last of the shingles. "I better be gettin' on home before dark settles in." He picked up his coat lying across a sawhorse and looked at John curiously. "What was all that bell ringin' about?"

"That," said John, "Was all about an angel of the Lord."

The following Saturday a crew of volunteers showed up to whitewash the building. John had thrown out an invitation to both classes, expecting a good response, but when twenty-nine eager scholars and some parents arrived, he caught his breath and explained, "We've got ten brushes, so you'll have to take turns. Those who aren't painting come see me and I'll find a job for you."

By the end of the day, everyone crowded around and admired the results of their labors. John stood in the middle, his clothes spattered white, his right arm so sore from painting he could hardly lift it. But his heart sang. The white clapboard walls and the bell tower contrasted starkly with the drab, unpainted shanties scattered along the bay. Yet they seemed to belong together, like a proud mother hen with her brood of chicks.

"It sure do look good," Jeb said, wiping his hands on a wet rag. "Do you think it'll be done fo' Eastah?"

"The Lord won't care if there ain't no door," Samuel said.

As John stood and surveyed the project, so near completion, a huge sense of satisfaction swelled up in him. "We'll have a door."

Except for the door and a few minor touches, the schoolhouse was about done. On Monday, John brought Browning down to the bay to show him the gleaming white building. "We're hoping things can be finished by Easter. What do you think?"

"The funds from the northern churches have paid most of the bills," Browning said, "but we are still a little short. It would be a shame to stop now, we are so close. I don't think we can approach local merchants again. Can you possibly come up with the balance?"

He handed John an invoice. Thirty dollars. Surely that amount could be found. Yet another appeal to the churches in Illinois and Michigan would take weeks for a response.

"I think I can," John said. "I'll let you know as soon as possible."

He hadn't meant to take advantage of Mr. Ware's offer so soon, but the man had been sincere, and the need was now. John wrote a long letter explaining how grateful he and the children were for his generous gift of the bell:

> *...And now we find we are short thirty dollars to complete the building. Is it possible you could help us...again?*

George Ware replied post haste:

...If you can take up a contribution or in any way raise one half of the $30, I will pay the other half in receipt of a letter from you advising me of the fact.

"God bless you, Mr. Ware," John said aloud. "We will do it."

He presented the idea to the evening class that very same day.

"Well, gentlemen, what do you think?"

"It'd sure be nice to have us a door," Samuel said, swatting at a mosquito.

A chorus of "Yes, suh"s swept through the room.

Jeb stood, scooped his cap up from where it lay on the bench, and said, "How much you say we got to pay?"

"Fifteen dollars."

Jeb reached into his pocket and pulled out some coins. Dropping them into his up-turned cap, he passed it to the man beside him. By the time the cap reached John, the center sagged from the weight of its contents. John dug into his own pocket and added to the collection. He didn't count the money, but knew, even if it was short, the rest would be attainable—from his own salary if nowhere else.

"Thank you. I believe you have just paid for the completion of the schoolhouse."

A great cheer arose. "Hallelujah! We done it. Praise the Lawd."

On Sunday, the bell in the tower rang officially for the first time, heralding a glorious Easter morning. John had attempted to continue church services and Sabbath school in the incomplete building, but it was awkward and attendance poor. Today, the entire Negro community crowded onto the benches. John scanned those present and thought of Ezra's tiny, bent grandmother who had refused to come to church meetings because she couldn't get up the stairs. There were a few steps here, but not many, not like the upper room in the warehouse. With deep gratification, John observed other elderly members of the community in attendance.

After a good sermon on the risen Lord, John led the congregants in a rendering of "I Know That My Redeemer Lives." His tenor notes rose above the attempts of others who struggled with the unfamiliar words and tune. At the end of the hymn, a hush fell, then a clear, lone voice began singing. *Chillun, did you heah when Jesus rose? Did you heah when Jesus rose?* Others joined in. *Chillun, did you heah when Jesus rose?* Soon the room rocked with claps and shouts.

Mary set her table in spite of all her foes;
King Jesus sat at the center place and cups did overflow.
The Father looked at His Son and smiled,
The son did look at-a Him.
The Father saved my soul from Hell
And the Son freed me from sin.

John, too, clapped and swayed to the rhythm, grabbed by the jubilation spreading throughout the room. This song of the freedmen said more than all the words his fledgling sermon ever could.

Energized by the day's events, instead of heading for the confinement of his little shack, John locked the schoolhouse door and began to walk toward the Chocolate Bayou. A thunderstorm had passed through, wetting the earth and rinsing the multicolored display of wildflowers, reminding him of his first venture onto this Texas prairie over a year ago, how awed he had been by the stark beauty, and how the pungent smell of the sage had spiced each breath. Birdsong had lightened his step along the way. And so it was again. He walked until the sun rested on the horizon before turning to retrace his steps for home. A wind played tag with his coattails and rustled the spindly limbs of the mesquite. By the time he reached the outskirts of town, twilight splintered the shadows along the roadway.

A group of horsemen emerged from a distance, and John watched with curiosity as others joined them, still too faraway to make out who they might be. Excited shouts drifted on the wind, horses whinnied, and the assembly gathered speed, galloping in his direction. As he watched them approach he noticed they appeared to be in some sort of costume—each dressed alike. A tremor crept along John's nerves. He had no reason to think this group might be seeking him, but still his mouth went dry. Hoping the distance and darkening skies had not yet revealed him to the horsemen, he slipped behind a bush, the only shelter immediately at hand. The group thundered by minutes later, obviously intent on a destination beyond where he stood. They were a sight to behold. Each rider—and there must have been at least a dozen— wore some sort of a white hood over his head with two holes cut for eyes. A ghoulish lot with obvious covert intentions.

John stood rooted until the sound pounding in his ears was no longer that of horses' hooves, but only of his own heartbeats.

Waiting until dark, he made his way home at a pace just under a run and locked his door securely behind him before groping his way to the bed where he sat in the dark, willing his heartbeats to slow. Here in the once longed-for solitude of his own place he had never felt so terribly alone and vulnerable.

That night, as his head lay on the pillow pressed against the hard metal of Jacob's revolver, every hint of a noise caused him to jump. Any moment he half-expected to look up and see a ghostly figure leaning over the bed, eyes peering out of blank holes.

John did not feel prepared for class the next morning, his brain foggy from lack of sleep. The moment the pupils began to arrive, he sensed something different. As each took his or her place, an abnormal hush hung thick over the classroom. By nine fifteen, only half the benches were filled. Even Mrs. Wallace crept in silently at the last minute.

"Where is everyone?" John asked.

His former landlady glanced around, connecting with the fear-ridden eyes of her classmates, then stood. In a shaky voice, she said, "Well, suh, Mistah Ogilvie, we had us a terrible fright."

"Yes, suh!" Jeremy jumped up, his rapid breathing wheezing out words, "Ghosts, suh. Ghosts riding on horses in the dark. We hear they looking for a nigger to hang and ... and ..."

John unconsciously picked up the Bible from his desk, clutching it until his knuckles paled, waiting for Jeremy to finish.

"And white folks who take up with coloreds." The boy slumped back on the bench, unable to look John in the eye.

Melinda started to cry.

Fear seemed to curdle the air, making it hard to breath. Still, it was John's place to calm shattered nerves. "I saw those ghosts last night, and yes they were scary, but they weren't really ghosts. They were cowardly men who hide behind sheets to scare others because they are afraid themselves—afraid of change. We need to pray for them and all of Texas and the South, while everyone adjusts to living together differently than in the past."

The tap, tap of raindrops knocked at the windows, and John continued. "The wisest thing to do is keep on learning. Let's continue with our lessons." He set the Bible down and picked up a primer.

No one moved, all eyes focused on their teacher, an unanswered question on each face.

"What is it?" he asked.

Heads turned, appealing to Mrs. Wallace, who stood at the rear of the room. Folding her arms across her bosom for support, she spoke in a quavering voice. "Well, suh. They—we—is afeerd you gonna pack up and leave on account of them riders."

John felt a stirring in he chest. *They are as afraid for me as for themselves.* The thought struck with the same intensity as though the Lord himself had spoken. Swallowing a rising lump in his throat, he scanned each pleading face.

"Well, lads and lassies, there is no need to worry. I have no intention of leaving Lavaca. You are too important to me."

Smiles appeared. A cacophony of voices rose, and primers were picked up and opened for the days lessons.

"Page thirty-seven," John said. "Jeremy, would you please read?"

Chapter 23

No one John spoke to actually knew first-hand of a lynching or of a Negro gone missing, nor, for that matter, any "nigger-loving" white folks beaten. But the night riders couldn't be forgotten. That John and the school were among the intended targets was certain, but the fact he had not been personally confronted or injured in some way must mean they meant to scare him out of town. Well, he wouldn't give them that satisfaction. As though to prove that point, he rang Mr. Ware's bell loud and clear each morning to herald the beginning of class.

Some of the students never returned after the scare, others denied their fears and courageously showed up for lessons, but good marks were few and tension remained high. John himself often felt wound as tight as the mainspring of his pocket watch. As the heat and humidity of June set in, he acknowledged his own need for a break. This year he would not attempt to continue school through the summer months.

Though he fully intended to return in the fall, he began planning a retreat to Minnesota. *I'll spend some time on the Cranston farm, see Lucy, and visit the American Missionary Association offices in Chicago, as well—meet the faces behind the signatures on my correspondence.* Just the thought lifted his sagging spirit, and he wrote to both the bureau and AMA telling them of his intentions. Return letters acknowledged his plans, and unlike the previous school year, even the bureau sent a timely payment for his services as a teacher, bringing its account current through the end of June.

A very welcome letter from the AMA, dated June 20, arrived a few days before his planned departure.

Dear Bro:

I enclose $100 on account. Please sign and return vouchers. I hope to see you safely here in Chicago ere many weeks. With your consent, we would like to arrange for your ordination while here.

Very Truly,
O.C. Sabin,
Asst. Treas.

My ordination? The thought made him dizzy with pleasure and crowned his desire to head north, knowing he would return a more proper preacher. However, as much as he needed a break, John harbored two fears: one was for the safety of his colored friends with the Ku Klux frenzy spreading, the other for the new school-church building that had been so long coming. It must not stand empty during his absence. Since its completion, he had emphasized that for church purposes it was to be a union building to be used by the different denominations as might be arranged by and among the freedmen. Gradually, this idea took hold, and when he finally packed his bag for his much anticipated trip, several groups had begun to make use of the room.

As for the safety of his students, there seemed nothing he could do, but perhaps his absence might abate the danger. He could only pray that all would be well throughout the summer weeks.

Early in July, John stepped onto the deck of the steam lighter *San Antonio*. Standing against the railing he waved at the small assembly of students who had gathered to see him off.

"Don' foget to come back," Jeremy yelled.

A white handkerchief fluttered in Mrs. Wallace's fingers.

Pablo waved both hands frantically, "*Adios, señor* teacher."

The gang plank swung upwards and a bellow of the ship's horn announced departure. As the starboard side eased away from the dock, a part of John felt like a shepherd deserting his flock, and for one long moment he had an urge to plunge into the bay and swim to shore. He stood on deck watching his three friends until they became mere specks.

At Indianola he transferred to the larger steamer, *I. C. Harris*. After maneuvering through Pass Cavallo, the ship entered the gulf waters and headed for Galveston. That bustling port city would be John's first stop. He had written Sarah Barnes about his trip and she had replied immediately. *Please spend a night here in our guest room. That will give us time to share our experiences teaching the freedmen.*

Her letter had been longer than usual, and she went on about a Captain Rathbun, who visited the school whenever his schooner was in port. She had mentioned him in previous letters and John had not thought much about it, but now he felt a wee touch of jealousy. He hoped the captain was a special benefactor of the Galveston school such as his George Ware, not a man courting Sarah Barnes.

***

In the harbor at Galveston, John stood on the dock, scanning faces for the source of the feminine voice calling his name. A hand rose and waved from a cluster of greeters at the far end of the boardwalk. "Mr. Ogilvie! Over here."

He picked up his bag and strode toward the group. As he approached, he recognized the lithe figure of Sarah Barnes, and next to her that of Miss Skinner. The two hurried toward him.

He couldn't keep from grinning at the enthusiastic greeting. "Good day, ladies. What a splendid welcome."

"We are glad you have come," Miss Barnes said. "You remember Miss Skinner?"

John tipped his hat. "Miss Skinner."

"We hope you plan to accept our invitation to stay in the teachers' home," Miss Barnes said. "I would very much like time to discuss plans for our new school building. I'm certain you could contribute some helpful comments, having recently been through the same experience."

"Aye," John said, "I will be happy to do that," though his thoughts at the moment were far removed from the trials and tribulations of building a schoolhouse; all the warm feelings he had experienced upon first meeting Sarah Barnes more than a year ago suddenly revived.

"Here comes our ride," Miss Skinner said, interrupting his flow of thought.

The clop of hooves joined the dissonance of the harbor as a public car pulled up. They climbed aboard, the driver clicked to the mule, and, with a lurch, they began rolling along 24th Street, crossing Strand, Mechanic and Market toward their destination.

After so many months in Lavaca, John marveled at the big city feeling of Galveston—the constant street activity, the large commercial buildings, and the stately homes so opposite from the little harbor town where he struggled alone to meet the needs of the freedmen.

The mule turned to the right on Broadway, and after a few blocks Miss Barnes called out for the driver to stop. "We'll walk from here," she said, as they climbed out of the car.

Two blocks more, and John recognized the teachers' home from his first visit to Galveston. Though the walk was a short distance, the moist June heat quickly sapped their energies, and they sat and rested for a while on the porch, relishing the breeze blowing in from the gulf.

"You should show Mr. Ogilvie the new school site," Miss Skinner said.

"Yes, after supper, when it is cooler, we can walk there."

They gathered around an oval table in the dining room. The aroma of food cooking, the pleasant female companionship, plus the homey atmosphere filled a longing John had felt since his arrival in Texas. The meal, prepared by Martha, a colored woman who hummed while she worked, consisted of roast beef, potatoes, gravy, biscuits and greens. John couldn't get enough, savoring each bite and taking more when a dish was passed his way. At the completion of the meal, they sat around the table conversing and sipping tea. A drowsiness overcame John, and he felt his head begin to nod. Miss Barnes rose from her chair.

"Shall we walk to the school site?"

John took a last swallow of tea to wash the fog from his head and joined the two women. Their stroll took them beside clusters of small, wooden homes where colored families sat on porches fluttering fans to ward off the summer heat. Many called out as they passed by.

"Evenin', School Mistis."

"Fine night fo' a walk."

One small boy followed for an entire block, skipping ahead, dropping behind, then dashing in front again, all the while flashing a huge smile at Miss Skinner and Miss Barnes.

"Are you doing your summer reading, Tobias?" Miss Skinner asked.

"Yes, Ma'am."

When the lad had scampered back to his own front porch, Miss Skinner remarked, "He can't sit still in the classroom either, but he wants to do well."

Several blocks later the group of teachers stood beside what appeared to be a shallow pond.

"This is it," Miss Barnes said, pointing toward the stretch of soggy, vacant land.

John felt his heart sink. "It's a marsh."

Sarah Barnes stood straight, her chin held high, and spoke with firm conviction. "It is available for a very good price," she said. "It can be drained and filled and will be very suitable, being near the colored district."

"And the money?" John said. "Where will that come from?" An ache grew in the pit of his stomach, knowing of the struggles that lay ahead for her in this huge endeavor.

"The bureau has promised money, plus I will be leaving for Connecticut shortly and, while there, plan to persuade congregations to assist financially with the new school."

John had to admire her determination, and perhaps she was right. The marshy property would certainly have very little appeal to other folks seeking real estate, making her goal more attainable. He had every confidence that this Christian lady could convince churches in her native New England community of the need. *I will give her any advice she seeks from me, but discouraging her will not be part of it.*

They sat up late talking of building schools, the bureau, and the challenge of teaching the freedmen. John told of the Ku Klux notices appearing in Lavaca during the past months and the terrifying effect it had on the scholars. The two women listened solemnly.

"A frightening thing," Miss Skinner said, then she told a story of horror in their own neighborhood. "It was a year ago. We heard a loud knock on our door and someone crying for help. A Negro had been terribly stabbed by some soldiers." She paused a moment shaking her head. "We found help for him, but he died praying for his Lord to save him."

"That was only one instance of three that happened within a week in Galveston," Miss Barnes said, "and there have been others since."

A clock chimed midnight, and Miss Skinner gave a start. "That late? I'm off to bed." She rose and headed toward a hallway.

John hoped for a few moments alone with Miss Barnes, but she also stood. "This has been most enjoyable, and I appreciate all your helpful suggestions, Mr. Ogilvie, but I'm certain you must be tired after your long trip. The guestroom is the first door down the hall. I hope you find it comfortable." She picked up a Bible and hesitated a moment. "Oh, and one more thing."

"Yes?" His heart skipped a beat.

"Breakfast is at seven. Goodnight, Mr. Ogilvie."

A short time later, John slid under the mosquito netting and lay between the cool sheets in the guest room. The pleasant scent of the women in the household clung to the bedding and lingered in the air. He sighed, thinking of Sarah Barnes and wondered again about the ship's captain she mentioned in her letters. His name had not come up once during any conversation today. Perhaps this Captain Rathbun, whatever his intent, had sailed out of her life.

Upon arising in the morning, John readied himself to leave, tending to his grooming and the re-packing of his satchel. He must be aboard the steamer to New Orleans no later than ten o'clock. In the dining room, he found the ladies of the house gathering for breakfast.

"Good morning, Mr. Ogilvie," Miss Skinner greeted him.

"Good morning. It looks like the sun will be shining again," John said, glancing out the window. Thunderheads piled in the distant horizon, but instead of threatening, their white billows added a bright contrast to the brilliant blue sky.

"Please have a seat," Miss Barnes said, motioning John toward a chair at the head of the table. "Breakfast is about to be served."

The women and John took their designated places as Martha wheeled in a cart laden with platters of hotcakes, sausage and fruit.

"Would you do us the honor of saying grace?" Sarah Barnes looked directly at John. The warmth of her gaze momentarily turned his thoughts to mush, numbed his capacity for speech. He nodded, bowed his head, and after a deep breath blessed the food as thoughtfully and with as must eloquence as his muddled brain allowed.

During animated conversation between bites of the warm, appealing food, a knock sounded at the front door.

"I'll get it, Missus," Martha said, hurrying through the parlor. She returned several minutes later with an envelope which she handed to its intended recipient. John noted the words *Miss*

Barnes written in a bold script on the front. An elegant gold seal held the reverse side firmly shut.

Sarah Barnes glanced quickly at the envelope and her cheeks flushed a soft pink. "Please excuse me a moment," she said. Rising from the table, she disappeared into the privacy of her own room.

Miss Skinner leaned toward John with a twinkle in her eye and whispered, "My guess is the brig *Florence* has come to town."

Martha giggled as she refilled coffee cups, then immediately wiped the grin from her face when Miss Barnes swept back into the room.

"Well, Mr. Ogilvie, this is most convenient. We will accompany you to the harbor and see you off, then continue on to the next wharf. Captain Rathbun arrived last night and has invited Miss Skinner and me aboard for lunch. I'm certain I have written you of him. He handles cargo between here and Liverpool and visits whenever his ship is in port."

"Aye, you have mentioned him. What a pleasant surprise for you," John said with as much grace as he could muster.

During the return ride to the port, the serious discussions that had engaged John and the two teachers the evening before now turned to chit-chat. As the mule pulled the car clear of the multi-storied buildings on the Strand, ships anchored at the various piers on Galveston Bay came into view. Straight ahead, the Morgan Line steamer *Josephine* waited to take John and other passengers to New Orleans. Against a longer wharf to the right sat the impressive schooner *Florence*, its tall masts reaching skyward, as though attempting to touch the very tips of the blossoming thunderheads. And into those clouds John's dreams of courting Sarah Barnes evaporated.

Chapter 24

Rice Lake, Minnesota, summer 1868

In spite of his many days of travel since leaving Lavaca, John's weariness vanished the moment he stepped from the Winona and St. Peter Railroad car at the Minnesota town of Claremont. The only passenger to disembark, he stood on the wooden loading platform a scarce two minutes before the engine's huge iron wheels began turning once again, rapidly picking up speed. The cylinders hissed, smoke spouted from the stack, the whistle blew and the train continued its journey west toward Owatonna, diminishing to a dark spot on the horizon, then gone altogether.

John brushed specks of black soot from his coat, picked up his bag and began the five mile walk to Rice Lake. He inhaled a deep breath, acutely aware of the smells and an immediate sense that this was Minnesota, not necessarily better than Texas, but very different. Though he had lived here for two short years, the familiar countryside still held the feeling of home. Only a trip to Scotland would have been more satisfying. He increased his stride, whistling a tune in rhythm with each step. He had walked a couple of miles when the squeak of wheels and the thud of hooves on the earthen roadway caused him to turn and squint into the lowering sun. A swirl of dust evolved into a wagon pulled by two horses.

"Whoa. Whoa, there." A bewhiskered man wearing overalls and a well-worn, homespun shirt pulled the reins taut. "I don't know where you're headed, but it looks like the same direction I'm going. Could you use a ride?"

"The hotel in Rice Lake, and a ride would be a kindness."

"You're about half there and I can get you the rest of the way if you're willing to be jostled a bit in this old crate."

John tossed his bag into the wagon bed. The man reached out with a calloused hand and helped him up onto the wooden seat.

"Name's Tanner. Ned Tanner."

"John Ogilvie. Glad you came along."

Once they were settled, the man snapped the reins and off they rolled along the country road.

"Visiting anyone in particular?"

"I plan to spend some time with the Cranstons. I worked there when I first arrived in America. Do you know them?"

"Carl? Of course. He's been around awhile. Does he know you're coming?"

"I wrote, but I've come all the way from Texas and couldn't tell them an exact date for my arrival. I'll head on out there tomorrow."

They rode for a bit without further talk, the continuous squeak of the wheels and the alternating clops of the horses' steps filling the silence. After a while, Mr. Tanner spoke again. "Say, I know you. Aren't you the feller who went south to teach the colored folk?"

"Aye, I'm the one."

"Them slaves hard to teach stuff to?" The question riled John; but it seemed to be asked without animosity, simply out of ignorance as to the capabilities of a people whose educational desires had been deliberately stifled for generations.

"Former slaves," he corrected. "Most are very good pupils and eager to learn." He tried to keep any hint of irritation from his voice.

"That so? I wouldn't of thought. Whoa there, Rocky and Jane. Whoa." The man went from their discussion to the situation at hand as though the two were somehow connected. "Well, here we are."

John jumped down from the wagon seat, retrieved his bag and tipped his hat. "Much obliged, Mr. Tanner."

"Glad to be of service." He nodded at John, clicked to his horses, and the wagon continued on down the road.

Travel weary, John settled into a room at the hotel. But as he lay on the bed, Tanner's notion that former slaves might not be teachable seemed stuck in his mind—nudging away sleep. The remark had hit a nerve, and he knew why. The same question had troubled his own thoughts when he left for Texas. He sighed and closed his eyes. *How ignorant we are. How much we assume. Dear Lord, help enlighten all the Tanners in this nation, and thank you for showing me the truth. Amen.*

Flora Beach Burlingame

***

The Saturday morning sun woke him at daybreak, but he felt no urgency to arise, content that his long journey now lay behind him. Carl Cranston claimed this day of the week for his Sabbath, and John intended not to let his presence be known until afternoon when church services were over. Making good use of his free morning, he sought out the village barber for a bath, shave and haircut.

"I feel like a new man," he told the barber, handing him several coins for his services.

"You look a mite better, too, if I may say so." The proprietor deposited the money in the cash register. "Tell Carl hello for me."

John lunched in the hotel saloon before checking out, and accepted the offer of a ride from a salesman who was heading north. Dropped off as near to his destination as the man would go, John began the one-mile jaunt along the grass-covered wagon trail. When the gate to the farm came into sight, and beyond it the house and the low barns, he felt a quickening in his chest and stepped up his pace. As he approached the buildings, he spied a figure pumping water from the well.

"Hello," he shouted.

The pump handle slowed and suddenly a whoop rang out.

"Papa, it's John! He's here!" Lucy Cranston set the bucket down and ran the length of the long drive. Catching up to John, she stopped short of flinging her arms about him, instead stood there, hands on her hips. "You're here," she repeated with a grin.

"Aye, that I am," John said, "and it seems you are, too."

He eyed her with a chuckle. She wore the same bloomers, her farm work attire, as when he had first seen her. Her brown hair escaped in wisps from the knot of it at her neck, and her blue eyes glowed with mischief and intelligence.

"I see medical school hasn't changed you one bit."

"Oh, but it has. I'm learning wonders, John, and I haven't many more months before I can help in a practice. I am home for only a week before I go back to the seminary. Here, let me take that. You must be tired after your walk from town." She grabbed John's satchel, not allowing him to protest, and led him toward the house.

He smiled and shook his head. She may have gained more medical knowledge, but outwardly she was just as he had remembered—boyish, head-strong, and determined.

Carl Cranston emerged from the cow barn, wiped a hand on his overalls and extended it. "Welcome, son. It's mighty good to see you again."

The firm, sincere handshake warmed John's heart. Noting the man's dusty clothing and heavy boots, John asked, "What's this? You're working on your Sabbath?"

"Animals still need to be fed and the cow milked. They honor no religion. Surely, you remember that."

The screen door squeaked open and banged shut behind Mrs. Cranston. "Welcome, John. Please come in and rest yourself. I've made up the spare bed for you in the attic. We trust you will stay awhile."

"Only if I am allowed to work."

Carl put a hand on John's shoulder. "I've already made plans for you to pitch hay, now that you are fully trained. I'll even pay you the same two dollars a day you earned before."

"Good. It's agreed."

The evening meal in the farmhouse was light, as usual for their Sabbath, and conversation during supper consisted mostly of catching up on news from around Rice Lake.

Afterwards they gathered on the porch, seeking respite from the warmth of the day. John and Lucy sat on the top step. Mrs. Cranston chose the rocker, and Carl brought a straight-backed chair from the dining table.

"Now, tell us about Texas," Lucy said.

"A lot of it is prairie, but not the same as this," John said, gesturing toward the grassland beyond the farm. "Southern Texas has its own peculiar vegetation."

"And your students? What of them?" Mrs. Cranston asked.

"They are of all colors and varying intellect, many as bright as pupils anywhere. They want to learn—are starved for it. And they are my friends."

"Is it true some teachers have been murdered by Ku Klux Klan members?" Lucy asked.

"Not in my part of Texas, though there have been threats."

He didn't mention his harrowing night on the water front when he first arrived nor the Ku Klux horsemen, but talked of the social disdain for the teachers of the freedmen, the intimidating notices, and the rock-throwing incident involving Ezra.

When he finished the telling, no one spoke. Carl's grey eyes reflected serious thought. His wife's chair squeaked rhythmically, her toes tapping on the wooden surface of the porch each time she pushed to rock. Katydids chirped, and a mosquito buzzed.

Finally, Lucy asked, "You're not going back, are you?"

"Of course. I'm not finished with my work there. We just got the schoolhouse built. What's more, I preach on Sundays and teach a Bible class. These folks are not only being taught their ABCs, I am honoring my vow to the American Missionary Association by promoting their moral and religious instruction."

"But what about your own future? Your own education? You had talked about going to divinity school when you had enough money saved. It will be difficult to do if you are dead." She crossed her arms and looked him in the eye.

John chose not to respond. The squeak and tap of the rocking chair ceased, and Mrs. Cranston excused herself, saying it was bedtime. Carl stayed put a while longer, then rose and bid them goodnight, carrying his chair into the house with him.

John and Lucy remained silently together on the porch stoop. A breeze talked to the katydids and a yellow moon surfaced on the horizon. The smell of new-mown hay scented the air.

Lucy broke the mood. "I still think you should reconsider your decision to return to Texas. The Lord may have called you there, but isn't he calling you to the ministry, too? That isn't any less benevolent, and it is certainly safer."

"I haven't given up that idea, Lucy. But there's more to it than the obvious. I have been putting money aside for my education and need more. Teachers of the freedmen don't get wealthy, though I should have enough in two or three more years."

"Two or three years? And after that how many years of schooling? You are more patient than I, John. I am glad to be almost done and ready to start the calling of *my* life."

"Doctor Lucy Cranston," John said. A touch of envy wriggled through him as he spoke. "Where will you be working?"

"There's a doctor in Detroit willing to take a woman in his practice. I hope to start there before the end of the year."

They talked for most of an hour until Lucy yawned, stretched her arms and stood. "In case you don't remember, we get up early around here. I'll see you in the morning."

Charcoal and Chalk

"Good night," John said. "I'll be coming in a wee bit."

After Lucy left, he sat there alone, drinking in the sounds and smells of the night. His thoughts drifted to Sarah Barnes, different from Lucy, yet both women equally strong in their commitments. Though he and Lucy were close, he never had any romantic inclinations toward her, nor she to him—so far as he knew. As for Sarah Barnes, John had left Galveston disappointed. He sighed. *Somewhere, sometime, the woman I'm waiting for will appear, and the education I want so very much will become a reality.* In the meantime, in spite of Lucy's urging otherwise, he would not let his pupils in Lavaca down.

As it turned out, John did not leave for Texas until the end of October. Two things prevented him from returning in a timely manner—his promised ordination in Chicago by the AMA and his too familiar nemesis, the lack of funds. Finally, he received notice from the missionary association that his ordination would take place at the Tabernacle Church in Chicago on Sunday, October 25, and that money for his return trip had been arranged. Though frustrated at the late date and afraid his pupils would think he had forgotten them, John felt joy in the renewal of his mission that the ordination would bring, and grateful for a means of fuller service upon his return to Lavaca. Yet anxiety alternated with joy as he wondered what awaited him in the new school year.

Chapter 25

Lavaca, Texas, November 1868

John pushed open the schoolhouse door and stood a moment to survey the room. He stopped here first, on the way to his wee home. Evidence of the facility having been put to use showed itself in rearranged benches, scattered stacks of books, and words of scripture scrawled across the large chalkboard.

He strode across the planked floor and, setting down his satchel, reached for a primer. Leafing through the familiar pages, he had already conjured up a lesson plan when the sound of footsteps on the stairs caused him to turn. In the front doorway, hands on her hips and a smile stretched across her face, stood Mrs. Wallace.

"I seen you sneaking into heah," she said. "We all figured you ain't nevah gonna come back, and heah you is."

She scooted into the room, her feet almost dancing. John held out his hands and grasped both of hers in his.

"Aye. 'Tis me, all right. There were delays I hadn't counted on, but here I am, and you are a very welcome sight."

"Suppah is cookin' and you is invited. We wanna know all what you been up to."

"And I want to know what's been happening in Lavaca, too. I'll walk with you to my place. Let me wash up and rest a little, then I'll be over."

His hut smelled musty, but everything was as he had left it. He began to unpack, laying clothing across the bed, until he came to the bottom of the bag. Carefully lifting a small, gold-colored box, he set it on the table, opened the lid and removed the packing around a porcelain cup and saucer. Delicate roses, painted in shades of yellow, decorated the pieces. John smiled as his fingered the gift. He had bought it in Chicago thinking it would look nice in Evelyne Duval's china cupboard, but suddenly he had another idea in mind. He returned the cup and saucer to the box and set it aside.

The final item extracted from his traveling case was a document. John smoothed the crisp parchment and laid it before him, reading once again the now familiar words.

> *This certifies that the American Missionary Association has appointed John Ogivlie a Missionary Teacher to the Freedmen in the State of Texas for one school year and hereby commends him to the favor and confidence of the Officers of Government, and of all persons who take an interest in relieving the condition of the Freedmen, or in promoting their intellectual, moral and religious instruction.*

The last phrase had even more significance to him since he had repeated the vows of ordination during the service at the Tabernacle Church in Chicago. He was now not only a teacher, but a *bona fide* preacher of the word of God. Of course, this was in act only, and though it made him feel more qualified than before, he still dreamed that in the not-too-distant future he would attend college and study to earn a divinity degree. Someday he would stand behind the pulpit in his own church, as had his father and grandfather before him.

After putting his few articles of clothing away, John turned and eyed the bed. He longed to stretch out for a while but knew if he did he would fall asleep and probably remain there until morning. For now, he needed to freshen up for the supper invitation.

A half hour later, he stepped out the door and walked the few yards to the Wallaces' shanty. Joe sat in his rocking chair on the porch, and familiar aromas floated through the front door accompanied by strains of *Rock-a my soul in the bosom of Abraham*, from Mrs. Wallace's throaty alto.

Joe stood, holding out his hand. "Pleased to have you back, suh. That woman is in there makin' somethin' mighty good. Come on in."

John shook the extended hand in greeting, then followed his host into the dimly lit room.

"You got heah jus' right. Suppah is ready." Mrs. Wallace set a steaming dish of grits on the table beside bowls of black-eyed peas, stewed figs, and biscuits and honey.

"Set yo'self down." She motioned to the bench where John always sat during his stay in their home.

"First, I have a little something for you," he said, handing her the gold box.

"Oh my!" Mrs. Wallace gasped and gingerly reached for the gift. "It's so pretty." She fingered the gilded box, her eyes glowing.

"Open it," John said.

She set the box on the table, lifted the lid and removed the cup and saucer. "Oh, my. I ain't nevah had nothin' so beautiful." She carefully set the china cup and saucer on a high shelf. "Where I can see it every day an' it won't get broke."

"Les' eat," Joe said. He spooned grits onto his plate, took a bite, then momentarily stopped chewing while John offered a prayer of thanks.

Mrs. Wallace looked to John, "Now, let's heah all about yo' summer."

He began with his stay at the Cranston farm. "It seemed like going home," he said. "Yet coming here gives me the same feeling."

"I reckon folks kin have more than one place to call home," Joe said.

"Was that your bes' time? You went to the big city, too," Mrs.Wallace said. "I knows that cuz of my pretty cup." Her eyes shone as she glanced at the shelf holding her gift.

"Being at the farm was good," John said. "But the most special time was in Chicago when I was ordained by the missionary association."

His announcement drew only silence from his host and hostess accompanied by puzzled looks on their faces.

"That means when I give sermons on Sunday, I am now more of a real preacher."

"Well, I'll be," Mrs. Wallace said. "Kin we call you Reverend?"

"Mr. Ogilvie or Teacher will still be just fine. I won't be a genuine reverend until I get a college education. This just makes it more official for now."

By the time John left in the dark of night, fog had crept in, swirling about him as he walked. Foghorns on the bay sounded their mournful call—repeated in a distant muffled echo. He welcomed the sound and the cool, moist air. As he lay in bed—his own bed—a prayer of thanksgiving escaped his lips. He pulled the quilt up to his chin and drifted off to sleep.

Fog still shrouded the bay the following morning. John built a fire in the stove to remove the chill. Heating a pot of coffee, he sipped the warm brew between bites of bread from a fresh loaf, baked just for him by Mrs. Wallace. He didn't linger long, eager to see what mail had collected for him during his absence.

The postal clerk handed him a bundle. "Glad you're back, Ogilvie. I was running out of space."

It really wasn't that much. Most of his correspondents knew of his whereabouts and approximately when he would return. He carried it home and deposited it on the table, then poured himself another cup of coffee before sitting down to sort through the envelopes. He read familiar return addresses: Captain Bailey from Indianola, Joseph Welch from Austin, and in a more feminine and precise script, Sarah Barnes, Galveston. John laid the first two envelopes aside and unsealed the third.

> *Dear Mr. Ogilvie,*
>
> *I trust you are safely back in Lavaca and school there has commenced. We have many students this fall and it seems I scarcely have time to breathe. Plans for the new school building are progressing well. Heaven knows, we need the room.*
>
> *We pray there are no more unpleasant incidents regarding prejudice against you and your school. Please keep us informed of the situation there.*
>
> > *Kindest regards,*
> > *Sarah Barnes*

John had not taken time on his return trip to seek out the teachers in Galveston. Though he had been sorely tempted to stay over and visit, he had been able to make quick connections between steamers. What's more, he knew that Sarah's heart belonged to a determined sea captain, and there was no point to inviting torment by putting himself in her presence.

The envelope postmarked from Austin held the annual form of the Bureau of Refugees, Freedmen & Abandoned Lands stating that his appointment as teacher "*will take effect November first, and remain in force until revoked by orders from this office.*" It continued to say he was to report to Captain F.W. Bailey, Sub Assistant Commissioner at Indianola, for his assignment to duty at Lavaca. The document was signed by Jos. Welch, Superintendent of Schools.

"Well," John said aloud, "it appears communication is improving. At least within the bureau, they now know who is who."

With raised spirits, he next opened the envelope from Bailey, noting the date of October 11, 1868. More than a month had lapsed since this had been posted. As he read the single sheet of paper, disbelief countered his positive mood of only moments ago.

> *Sir:*
>
> *I have received a letter from the Supt. of Education B.R.F.& A.L. at Austin, Texas, asking for replies to the following questions:*
>
> *"Do the Freedmen of Lavaca own a lot of ground for school purposes? What effort, if any, has there ever been made by them to obtain or build a schoolhouse?"*
>
> *I suppose that you are acquainted with the facts and will be much obliged if you will give me the necessary information.*
>
>

Respectfully yours,
W. Bailey
>

John sat stunned, recalling the correspondence with Wheelock in Galveston, plus letters to other assistant commissioners, the promise from Mitchel for money to build the school, and a visit to the actual site by Bonnaffon. Surely there were records of all this within the bureau somewhere. He felt his face grow hot with anger and frustration.

He searched his desk for a blank piece of paper, dipped a pen into the ink well and immediately began scratching a note to Bailey. His reply was curt and to the point. *Of course there was land for a school and a schoolhouse built on it—mandated by the bureau and built under difficult circumstances without any of the promised financial help. As for particulars, they could check their own records.*

He spent the rest of the morning at the school, sweeping the floor, arranging benches, and sorting through supplies. As he worked, his emotions seesawed from anger to disbelief to shame that his hasty answer to Bailey was not befitting a newly ordained preacher, but when he mentally reread Bailey's letter, his anger rose again.

John's ire purged any fatigue from his long journey and by morning's end he had everything prepared for the new fall school session. He spent the afternoon tacking notices around town to announce the commencement of the freedmen's school. If word hadn't spread to those in outlying areas by the end of the week, he planned to hire a horse and call on them himself.

His eagerness to start the instruction, so long delayed, was countered by worry that those citizens of Lavaca who left threatening notes to *Carpet Bagger* enemies might re-emerge. But when he rang George Ware's tower bell, and classes began, those fears were shoved aside by the appearance of freshly scrubbed, smiling scholars. Familiar faces of all ages, plus a few new ones, filled the benches.

"We thought you lef' for good," Patsy said, as she carefully arranged the skirt of her new frock.

"I knew he be back," Jeremy countered. "I ain't learned all my words yet."

The happy banter caused John to chuckle—it all felt so natural. Mrs. Wallace assisted in distributing slates, which the new pupils received with wonder in their eyes.

"We'll begin with review," John said. "Those of you who attended last year, put your name in the upper corner, then write about your summer. I will come around to the newcomers and help with the spelling of names."

In spite of first day excitement, things settled into a routine. The mood felt right, and for now John's mind filtered out bureau complications and white-sheeted ghouls. The hours flew and it seemed class had barely begun when it was time to wrap up lessons for the first day. The pupils left in good spirits and all appeared eager to return—especially the new ones. One little bright-eyed girl of perhaps seven hung back after most of her classmates had left. Holding her slate out to John, she spoke in a shy whisper.

"Kin I take it home to show Mammy this here word is me?"

"Aye, you may, lassie," John said. "Just be sure to bring it tomorrow so you can learn new words."

Off she ran, clutching the slate so close to her chest John feared the name would be erased by the time she reached home.

He stayed at school and ate a hasty supper while he prepared for the evening class. A full hour before lessons were scheduled to begin, the door swung open and in walked Samuel.

"Evening, Mr. Ogilvie."

John jumped up, his wide smile matching that of this capable student. "Samuel, it's good to see you." Their hands clasped in an enthusiastic greeting, and John motioned to a bench. "Come sit and tell me about your summer."

"Been workin'," Samuel said, "That's about it. Though at night I still practice my numbers and readin'. I believe I'm gettin' right advanced." His voice held no hint of boasting, but pride shone in his eyes.

That pride slid right into John's heart.

Typically of Samuel, his attention turned away from himself. "What about you, suh, how about your summer? You lookin' like you worked same as me."

"Aye, Samuel. I've been pitching hay."

"Pitching hay?" Samuel laughed. "Wait 'til I tell the others about that." He shook his head and laughed again, as though the idea of a teacher doing field work was beyond belief.

"And I also received an ordination from the missionary association." Of all his students, Samuel would appreciate this the most.

"Oh, suh. That is fine. Real fine." Samuel's expression softened. "You know, someday I'm goin' to be ordained, too."

"I believe you will be, Samuel."

Their talk continued for the rest of the hour, a sharing of common thoughts and goals, as though their dreams and skin color had blended to one. As though they were almost on equal footing.

The other men arrived on time, all greeting John heartily and ready to continue their learning. They had worked hard at their studies and some were now ready for more advanced lessons in multiplication, division and grammar. Each step up by a pupil brought to John the same excitement he experienced when he himself had progressed through school. It would be a good year; he felt it in his bones.

Later that night, as he readied for bed, his gaze drifted to the letter from Bailey resting on the table. He sighed. *Perhaps I over-reacted in my response to the questions regarding the existence of a schoolhouse. I should at least inform Captain Bailey classes have begun.* Before turning down the lamp wick, he sat and composed another letter to the agent.

Bailey replied shortly to the two notes. Along with the standard forms for a monthly report as to the number of students under John's tutelage, he enclosed the original letter from

Superintendent Welch containing the queries as to whether the freedmen in Lavaca owned land and a schoolhouse. The letter began: *"Please make diligent and thorough inquiries for the following points ..."* With the lapse of a little time and the help of prayer, John made an effort to answer these seemingly unnecessary questions without agitation. He had no bones to pick with Bailey—the man was probably equally as frustrated—and everyone was trying to work under difficult circumstances.

A letter from the AMA shortly thereafter helped. Jacob Shipherd again advised him of the churches that were interested in supporting him for the school year. John paid special note to the names of the congregations: Winnebago, Port Bryson, and Stillman Valley (Hale PO), Illinois. The same folks who saved the schoolhouse. *May God bless them.* But it was one paragraph in particular that drew John's attention:

> *As a whole, the reports last year were admirable, and resulted in doubling the interest of Northern friends in your work. They will seldom respond directly to you, as the thirsty earth never gives audible thanks for the showers that freshen it; but our eyes see as prompt and gladdening growths of blade and flower in the fields upon which your fresh words fall, as your eyes trace after the most welcome summer rain. "Cast not away, therefore, your confidence, which hath great recompense of reward.*

Contrary to the statement *They will seldom respond directly to you ...* John's churches had indeed given "audible thanks" in the form of money, for which he would be forever grateful.

Chapter 26

Sundays took on a new meaning, a new challenge. Though eager to preach every Sabbath, John was unable to do so. The new building had been promised as a place of worship and preaching for the colored folk, and they took full advantage of this during John's absence. He still taught the Bible school class but now shared the pulpit.

Among those freedmen who spread the word of the gospel was an ancient darky called Uncle Booker. Having been emancipated and then left to eke out a living on his own at an advanced age, the man had very strong opinions that worked their way into his talks. Though Uncle Booker sometimes failed to include scriptural references, John usually gleaned words of wisdom from this man and also from the other freedmen willing to preach.

Anticipating Sunday's sermons provided a topic for lively conversation at the Saturday supper table John often shared with the Wallaces. One such evening, Joe turned to him and remarked, "I heah Brother Booker done got hisself arrested."

"Arrested? What on earth for?" John asked.

"He done stole a suit of clothes from the general dry goods and clothing store."

"No. You must be mistaken," John couldn't believe what he was hearing. He respected all men who chose to share the pulpit.

"Nope. It be the truth," Joe said.

"He's scheduled to preach tomorrow," John said. "Looks like I'd better find someone to take his place."

"Won't need to. He done been tried, found guilty, fined ten dollars, and let loose. He be there tomorrow."

"Where'd he get the money? He's dirt poor."

"Some friend done that for him."

John shook his head and wondered as to the content of Uncle Booker's sermon the following day.

Word spread of the old man's run-in with the law and the schoolroom filled to bursting for his sermon Sunday morning. John stood in the rear, anxiously anticipating the subject of the day's talk, still finding it difficult to believe the man had committed a crime. What a perfect opportunity for a true Christian message of penance.

The wrinkled and stooped white-haired Negro, wearing a tattered coat, approached the lectern, cleared his throat and began.

"I knows you all heerd 'bout what I done, and I ain't one bit sorry. Them white folk got no call to punish me for taking what is rightly mine." He proceeded to elaborate on his arrest, trial, fine, and the persecution he had suffered at the hands of the white folks. John listened to the so-called sermon with great concern, especially when the congregation added exuberant "Amens" and "Yes, suh!"s

At the close, most of those in attendance avoided eye contact with John, and many approached Booker with a hearty handshake. John slipped unnoticed out the door and marched home where he sat on his bed, head in his hands, and contemplated Booker's message to his brothers and sisters. Feeling responsible for the services in the school building, he resolved to visit Uncle Booker during the break between his morning and evening classes the following day. *A preacher of the word of God must not be condoned for breaking the law.*

And so, at two o'clock on Monday, John walked the three-quarters of a mile from town to the place Booker called home—a wretched abode half dug out of the earth and the other half fashioned from sod. Seating himself on a crude bench just inside the open doorway, he told Uncle Booker why he had come, expressing his surprise at the man's conduct and subsequent preaching.

The old man listened patiently. When John finished, Booker sat quietly for a few moments, sighed, then spoke. "Brudder Ogilvie, you don' understand." He rose and motioned for John to join him. "Come. Ah'll show you."

John followed, the two of them taking a path along the sluggish waters of the Chocolate Bayou. Soon a mansion appeared in the distance, its white walls sharply contrasted against the chaparral. Beyond it stretched cultivated fields. Uncle Booker stopped, and pointing toward the impressive building, raised his voice and said, "Does you see dat house?"

"Aye," John said.

"Me and my boys built it. Does you see dat plantation?"

"Aye."

"Me and my boys made it." Then turning to John he added, "Brudder Ogilvie, my sons have been all sold away from me and I dunno whar dey am. I am old and not able to work. I am sot free and have no one to look to. Brudder Ogilvie, de man dat own dis plantation owns de store dat you say I stole the clothes from, and I don't call it stealing to take anything of his'n dat I kin lay my hands on."

John slowly exhaled and a tightness worked its way across his chest. There had been times since his arrival in Lavaca when he felt terribly inadequate to do the job he was sent to do, and this was one of them. He had come to teach, and yet he had so much to learn from those who had been "sot" free. John laid a hand on the shoulder of the older man, then with nothing more to say turned and retraced his steps to town, a prayer in his heart for compassion and understanding for that which he had not himself experienced.

***

One Friday, after the day session ended, John stayed late at school to catch up on lesson preparations. He occasionally did this. With no evening class, he was relaxed and munched on a light supper while he worked. Tonight was a little different in that Samuel planned to join him later. A large crate stood at the head of the classroom. Inside was a new chalkboard, bigger and of better quality than the one it would replace—another generous gift from George Ware. He'd ask Samuel to help him uncrate and hang it. John chuckled as he thought of the stir of excitement this new addition would create on Monday morning.

It was late autumn and the wind had gusted erratically all day, bringing with it the hint of a northeaster. John lit a fire in the wood-burning stove, something he rarely did, but a chill circled through the air. He stoked the flames and added another piece of wood. The heat felt good. A burst of wind rattled the door, followed by a muted thump from somewhere outside. John walked to a window and glanced out expecting to find a fallen tree. Darkness had settled in and he could see very little. He pulled his watch from his pocket, a quarter to seven. It was getting late. Samuel should be here any minute now. Returning to his desk, he sat and picked up a book. Another noise outside, not the wind this time, caused him to look up. *Ah, Samuel has finally come.* He waited for the door to open. It did not.

The smell of smoke gradually filled his nostrils. He rose and checked the damper, but there appeared to be no smoke escaping from the stove. Now he heard voices rising above the wind. Samuel? The smoke grew thicker. Once again John walked to the window. This time he could see something—an orange glow rising from below. The unexpected color swirled and grew. For a second, John didn't move, then the awful realization swept through him.

"Fire!" He yelled and pushed open the door so hard it slammed against the wall. Stepping out onto the landing, his heart stopped. The bottom step was already burned through, and flames lapped angrily up the side of the schoolhouse. Running down the stairs, John stomped on the burning boards with his boots. He pulled off his coat and used it to beat out the flames. "Fire!" He hollered again. Dropping his coat, he snatched up a bucket they used for drinking water and ran toward the bay. He had not gone far when someone grabbed him from behind, jerking him to a stop. As he struggled to free himself, a coarse, woven sack was shoved over his head. His arms were bent behind him at such an angle that the immediate pain caused a scream to rise in his throat.

A low, menacing voice growled, "Best you cooperate, teacher, or you'll be more than sorry." John was thrown to the ground and a rope twisted around his feet, his wrists tied behind his back.

"Tie him good," someone snickered.

"Quick," another voice said. "That there fire's gonna get folks here."

John felt himself being lifted and flung up. He landed stomach down on what he guessed was the rump of a horse. The breath was knocked out of him, the pain so acute he thought he would vomit. Someone settled in a saddle next to him and, with the clink of spurs, they were moving. Not fast at first—plodding quietly along the sand of the bay. Then they were at a gallop, jostling John to the point of agony. He drifted in and out of consciousness. One strong jolt caused him to cry out. The man in the saddle laughed. It seemed to echo in the wind, or was that another man close by, joining in on the fun?

John had no idea how long they traveled. It seemed like forever, but he supposed it had been only ten or fifteen minutes. When the excruciating ride came to a halt, someone pulled at

John's legs and he fell to the ground, landing hard on his side. He lay there stunned.

"What's the problem, preacher-teacher? Didn't you like that little ride?" More laughter. John recognized the husky voice of the man who had tied him up.

Another voice, younger and anxious, said, "We've got to get him in the barn and out of sight."

John was dragged across brush and rocks. The creak of hinges mingled with the noise of the pending storm, and he was pulled into an enclosure and settled against a rough wall in a sitting position. At first it seemed warm without the wind blowing across him, but that didn't last long. In addition to his scrapes and bruises, the cold bit at him, and he wished for his coat that lay somewhere by the schoolhouse. He heard a door slam shut. For a moment he thought he had been left alone, then someone coughed and he smelled cigarette smoke.

"So, what now?" The younger voice again.

"Let's jest sit tight till that there schoolhouse is burnt down. Then we'll decide what now."

John's muddled thoughts came into focus and he remembered the smoke and flames. *Dear God, no. The school.* He had trouble breathing behind the fabric that covered his face. His hands throbbed—the ropes were too tight. He had no feeling in his feet, and his side hurt where he had hit the ground. He felt nauseous. "Water," he blurted, his voice muffled.

"What's that you say, preacher?"

"Water."

"Water? You come barging down to Texas where you don't belong, interfering in our business and you expect favors?" This from the gravely-voiced man.

"He's a preacher? I thought he was a teacher. I thought he taught the coloreds at that school." The younger voice rose in volume.

"Teacher, preacher. All the same."

"Not so. My ma says you gotta respect preachers. They know all about what's in the Bible and what God tells us to do."

"Oh, hell, kid, get off of that talk. There ain't no God."

Silence, at least no talking. John figured there were only two of them now. At the schoolhouse he had sensed more. He could hear raspy breathing—probably the older man. And he heard something else—rain on the roof, scattered drops at first, then more, beating down steadily and hard.

Boots with spurs clomped across the floor. The door squeaked open; a rush of rain blew in on the wind and it felt like a sideways waterfall, soaking John's clothing. The door slammed shut.

"Damn rain will put out that fire."

The boots and spurs stopped in front of John and a sharp toe kicked his leg. John sucked in his breath and bit his lip. *Dear Lord, give me strength for what may come.*

"If the school's burnt down, will you let him go?" The younger man asked.

"Don't see's how we can. He's just fool enough to stick around and teach the coloreds in that there warehouse again or some such place. Nope. I think we should throw him in the bay. He'll die quick, all tied up like that. Ain't no tree big enough around here to hang him, and shooting's noisy and messy."

"Anyone kill a preacher and they go to Hell for sure." The other voice held a note of alarm.

A growl came from the throat of the older man. John heard him spit. "Ain't no hell, no heaven neither. Dead is dead, and you got a yella streak I don't like, Gavin. Yore daddy'd be ashamed. You gonna chicken out on me? You was all excited about this an hour ago when you helped me and the others light that fire. This was our part of the bargain, to take the teacher, and we ain't going to let the rest down."

No answer. The barn became quiet again except for an occasional patter of the diminishing rain. *So this is it. All those warnings were more than threats. By morning I'll be lying at the bottom of the bay.* Words from the recent past crawled through John's brain. *You're not going back, are you?* He could still picture the look of alarm on Lucy's face as she spoke. *What about your future? Your own education? It will be difficult if you are dead.* Now it seemed he had no future. Had he been right to return to Lavaca? Of course. *I knowed you'd be back,* Jeremy had said. *I ain't learned all my words.*

Anger pulsed through John. He tried wiggling his fingers, but the pain at his wrists was so intense he thought he'd faint. He moaned involuntarily.

Deep laughter. "You hurting, teacher? Well, won't be for long. We'll put you out of your misery."

A horse neighed, then snorted. Spurs jangled. Boots stomped. "I'm gonna take a ride back aways. See if the school's burnt down and if there's folks about. Can't dump the teacher in the bay if there's a crowd. You keep an eye on him while I'm gone." Clopping hooves joined the boots. The barn door opened and closed.

A spark of hope lit within John. He was alone with one man, a boy really, whose conscience wrestled with the thought of killing a preacher. "Laddie, could you loosen these ropes on my legs a wee bit? I have no feeling in my feet."

"Don't pull that trick on me. I ain't dumb, you know."

The barn went quiet again. The only sound a steady drip, drip —residue of the rain off the eaves—and breathing: John's own, that of a horse, and of his young captor. John couldn't stop shivering from the cold. He tried to move to get the blood circulating in his veins, but the constraints forbid it. "Do ye have a blanket, laddie?"

"Shut-up. My uncle says we ain't offering you no favors."

John shifted his weight. In the places he wasn't numb, he hurt —a deep, throbbing pain. He closed his eyes and prayed a silent prayer, then spoke aloud. "Sounds to me like you believe in God, laddie." His words came out thin, and he had to stop in mid-sentence to take a shallow breath.

"It's my ma's Bible that says that, not me."

"You have a very wise mother."

"Leave my mother out of this."

"Does she know what you are doing tonight?"

"Shut up."

"Burning a school where young people are taught to better themselves?"

"They're niggers."

John found a surge of energy that momentarily over-rode his pain. "Skin color's got nothing to do with it. In their heart and soul they're folks just like you. How old are you, lad?"

"Seventeen, but it's none of your damn business."

"Seventeen and you're about to kill a man?"

"You ain't a real preacher, so it don't matter."

John took in another painful breath and continued. "Your mother's Bible says thou shall not kill. That's anybody—man, woman, or child. It has nothing to do with preachers. That's God talking, Gavin, and in spite of what your uncle says, there *is* a heaven and a hell."

There was no response, just a rustling of hay. For a few moments John's strength waned. He took a series of shallow breaths—less painful than deep ones. He closed his eyes again—he couldn't see through the sack anyway—and began to pray, this time as loud and clear as his condition allowed. "Dear God, please save me from death and save this promising young man from Hell. In Jesus' name, I pray, amen."

Silence, then more rain on the roof. John was spent and he could not control the shaking. "So cold," he mumbled.

A few moments passed, then he was aware of movement and some noises he couldn't identify. Footsteps approached him, and something heavy and musty-smelling was placed over his shoulders. "It's for a horse, but it'll keep you warm."

"God bless you, lad. God bless you."

As the boy adjusted the blanket so it fit more snuggly against John's shivering body, the door flung open. A horse stomped in, snorting and breathing hard. Boots hit the floor and a voice bellowed. "What the hell are you doing? I turn my back on you jest once and you're pampering the enemy."

"He was cold. It won't hurt nothing."

The uncle muttered something under his breath, but the rain had picked up again, making it impossible to understand the words. John waited for the blanket to be snatched away. It didn't happen. Long minutes passed before the wind and rain slowed enough for his captors to talk

"Was the schoolhouse burnt down?" The boy asked.

"I didn't get that far. Folks were milling about all along the shore, and I near got drowned by the rain." Conversation ceased for a few moments and cigarette smoke wafted through the barn. "I'll go out again in a bit when the weather has settled some. And you're going with me this time. I can't trust you here alone with the teacher. He don't need guarding anyhow. He ain't going nowhere all trussed up like that."

They waited. Eventually, the howl of the wind turned to a muted moan, unaccompanied by rain. "Come on, boy. Let's see what's going on." Once again the horses were led through the barn, and the door opened and closed.

John was thankful to be alone. The thick blanket had eased the biting cold, and he relaxed a little. Yet he knew Gavin's uncle was correct—he could not free himself. He had attempted a number of times to wriggle out of the ropes and it was useless. He had even tried to work the burlap sack off his head by rubbing it against the rough wall—a futile exercise. He lapsed into prayer. The next time the door opened, he would most likely be dragged to the bay and to his death. *Please, Lord, let it be swift.* A calm descended upon him. He believed in a life hereafter. His struggle now was not with a fear of death, but against leaving behind an unfinished task: his pupils as they grew in their independence and education.

The barn door creaked and a gust of wind whipped at the sack on John's face. All his muscles went taut. He swallowed hard, waiting for the voices that would discuss his fate. No one spoke. The hay beside him crunched. John felt a tug on his mask, and it was off. He gulped at the air and blinked, his eyes trying to focus in the dark barn. A form knelt at his feet loosening the ropes.

A low, familiar voice said, "Mistah Ogilvie. You going to be outta here in a jiffy."

"Samuel!" John cried.

"Shhhh. We gotta be quiet."

The big man worked on John's wrists. Relief and pain swept through his freed hands as the blood returned to his fingers. Samuel lifted him to a standing position and John collapsed, unable to stand. "My feet. I can't feel them," he whispered.

So Samuel picked him up, flung him over his shoulder, and moved swiftly and silently though the door, into the wind and amongst the trees.

Twenty minutes later, after cautiously skirting the shore and staying well away from town, Samuel laid John on a soft bed, Samuel's own. Ellie took off John's boots and massaged his feet until he regained feeling in them. She washed and bandaged his wrists where the rope had cut through the skin. "They looks bad, but ain't deep. I expects they will heal fast."

"You're a good nurse, Ellie. I'm much obliged."

"This ain't nothing like what you been doing for my Samuel. Now you best rest."

"The school?" John asked, dreading the answer.

"It's still there, suh. I just came from checking," Samuel said. "A little charred in places, but nothing serious. It peers a few buckets of water and all that rain done put it out." He told how he had reached the school to help unload the new chalkboard just as the horsemen rode away with John. "Joe and a couple of others heard you yell fire and got there right after me. I told them to put out them flames. I was going after you. I been hidin' out aside that barn, waitin' for the time I could get you outta there."

For the first time since the beginning of that awful night, John choked up. Through all his prayers, God had been with him. He brought the rain that put out the fire and hampered plans for his demise, His written word had influenced a conflicted young man to comfort John at a critical moment, and He had brought Samuel to rescue him. What was it Sarah Barnes had written after he survived yellow fever? *"Surely, the Lord has more work for you to do on this earth."*

He drifted off to sleep and didn't wake until the sun was high in the sky.

Chapter 27

"So, are you going to be leaving us?" These surprising words came from the mouth of the postal clerk on an afternoon in mid January.

Startled, John stared at the man. "Should I be?" It had been two months since the fire at the school and his abduction. Surely, anyone who knew about it, including the Ku Kluxers, understood by now that he was not going to be scared away, and he had yet to come across a young man named Gavin or his raspy-voiced uncle.

"Well, it seems logical with the Freedmen's Bureau folding and all," the clerk said.

This was an entirely different matter. "I think you are mistaken. Things are progressing well here."

"No mistake. The official word has it that Reynolds and his people have packed their bags and the bureau closed its doors all over Texas. In all the south, so far as I know."

John bristled at the comments so carelessly tossed out by the man. Granted, the clerk always seemed to know what was going on and was certainly in a good position for it—casting his eyes on everyone's mail even before the recipient saw it. But there had never been any evidence of tampering with John's correspondence.

"You have some misinformation. If that were so, I would have heard. Any mail for me?"

"Nope. But then there wouldn't be under the circumstances. Not from the bureau, anyway. Would there?"

Irritation prickled under John's collar, and he chose to ignore this last remark, at least outwardly. He tipped his hat and left. He would not put any credence in the rumor until he heard it from a proper source.

His first official word regarding changes in the bureau arrived the following week. When checking for mail, the clerk, without comment, handed over an envelope containing the bureau's familiar return address from Austin. John restrained an urge to say, *"See, I told you so."* Then with a spasm of doubt, it occurred to him that rather than one more piece of ongoing correspondence, this could be a final notice and perhaps the clerk was thinking the same thing.

Back in the schoolhouse, John opened the letter. It was a printed order typical of others John had received during his two-year tenure as a teacher of the freedmen. The first thing he noted as his eyes swept the page was the very bottom line, which read *By command of Brevet Major General E. R. S. Canby*—not General Reynolds. John tensed.

Returning to the top of the paper, he began to read. By the third line he felt himself relax as the meaning of the words filtered through his anxiety.

> *...for the better organization of the Educational Department of the Bureau of Refugees, Freedmen and Abandoned Lands, State of Texas, the following School Districts are hereby constituted.*

The schools would not be closing. Four districts had been established, each including specific military posts; Indianola, and thus Lavaca, fell in No. 2. The Assistant Superintendent assigned to his district was a Mr. William Sinclair.

The document continued:

> *The Asst. Superintendents assigned under this order will immediately proceed to their stations, and make a thorough inspection of the freed schools in their School Districts....*

So, he would be meeting Mr. Sinclair in the near future. No bureau official had visited his school since Bonnaffon a year-and-a-half before. Bailey didn't even come when the bureau hierarchy was questioning whether there in fact was a school in Lavaca.

John grabbed a piece of chalk, marched to the chalkboard and wrote in a large, flowing script, *Welcome Mr. Sinclair*. Dusting off his hands, he stood back and viewed the greeting with satisfaction.

The door opened and in strode Samuel, who stopped with a start when he caught sight of the board. "Welcome Mr. Sinclair?"

He turned to John with a wary look on his face. "Who's that? Not the name of a new teacher, is it, suh? You ain't leavin'?" This was a question Samuel had asked several times since his rescue.

John laughed. "No, Samuel, I am not leaving. That is the name of the Assistant Superintendent of Education for the Freedmen's Bureau, and he is going to come visit our school."

John learned in short order it was true that other functions of the bureau in Texas had indeed ended, effective as of December 15, 1868. Only the educational portion remained, and Major General Canby, now responsible for this final phase of assisting the freedmen, had taken over as military commander on January 1, 1869.

Assistant Superintendent of Education William H. Sinclair immediately made points with John when his first piece of correspondence from the man, a circular sent to all the teachers in District 2, stated only one copy of the monthly report need be sent. *"Duplicates are unnecessary,"* he wrote.

"Praise the Lord! Thank you, sir," John said, bouncing his verbal comments off the inner walls of the school.

***

Two months passed before Sinclair's anticipated visit. The assistant superintendent greeted John, then proceeded to explain the reason for the delay in coming. "I made the rounds of the schools north of Galveston first—those in the Hempstead, Bryan, and Columbus military districts. From here I'm on to Corpus Christi. That's a lot of territory to cover."

Sinclair stood at the doorway, looking around the classroom as he spoke. By the dark hair graying at the temples, John guessed him to be about forty years of age. His military bearing made him appear taller than he actually was, and he exuded authority. John immediately liked the man, although he felt a little intimidated by him.

"Looks like you have a school to be proud of here," Sinclair said. "A tower with a bell even."

"Aye. The bell was a gift from a strong supporter from Massachusetts, now living in Indianola—George Ware." John followed as Sinclair strode the perimeter of the room. "We have seventy scholars, all ages, mostly Negro, but there is a Mexican boy and two little Anglican girls, twins."

"I understand you raised the money and built this place single-handedly without bureau help. That's quite an accomplishment, Ogilvie."

"Aye, sir, well, no, sir. No help from the bureau, but lots of help from some local merchants, some Northern churches, and the freedmen themselves."

"Excellent." Sinclair surveyed the room once more. "You have an evening class?"

"At five o'clock."

"I'll check into the hotel, get some supper, then return to sit in on the lessons. I'll also spend some time tomorrow with your day scholars before I head on down the coast."

John could have hugged every student individually after Sinclair's visit. They each not only behaved properly, but performed their very best for the assistant superintendent. Their pride was his own, and when Sinclair left on the boat to continue his school inspections, the trials and challenges of John's two years in Texas seemed minimized. *Surely, my relationship with the bureau will go smoothly from here on out.*

Sinclair's visit had a settling effect on John. Recognition by the bureau caused him to feel less alone in his accomplishments. The AMA had always been very supportive, but theirs was a long-distance relationship. Now that the bureau had actually witnessed and commended the progress in Lavaca, he even began to feel a little like he belonged in Texas—except for one thing. Deep in his heart he was a Scotsman, and he missed his homeland. He longed to see his father again, and since his near encounter with death, he understood that life is fragile and tentative.

He wrote his father often, telling of the progress and complications with the school, talking of his pupils, and trying always to sound cheerful. He left out references to the Ku Klux Klan and other dissenters, and never mentioned his abduction or that he slept with a gun. No point in causing a worry his family could do nothing about.

It took long weeks before replies came, the distance being so great. Early in 1869 he wrote home telling of the changes in the bureau and of Sinclair's visit, and in a moment of melancholy concluded with *"I have grown fond of this place, but nothing ever quite removes the ache in my heart for the land of my boyhood."*

Whenever he posted a letter to Scotland, he counted the days until it could possibly arrive, marking the approximate date on his calendar, then imagined peering over his father's shoulder while the man enjoyed a message from his faraway son. John anxiously awaited replies, allowing ample time for the senior Ogilvie to sit down some damp, Scottish evening to write, and the return letter to travel across the sea.

It was late spring when a response came to his letter:

> *Dear Son,*
>
> *Your welcome letter arrived today. The news you relate is of much interest, but the sentence which affected me most was the "ache in your heart" for Scotland. It has been more than four years since you left here and we long to see you. Could you possibly come home when your pupils take a break for summer? I am now sixty-nine years of age, and my health is beginning to fail. It would be grand to see you once again.*
>
> *Your Affectionate Father*

John's eyes teared as he read the poignant message. That night he slept a restless sleep, dreaming of Bannockburn and of Stirling Castle perched high on its stately hill, shrouded in a morning mist. And if his father's message weren't enough to occupy his thoughts, the very next day another unexpected letter arrived to add to his emotional turmoil, this one from Sarah Barnes.

> *Dear Mr. Ogilvie,*
>
> *Progress on the schoolhouse continues, and if all goes well the building will be ready for the fall session, although each day some complication seems to arise with which I must contend. In the meanwhile, the number of scholars here has multiplied greatly since the new year began. It is all we teachers can do to keep up. I'm afraid Miss Skinner gets more than her share because my strength often fails me.*
>
> *Captain Rathbun visits each time he is in port and on more than one occasion has asked me to marry him. At first I could only tell him no because of my duty here to carry on the work of our Lord. However, my resolve is weakening, and before my health is more seriously impaired by these obligations in Galveston, I may accept his offer.*
>
> *The reason I am sharing such personal information is to ask if you would consider taking charge of the work*

*here. I would feel so much better knowing things were left
in your capable hands. You have plenty of time to think it
over as I am certain I will stay until the completion of this
session through the end of May.*

I pray you will give this some serious consideration.

Sincerely,

Sarah Barnes

John reread the message a half-dozen times. Captain
Rathbun's intentions were no surprise, nor even Miss Barnes
weakening to his proposals. But the suggestion that he, John, leave
Lavaca and take charge of the freedmen school in Galveston sent
his pulse racing.

As he tended class that day, his thoughts on the matter put
before him by Sarah Barnes kept going off in a hundred directions,
tangled together with his father's request that he take a trip home
to Scotland.

"Mistah Ogilvie!"

An insistent voice brought John's focus back to the scholars in
the night class. Though he stood at the head of the room he was
sorely neglecting his duties while he pondered these dilemmas
presented by two letters in as many days.

"I cain't do this heah 'rithmetic. They's too many numbers."

"He be right, suh," another voice joined in. "It don't make no
sense."

"Are others having trouble, too?" John asked.

Several "Yes, suh"s resounded across the room, and with great
effort, John shut out thoughts of Galveston and Bannockburn and
proceeded to assist his pupils. He wrote the problem on the
chalkboard and went over it several times. When it clicked and
"Yes, suh"s sprang from the excitement of it, John felt the surge of
accomplishment and pride in his scholars he always did at such
times. Going to Scotland for a few weeks was not a problem, but
leaving this group to teach in Galveston was another matter. *If I
leave, will it appear that I'm running? And whoever replaces me
will surely be put in harm's way as well.* His thoughts were in a
turmoil. Yet he knew that teachers of the freedmen were at risk no
matter where they taught, even in Galveston.

He first wrote to his father, saying he would do everything in
his power to be there for summer break. As for relinquishing the
school at Lavaca and stepping into the shoes of Sarah Barnes, that

question he pondered for several more days, then put pen to paper, indicating the direction in which he was leaning.

> *Dear Miss Barnes,*
>
> *I am deeply troubled to learn of your failing health and equally flattered and humbled that you consider me capable to continue what you have so successfully begun in Galveston. Although the ultimate decision will be up to the bureau and the AMA, if they so approve, I will accept the transfer provided I am assured the school in Lavaca will be left in good hands.*

He ended with a strong, sweeping signature that did not reveal the emotions in his heart over this decision. Before he could dwell on what he had written one minute more, he sealed the envelope and left the schoolhouse for the post office.

As he strode up Main Street, the pleasant voice of Evelyne Duval called to him.

"*Monsieur* Ogilvie. How good to see you."

He smiled and waited while she hurried to catch up to him.

"Good afternoon, Evelyne, and how are all the Duvals?"

His former landlady caught her breath before answering, "We are doing well and were discussing you only this morning at the breakfast table. How are things at the school?"

"All is presently under control."

"No further problems from, well, you know, that terrible society?"

"Not at the moment, and the scholars are doing well."

"The freedmen are fortunate to have you. Truly they are," Evelyne said with great sincerity showing in her eyes.

Suddenly the letter in John's pocket seemed to weigh him down. He wanted to tell her that in all probability he would be leaving Lavaca. Yet, he couldn't.

Changes had occurred in the ranks of the American Missionary Association also. John now corresponded with a new district secretary, General Charles H. Howard. The general, who succeeded J. R. Shipherd in the Chicago office, was brother to O.O. Howard—head of the Freedmen's Bureau. *This should be a good thing*, John thought when he learned of it. A positive move, though it meant he must write to a total stranger of his wish to travel to Scotland, as well as of the appeal from Sarah Barnes and his willingness to take her place. Surely, his good rapport with Howard's predecessors at the AMA would speak well for him.

John often found himself rooted in one place, deep in thought, staring out the window, watching the sea birds swoop and dive. He felt a kinship to the water now, having lived so close to it the last two years. At least he would still have that in Galveston, being right on the gulf.

"Mistah Ogilvie, you sure got something on your mind," Samuel said as school closed one evening. "I hope it's not trouble." Worry swam in his dark eyes.

"No, it's not trouble. It's decisions."

"Decisions can be mighty burdensome. Have you talked to the Lord about it like you tell us to do when you preach on Sundays?"

John smiled. "Samuel, you learn your Bible lessons well. I have talked to the Lord every day, and He's helping me through this, but I think He wants me to struggle a wee bit."

"Well, suh, you surely seem to be doing that."

"Aye, you are right. I'll try harder to listen to my own sermons." He never ceased to marvel at the insightfulness of this exceptional pupil.

"You do that, Mistah Ogilvie. I expect those worry lines to be gone next class time. Good night, suh." Samuel plopped his cap on his head and walked out the door.

Once alone, John unconsciously wiped his hand against his forehead as though he could erase the tension that pulled him between Lavaca and Galveston. Then he laughed at the gesture and his anxiety. He hadn't even been offered the position yet. All this mental tussle might be for naught.

Chapter 28

On a blustery, wet April afternoon, John's first letter arrived from his new AMA contact, General Charles Howard, addressed, from all places, Galveston, Texas:

Mission Home, April 19, 1869
Galveston, Texas

Mr. John Ogilvie
Port Lavaca, Texas

Dear Brother,
On first coming to Galveston, I had some expectation of visiting you.

Indeed I went so far as to plan a tour from Austin to San Antonio and thence to your place and Indianola – but I am back from Austin and find I have no more time for Texas this season...

If we get the schoolhouse completed here there is thought of asking you to come here with two lady assistants and with more jurisdiction of other schools. In that case what would be the prospects for a teacher in Lavaca—Do you know of any one there who would keep up the school?

...There is no objection to your going to N.Y. direct and thence to Scotland if you still think it best. I would like to know more about your field at Indianola—Please write me at Chicago 29 Lombard Block. You can address Bros. Sabin or AMA Treasurer until I hear from the new appointee—probably. S.N. Clark.

Fraternally, C.H. Howard

Charcoal and Chalk

It wasn't a definite promise, but John felt he could assume his fall assignment would be the new Barnes Institute in Galveston. He'd be daft not to accept. Not only would it be a promotion, it was a definite vote of confidence in his abilities. He glowed in the thought, then admonished himself. *"Careful, pride goeth before destruction, and an haughty spirit before a fall."*

The question regarding his replacement in Lavaca perplexed him. His own assignment came from the agencies and surely they could again find a suitable person to continue with his work. In the meantime, he must begin to prepare the pupils for his departure.

***

April turned to May, bringing warmer days. The feel of summer crept into the air. John sensed a restlessness in the scholars as they anticipated a break from studies. The thought of leaving his pupils still troubled him, but with each piece of correspondence from the AMA alluding to his relocating at Galveston, the more energized he became at the prospect.

He told Joe and Mrs. Wallace first. They must not hear it as either rumor or fact from another source. It was on a Saturday evening after the meal he so often shared in the older couple's shanty. Joe sat in his rocker on the porch plucking on his fiddle, and Mrs. Wallace and John brought out chairs to join him. A damp May breeze swirled up from the bay bringing a scent of fish. Gulls called and flapped their wings, landing along the shore to pick at oyster shells scattered about the sand. John sat with his two friends for a full ten minutes without speaking, relishing the satisfaction of a meal shared. Finally he cleared his throat, and began.

"Looks like I may be leaving Lavaca to teach elsewhere."

Joe's rocker stopped creaking. "What's that you say?"

Mrs. Wallace grabbed the hem of her apron, keeping her gaze toward the bay, as though not hearing.

John continued, overriding a lump in his throat at this initial reaction. "There's going to be a vacancy at the freedmen's school in Galveston. They are looking for a new principal. There's talk of me going."

"An you would do that?" Joe looked at John, disbelief written across his wrinkled features.

"I've been giving it a lot of thought—don't know for certain yet."

Mrs. Wallace turned to him, glaring, a pained expression in her dark eyes. She'd heard, all right. "An' who you 'spect will teach us heah if you goes?"

John tried to quash the guilt rising within him and averted his gaze to a piece of flotsam bobbing in the water. "The American Missionary Association that sent me here will find a replacement. There are good teachers who would be glad to come where there is a new school building and scholars doing so well." He hoped his voice didn't sound as though he were trying to convince himself as well as his hosts that all would be okay.

"When you a-goin'?" Joe sat with his arms crossed. To him it was obviously as good as done.

"I will leave Lavaca in a few weeks when school is out for the summer. First I plan to go to Scotland and see my father. When I return in the fall, it will probably be to Galveston."

Mrs. Wallace released a long, slow sigh. "I 'spects I'll quit then. I knows lots 'bout reading and 'rithmetic now. Don' need no more."

Her words jabbed at John's heart. "None of us ever know enough, Mrs. Wallace, and the new teacher will need your help. I couldn't have done it without you."

They sat a while longer not saying much. Joe's chair commenced its creaking, the gulls continued squawking, and an incessant mosquito whined about. A half hour later, John said goodnight, the darkening sky adding to his doubts as he trudged the few yards home.

The following morning the bright sun helped scrub away his doldrums, and after rereading the correspondence leading up to his decision, John felt right about it once more. As long as a teacher taught at the school here, the pupils were preparing for a better life. He needed to look toward his future, too, and moving to Galveston seemed a step in the right direction.

That evening he knocked on the Duvals' door and, after being ushered into the parlor, John repeated his story. The French family took the news more calmly and wished him well. Evelyne kissed him on the cheek and John detected moistness in her eyes, but he sensed in spite of their early friendship, they were perhaps even relieved he would be leaving.

Now that the Wallaces and Duvals had been informed, John began to drop hints to his classes that perhaps he would not return in the fall. From some he received puzzled looks—as though they had heard wrong. Others simply ignored his comments. But word was out and he knew they knew.

A week before the close of school, Melinda and Ophelia Houck approached him after class.

"Teachah, could we please borrah your Bible for a time?"

John raised his eyebrows at the question, glancing at the dog-eared book on his desk. It went everywhere with him—indeed, was a very part of him. He hesitated before replying. "Well, now, and what would you be wanting with my Bible?"

The girls giggled, and Ophelia said, "It be a secret, but we promise to bring it back."

John's first inclination was to refuse, then he shamefully checked his feelings. Even if these lassies didn't return it, what better memento of him to leave behind than his Bible?

"Pleeeese, suh?"

Embarrassed at his own hesitation, he smiled, picked up the book, and handed it to Ophelia.

The last day of school arrived too quickly. Those who had refused to believe now had to accept the fact that their teacher would in all probability not be back. Determined to leave on an upbeat note, John made a party of the remaining hours. They sang favorite hymns and played games. As the clock approached two in the afternoon, Ophelia and Melinda stepped to the front of the classroom, hands tucked behind their backs.

"Mistah Ogilvie, we got somethin' fo' you," Ophelia said.

"Close your eyes," Melinda added.

John obeyed, and as he stood there unseeing, the shuffling of feet, scraping of furniture against the wood floor, and whispering voices teased his ears.

"Now," Ophelia said.

His eyes popped open to see the entire class circled around him. Melinda handed him a book covered in the same calico as her primer.

"Oh ho, what have we here?" John asked.

"Look inside," someone prompted. He opened it to the title page and immediately recognized his own well-worn Bible. A grin sprang to his face.

Jeremy jumped up. "Now it don' look so bad," he said, his voice high pitched with the excitement of it all.

"An' it will be protected," Melinda added.

"Look some more," Pasty called out.

John turned a page and several papers fluttered to the floor. He stooped to pick them up, then grinned more broadly when he saw what he held in his hands. With ink, each scholar had signed his or her name. There were some splotches, to be sure, but forty-three signatures covered the pages: some tiny, some too large, some awkward and almost illegible, but there nonetheless. A few of the more advanced scholars wrote messages, someone even added an arithmetic problem.

"This is splendid," John said, swallowing a lump rising in his throat. "The best present I ever had." He knew they must have had help. He scanned the room till his gaze locked with that of Mrs. Wallace who stood back from the group. He smiled and nodded. His able assistant, former landlady and friend, smiled back, then looked away, hiding her face behind her hands to conceal tears sliding down her cheeks.

The evening class proved less emotional, at least outwardly. Several chose not to come. Those who did stoically shook John's hand, wishing him well. This was not a group to fuss over change. One by one they left the building until only Samuel remained. As was their normal routine, he and John organized the room—stacking books, erasing the board, and tending to whatever else was required. Tonight, their last night together, a silence hung between them. Finally, there was nothing else to be done.

"Well, Samuel, I hope you know what a help you have been, not only in the classroom, but in my spiritual life," John said. "And you saved my life. That is the ultimate gift, and no thank-you is enough."

"Yes, suh." Samuel looked away. It was the first time John remembered him lacking for words.

"I'm counting on you to show the new teacher around and expect you to continue as assistant. Here, I have something for you." John reached into a pocket and pulled out a piece of paper.

Samuel reached for it. "Is it your address, suh? I want to write you."

"I'll send my address as soon as I know it. That won't be until fall. This is a letter of recommendation. It tells whomever you wish to present it to of your qualifications. You are going to make your race proud, Samuel."

Samuel tucked the paper into his own pocket. He did not read it in front of John. "Thank you, suh. You been a good teacher and a good preacher, too. Someday I will be like you." He shook John's hand one more time, then turned abruptly and hurried out the door.

That evening John spent several hours reading from his calico-covered Bible. When he finally turned down the lamp wick and climbed into bed, the faces of seventy scholars, young and old, crowded into his dreams.

He awoke early and ate a light breakfast before strolling away from town toward the Chocolate Bayou and the prairie. A few remnants of spring wildflowers brightened his path, and the buzz of insects accompanied his steps. He breathed deeply and slowed his pace to enjoy the countryside. This place had taken some getting used to, but had wormed its way into his soul.

His direction took him to the burial grounds for the colored folk. Removing his hat, he clutched the brim tightly as he stood before the wooden marker of Ezra's spunky grandmother. He spoke a prayer for her spirit and one for Ezra, wherever he might be. Next he walked to a second cemetery where he sought Neal's grave. There he knelt before the mounded earth, now scattered with Texas Blue Bonnets.

"Goodbye again, special friend. Thank you for the laughter and fun we shared. I shall never forget you."

Returning to his hut, he gathered together the household items so generously loaned by friends and made the rounds through town to return them, presenting each family with a book of songs in return for their kindness. The bed, chair, and chest of drawers would remain in the house. Evelyne and Pierre had told him to leave them there.

His plans were now set. He would leave Port Lavaca early the following day with a stopover in Galveston for two days as requested by Sarah Barnes in her most recent letter, which in part read:

> *Dear Mr. Ogilvie,*
>
> *I am so pleased that all is falling into place for you to begin your tenure in Galveston this coming fall. I now have one more request of you. Captain Rathbun is due to sail into port here on June 29th and we will be married the following day. As I understand it, you will be passing through about then on the first leg of your journey to Scotland. If it is at all possible, could you please serve as the Captain's groomsman? Miss Skinner will be my*

bridesmaid and I have asked the Baptist minister to administer the vows of holy matrimony ...

When John first read the letter he had smiled at the irony of it. Did he really want to be a part of this wedding? Aye, if that was what Sarah Barnes desired. He would have to forget what might have been and look ahead to his trip to Scotland and the challenging horizons in Galveston come September.

Supper this final evening was to be with the Wallaces. In preparation for his farewell, John had washed and mended Mrs. Wallace's quilt, which, in spite of her argument to the contrary, he knew was not an extra. He could do without it for his last night in the hot and humid June weather.

Next he carefully wrapped and tied Jacob's revolver into an unrecognizable bundle. There were times after the K.K.K. notices were posted that the tension ran so high John had resorted to bringing the gun to church, hiding it on a shelf beneath the pulpit. He wondered about its usefulness. *It wasn't with me when I really needed it. They probably would have found it in my possession; and even if they didn't, I couldn't have used it with my hands tied behind me. And I could never shoot a seventeen year old lad. How do I justify the right to defend myself, if it means taking a life, and going against my calling?* Thank God, he'd never had to find out, and he had no intention of taking the gun to Galveston.

At six o'clock that evening, laden with the two items to be returned, plus a song book for his host and hostess, John left for the most difficult of all his good-byes.

Chapter 29

Bannockburn, Scotland, summer 1869

In the four years since John left Scotland, his father had grown more bent and frail, though when their hands clasped on greeting, the old man's grip still felt strong. John's half-brothers, Andrew and Alexander, were full of questions.

"Tell us about America," twenty-two year old Andrew said. "Are ye rich?"

John laughed. "Not yet." He thought of the two dollars a day he made pitching hay in Minnesota, often more than twice what he saw teaching the freedmen in Texas.

"What's it like, America? And are you really teaching colored folk?" Alexander's eyes shone bright with eagerness. Now fifteen, he hung on John's every word with wonder, obviously awestruck that his older brother had ventured across the ocean to a different life.

They sat in the modest home at the hand-carved wooden table, worn from generations of family members. Their father smoked a pipe and smiled while John answered questions. Rain pattered softly on the thatched roof and Isabella, John's stepmother, hummed as she basted a fresh leg of lamb as it roasted on the hearth. The aroma caused John's mouth to water and filled his mind with memories. It felt so comfortable, so right, as though he had never left.

The first Sunday he attended church was especially poignant. His family sat together at St. Ninian's, his father no longer in the pulpit, and his grandfather long gone to his final rest. Townspeople turned to look at John, smiling and nodding. He could almost hear their thoughts. *It's young John Ogilvie, a man now, come home.* The stone sanctuary was cold and damp, as it had always been. The softest cough or whisper echoed off the high-pitched ceiling. John found the routine service too formal, and had to catch himself from responding with a loud *"Amen"* at one particular sentence wrung with feeling by the preacher. Music bounced off the walls, and the sound wrapped around John like a comfortable shawl. He sang the hymns with gusto, releasing his frustration at the rigid ritual. He chuckled at his own reaction, remembering the shock he felt at the first service he attended in the Negro Baptist church in Galveston. He now thought, *the joyous spontaneity of my colored friends in Texas seem a more fitting relationship with God.*

After the benediction, old acquaintances made a point to find him in the narthex to shake his hand or slap him on the back. Each with the same question, "And will ye be staying, lad?"

As John strolled the familiar lanes of Bannockburn, with Stirling Castle keeping sentry on a distant hill, something was missing—a yearning within him, not unlike that he had felt from the moment he set sail to America and watched his native land slip away. *Aye, this was home, but I've found other homes, too.* What's more, he had found other people, and just as he had sorely missed Scotland these past few years, he now missed those places and those people.

To return to his homeland had been good, finding everything as it had been—the chance to weave together old memories with new. He discovered joy in the familiar: twin chimneys on the buildings, hills purple with heather, and the poetry of Robby Burns. But there were reminders, too, of why he had left. The miners, black from coal dust, their eyes dull from exhaustion at the end of the day, with only a few coins in their pockets to show for their labors. The sparse furnishings in the family home, his father's patched clothing. The poverty. Andrew worked in the nearby mill and contributed to the family coffer. Aye, everything was as he had left it. Thus, when the question arose, *"Will ye be staying, lad?"* The answer was no, a surprise perhaps to others, but not to John. He had never intended to stay, and though he had suffered many bouts of homesickness in America, returning to Scotland had put that yearning in far clearer perspective.

When time came for him to leave, he knew in his heart this was a final goodbye to his father. He would not be returning to Scotland soon. His calling, the giving of himself and introducing the Lord to those less fortunate, lay in a distant land.

His father's parting words as they embraced were ones John would not forget in a lifetime. "I'm proud of ye, lad. 'Tis good to be proud of one's children. A man can't ask for more than that."

As John swung up into the carriage, his father handed him a small book bound in red—*The Poems and Songs of Robert Burns.*

"So ye never forget your homeland," he said, tears brimming in his eyes.

"I never will, Father," John said. "It is a part of me." He clutched the precious book to his chest.

As the carriage gathered speed, taking him away from the place of his birth, he lifted his hand and waved, not pausing until the man who had influenced him so deeply was gone from sight.

His thoughts turned to his new role in American. He could only guess what unknown challenges would face him on his return.

John Ogilvie Stevenson, Teacher of the Freedmen, Lavaca
and Galveston, Texas, 1867-1872

Anna Keen, Teacher of the Freedmen, Galveston, Texas,
1871-72

Commission appointing John Ogilvie Stevenson as a to teach the freedmen in Lavaca, Texas

Courtesy Rosenberg Library, Galveston, Texas

Headquarters,

BUREAU REFUGEES, FREEDMEN & ABAND. LANDS,

State of **Texas,**

GALVESTON, TEXAS, March 7, 1867.

SPECIAL ORDERS, }
   NO. 28. }

[EXTRACT.]

1. JOHN O. STEVENSON, Teacher of Freedmen's School, will proceed to Lavaca, Texas, and organize and teach a school for Freedmen at that place.

    *   *   *   *

BY COMMAND OF BV'T MAJ. GEN. GRIFFIN, ASS'T COM.

       J. T., KIRKMAN,

       1st Lieut. 26th U. S. Infty, A. A. A. G.

OFFICIAL :

       1st Lieut. 26th U. S. Infty, A. A. A. G.

To. John O. Stevenson,

Galveston, Texas.

Special orders from the Freedmen's Bureau sending John Ogilvie
Stevenson to Lavaca, Texas

Courtesy Rosenberg Library, Galveston, Texas

Headquarters,
BUREAU REFUGEES, FREEDMEN & ABAND. LANDS,
State of Texas,
Galveston, Texas. June 19, 1867.

CIRCULAR
No. 6.

The Schools for Freedmen in Texas will close, for the customary summer vacation, on the 30th inst., to resume on the 1st of October.

Teachers desiring to continue their schools through the vacation, can do so on a self-sustaining basis, prescribing and collecting such fees as they think proper. They will be allowed the use of the school furniture now in their respective school buildings, and will continue to make the customary reports, the Bureau furnishing school rooms and paying rents of the same.

Such teachers as propose to continue schools under the above terms, will report the fact promptly to the Sub-Assistant Commissioner, in whose Sub-District they may be teaching, and to these Headquarters.

Those instructors who accept the offered vacation will report at once to the Sub-Assistant Commissioner of their Sub-District, who will take charge and hold all furniture and apparatus, property of the Bureau.

CHARLES GRIFFIN,
Bv't Maj. Gen'l U. S. A., Ass't Com'r.

Official:

1st Lieut. 26th U. S. Inf'ty, A. A. A. Gen'l.

Circular received by John during his first year in Lavaca, TX. while he was contemplating keeping the school open.

Courtesy Rosenberg Library, Galveston, Texas

Sir

I am in receipt of a petition from Galveston, referred to me by Hon. W. H. Sinclair, recommending you for the appointment of Superintendent of Education for the State.

I will place this petition, together with the resolutions of the "Republican Association of Galveston" which were also enclosed on file for reference, and when the time comes for making the appointment mentioned, your claims will receive respectful consideration.

Respectfully
Edmund J. Davis
Gov.

J. O. Stevenson Esq.
Galveston Texas

Response from Governor Davis regarding John's petition

Courtesy Rosenberg Library, Galveston, Texas

☞ ATTENTION!!! ☜

Fall of 67

Brethern of the Klan, and friends of the South! When the banner under which our heroes fought and bled was lowered from her proud position by overpowering numbers, we took the hands of our enemies once more in friendship, and listened to their promises, seemingly fair and honest. We resolved to let "the past be buried in the eternal past;" yea, shut out from sight our barren fields and desolate homes, and to forget whose guns contained the bullets that sent our brave and fair to their last resting places. Look around you now! See how their promises have been fulfilled! See upon what quicksand our hopes were built! Time has rolled around and finds us under the worst tyranny in the world. To Southern and working men, there is no fear. To "Carpet Baggers" enemies to our blood and country, we say, beware! You are clogs on the wheels of our prosperity. To you we may have smiling faces and extended hands, but our hearts are envenomed and we will act accordingly.

The 15th Legion of Lone ☆ are commaded to meet again. New members to be iniated. Personal business of great importance to be transacted. By order of

GRAND CYCLOPS.

Ku Klux Klan threat, fall of 1867, from the scrapbook of John Ogilvie Stevenson

Courtesy Rosenberg Library, Galveston, Texas

CORPS OF TEACHERS.

HIGH SCHOOL.
J. O. STEVENSON,

GRAMMAR SCHOOL
MISS A. M. KEEN,
Graduate of Forest Hill Seminary. Rockford Ills.

INTERMEDIATE
MISS M. A. E. NICHOLS,
Of Racine High School, Racine Wisconsin.

PRIMARY
MISS H. L. LANE,
Graduate of Holyoke Seminary, South Hadley Mass.

BOARD OF TRUSTEES.

WASHINGTON GREEN. - - - - - - - - President.

GEO. TERRY, - - - - - - - - - - - Vice President.

Alfred Perkins,	Gen. C. H. Howard,
Madison McKinney,	Rev. Wm. Howard, D. D.
Richard Grandison,	Mrs S. M. Rathbun,

J. O. STEVENSON, Secretary.

NO. OF STUDENTS.
Primary 28, Intermediate 45, Grammar 50, High School 10
TOTAL No. OF SCHOLARS 133.

Courtesy Rosenberg Library, Galveston, Texas

GENERAL COURSE OF STUDY.

PRIMARY DEPARTMENT.

SECTION A.	SECTION B.
Alphabet, 1st Reader...	Spelling, 2d Reader, Writing...... ......
Slate Writing......	Primary Arithmetic, Primary Geography

INTERMEDIATE DEPARTMENT.

SECTION A.	SECTION B.
Spelling, 3d Reader, Writing...........	Spelling, 4th Reader, Writing...........
Felters Addition and Subtraction.......	Felters Multiplication and Division......
Introduction to Geography.......	Geography, Primary, English Grammar..

GRAMMAR.

SECTION A.	SECTION B.
Spelling and Defining, 5th Reader...	Spelling and Defining, 6th Reader, Writing
Writing English Grammar................	Quackenboss' English Composition.......
Davies Elements of Arithmetic..........	Davies Practical Arithmetic... ....
Geography, United States History........	Geography, History................. ......

HIGH SCHOOL.

SECTION A.	SECTION B.
Derivation of Words, Advanced English Composition....................	Not yet required.... ....
Latin Grammer and Reader.............	
Elementary Algebra, Physical Geography.	

Courtesy Rosenberg Library, Galveston, Texas

Flora Beach Burlingame

K. K. K's.

'The Moon is low,--
The Bull is rampant.
St. Mark: the Hour
S. X.
By order of the
KHENGIS KHAN,

Galveston Tex

BARNES

INSTITUTE,

SPRING TERM

THIRD SESSION.

J. O. STEVENSON, Principal.

March 31, 1872

Courtesey Rosenberg Library, Galveston, Texas

Cartoon clipped from a newspaper (date and paper unknown),
from the scrapbook of John Ogilvie Stevenson

Courtesy Rosenberg Library, Galveston, Texas

Chapter 30

Galveston, Texas, September 1869

John stepped off the steamer at Galveston and into his new role as headmaster of the Barnes Institute. He approached the bureau office with broad and purposeful steps, spurred on by the thought of new scholars to meet, a staff to assist him, and the constant activity of this bustling city. He entered the building and a stranger at the desk looked up.

"Major Stevenson?" John asked.

"Yes." The man stood as he spoke.

"John Ogilvie, sir, reporting for duty at the Barnes Institute." He handed the assistant superintendent of schools for the Freedmen's Bureau a letter of introduction. "General Howard suggests we might keep house together, for the sake of economy," he said, sizing up his potential roommate. Taller and older than John, the major's handshake conveyed confidence and strength.

"So, at last we meet," Stevenson said, after reading the letter. "I too have heard from Howard suggesting we room together. I am currently renting a small house. The furnishings are minimal, but it should accommodate the two of us nicely, and it will be to the financial advantage of both the AMA and the bureau. I will be honored to have you join me there. General Howard speaks very highly of you."

The Major motioned for him to sit. "The new schoolhouse is still under construction and won't be ready for the fall term, but I am trying to push it forward the best I can. Miss Skinner has returned from her summer break, and a Miss Williams will be arriving shortly to handle the primary grades." He brought John up to date on the bureau's activities in Galveston and asked him questions about his tenure in Lavaca.

After an hour of talk, the major pulled a key from his pocket, scribbled some instructions on a scrap of paper, and passed it over to John. "Here's how to find the house. It's not far. Feel free to make yourself comfortable. It will be a couple of hours before I get there."

John rose and picked up his bag. "Thank you. It will be good to rest a wee bit. Then perhaps I'll walk over to the school site and check on the progress."

To John the major's house seemed luxurious after the tiny hut in Lavaca. It consisted of a sitting room sparsely furnished with a settee, a straight-backed chair, and a desk. The small kitchen held a dry sink, a table and two chairs, a wood-burning cook stove, *and real built-in cupboards—not made from packing crates,* he observed with a smile. A curtained opening led into an attached washroom, which in turn had its own exit to the outside. Behind the house, in the fenced yard, stood a privy. Best of all, two bedrooms meant he and the major each had their own private space. John set his bag down in the one obviously unused.

He stretched out on the bed, but was too wound up for a rest. Within a half hour he was out the door strolling down 29th Street. Turning right onto Avenue M, he caught his breath. A two-story structure rose beside the marsh—Sarah Barnes' dream taking shape. John cautiously walked through the building-in-progress, mentally mapping out the rooms and their intended functions. He lingered for a while, imagining the pupils and lessons to be taught here in a few weeks' time. Finally, content with his exploration, he retraced his steps toward the major's house. But first he had one more stop to make before the day ended—the teacher's home where he had stayed during his last visit to Galveston. Upon recognizing the modest building, he stepped up to the front door and announced his presence with a firm knock.

Martha, the housekeeper, greeted him with enthusiasm. "Mistah Ogilvie, I knew you was goin' to get heah by'n'by. Mail has come for you addressed to the school." She scurried to a sideboard, retrieved a white envelope, and handed it to him. "I'll tell Miss Skinner you is heah."

While John waited, he turned the envelope over to examine the return address: Samuel Canfield, Lavaca, Texas. With a smile on his lips, he pocketed the piece of mail to read later.

"And here you are all the way from Scotland, at last." Sarah Skinner swept into the room, her hand extended. "Won't you please stay for a cup of tea?" She motioned toward the dining room table. "It will only take a minute to steep, and we have some fresh biscuits to go with it."

Flora Beach Burlingame

The last time he had seen Miss Skinner was at the wedding that had taken place here in Galveston prior to his visit to his homeland. She had served as Maid of Honor for Miss Barnes, and John, fulfilling his promise, stood beside the Captain as the Groomsman. Reflecting for a moment on that event, John smiled. Though thin and pale from overwork, Sarah Barnes had been as radiant as any bride. Dressed in a simple gown of beige silk, a string of pearls at her neck, she held a small bouquet of yellow roses. The Captain may have had to persuade her to marry him, but as they spoke their vows, John acknowledged the match was right. The two were obviously very much in love, and rather than being remorseful at losing a woman who had never been his, he had left Galveston feeling glad for Sarah. She was in good hands.

Now, he, Miss Skinner, and Martha sat at the table, partaking of the mid-afternoon refreshment, and talked. "I met with Miss Barnes—Mrs. Rathbun—while in New York on my return from Scotland," John told the women. "Her health is greatly improved and her energy returning. The captain is taking good care of her."

Martha shook her head, "She jus' fretted too much 'bout the building of that school, and she worried 'bout the students jus' as if they was her own chilluns. It's no wonder she was wastin' away."

"Did she tell you of our problems getting the school built?" Miss Skinner asked. "We had hoped to start classes there in the fall, but now it looks like it won't be until the first of the year."

"Aye, that she did, and Major Stevenson mentioned it also. She also talked about the pupils—the good scholars and the mischievous ones."

"There are certainly those," Miss Skinner said.

"We'll manage," John said. "I've seen all these problems before." The clock struck five; he rose and excused himself, eager to return to his new home and read Samuel's message before Major Stevenson arrived.

Once in the house, he lit the kerosene lantern that hung above the kitchen table, pulled up a chair and retrieved the envelope from his pocket. Breaking open the seal, he unfolded the single page within. Samuel's bold lettering seemed to jump at him:

Dear Mister Ogilvie,
We are still waiting for a new teacher and none has come. It is most important that someone be here soon or that you come back.
Your friend, Samuel

207

John's enthusiasm for his new role plummeted. *Have I let those precious scholars down after all?* Rubbing his hand across his brow, he closed his eyes and breathed deeply, sitting prayerfully for a few moments before taking the note to his bedroom and placing it on the nightstand.

The front door opened and in walked Louis, carrying a large bundle. "Sorry to be late. I hope you didn't fix a meal. I stopped off at the fish market for mackerel and got us some bread at the baker's, too."

John hadn't even thought about supper, and sheepishly responded, "No, I'm afraid I wasn't that considerate. I'm much obliged. We need to discuss meals and how to share that responsibility."

Louis made a pot of coffee and brought out plates and flatware. The aroma of fish, breaded and fried in pork fat, filled the room. John pulled a chair up to the table and sat opposite Louis. "I m a lucky man," he said. "I have found a good cook as well as a congenial housemate. Now tell me how you got involved with the bureau?"

"As you know," Louis began, "most of its personnel are from the military. Being an army man, I chose to continue my career in this manner, and eventually ended up working in the area of education rather than some of the other helps the bureau offered the freedmen. My first assignment was as an agent in Columbus." He studied John a moment while he chewed and swallowed a bite of bread. "What about you? How did you get involved teaching the freedmen when you had hardly set foot in America?"

John wanted to hear more about Louis, but figured that would come with time, so he replied, "It had to do with two influential men—my father and one very persuasive preacher from the American Missionary Association." Yet it had been more than that. The thought of lifting these former slaves out of despair and into hope, in the name of the Lord, was a powerful motivator.

At eleven o'clock John began to feel his long day. "We have lots of time to learn more about each other. I need some sleep, and tomorrow I'll have supper ready."

In his own room he prepared for bed, placing his coat and trousers on a wooden hanger in the wardrobe. As tired as he was, his thoughts drifted back to Samuel's letter. *Is it my responsibility to ensure the continuing education of the freedmen there? No, I think now my duty belongs in Galveston with a new group of scholars, and I do have a limited time to ready myself.* Guilt stabbed through his mental debate. *Aye, pride has played a part in my coming here, I cannot deny this...and the pay. But more is to be earned in Galveston, and I will need this if I am to achieve my own goals of a college education.*

He poured water from a pitcher into a basin and washed the day's dust from his face, neck and ears. As he wrestled with his conflicting thoughts he focused on the reflection in the chipped mirror hanging on the wall. He no longer saw the image of a young, inexperienced Scotsman. He had a substantial beard, and the hint of creases appeared at the corners of his eyes. At twenty-eight a maturity showed that hadn't been there when he first arrived in America.

Pulling on his nightshirt, John knelt. *Dear Lord, please help me find the answer to this troubling question.* Once in bed, he stared through the darkness. The familiar faces of Samuel, Jeb and the other men from his night class in Lavaca hovered above, an expectant pleading in their eyes, and behind them clustered Jeremy, Ophelia, Patsy and all their classmates. The cruelty of teasing them with the beginnings of an education then walking out for his own betterment twisted a blade in his heart.

Neither the bureau nor the AMA had come up with a teacher. *Who in Lavaca could or would assume this role now?* John had pondered this question since first learning of his transfer to Galveston. After going through a scant list of possibilities many times over, two names always remained—Samuel and Mrs. Wallace. They were both respected by their peers and advanced in their studies. *But will they do it?* He wondered. *I can provide material for instruction and advise them whenever necessary. And perhaps those who objected to the freedmen being educated would feel less threatened if they were taught by their own.* A sense of resolve slowly settled over John, and before he slept, he knew how he would respond to Samuel's plea.

"If there is a steamer to Indianola leaving today, I may have to take back my promise of supper. I need to go to Lavaca." John waited until his housemate, assistant superintendent of schools for the bureau, drank his first cup of coffee the next morning before telling him of his decision.

Louis raised his eyebrows. "Lavaca? Your responsibilities there have ended, Ogilvie. With school scheduled to begin here in mid-October, you hardly have time to prepare without traveling about in the meantime."

"Aye, but there seems to be some confusion as to the assigning of teachers there. I felt it was the job of the AMA, but apparently no one has reported." He pulled Samuel's letter from his pocket and passed it across the table to Louis.

As the major read, a frown furrowed his forehead. "Hmmm. We do have a dilemma. I too thought the missionary association was sending someone. Do you have a teacher in mind?"

"If enrollment stays the same or increases at all, the job is too much for one person. Two of my more advanced pupils, who served as assistants, could probably handle the classes, though it might take a bit of persuasion."

"I guess it's worth a try. Will a week give you enough time?"

"Aye, with much prayer and a wee bit of luck, I believe so."

Chapter 31

The steam lighter eased up to the pier at Lavaca. Once off the boat, John strode down the gangplank and along the familiar wharf toward the schoolhouse. As he approached the building, several children were playing tag nearby. Suddenly one tall boy stopped and stared.

"Teacha?"

John turned in the direction of the voice. "Jeremy! You've grown. And it's only been a summer since I last saw you."

The boy broke into a huge grin. "You be back."

"Well, not for long, laddie. I've come to visit and see how things are." He didn't dare promise a teacher yet.

A pout formed on Jeremy's lips. "We be waitin' for school to start up."

"Aye, so I've learned." In order to derail the challenge in the boy's eyes, he quickly asked. "Who are your friends?"

"This here be Micah and his brother Lucas. They come just this summer." He pointed at each one, then swept his hand toward John saying, "This be our teacha."

John decided against correcting the last statement and held out his hand to shake that of the newcomers. "I'm honored to meet you," he said.

The boys giggled at the solemnity of it, and dutifully shook John's hand, then followed him as he took the few stairs to the schoolhouse door, opened it and stepped into the building.

Everything appeared neat and orderly. A stack of Bibles lay on the table next to a vase of slightly wilted daisies. A hand-carved wooden cross hung on the wall at the front of the room, a new addition since John's departure, obviously made by some parishioner's artistic and loving hands.

John removed his hat. Suddenly everything that had gone into the creation of this place rushed at him. He swallowed down a lump and cleared his throat before he spoke. "I see church services are still held here."

"Yes, suh."

"That's good," John said.

"Yes, suh." Jeremy nodded his head. "Tha's mostly good, but sometime the sermons be too long."

"Tha's right," the others joined in.

John smiled at the boys. "Which means you are attending church. That's good, too."

"Mostly," Jeremy said.

"And Sabbath school? Is there still Sabbath school?"

"Yes, suh. Samuel be the teacher, and it ain't so bad."

John laughed with relief. Good, dependable Samuel. He stepped toward the door. "I have some visiting to do, but perhaps I will see you again."

The boys apparently weren't about to risk his disappearing, for as John left the school grounds they clipped his heels all the way to the Wallaces' shanty. John stepped onto the porch and rapped at the door. When no one answered after repeated knocks, he took a moment to write a short note and pushed it onto a nail head protruding from the door frame. As he continued on up the bluff toward town, the boys still shadowed him. Finally, John turned to them. "I enjoy your company, lads, but I have business to tend to. I'll meet you back at the schoolhouse later."

"Yes, suh," Jeremy said, his lips puckered in another pout.

At the blacksmith shop, a shirtless Samuel shaped a red hot horseshoe. His black shoulders glistened from the heat of the furnace. When John stepped up, the man's eyes widened in disbelief before a grin brightened his entire face.

"I don' believe it. My prayers done been answered." He dropped the horseshoe and grabbed hold of John's hand. "You is— are—a sight for sore eyes."

"Hello, Samuel."

"Is you really back?"

"No, I'm sorry, I'm not, but we need to talk. Can you take a break?"

***

At first Samuel was stunned at John's proposal that he take over the night class, then the more John encouraged him, the more excited he became. "Does—do—you really think I can teach?"

"I know you can. I will stay a few days and help draw up a lesson plan for each level. You have books and you read well. You can do it."

They agreed to meet the next evening at the schoolhouse to get organized. By the time John left, Samuel was shaking his head in disbelief and mumbling over and over, "I'm going to be a teacher."

When John approached Wallace's shanty once again he knew he was expected. The familiar aroma of Mrs. Wallace's cooking enticed him to pick up his pace.

On the porch, rocking away, sat Joe wearing a wide grin. "Here he come," he sang out.

The door flung open and Mrs. Wallace stood in the entry, hands on her hips. "Well, it's about time you come a-visitin'. I figured you done forgot us. I hope you is hungry."

"Aye. My stomach is rumbling for a bite of your good cooking."

During supper they talked about Scotland, Galveston, and the goings on in Lavaca since June. John kept waiting for the right moment to approach Mrs. Wallace about teaching. She presented that opening herself.

"So, do we have us a teacha yet?"

"That's why I'm here," he said, looking her steadily in the eye. "I think we do."

She took more convincing than Samuel, her first response being an adamant, "Mercy no. I nevah could do that."

But the idea began to appeal, and the flattery of it gradually overtook the denial of her ability. Plus there would be pay.

Joe gave the final push. "Fo' heaven's sake, woman, jest do it."

That night John stayed in his familiar hut. It was now Jacob's place, but the young man was gone and John slept alone. It was a good sleep. His mission had been accomplished. He awoke early, refreshed and eager to get on with the day. Following breakfast with the Wallaces, he took off for the schoolhouse. He was to meet Mrs. Wallace there later in the morning and wanted to look over the supplies and start some lesson plans for her.

At a quarter to nine, Jeremy and his friends showed up. "You never came back, so we all went on home," he said, a hint of distrust in his voice.

"My errand took longer than expected, Jeremy, but I'm glad you're here. I have a job for you. How would you three like to earn some money?"

"You ain't funnin' us, is you?"

"Not at all. I need you to take care of some very important business."

The boys' sullen demeanor somersaulted. They crowded around John as he wrote and dispersed several notes among them. "Deliver these to as many of the adult scholars, day and night, as you can find. School's going to start soon, and we're going to have a meeting about the new teachers tomorrow night. We want as many folks to know as possible. When you return, I will see that you each get a coin." Papers clutched in their hands, the boys dashed off.

The sessions with Mrs. Wallace and Samuel went well, each appearing more confident as John explained and organized lessons. By the following evening they were ready to be introduced as the new teachers.

At a quarter to five John rang the tower bell. The strong, melodic bongs reverberated throughout the community and soon familiar faces entered the door. Each person in turn greeted John, then found a place on a bench. When it appeared all had arrived, John took his customary position at the front of the room and addressed the crowd.

"As you know, I have been assigned to teach in Galveston, but the scholars here hold a special place in my heart, and when I learned a teacher had not yet been assigned, I felt it my duty to find somebody. Fortunately, we have right here in Lavaca two qualified people who will make fine teachers. They have helped in the classroom and are willing to continue in my place. Mrs. Wallace and Samuel, will you please come forward?"

As the two took their places up front, a murmur rose in the room. John couldn't tell if it was from pleasure or disappointment. Mrs. Wallace started to tremble, and for a moment John was afraid she would walk out the door.

Samuel saved the day. Raising his hand, the big man spoke. "Brothers and sisters, let us pray." And pray he did, raising his deep voice to the heavens, asking for guidance and strength in "this most important role" and "dear Jesus, help me and the most capable Mrs. Wallace pass on the learning we got from Mr. Ogilvie to all God's colored scholars in the town of Port Lavaca."

When his ten minute supplication ended, cheers and claps thundered through the room. Folks came forward and shook the hands of their new teachers, some with tears rolling down their cheeks. John stood to one side, awed at Samuel's charisma and sense of timing. Any doubts he had harbored about this man's capability were swept away like feathers on a swift tide.

Once order was restored, John announced classes would commence a week from Monday. "Please spread the word and let all your friends and any former pupils know."

He answered queries regarding books, lessons, starting times, and other school related matters to the satisfaction of both the new teachers and the pupils. After a half hour or so, the questions diminished and the room quieted except for an occasional shuffling of feet or rasp of a cough.

"Anything else?" John asked.

The air stirred with a tenseness—a feeling of anticipation. That school would finally begin was surely a part of it, yet something else was afoot. Something not resolved. As John scanned the faces his gaze came to rest on Samuel who turned and looked at his fellow classmates. Several heads nodded.

Samuel rose from his front row seat. A hush settled across the room as he cleared his throat. "Mistah Ogilvie. There's one more thing."

"Yes, Samuel?" A tiny spark of anxiety lit up in John.

"It's about voting. You done told us about the amendments to the Constitution saying we got a right now to do that and we expects to next month. We want a sheriff, and a senator, and governor what cares about us."

Voices began to rumble across the room, first low, then building up volume.

"Yes, suh."

"Dat's right."

"We is free and gets to vote now. Ain't nobody stopping us."

Samuel raised his hand and the commotion subsided enough for his voice to be heard. "We is hoping you can help with the right names to mark and be here when it comes time to vote so there won't be no trouble."

The rumble began again, resonating with determination. John felt it flow through his own body, limb to limb. He was witness to a critical turning point for these men. Caught up in the excitement, he exclaimed, "Aye. I'll come and help anyway that I can," though he wasn't certain his presence would keep away trouble.

A cheer erupted. Men stood and shook John's hand and slapped each other on the back. They were to have a voice in the government, and John felt the thrill right along with his pupils.

Chapter 32

At supper, the evening of his return to Galveston, John told Louis of his success in finding teachers for the school in Lavaca. "And the men want me to return to help them with voting in November." He still felt the excitement of it as he spoke.

"It's going to be a lively election," Louis said. "In case you haven't heard, while you were gone, Governor Pease resigned."

"Two months before the voters go to the polls? What's the point in that?"

"You know he was only a provisional governor appointed after Throckmorton's removal from office. He supported Hamilton for the upcoming gubernatorial race, but General Reynold's push for Edmund Davis instead has got his ire up. It's good your Lavaca men are so eager to vote. It's critical that the Radical Republicans get as many men in office as possible in order to continue the rights of the freedmen. We need Davis in there."

John had ignored political activities during reconstruction. His main focus was getting the school going in Lavaca. Now he could foresee stimulating times ahead, and his own involvement was inevitable. Louis was familiar with pivotal people in both the bureau and the government, and for the first time since coming to Texas, John was in the thick of things.

Alone the following morning, he pulled a chair up to the desk in the sitting room and organized his papers and correspondence. On top of the stack he placed the one piece of mail that had arrived during his brief absence, his annual Certificate of Commission from the AMA. This one differed from the others in that it certified his appointment as a *Missionary Superintendent* instead of *Missionary Teacher*. A swell of pride as he read the document was quickly curbed by his awareness of the added responsibilities it implied.

With the new building still incomplete, school would continue at the Baptist church where Sarah Barnes and Sarah Skinner had taught. John had arranged to meet Miss Skinner there at ten o'clock that morning. He arrived a few minutes early, unlocked the door, and surveyed the room. The long, narrow space, crowded with benches, was reminiscent of the makeshift school in the warehouse at Lavaca. He shook his head. The need for the new building in progress was very apparent.

Miss Skinner quietly entered and stood beside him, seemingly reading his mind. "When school ended last spring, we had an enrollment of well over one hundred pupils," she said. "Of course not all attended everyday, and it also included our night classes, but I am sure we can anticipate at least that many again this fall."

She paused a moment, brushed back a lock of hair from her forehead and gazed across the empty benches. "I'm glad you will be teaching the night classes, Mr. Ogilvie. That became very difficult for Miss Barnes—the long hours."

"You know the missionary association is sending another teacher to help," he said, "a Miss Williams. She will teach the primary students. According to Miss Barnes, you are proficient at the intermediate level. That leaves the advanced and evening scholars for me. We can do it."

"Praise the Lord. I had hoped against hope for additional teachers," Miss Skinner said, relief evident on her face.

Being in a classroom spurred John's enthusiasm, and after the initial cleaning, he and Miss Skinner sorted through supplies. He was impressed with the array of subjects offered, more than he was able to manage alone in Lavaca: spelling, reading, writing, grammar, arithmetic, geography, history, and for the most advanced levels, Latin. But far too few texts for each subject.

"I see not enough teaching materials is a problem here, too," John said.

"We never have enough," Miss Skinner said. She sighed and lowered herself to one of the benches, her long skirt draped gracefully to the floor.

John leaned against the wall opposite her. A welcome breeze flowed through an open window as they rested from the tasks at hand. He studied his assistant—a tall, plain woman probably several years older than he. She seemed truly dedicated to this benevolent teaching career. He admired her for that and was grateful she was here to help with his adjustment to the Galveston school. However, she held no special appeal for him as had the former mistress of this institution. For a moment, a sense of longing seized him. Maybe somewhere in this city full of people he would cross paths with a woman to share his dreams and future. He shifted his thoughts. For now, he must forget such notions and concentrate on his obligation to the freedmen.

"In regard to supplies," he said. "I'll talk to Major Stevenson and see if something can be done.

Two days later, Miss Williams arrived to complete the staff. A short, honey-haired woman, she had taught for a brief time at another freedmen's school. She appeared tired from her trip but eager to begin her new teaching assignment. With his staff complete, John was ready and anxious for school to open.

***

On October 11, 1869, classes began on schedule. John asked Miss Skinner to open with a prayer, and she in turn introduced John and Miss Williams. That first morning, each pupil was tested to determine in which level they would begin. This also gave John an opportunity to become acquainted with all the scholars.

"Henry Wilson and Willis Reedy are inclined to aggravate one another," Miss Skinner had told him. "They are good boys but get on each other's nerves and sometimes disrupt the class. A man's presence will be a beneficial influence."

Miss Skinner had also mentioned outstanding scholars. During roll call John stayed alert for the names Violette Green, Ada Newel, and Adeline Westly in particular. He looked for these girls and was rewarded with bright smiles and an infectious eagerness for learning. He sensed right away these would be special, like the Houck twins and Patsy Harper.

The students of the night class differed from Lavaca in that most of the adults worked as domestics in homes about Galveston and included several women. The male contingency seemed to especially welcome the idea of a man for a teacher. A few stood out immediately. Violette Green's father, lanky Washington Green, wore a suit with pants that rode up on his long legs, and, though reserved, he carried with him an air of dignity. Another pupil, Alphonse, seemed self-assured with a sense of humor that offered a welcome break from the often serious atmosphere. John knew the sea of faces would eventually become individuals, each with his or her own unique contribution. Yet he missed the familiarity of Samuel, Jeb, and others. *Be patient,* he told himself.

John and Louis saw little of each other that first week. Their schedules were out of synchronization from early morning until

John returned late from his evening class. Finally, on Friday night they had some time to relax and visit.

"What do you say we take a tour of Galveston tomorrow?" Louis suggested. "She is a fine city with lots to do and see. You will learn it is quite a different place from Lavaca—or anywhere else, for that matter."

"I'd like that. I've seen some of the island, but don't really know too much about it." He recalled a picnic on the beach during his first visit here en route to his assignment in Lavaca: the rippling waves against the sand; the laughter of Miss Barnes and Miss Skinner; and, during the trolley ride to get there, the scorn directed at the "nigger teachers." He remembered that most, how it had tainted their outing even though the ladies pretended it didn't matter.

"We'll hire a carriage, and I'll give you some history along the way," Louis was saying.

John brought his attention back to the current place and moment. "Aye, let's do it."

They were out the door at ten the following morning after a leisurely breakfast. A crisp breeze blew off the gulf, teasing their coattails as they walked to their first destination, the Custom House. The striking Greek Revival structure was familiar to John as it served as headquarters for the bureau and also housed the post office and courthouse.

"Looks like this place didn't exactly escape the war," he said, noting crumbled mortar and a chipped stone wall.

"The damage occurred during the Battle of Galveston in 1863—just two years after the building had been completed," Louis said. "The Confederates regained control of the island during that conflict on January first. The Union forces had taken it only a few months before."

Louis hailed a carriage. To John's surprise, the driver was Alphonse from the evening class. He flashed John a wide smile and tipped his hat. "Good morning, Mr. Ogilvie."

"We'd like a tour of this beautiful city," Louis said, and he and John settled into the comfortable leather seats.

"Yes, suh, at your service." With a flick of the reins and a "Gid-ap" to the sleek brown mare, Alphonse put the carriage in motion through the impressive downtown district. "This heah be the Hendley Buildings," he said, pointing to a row of long, tall edifices with a tower on a common roof.

"The tower was used to keep watch by the Confederates for enemy ships during the war," Louis added.

The carriage made a left turn at 24th Street and again onto Church, rolling along into a residential area where elegant Victorian and Greek Revival style homes stood side by side. John gave a low whistle. "There's money here."

"Yes, indeed," Louis said.

They rode to the gulf, stopping to ponder the gray-blue sea that stretched on forever. Then off they rolled again, returning to The Strand where the carriage dodged streetcars and pedestrians. Among the many folks hurrying about the business district, a nattily dressed, light-skinned Negro stood out.

"Hello there, Ruby," Louis called.

Glancing toward the carriage, the man smiled in recognition and waved. Alphonse tipped his hat to the impressive-looking gentleman, and that too was acknowledged before he disappeared into the doorway of a mercantile.

"George Ruby," Louis said, turning to John. "Now there's an extraordinary Negro for you. I'm sure you've heard of him. He worked for the bureau for awhile and served as delegate to the recent state constitutional convention. He is currently deputy collector of customs here and president of the Union League."

"So that's The Ruby," John said. "I have heard of him. He's a man I would like to meet sometime."

The carriage slowed to a stop, back where they began. They each thanked Alphonse, handing him extra coins.

Louis turned to John. "How about dinner at one of the restaurants along The Strand?"

As they strode along the boardwalk toward the center of the bustling commercial district, two young women approached in the opposite direction. One, quite pretty, with yellow curls and wearing an expensive-looking blue frock, cast a coy smile at John. Her dark-haired companion, cheeks flushed, seemed to deliberately avert her gaze when they passed by.

Louis whispered, "Hmmm, not bad. One for each of us."

His comment surprised John, who broke into a grin. But in his opinion these two women in all their finery couldn't hold a candle to Sarah Barnes.

"Of course you know,' Louis continued, "high society ladies won't have anything to do with us—Radical Republicans working for the Freedmen's Bureau."

The truth of Louis' remark struck John like a hard slap. *It's a fantasy land*, he thought. On the surface all seemed worry free in this fair city. One could easily be oblivious to any undercurrent of prejudice, inequality, and ugliness. Yet for sure it was there. *Aye, it is there.*

Dining out was a rare treat for John, an extravagance not in his budget, but it was a satisfying conclusion to an interesting morning. Though fish was the main item on the menu, he'd had plenty of that in Lavaca and chose instead a tender steak with potatoes. He savored each bite. "Weak soup and toast tonight," he warned Louis.

"Suits me, as long as you fix it."

When they paid their checks, Louis said, "If you don't mind, I believe I'll walk back to headquarters and finish up some paperwork. I'll be along later."

John didn't mind at all. He had correspondence of his own to do.

Once at the house he began a letter to General Howard telling of his trip to Lavaca and asking for certification of the two teachers he had put in place. *Surely, this will please him*, John mused. After all he had just saved the AMA all the work of placing suitable teachers for that remote location. He sealed the letter with a feeling of satisfaction.

He had one more letter to write. Before his trip to Scotland, his good friend and benefactor, George Ware, had been kind enough to advise him as to the best route to New York. John had not yet acknowledged this kindness, nor had he let the gentleman know he now resided in Galveston. He owed him that. Once again he dipped his pen in ink. *Dear Mr. Ware...*

The days sped by as though the hands on a clock had been wound too tight, then released like a top. The extra responsibilities and additional scholars made for a long, tiring week, in spite of there being two other teachers. John's assumption of an increase in salary still remained without confirmation from the AMA, and with the bureau easing out of the south altogether, the missionary association now provided his main source of income. He had asked about it in his recent letter to General Howard and anxiously awaited a reply to that and other questions.

Answers arrived on October 23.

Flora Beach Burlingame

Dr. Bro. Ogilvie,

Yours of the 15ᵗʰ rec'd... Glad you went to Lavaca. In regard to those teachers—as far as to commission—are they Christians and competent teachers?

...As to your salary, we will not object to an increase—though this happens to be the hardest time with us since you came into our service. But as we expect you to remain all the year I would suggest that we pay you yearly $400 and expenses.

If this is satisfactory we will make the change for the year beginning October first.

Very Truly & Fraternally,

C.H. Howard,

Sec'y

Four hundred dollars a year plus expenses. This was indeed good news. If he were a drinking man, John would have celebrated with a shot of something stimulating. Instead he ventured out into the cool gulf breeze, marching for blocks, humming a tune. Yet beneath his rejoicing lay a subtle awareness he would earn this extra pay.

Chapter 33

Each day more political billboards surfaced about town and tension mounted. Anxiety and excitement simmered among the Negroes. The idea of walking up to the polls and voting epitomized the very concept of freedom and made it a reality.

John could feel it in the classroom, especially among his evening scholars. "Don't forget, the more you concentrate on your studies, the more you will be able to prove your capabilities to the skeptics," he reminded the men.

"Mr. Ruby, he be talkin' at the meetings about where to put our mark on the paper," Washington Green, usually quiet, found much to talk about with only a few weeks remaining before the big day.

John's ears perked at the mention of Ruby's name. "When do you meet?" he asked. "The League, I mean." He was aware of the group that formed to assist the colored men with voting. In fact, he had just recently learned Louis was one of the organizers.

"We meet mostly Saturday nights," Alphonse said.

The League supposedly met in secret, but these scholars apparently had no qualms about an open discussion of the matter in John's presence. He was on their side. This warmed him greatly.

"Would you gentlemen allow me to accompany you next time?"

"I 'spec's that'd be all right." Washington cast an inquiring glance toward his fellow scholars and received several nods.

And so three nights later John stepped into the cool November night air and joined five Negro men as they walked toward the harbor. Low murmurs of conversation mingled with the soft moan of the wind, though no one talked much. John kept his hands thrust into his pockets to keep them warm. The remains of rope burn scars could still be seen on his wrists, but he never talked about them, or their reason for being there.

"Feels like one of them blue northers," one man muttered.

"Sure do," another voice responded.

The cold seemed to heighten the buzz in the pit of John's stomach. He glanced at Washington's face as they passed under a flickering gas street lamp. A taut muscle worked in the man's jaw and his dark eyes reflected a sense of purpose. There was no doubt these men experienced strong feelings, ones he could not begin to compare fairly with his own. Only a few short years ago they were owned by other men, property in the same class as the master's mules, and now they prepared to vote on an equal footing with those for whom they had once slaved. As they approached the warehouse on the harbor's edge, John's lips moved in quiet prayer, gratitude for his own background and a supplication for the future of these determined men.

They stepped into the huge, dimly lit space out of the wind, and though not heated, it seemed warm. Men of all color milled about. Somewhere over the din a gavel banged and the rows of benches began to fill. The banging was repeated and silence rolled across the assemblage like a muted wave. A single voice now resonated through the warehouse. John strained to see through the crowd. On a platform stood George Ruby, looking as elegant and upper class as he had the day John first saw him. He began to speak in a vibrant voice devoid of any southern drawl, his grammar and use of the English language impeccable. Full attention was afforded Ruby as he spoke of issues and contestants on the docket for the statewide election. A vote for Edmund Davis for governor meant a better future for the freedmen. Ruby for state senator was a given.

John pulled his watch from his vest pocket, flipped open the cover and checked the hands while he waited for his pupils and their friends at the warehouse door. Ten o'clock. The meeting had gone on for two hours, providing tremendous insight into the political mood of the state of Texas, Galveston in particular.

The wind had lessened by the time the meeting disbanded, releasing some of its bite, as the men retraced their steps. Stimulated by the subject matter of the meeting, comments overlapped one another, unlike the quiet mood that had accompanied their previous walk.

"That Ruby, he sure knows 'bout most anything."

"He be educated, like Miss Barnes and Mistah Ogilvie is helping us to be."

"He from up north. It be different there. He ain't been where we been."

"But he knows where we is headin' and cares 'bout that."

Their numbers and voices diminished the further they walked until five remained. John listened intently to the comments, still learning. Rounding a corner, their pace suddenly slowed. Up ahead, lined across the width of the street, a band of men moved deliberately toward them. John stopped. Washington followed suit, as did the others. A three-quarter moon in the night sky eased away from a cloud, its glow revealing white, angry faces. The line of men advanced until a space of only a few feet separated the two groups. One of the aggressors stepped forward, hands on his hips, his mouth stretched in a jeer.

"Well, look what we got here. A nigger-loving teacher."

John's thoughts on how to respond lay momentarily trapped beneath the rhythmic pounding of his pulse as he recalled his harrowing abduction in Lavaca. Then common sense and a prayer took over.

"Good evening, gentlemen," he said, his voice calm and steady. "Can we be of help?"

"Hah! Hear that fellows? Can they be of help?" The spokesman said, turning to his comrades. Belly laughter came from a couple of the men. The others stood scowling, feet apart.

"How about stepping aside, so's we can get by. You and these here darkies don't own the street, you know, in spite of what you teach them."

John made eye contact with Washington and nodded. Silently, the five moved to the right, pressing against a building. The white men strode past taking up the entire street, accompanied by a strong smell of whiskey. Each cleared his throat and spat while passing within inches of John and the others, the foul expectorate striking trousers and shoes.

When the laughter and vulgar language grew faint, Washington removed a handkerchief from his pocket. Kneeling, he began wiping John's shoes. "I's sorry, suh."

"No!" John said, anger rising within him. A look of surprise in Washington's eyes made John feel ashamed, and he laid a hand on the man's shoulder, fighting to control his emotions. "I'll take care of that, and don't be sorry on my account. We're all in this together."

For the remainder of the walk home no one spoke, though John observed clenched fists and lips set in a determined firmness. As for himself, he felt drained, and after entering his house and locking the door behind him, admitted he had not known such fear since the night of the fire and his time spent inside of that barn in Lavaca.

Louis was off to Houston on business, meaning John was alone. Sitting by lamplight, he read the Bible far into the night, solace for the ugly scene he had just witnessed.

Dawn brought sunshine and a more subdued breeze, the cold front having passed through. *Sunday, blessed Sunday.* Church school class and then a rousing sermon by the Baptist preacher kept John's focus away from the surly malcontents of the previous night. However, the scripture lesson caused him to leave the service feeling less than Christian. The words of Matthew 5:39 cycled through his mind: *"But I say unto you, That ye resist not evil: but whosoever shall smite thee on the right cheek, turn to him the other also."* By stepping aside and allowing the belligerent group to pass, he and the others had indeed turned the other cheek. Yet John felt a strong urge to punish each man who had spat on his companions the night before. For these thoughts he asked forgiveness.

When he returned to the cottage late in the afternoon, John spied Louis' coat flung across the settee in the sitting room. "Hello there," he called out. His housemate stepped from the bedroom stocking-footed, his shirt unbuttoned at the neck and sleeves rolled up casually.

"Good to have you home," John said. "How was your trip?" He sat and leaned down to unbuckle his shoes as he spoke.

"Tolerable. How did the meeting with Ruby go?"

At that moment John suddenly realized the importance of his relationship with this new friend. For two and a half years he had never been able to share his innermost thoughts and fears, not even with Neal, and certainly not with the Wallaces. Now the words came tumbling out. He told of the camaraderie of his group of pupils as they marched to the warehouse, the fine and convincing speech of George Ruby, the excitement of the men on their return, and the unpleasant finale. "They were drunkards," he said. "If they had been sober the incident probably would not have occurred. I don't plan to dwell on it."

Louis looked him steadily in the eye, shook his head solemnly, then said, "Don't be so sure, John. Things here in Galveston often appear calm and civilized, but we can't outguess what's brewing below the surface. Before coming here I served as assistant superintendent of schools for the bureau stationed out of Jefferson in northeast Texas. That area is littered with outlaws set upon ridding the state of freedmen and unionists. I never felt safe. It's better here, but I've learned to be wary."

***

The following week, John's thoughts regarding the election mingled with his lesson preparations. He often had as much trouble as his students staying focused on the Latin text or arithmetic problems. Then a letter from Samuel dropped him right into the political pot.

> *Dear Sir,*
>
> *We are looking forward to your help when we go to the polls. The election has even more importance to me now. There is an opening for Justice of the Peace at Lavaca and I aim to run for that office. I feel I am most qualified and many others think so, too. I know the Lord will be with me in the coming weeks. Pray for me.*
>
> *Your brother in Christ,*
> *S. H. Canfield*

John's reaction to this unexpected news shifted from pride to astonishment to fear for Samuel's safety. What was the man thinking? Capable and qualified, yes. But John doubted the general population of Lavaca would agree. Few Negroes had made inroads into public office, and though an admirable scholar, Samuel was no George Ruby.

John paced the floor of his small bedroom, slapping the letter against the palm of his hand. He felt a strong paternal urge to write Samuel and say, "Don't do it." Yet John had spent many classroom hours talking to his pupils about equality. No, he could not in clear conscience tell Samuel he had no right to toss his hat into the political arena. He would leave well enough alone.

November 30, election day, was drawing near, and John had every intention of being in Lavaca for this crucial and exciting event. However, he still needed information on names that would appear on the ballot there. George Ware had responded to John's recent letter:

> *...Was surprised to learn that you were not to teach at Lavaca this season, but it seems you are called to fields of*

enlarged usefulness. May the greatest success attend your labors.

Here, John thought, was someone who would know the best choices of candidates for the Negro men in Lavaca. He took out pen, ink, and paper and began a note to the man who had done so much for the freedmen's school there.

The wind kicked up again all week. Not that it really ever stopped blowing. Sometimes it was just more noticeable—stronger and howling like a pack of wild dogs. John observed the younger scholars always seemed more agitated on such days. They talked out of turn and the boys deliberately prodded one another until a scuffle usually occurred. Miss Skinner rapped her pointer on the desk often, and John paraded along the rows of benches so as to be very visible.

Midweek, when the group came in from recess, a printed billboard skittered in through the door on a stiff gust of air. One of the newer pupils picked it up and studied the words.

"What's this say?" he asked.

"Hand it to Adeline," Miss Skinner instructed. "She will tell us."

The girl reached for it and began reading. "A Vote for Edmund J. Davis for Governor is the right vote for the future of Texas." Adeline scowled at the words for a moment. "What's all this 'bout voting?"

"An important election is coming up," Miss Skinner said, "and this time the Negroes will help choose among the candidates." The pitch of her voice rose on the second phrase, and she smiled broadly.

Adeline's eyes lit up, brightening her entire face. "We get to vote?"

"Not us. We ain't old enough," said Violette.

"You never goin' to vote," chimed in Willis. "You is a girl."

"That ain't so. I will too vote."

"No, you won't."

"I's as smart as you—maybe smarter. That's not true, is it teacha? I will get to vote!"

"I'm afraid Willis is right," Miss Skinner said. "Even Miss Williams and I are not allowed to vote. Only men have that privilege."

"Ha!" Willis said crossing his arms in victory.

"It ain't fair," Adeline said.

John strode to the front of the room. "You are right, Adeline. It isn't fair. But I believe someday you *will* get to vote. However, one victory at a time, and right now we are glad that your fathers and older brothers will help decide who will run the government."

He heard the girl whisper again under her breath, "It ain't fair."

"Time for spelling," Miss Skinner said, ending for the day the lesson on voting rights.

***

John boarded the steamer for Lavaca on November 29. He had not received a response from George Ware regarding candidates. The November air blew in chilling gusts and therefore most of the trip was spent inside the vessel, stifling John's energy and anxiety. He hoped there would be enough time at Indianola between boats to seek out Ware and talk to him personally. But the steam lighter waited for the passengers of the *St. Mary* to transfer their luggage and immediately chugged up the channel to the Port of Lavaca. When the boat nudged against the wharf, John squelched a sudden urge to leap onto the gang plank and dart to the schoolhouse. Instead he moved in step with other disembarking passengers, increasing his stride as he approached the end of the dock.

"Mr. Ogilvie," a voice called from behind.

John turned and recognized the familiar face of the postal clerk. He stopped and waited while the man, carrying a heavy mail bag, struggled to catch up.

"Mr. Ogilvie," he puffed, "this is most fortunate. I have a letter waiting for you at the post office—delivered yesterday."

With a mix of relief and anticipation, John accompanied the clerk to retrieve the letter. It was from Ware, who obviously had taken no chances on it arriving in Galveston too late, gambling that John would somehow connect with the mail here.

John tucked the letter in his waistcoat and headed away from town toward the Chocolate Bayou. He wanted to read the content in private. As he walked, the scent of mesquite and sage brought a rush of memories and a sensation almost akin to homesickness. He found a quiet spot to sit, opened the envelope and pulled out four pages covered with writing. An additional paper dropped to the prairie sand beside him. Grabbing it before it sailed away in the breeze, John held it in place with a rock, returned his attention to the letter, and began reading:

J.Ogilvie, Esq., Lavaca,

Dear Sir:

...I Enclose you the Republican Ticket—all on one paper—for State officers, for the 4th Congressional District, for State Senate and Representatives, also for the county officer as clerk of the District Court, Sheriff, and also for the Justice of the Peace Precinct No.2 which is Lavaca.

The letter talked about specific candidates and expounded at great length on the inefficiency of the current county sheriff, advocating the Republican candidate for that office. He continued:

I am very glad you have come over so to be here at election day, as your influence will be very powerful for the Republican cause. The colored men of Lavaca are much more like <u>real sensible</u> men than here in Indianola for we find the colored men here are permitting themselves to be 'bamboozled' by liquor and money bribes, to voting for the democratic-whiskey-gambling gang...

John had to chuckle at the man's incendiary words. He lay the letter aside and picked up the ticket from beneath the rock, scanning the list of candidates. The names for state offices were familiar, being ones extolled by George Ruby and Louis. Some of those for local positions John recognized, others he did not. One puzzling point—the name of Samuel Canfield did not appear as an option for Justice of the Peace in Lavaca. Samuel's letter announcing his intentions to run for that office had rung with excitement. Something or someone had obviously changed his mind.

John couldn't sit still any longer. He had information to share and there were questions to be answered. Gathering up the papers, he put them in his coat pocket and headed for town. The emotions running through the written words in Ware's letter served to stimulate him, though he couldn't shake the nagging feeling that he was marching to battle.

Chapter 34

First stop was the blacksmith's. When Samuel saw John approach, he broke into a wide grin, wiped his hands on a cloth tied around his waist and reached out to grab John's hand with a firm shake. "Thank you, suh, for coming. I've talked to as many colored men as I could and we plans to meet at the schoolhouse tonight. I told them you'd be there."

That evening the school room bulged with eager men. The air smelled of tobacco and sweat, the atmosphere so charged John felt if he lit a match the place would explode. He had come early and duplicated the Republican ticket on the blackboard, but from the comments of the assembly it was obvious these men knew for whom they planned to cast their votes. From John they needed not direction but the support of a white man experienced at voting. John had never voted in America. He was not a citizen—a fact he chose not to reveal at the moment.

Though some of the men in the room were unfamiliar to him, most had been pupils in his evening class. When all seemed present, Samuel whistled loud and sharp, bringing the noisy throng to attention. "Brothers, as you all know, tomorrow is one of the most important days of our whole lives. Because of us, Texas is going to get a government what cares about colored folk."

A cheer erupted, and foot-stomping rumbled across the wood floor. For a full five minutes even Samuel's shrill whistle couldn't stop the jubilation. Once a calm settled in, he continued. "Most of you know Mr. Ogilvie personally, and those of you who don't surely know *about* him. This here is the man who taught most of us to read and write so's we can vote smart. He has come to help us." With a huge smile, Samuel turned to John, gesturing for him to take over.

"Good evening, gentlemen," John scarcely got the words out when pandemonium broke loose again, this time in a round of cheers and clapping. He grinned and held his arms up, motioning for quiet. Within seconds he had the full attention of everyone in attendance. He tried to look serious; the occasion certainly called for it, but he couldn't keep the smile off his face. These were his pupils, they knew it and he knew it, and he was here to teach one more lesson.

Picking up a pointer he focused on the blackboard and the sample ballot he had drawn. "Here are some names you might want to consider when you go to the polls tomorrow. Names of candidates who believe in equality for the freedmen."

Whistles and clapping erupted again. John waited, allowing the excited response to work through the crowd and cool to a simmer. Continuing, he expounded on the virtues of the candidates as per comments by Louis, George Ruby's speech, and the letter from Ware. The men listened intently, some scribbling notes. When John finished, he answered questions the best he could until no more came forth.

"Well, are we ready?" he asked.

A unanimous "Yes, suh!" filled every corner.

"We'll be voting in Indianola, the county seat. Malcolm Frank has agreed to loan us wagons. We'll meet here at eight o'clock tomorrow morning and walk to the livery."

Samuel joined John at the front of the room. "One more thing. We must keep in mind to be peaceable at all times, even when white folk hassle us about being there."

Subdued murmurs of "Yes, suh" scattered through the room.

Samuel continued, "Let's pray to Lord Jesus about tomorrow."

At his concluding *"Amen,"* more amens followed and a clear tenor voice began to sing: *"I'm a soldier in the army of the Lord. I've had a hard time in the army of the Lord, I'm fightin' for the rights in this army, I'm fightin' for my rights in the army of the Lord, I'm a soldier in the army of the Lord."*

All voices joined in, and goose bumps crawled along John's arms as he observed tears flowing on black faces. His own eyes stung, and he marveled at Samuel's control. Charles Howard had expressed concern that the new teachers might not be Christian. With Samuel Canfield at the helm, these men were certainly getting lessons from the Holy Book. *Surely, with the Lord on their side, things will go right tomorrow.*

John spent the night once more in his vacant hut. Long after he lay in bed, he heard the squeak of Joe's rocker on the porch next door. At one point, Mrs. Wallace called out, "Joe, you git to bed."

"Cain't sleep," came the reply, and the squeaking continued.

With very little rest himself, John rose early the following morning and joined Joe for a quick breakfast, before they both hurried to the schoolhouse. There, a congregation of restless men had already gathered.

"This is it," Samuel said, the expression on his face a peculiar mix of cheer and anxiety.

John looked around the group. "Where's Jeb and Raymond?"

Samuel shook his head. "I don't hardly expect them. Last night Jeb told me their master—um boss—on the ranch where they work, said if they took time off to vote they'd lose their jobs. That job is mighty important." His dark eyes sparked anger as he spoke, and a vein tightened visibly in his neck.

John felt sick. "If I had known, I would have gone out there and talked to the man."

"And maybe got yourself kilt," Samuel said, sullen-faced.

How many more freedmen had received such threats? John's blood ran hot as he pondered the question.

They waited until fifteen after eight, but the two missing men didn't show. Before descending the schoolhouse stairs for their march into town, John stood at the doorway and held up a hand for attention. There was no need to demand silence. This morning, quiet seriousness pervaded the group.

"Let us pray to God for strength and wisdom on this important day," John said. Hats were removed. All heads bowed for a few words to the Almighty, then, leading the way, John stepped out the door, every muscle taut with anticipation.

A hushed, prayerful state endured as they walked with dignified strides up the bluff to Main Street and on to the stables at the edge of town. Frank was waiting with two wagons. The men piled in the back. Sam drove one with John sitting beside him, and Malcolm Frank himself took the reins of the other.

A squall had passed through during the night leaving behind puddles and the scent of new mud. The wind tossed leaves and twigs about, intensifying the angst that had settled in John's stomach. No one spoke as they jostled fifteen miles over the rough road.

When the wagons pulled up to the courthouse in Indianola, John breathed a little easier. A man in military attire stood guard at the doorway. A rifle slung over his shoulder glistened in the sunlight. John clutched his own weapon of choice, a Bible. Not so visible was the constant prayer on his lips and in his heart.

Near the front steps, a column of men waited their turn to enter the building and vote. Every segment of the white population was represented, from businessmen to farm workers. John's group approached, heads held high, ready to join the line in proper sequence. All eyes looked to the freedmen as they stepped forward, Samuel leading the way. A cattleman, his clothes grimy and dusty from his pointed boots to a well-worn Stetson, called out, "Go git in your own line, boy." He motioned with his thumb to the left of the building.

"Yeah," someone scoffed, "this here is for whites. Go where y'all belong."

"That'll be the day," another man said, and laughter ricocheted through the waiting throng.

"Don't cause trouble. They got a right to be here," a familiar voice spoke up. George Ware stepped forward. "Ogilvie. Good to see you. I hope you got my letter." John grasped the man's hand, relieved to find a friend in this hostile crowd.

"Aye, the postmaster found me as I got off the boat. The information was much appreciated." He glanced about, cautiously. This was a risky conversation where they stood.

"Good," Ware said.

Though John welcomed the moment of congeniality, his anxiety did not ease, and when his students disappeared around the corner of the courthouse, he excused himself and hurried to join them.

A sign tacked above a side entrance read:

"COLOREDS VOTE HERE."

John clenched his jaw at the injustice of it. They could vote but this certainly wasn't equality. His knuckles clutching the Bible showed white. *Dear Lord, let there not be trouble.* He was relieved to see another soldier was posted by the side door.

The men from the evening class stood in line with a number of Negroes John did not know. All waited in an orderly manner, parading at a measured pace with Samuel in the lead. John positioned himself a few yards away, where he could observe but not be so noticeable. A couple of sheriff's deputies, guns in holsters slung on their hips, sauntered about, keeping a close eye on the voters, especially the coloreds. Their presence wasn't quite as reassuring to John as that of the soldiers.

At a table near the door sat a large, pleasant white man who asked Samuel to sign his name in a book, then handed him a ballot, directing him into the building. John choked up as he watched. It seemed like forever until Samuel reappeared, raising his hands over his head in a gesture of victory, a radiant smile spread across his face.

John stepped forward and clasped Samuel's hand with a firm grip. "Congratulations," he said. The emotion of the moment blocked any other words fitting for the occasion.

As each man in turn approached the table, signed his name, and stepped into the building to vote, it took a full ten to fifteen minutes for him to reappear. John grew fidgety during the wait, but guessed each was carefully studying the ballot before marking it. Gradually, after the first hour, John began to relax. Except for the few earlier remarks by the white voters, things seemed to be progressing trouble-free. Eventually, rather than stand rigid in the shadows like a sentry guarding his troops, he walked up and down the line, talking with the men to help ease any tension.

"Got it all figured out?" he asked Joe.

"Sure do, Mr. Ogilvie. Sure do."

A sheriff's deputy materialized beside John, right hand on his hip, close to his weapon. "It's against the law to talk to these folks here about voting," he said.

"He ain't doing that," Joe spoke sharply.

The deputy took hold of John's arm. "Listen, Bible-totin' teacher, I suggest you stand aways from here if you don't want to end up behind bars."

John pulled his arm loose from the man's grip, and walked with a resolute stride to a low fence several yards away. He leaned against the railings for support, his gaze never leaving the deputy who paced along the line of Negro men.

A damp fog crept up from the bay, curling into every cranny, slowly rising like steam from a hot bath, but bringing instead a biting cold. John pulled up his collar and shifted his feet for circulation as he watched his friends move ghost-like through the translucent mist. The cold November air did nothing to dampen their spirits. As each completed his historic journey from subservience to a decision-making member of society, they emerged through the fog to shake John's hand in warm jubilation.

When they returned to Lavaca, the men gathered together once again at the schoolhouse. Comments and individual experiences were exchanged, the mood as bright as the ringing of

Mr. Ware's tower bell. Wives and mothers brought potluck, spreading the dishes out on clean cloths across the benches and the teachers' desk. With doors and windows shut against the chill damp air, conversation bounced along the walls. The seriousness of the night before was gone. Reaching for a piece of Mrs. Wallace's cornbread, John stood aside, scanning the room and enjoying the atmosphere.

Joe approached him. "When do y'all 'spect we'll know who done got elected, Mr. Ogilvie?"

"Might be days—maybe longer—though you'll probably learn about the local offices sooner."

Joe shook his head. "I 'spects I won't sleep much 'till I knows."

There were moments when John wondered if the votes of the colored men would really be counted. There was much bitter talk across Texas against the radical Republicans pushing to get their candidates into office. Samuel had mentioned on the way home that the word *Negro* was printed on the top of each of their ballots, so there was no question, at least in Indianola, which box contained the colored votes. John could only trust the white men working on their side to see that everything proceeded correctly and all votes were counted.

A smiling Samuel approached John, breaking into his thoughts. "Thank you again, suh, for coming all the way to be here. It sure helped us all."

"I was glad to come. But to be honest, you didn't need my help. Every man here was capable of marching to the polls and voting properly. With your leadership, Samuel, the freedmen are doing fine in Lavaca." He looked steadily into the man's eyes. Was now the time to ask Samuel why he hadn't run for public office? John hesitated just long enough that the responsibility was taken from him.

"You may be guessin' why I didn't run for Justice of Peace like I said I was."

"Aye, Sam, I did wonder."

"Well, suh, it ain't real simple. Let's jus' say, I weren't ready." He lowered his eyes as he spoke the last few words.

John grasped his friend's shoulder. "Maybe not this time, Samuel, but you will be ready someday. Of that I am certain."

Samuel resumed his smile and turned to acknowledge a statement by a nearby classmate. John looked on, also smiling, yet understanding he had not been given a complete answer to the reason for Samuel's withdrawal.

Chapter 35

At home in Galveston the following day, Louis greeted John with enthusiasm, and even before he had a chance to unpack, he was assailed with questions.

"Well, partner, you appear to be in one piece. How did the voting go in Lavaca? Any problems?"

"A few minor situations—cat calls, that sort of thing—but all in all it was good. Of course, having some military personnel there helped. How about here?"

"The same. It was quite a day."

They talked well into the night, leaning back in the kitchen chairs, their stocking feet propped on the table. The lamplight sputtered more than once, and John kept turning up the wick. Louis began to nod off when the clock chimed midnight.

"Pardon me for boring you," John said with a grin.

Louis yawned. "Forgive me. I'm certainly not bored, just spent. I stayed up a good part of last night celebrating with half the Negro community at a party for Ruby."

On Monday morning, it was back to work. Before the pupils arrived, Sarah Skinner and Miss Williams besieged John with the same questions he had heard from Louis. They listened eagerly and he sensed an increased respect toward him for his endeavors in Lavaca. This welcome gave him a sense of belonging in Galveston, a relief since he still grappled with the awkward feeling of being a newcomer.

The children began to arrive, and Adeline Westley rushed forward. "Mistah Ogilvie, you is back!" You would have thought he had been gone for a month.

John patted her head of tight curls. "Good morning, Adeline. You are in fine spirits today. Does this mean your spelling words are all learned?"

The little girl released her hold on him and stepped back, looking up to meet his gaze with sparkling eyes. "Yes, suh. Jes' like always."

This was true. Adeline always knew her spelling words. She epitomized his reason for being here, and the warmth of her greeting reaffirmed it.

In the evening class, a new attitude seemed to fill the room. John let the men talk about how it felt to vote, to be part of a decision-making process. He sensed that even more than schooling, this act gave them purpose and hope for the future.

Everyone in Texas waited each day for the final count for who would be Governor of the state. John was as caught up in the politics as though he were a native Texan. A letter from Charles Howard, dated December 3, brought his focus back on track:

> *Dear Brother,*
> *I am much pleased with yours of the 25th. Isn't it possible for you to be elected Supt. of the S.S. or assistant, so that you can bring it to a higher grade?*
> *Please write me what you hear from Lavaca.*

This was a response to John's report written the end of November before the election. So much had happened since then he had to sort through his thoughts and backtrack to remind himself where he had left off when he last wrote to Howard. He immediately put pen to paper, spelling out what he had been repeating to everyone since his short but eventful trip to Lavaca.

It was Saturday, and ignoring a light rain he walked to the post office to mail his reply. There he was handed a letter postmarked *Indianola*. Inside were a short note and two newspaper clippings:

> *Thought you would be interested in these,*
> *George Ware*

John pulled out the first of the two articles and began reading:

> *The Yankee carpet bagger negro school teacher of Lavaca, that walked arm in arm with the negroes to the polls, having gotten through with his mission, left on the* St. *Mary yesterday. He has no further use for the darkies, having filled his pockets and accomplished the errand he*

*was sent out here for. When will the colored people learn
sense; learn that they are the victims of Yankee greed? We
fear never, until they have alienated themselves from all
protection with the people of the South. They just abide the
consequences, be they what they may.*

Indianola Bulletin.

If John had been a swearing man he likely would have let fly a
few flaming words, but he was more inclined to laugh at the
absurdity of it. If nothing else, this ridiculous piece of journalism
gave him insight into the volatile situation he had walked into and
out of without any serious incidents; more than ever he
appreciated that things had gone as smoothly as they had.

Still riled over the first article, he picked up the second. His
heart skipped a beat as the name S. H. Canfield jumped at him
from the bottom of the column and he quickly scanned the words
from the beginning:

*Justice Of The Peace: It will be seen from the appended
note that S. J. Canfield (colored) was laboring under a
misapprehension of fact when consenting to the use of his
name for this office. Since he has ascertained the facts and
the important duties devolving upon this officer knowing
his incompetency and the impropriety of his serving, he
declines the office and will not consent to qualify:*

To the Editor of the Commercial,
Sir:
*I desire to state that I only consented to the use of my
name for Justice of the Peace in Lavaca from the statement
made to me that there were to be two Justices and that I
could act in connection with an experienced officer. I have
now to state that I do not desire the office, nor will I consent
to serve or qualify for it. Respectfully, etc.*

S. H. CANFIELD.
Lavaca, Dec. 4ᵗʰ 1869.

John's fingers curled into a fist, crumpling both articles. His
face burned with the humiliation Samuel most surely had felt at
such a public announcement. John shook his head and stared off
in the distance, fighting back anger. *Samuel, you would have*

made a great justice of the peace. You and I both know that, his thoughts raged.

Thrusting the papers into his pocket, he walked away from the post office. He continued on for blocks in the drizzle, away from the city center, until he stood on the sands of the gulf. The wind tore at his coat and flapped the legs of his trousers, and wavelets rushed to his feet, receded then rushing in again. He walked against the gale until all energy had been drained from him, and he eased down onto the damp sand where he sat, head bowed in a prayerful state, simply listening to the sigh of the wind and the lap of the water.

I must learn to expect these disappointments. Acceptance of men like Samuel into the white community will be a slow process. He looked out across the water for a long while, the wind pressing at his eyes and ears, and into his lungs, bringing with it the scent of the sea. Then, feeling both renewed and calmed, he walked toward home.

John sidetracked to check on the progress of the new schoolhouse, something he hadn't done for two weeks. The muffled pounding of a hammer drew him inside the two-story brick building, where he found Alphonse and Washington hanging shelves.

"You gentlemen have been working hard. It looks almost complete."

"Yes, suh. It's mos' done, Mr. Ogilvie," Washington said, his face shining with pride. "Jus' a few more odds and ends and we kin move in."

"Do you think it will be ready by the first of the year?" John's voice reflected his enthusiasm.

"Don' know why not."

John walked the length of the large downstairs classroom, which would also serve as a general meeting room. His footsteps echoed across the well-sanded floors as he ran his hand along the edge of the chalk board mounted on the walls. He strode through a short hallway toward the rear of the building, opened a door and entered a much smaller area. This would be his office. *My desk and chair here, a bookcase there.* He could see it all clearly. Walking to the window, he gazed out at the view that stretched—interrupted by only a scattering of buildings—to the gulf.

Upstairs he surveyed the two additional classrooms. The intermediate and advanced pupils would gather here, away from the clamor of the larger, beginning classes. *Thank you, Sarah, for your diligence. You would be proud of the results.* He headed home in a much livelier mood.

Louis sat reading and looked up when John walked in the door. "Well, did you get lost on the way to the post office?"

"Not at all." He would show Louis the upsetting newspaper stories later. "I took a detour by the new schoolhouse. It looks like we can be moved into the Barnes Institute by the first of January." He sat on the settee opposite his friend.

"I looked it over just last week, and I think you're right," Louis said. "We need to start planning a dedication. What do you think about Senator George Ruby as a guest speaker?" Eagerness resonated in his voice.

"Aye, that would be grand. Do you think he'll come?"

"I don't know why not. It'd be good publicity for him as a new Senator. I'll ask him."

***

1870 was drawing to a close. Christmas decorations appeared in store windows along the Strand, and carolers filled the evening air with harmonic strains of familiar hymns. The trappings of the season reminded John of the successful pageant performed by his Lavaca students. He mentioned it to the lady teachers, who immediately took to the idea, and a part of each day turned into a flurry of rehearsals, sewing of costumes, learning scripts and songs.

All of the girls wanted to be Mary, and when one was finally chosen, twenty others sulked. To help soothe the crisis and keep the Christmas spirit on track, each of the also-rans was transformed into angels with a speaking part.

"The play is a little long," Miss Skinner said, as they sat together in the church hall after an exhausting day. "But I think everyone is content."

"There will be more happy parents, too," John remarked. "They won't mind a lengthy performance if their child has a line to recite."

Miss Williams agreed. "Now if only the wise men remember their parts, and Andy stops baaa-ing during everyone else's lines, it will be a success."

They laughed, and it was a good release from their hectic schedule. The classroom looked as though the wind off the gulf had whirled through leaving nothing in its place, a tolerable situation because only a few more days remained in which to teach in this insufficient space. The pageant would take place on December 23—only four days away.

That afternoon, Howard's response to John's letter of December 8th arrived. Its contents surprised and disappointed him, in fact, aggravated him:

Mr. J. Ogilvie,

Dear Brother,

... am glad that you assisted Genl. Davis in the election. We are still uncertain whether he is governor, but hope so. Please give some definite information on that point.

...In the general absorption in politics, is religion forgotten? Tell me about your S.S. describing minutely some single Sabbath. Do you have family prayers at the homes?

...Please do not rely on Maj. Stevenson to do all the writing.

Yours truly, C.H. Howard

John bristled. *Religion forgotten?* Howard had encouraged him to assist in the election. And amidst all the political activities, John had been elevated to Sabbath school superintendent, as Howard had desired.

Family prayers were another matter. *After the move to the new school and when things have calmed down, I will pursue home visits. Somehow I will find the time.*

The final remark in Howard's letter annoyed him the most. John wrote to the missionary association at least as often as Louis. He always took prompt care of his own correspondence. If Louis reported on the same subjects, it had nothing to do with John neglecting his duties.

As to the election, he had no definitive answer about Davis, nor did any of Texas, there still being some question as to who had been elected governor and ballots still being counted.

John sighed, laid his pen aside, and stretched. It was unlike him to feel this negative about a letter from Howard. He attributed his irritation to nothing more than lack of sleep. Yet thinking through the written comments raised his ire again. Reaching for his Bible, he read for an hour before he calmed down enough to pull out pen and paper to answer the questions thrown at him.

On Wednesday of that same week, John left school in the late afternoon for a quick meal at home before returning for his evening class. Drawing near the house, he observed a well-dressed man leaning against the door frame. The stranger straightened and removed his bowler as John approached.

"Mr. Ogilvie?"

"Aye." John eyed him with curiosity. He looked vaguely familiar.

"May I have a word with you?" The man asked. "I have a proposal which I think you will find very appealing."

"I didn't catch your name," John answered with caution.

"Tucker, Ernest Tucker. We met at a rally for George Ruby."

"Of course, please come in." John opened the door and motioned for the man to precede him, still trying to recall the face from that particular evening, now weeks ago, so crowded with new acquaintances.

"What's on your mind? My time is limited as I need to return to school shortly." John offered the man a chair and sat opposite him.

Mr. Tucker cleared his throat. "I'll get right to the point. We have a vacancy at the customs office, and your name has come up as a candidate for the position. The pay is good—better than you are getting now, I can assure you."

John almost fell off the chair. Where had *this* come from? He stared at the man, momentarily rendered speechless. Pulling himself together, he held up a hand. "You need go no further. I'm flattered at your offer, but I'm not seeking another job."

"You're not giving this much thought, sir. Accepting such a position would provide prestige in the community and perhaps a stepping stone to public office in the future, should you so desire, of course."

John couldn't help but chuckle at the absurd suggestion. "I have no political aspirations, Mr. Tucker." He stood and held out his hand. "Thank you, but the answer is no."

The man also stood. "Think it over. If you change your mind come look me up." He handed John a business card, tipped his hat, and showed himself out.

After his surprise visitor was gone, John stood in near disbelief, contemplating the short exchange that had just taken place. He thought of his minuscule savings and his dream of college. Maybe he was daft not to accept a more lucrative position. He shook his head and thought,

Oglivie, you cannot entertain such a thought. There are pupils to teach, a Christmas pageant to oversee, a new school is nearly ready, waiting to be filled, and how can I justify leaving for a better paying job and a political future? I must keep foremost what my goals really are.

Chapter 36

The pageant was a grand success. The children and parents loved it, even though Andy baaa-ed the entire time and woke the baby Jesus, who then commenced to cry for most of the program. After a bountiful potluck, the evening concluded with the singing of favorite hymns and spirituals.

Following the festivities, John walked home in the brisk night air, his gait in rhythm to strains of *"Oh, chullun, Christ is come to heal you of yo' danger,"* which rolled around inside his head nonstop. As much as he loved the familiar Christmas music of his boyhood, none of them moved him like the emotional songs wrung from the very souls of the colored folk. *"Pray that you may be reconciled to the Child that lay in the manger,"* he continued. Things couldn't be better; the uplifting evening with parents and students, Christmas Eve tomorrow, and the beginning of a New Year in the Barnes Institute following the holidays.

John and Louis both slept late the following morning—a luxury even for a Saturday. The ever-present wind brought with it squalls throughout the day, and John worked on a lesson for the Sabbath school class. He also took time to write Howard, telling him of the events of the past week, including the job offer he had received. *...And the institute is ready for classes. What a glorious place to teach with room enough for all the scholars.*

Christmas break began the following Monday. John and the men from the evening class transferred desks, benches, books, and other supplies to the new building on Avenue M. When the last remnant of the school for the freedmen was emptied out of the church hall, John thanked each man individually, clapping them on the shoulder and shaking hands.

He stayed behind, too keyed-up to call it a day. Sitting at the teacher's desk in the room for the intermediate scholars, his gaze scanned the space with satisfaction. "Thank you, Miss Barnes, and thank you, Lord," he said aloud. In a sudden burst of energy he strode to a crate, pried off the lid, and began to unpack. He was organizing books onto shelves when he heard the front door open and close. Two seconds later, Miss Williams entered the room, her brown muslin skirt swishing quietly with her steps.

John smiled upon seeing her and asked, "What do you think?"

"It will be an immense improvement. We are so fortunate." She picked up a few books and joined him. When the texts had all been neatly placed in their new location, John reached for a box containing slates. Glancing about the room for a practical spot to store them, he became aware of Miss Williams quietly standing nearby, her silence demanding his attention. He set the slates down and turned toward her.

"Is there something on your mind, Miss Williams?"

"Well, yes, Mr. Ogilvie. May I talk to you for a moment?"

"Certainly." He motioned for her to sit on a bench and he sat in the next row facing her. "Is there a problem?"

"I'm sorry to bother you with this, but it's the money. I haven't received any pay from the missionary association or the bureau for this year, and the AMA still owes me for a good portion of last year. I simply haven't any funds left."

John's thoughts rushed back to his early days in Lavaca and his struggles with delinquent salary. A slow response from the bureau was no longer a surprise, but the missionary association had a much better record at mailing promised pay.

"Have you been sending in your reports and vouchers?"

"Yes, on a regular basis. There must be a mix-up somewhere. I was hoping you could provide a word on my behalf."

"I'll tend to it right away. In the meantime, I will be happy to loan you a few dollars."

Miss William's cheeks turned a deep pink at the suggestion. "Oh, no, sir, Miss Skinner has helped me out. I certainly wasn't implying you should do so."

"I'm sorry if I offended you. My only intent was to assist until this was resolved," John said. "I'm glad you came to me, though I wish you had done it sooner."

"I didn't want to seem mercenary." She appeared flustered and hesitated a moment before continuing. "I just thought, in your superior position and all, you would have more influence than I."

John reached for her hand and gave it a squeeze. "Don't worry, Mary, we'll get this taken care of as soon as possible."

Miss Williams blushed again and stood. "Thank you, Mr. Ogilvie. Thank you very much." Averting her gaze, she gathered her skirts and hurriedly left the building.

John watched her go, surprised at her hasty exit. Picking up the slates, he mulled over the incident. He understood the woman's concern about not receiving pay, but was perplexed at her obvious nervousness in approaching him. She was a strong, capable woman—a trait of all the teachers who chose to teach the freedmen. *Do I come across as some kind of ogre that they can't bring their trouble to?* As he put away the last slate, he reflected on his impromptu grasp of Miss Williams' hand. A spontaneous gesture done in empathy, he suddenly realized it could be mistaken for something more intimate, especially since he had called her by her given name. He may have committed a grievous error.

John finished his unpacking of supplies and left for home. The first thing he did was sit at the desk and write to Howard regarding Miss Williams and her absent pay, stating it was of *utmost importance that this dedicated teacher receive her salary as soon as possible.*

That evening, John and Louis went over the schedule of events for the dedication of the Barnes Institute, now only two days away.

"It looks like everything is under control. It will be a splendid affaione to make Galveston and the freedmen proud," Louis said. Given to dramatics, he paced the room and gestured with his arms as he spoke. "Maybe you and I should compare speeches so we don't end up saying the same thing."

"My words will be succinct and to the point, and I hope yours are, too," John said. "We should let Ruby and the other dignitaries be the longwinded ones."

"Where's your enthusiasm, John? Now's the chance for your virtues to shine, and to speak out on what you care about."

"My virtues may be sliding somewhat," John said, thinking back on his private discussion with Miss Williams.

"What the hell are you talking about? You are the most virtuous man I know—it's almost nauseating. Sometimes I think I have four housemates, you and the Trinity." He reached out and gave John a playful punch on the shoulder. When John didn't respond in a like manner, Louis studied him thoughtfully. "Maybe you had better explain that last remark. You really don't seem yourself."

John told him about the conversation with Miss Williams and how he had on impulse taken her hand, a definite breech of principal-teacher etiquette. "If she discusses my impropriety with Miss Skinner and it gets back to the AMA, my job is as good as lost."

To John's dismay, Louis laughed. "You are even more naïve than I thought. It sounds to me as though that woman is smitten with you."

"No!"

"Now, John, you said yourself she is a strong woman, yet she was timid about approaching you with a problem. Money troubles are very personal and definitely something none of us want others to know about. Don't you see? If she has eyes for you, it would make it doubly hard to discuss it, yet you are the only one who can help her. Poor woman, love can be painful at times." Louis shook his head sympathetically, as though he were an authority on the subject. He continued his pacing with a sly smile on his face. "Fear not. If Miss Williams is in truth pining for you, she isn't going to do anything to jeopardize your position as principal of the Barnes Institute. Perhaps you should consider the whole picture. The lady may not be a striking beauty, but she is intelligent and admirable. Maybe she is the answer to your dreams." Louis spoke the latter with a hint of mischief in his voice.

John scowled, rose, and strode to the desk. He pulled out the chair and sat, trying to ignore the quiet chuckles of his housemate.

***

The entire staff met early on January 3rd to ready the school for the dedication. The women had collected evergreen cuttings, and with the boughs they crafted the word *WELCOME* in the vestibule of the building. Benches lined both sides of the large downstairs classroom, leaving a center aisle, and chairs were placed on a platform to accommodate the speakers. The air seemed weighted with the importance of the event.

"Six speakers, and three of them preachers. The little children will be squirming before this is over," Miss Skinner said, reading one of the printed programs.

"The parents will watch them. They'll behave," John said, hoping he was right.

Preparations were completed an hour before the scheduled time for the event. John and the others stood at the back of the room, surveying the results of their labors.

"What do you think?" Miss Skinner said, referring to large scripted words she and Miss Williams had posted at the front of the room. Framed in greenery, it read: *Malice to None, Charity to All.*

"Well done, ladies," John said. "Well done."

"Sarah would be so pleased," Miss Skinner said softly, tears glistening in her eyes.

And then there was nothing to do but wait, which was difficult and made the time lag. Unable to keep still, John swept up a few remnants of the greenery and deposited them out the rear door. On returning to the building, he encountered Miss Williams. He had casually observed her throughout the morning, as he searched for hints of her feelings toward him, either reproving or otherwise, in regard to his actions of the previous day. She looked plain and proper in an unpretentious gray dress, her blonde braids fastened together at the back of her head. In the bustle of readying the building, he had not spoken directly to her, but now with the two of them alone for the moment, he felt obliged to do so.

"I have written to Charles Howard regarding your concern and expect you will hear from him shortly."

"I wrote to him also," Miss Williams said. Her response seemed cool. John sensed no hint of affection toward him. An ominous chill trickled down his spine as he guessed what her letter to Howard might contain.

"They're coming," Miss Skinner's voice carried from the other room. Miss Williams hurried toward the vestibule and John followed, trying to curb a tightness in his stomach.

It had been arranged that he and Louis would greet guests at the front of the building, directing them inside where the ladies would show them to their appropriate places. First to arrive was the Reverend Reed of the African Methodist Episcopal Church, accompanied by his wife, a severe looking lady whose black dress trimmed in white resembled her husband's clerical attire. Immediately behind the Reeds skipped Violette Green, tugging on her papa's hand. The fifth-grader wore a white frock bedecked with ruffles and pink ribbon, a purchase, John sensed, that may have taxed the family's limited finances. Other children, too, appeared in new or freshly laundered Sunday go-to-meeting clothes. This was a proud moment for everyone.

Shortly before ten o'clock, a shiny plum-colored carriage pulled up to the door. The driver held firmly onto the reins against a lively bay as his passenger opened the carriage door and stepped down onto the walkway. Ruby looked very much the senator, his face, lighter in color than most Negroes, framed by mutton-chop whiskers. A striped bow tie added splash to his attire.

Louis hastened forward, offering his arm. "Senator Ruby. We are honored by your presence."

The senator smiled and doffed his hat. "My pleasure."

Louis turned to John. "You remember Mr. Ogilvie, principal of the institute?"

John held out his hand and received a warm, firm grasp from Ruby.

As the three men entered the schoolhouse, a hush fell. Louis led the guest of honor to a seat on the platform, and the other speakers followed, taking their places. The murmur of voices dwindled to silence and the Reverend Reed stepped forward.

"Let us bow our heads in prayer, as we humble ourselves before the Almighty on the dedication of this most wonderful house of education." And so the ceremonies began.

***

It was a grand beginning to the New Year, and the spirit of the event stayed with the teachers and the students for the remainder of the week. The new facility prompted good behavior, even from the most mischievous boys, and in the evening class John noted the usual weariness seemed lessened. Several of these scholars had assisted with the completion of the building and displayed a well-deserved pride in that fact. Alphonse especially made a point to show off his carpentry.

"These here shelves, I cut, sanded and put up level for all them books," he beamed.

"You just braggin'," Washington said good-naturedly. "I helped with the roof. That's most important, so the rain don't come in."

"Aye, it's all important," John said. "You did fine work, and with the instruction you are receiving here, you will be able to understand and read contracts and get better jobs." He hoped his words weren't empty promises, though he sometimes feared the intentions of the bureau and missionary association were too idealistic, given the anti-Negro feelings in so much of the South.

"Did ya'll see this?" Washington held up a clipping from Ferdinand Flake's newspaper. It was an article telling of the dedication of the Barnes Institute. John and Louis had pored over it the evening before, commenting between them that it represented the event and the new institute in a positive light.

"Read it to the class," John said.

Washington paraded to the front of the room, cleared his throat, and with great theatrics began reading. The first few sentences explained the affair and told of the decorations hung about the room and of the dignitaries present. Washington read on, stumbling over a few unfamiliar words, but for the most part doing an exemplary job. Those who had not seen the story listened with rapt attention.

> *"...The opening address was delivered by Capt. L. W. Stevenson, giving a history of the building, and the praiseworthy efforts of Miss Barnes in obtaining a lot, the total cost of the building, furniture and school apparatus, amounting to $9,000.*
>
> *Addresses were also delivered by G. T. Ruby and Wm. Townsend, on the importance of education and knowledge, and the large field for laborers in the work...*
>
> *J. Ogilvie addressed the children and young men. The dedication was well attended, and the audience exhibited marked attention to the exercises and addresses."*

When Washington concluded, the entire class clapped and cheered.

"We is somebodies, now. Ain't that right, Mr. Ogilvie?" Alphonse said.

"Aye," John replied. "The Barnes Institute is an important part of Galveston." He smiled at the group before him, feeling now a solid connection with the pupils in this class.

His relationship with the staff—the lady teachers—was a different matter. A strained politeness dominated their conversation in his presence. He wondered if the incident with Miss Williams was the cause. He waited anxiously for Charles Howard's reply to his letter and, more particularly, the response to that of Miss Williams.

Chapter 37

A week after the start of school in the new year, the postmaster handed John an envelope with the familiar Chicago return address. He pocketed the piece of mail, choosing not to read it until he was safely in the privacy of his home, and before Louis arrived. Once there, John tore open the envelope and hurriedly unfolded the enclosed page, rapidly scanning Howard's scrawling script, then sighed—not the letter he had expected. This was a response to one John had sent several days prior to the note concerning Miss Williams:

> *December 27, 1869*
>
> *Dear Brother,*
>
> *...Yours of the 20th here welcome. I like to know the details of your school. If you think it best, AMA might put a stove into the new building. Could you not raise funds for such a purpose there?*
>
> *We feel under obligation that you did not leave us on receiving a tempting offer. The Lord reward you....*

John had nearly forgotten the visit from Mr. Tucker. Well, if nothing else, declining the offer of a job at the Custom House pleased Howard, and the Lord had already rewarded him with a spacious new school. As for the stove, he supposed they could put one downstairs; however, except for the occasional northerner, the temperature seldom dropped to where a heat source was necessary, even during the dampness of the fog. He would decline this offer and save everyone money.

Three days later, another letter from Howard arrived. This *had* to be about the pay for Miss Williams. John ripped open the end of the envelope allowing a check to slip out and drop onto the desk. Retrieving it, he puzzled at the figure, $100, his pay, of course, but a larger amount than usual. He read the message, brushing through the preliminaries:

> *Miss W. asks for 15 dollars—I send you $100 from which please pay her 15 or 25 dollars as she may desire... I was a little surprised to find we were owing her so much on last year. If she is willing, I will settle with her by a promissory note at 8% interest.*

The two-page letter continued to talk about vouchers, the employment dates of Miss Williams, and a statement as to how the treasurer, Major Clark, had been extra busy. As John read, he felt lighter by the minute, relief rolling off him like raindrops on a slicker. The postscript provided the final hurrah:

> *Please thank Miss Williams for her church letter and wish her, with the rest, a Happy New Year.*

John set the letter down, leaned back in the chair, and between bursts of laughter he shouted, "Happy New Year!"

The door clicked open behind him, and Louis stepped inside.

"Well, happy New Year to you, too, but for your information this celebration is more than a week overdue."

John jumped up, cleared his throat and said, "Listen to this," and read the letter aloud, to which Louis showed no great surprise.

"Didn't I tell you?" He clicked his tongue in mock disbelief at John's concern. "For a man of God, you worry over trivia. Seems to me if you practiced what you preached, this entire debacle would have been placed squarely on the shoulders of the Lord, and you could have gone about free of worry."

"Aye, you are partially right, Louis, but after handing my troubles to the Lord, it is still my responsibility to resolve the consequences of my own blundering."

To this, Louis had no response.

Though John had planned to spend the remainder of the afternoon preparing for his evening class, he instead hurried to town to cash Howard's check before the bank closed for the day. A quick, early supper allowed him to stop by the teachers' home on the way to the institute.

Miss Skinner answered his knock. "Why, Mr. Ogilvie, please come in."

He stepped into the parlor. Glancing toward the dining room, he observed Miss Williams seated at the table. He had obviously interrupted their evening meal.

"I'm sorry to bother you," he addressed Miss Skinner, "but I have some news for Miss Williams."

At the mention of her name, the young woman immediately rose and approached him. "Good evening, Mr. Ogilvie. I couldn't help but overhear. Please have a seat," she motioned to a chair while she and Miss Skinner settled on the settee.

John would have preferred it to be just himself and Miss Williams, but obviously the two women had no secrets, and perhaps it was best Miss Skinner witness his professional handling of the matter. He handed Miss Williams twenty-five dollars. "From General Howard," he said. "I heard from him just today." He told her of the other provisions in the letter.

"I will write him immediately and tell him my preferences," Miss Williams responded in a soft voice. Her bosom rose and fell in a great sigh as she clutched the bills, and her usually cool demeanor broke into a wide smile. "Thank you for all you have done."

John quickly stood. "You are welcome. It's all part of my job. If there are any other problems, let me know. Now, if you'll excuse me, I need to get on with the evening class."

He strode to the door, opened it, and stepped into the night air, but before leaving turned and addressed the ladies once more. "Oh, and Howard says to tell you happy New Year."

***

"I'm not hearing much about a certain lady teacher these days," Louis said one afternoon.

"The salary issue has been resolved," John said, "and as for my relationship with Miss Williams, you missed the mark, my friend. I don't believe she is romantically inclined toward me, and she is definitely not the one I'm seeking. I'll know when Miss Right comes along."

In addition to balancing professionalism and an amiability with the staff, plus the day to day problems that arose among the pupils, the weather, too, brought challenges. John's initial unease about the school site being situated in a marsh proved to be a legitimate concern. Whenever a significant rain swept in off the gulf, the area surrounding the school grew soggy, and if the inclement weather persisted, a lake would form. Fortunately, the building had been constructed with this problem in mind, but it still severely limited outside activities and tested John's patience. When writing his weekly letters to Howard in Chicago, he often referred to the weather, prompting curious responses from the district secretary:

January 8, 1870

The idea of there being any hesitation about having a stove seems strange to us where this morning the thermometer ranges below zero.

And in reply to the damp surroundings following a storm:

January 21, 1870

Is any part of the house (Barnes Inst.) under water or is it only the grounds? How high are the posts on which it is founded? Could you not have a plank approach made by the Bureau to enable you to reach the building without wetting your feet?

John had to chuckle at the suggestion of a plank. One had long been in place.

"Tell him you want boots for all the staff, and students," Louis said. "Or better yet, how about boats?"

They made the best of the situation, and the scholars seemed undeterred by the inconvenience. The ladies refused to complain, lifting their skirts while "walking the plank" so as not to muddy their hems. John had to remind himself that the reason the land had been available was because no one else wanted it, and thus—mud or not—they had a school.

Outside of the walls of the Barnes Institute, significant changes were taking place, not only in Galveston, but in all of Texas. On January 8, still waiting for the official results of the election, Edmund Davis was appointed provisional governor. Though this pleased John and Louis, many Texans were not happy with the situation. There were accusations of irregularities at the polls. A substantial number of registered white voters had not cast ballots due to closed polling places or intimidation by troops posted at those that were open. Radical Republicans who had encouraged the Negro vote were not popular with a large segment of Texas society, not only the Democrats, but moderate Republicans as well. John could feel the tension building since the election. In some circles he was respected and honored for his role as principal of the Barnes Institute, yet there were still many who chose not to associate with the "Yankee teacher", a shunning that seemed even more acute in recent days.

"Looks like we've been dropped in the middle of a hornet's nest," Louis said after perusing the paper one evening.

Though his roommate thrived on controversy, and John welcomed challenges himself, he understood his own role to be that of a peacemaker. Thus he found Louis's gleeful view of a *hornet's nest* unsettling.

"We may have encouraged the black vote, and rightly so," John said, "but we can't be held responsible for the whites who didn't go to the polls, nor are you and I accountable for any indiscretions that may have occurred."

"You are right. Now just convince Hamilton's followers of that."

"I plan to stay out of the fracas as much as possible and simply do what I came for," John said. He promptly opened a text book and began preparing lessons.

When Louis arrived home the following evening, he tossed a copy of the *Galveston Daily News* onto John's lap—a particular page and column folded and marked.

"What was your remark about staying out of the fracas? Looks like you have been keeping secrets from me," Louis said, his attempt at pretending hurt betrayed by a glint of humor in his eye.

John picked up the paper and began to read the marked piece aloud.

Chief of Police
The determined efforts to have the Chief of Police removed are, at last, likely to prove successful. Dispatches received last night foreshadow the early appointment of a successor to Capt. McCormick, who has served honestly and faithfully for the last two years. It is not known who will receive the baton of the Chief, the contest lying apparently between Mr. Ogilvie and a Mr. Ketchum. If there is anything in a name Mr. Ketchum ought to stand the best chance, as no more appropriate cognomen could be suggested for an officer whose peculiar business it is to catch such vagabonds and rascals as may be found lying

around loose in the corporate limits of the city. The Mr.
Ogilvie spoken of is probably the gentleman who has been
teaching the freedmen's young ideas how to shoot in the
government schools...

John almost choked from laughter over the last sentence. "It seems I have been keeping secrets from myself as well. Can a person run for office without his knowledge? How does Chief Ogilvie sound to you? I wonder if it pays better than teaching the freedmen's children how to shoot?"

By now Louis was laughing so hard it was several minutes before he could gain control of his wits. "I'll help you compose a response, Chief John. This is too good to pass up."

The two worked on carefully chosen words in lieu of the lessons John intended to prepare. Then he, himself, delivered the results of their labors to the paper.

The following morning when he stepped into the classroom, Miss Skinner handed him her blackboard pointer, "Here, Chief Ogilvie, is your baton. There are a few unruly boys requiring discipline."

Miss Williams suppressed a giggle. John welcomed the relaxed atmosphere tinged with humor, something he had sought and up to now had not quite achieved with his lady peers. If it took bad newspaper reporting to bring it about, so be it.

As for the unruly boys, they weren't so certain. "Is you really running fo' Chief of Po-leece?" Willis stammered, his dark eyes wide.

John sensed the law did not necessarily represent something positive for these people. "No, Willis. You can rest assured I do not plan to be Chief of Police of Galveston. Being principal here is challenge enough."

"How come you ain't teaching us to shoot," Henry said, eyeing John with suspicion, mixed with a hint of hope. "The paper say you doin' that."

"You know shooting is not what this school is all about. The newspaper was making fun and also made a mistake. I am pleased to see that some of you read the paper. That is why you are here, to learn and become aware of the goings on in your community. Your assignment for this evening is to read the paper again and see if you can find my name."

The next day a handful of clippings were thrust at him as students entered the classroom. John gave Violette the honor of reading the rebuttal:

The Amende Honorable

Speaking of the probable successor to Chief of Police McCormick, yesterday morning, we mentioned on what ought to have been good authority the name of Mr. Ogilvie, in connection with that office. The modest instructor of juvenile Ethiops disclaims all idea of having honors thus thrust upon him, and wishes us to disabuse the public mind in that regard by publishing the following card, which we do very cheerfully, and would be glad to extend the same courtesy to all others whose names have been used in connection with the office:

Having had my attention drawn to a paragraph in your local news of today, headed, "Chief of Police," in which the statement is made that the contest for the baton lies apparently between Mr. Ogilvie and a Mr. Ketchum, and as there seems to be an idea in the Local's brain that I am the aforesaid Mr. Ogilvie, I would state for the benefit of your readers that, "the gentleman who has been teaching the freedmen's young ideas how to shoot" has never been, and is not now a candidate for any office.

Respectfully, J. OGILVIE

"That story made my papa mad," Willis said. "He said they's making fun of us and callin' us names."

"My papa says it's about who we *was* not who we *is*," Violette added.

"What is Ee-thee-ops, anyways?" Adeline asked.

Miss Skinner gave John a sideways glance, which seemed to say, "Now look what you've done."

That had been John's exact thoughts when he read the amendment to the Chief of Police article the evening before, not knowing, of course, when he made reading the paper a class assignment, that the editors of the *Daily News* would preface his own response with such mockery of the students. He had spent a good portion of last night figuring out how to handle the consequences. This morning he felt prepared. Directing attention to the world map on the wall, he handed the pointer to Violette.

261

"Show us Africa," he said.

For the next hour he talked about their ancestry, where they came from and why they left Africa. Though they had undoubtedly heard of their origins from parents, everyone listened. At recess, instead of whoops and hollers and pushing to get out of the room, the students moved as one, conversation among them a low hum, generated, John hoped, by a renewed awareness of who they were, and perhaps some anger to propel them forward and prove themselves.

***

A new schoolhouse was only the beginning of changes to mark the months ahead. On March 30, 1870, Texas was readmitted to the Union, and civilian rule of the state replaced that of the military.

"This is a banner day for Texas," John said, as he and Louis discussed the situation that evening. "But what does it mean for you, Major, and the bureau in general? And what about your support of the schools for the freedmen? Do the benevolent societies go it alone now?"

"That's a good question. Rumors from the government say we will be out by the end of this school term."

"I suppose I'll be finding a new housemate," John said with a sinking feeling. "Where will you go? What will you do?"

"I'm still thinking on that," Louis said. "But, rest assured, you will be the first to know."

On April 28, Edmund Davis was inaugurated as governor of the state, official acknowledgment of his eight hundred vote win finally conceded by the opposition. John made a point to see that the students were aware of the history-making events taking place around them. The restless young men in his evening class saw the changes as exciting, yet frightening. It was often difficult to anticipate what each political twist and turn would mean to them in their new status as freedmen.

Chapter 38

Though the bureau was phasing out, the missionary association made it known it had no intention of abandoning the schools and teachers now in place to educate the freedmen.

The port of Galveston served as a stopping off point for AMA personnel and teachers en route from the north to various destinations in Texas. They sometimes spent a night or two at the teachers' home, and John and Louis were usually invited for a meal when such guests passed through. On one such occasion, John particularly enjoyed an evening with Mrs. Julia Nelson from his adopted state of Minnesota. She was a no-nonsense widow who carried a little extra weight. Dressed in a no frills blue frock, she sat straight with an air of self-assurance.

John liked her immediately. "You'll find living in Texas a different experience," he told her.

"I've had a hint of that already. I taught briefly in Houston last year, then had to leave due to illness. But I am well now and ready to start again." She met John's gaze with confidence.

"In Houston?" he asked.

"No, I have been assigned to Columbus—at a school by myself." An eagerness snapped in her eyes, and John sensed a stoicism that would pull her through difficult times.

Later that evening, back in their own home, Louis remarked, "Mrs. Nelson has a challenge ahead of her, but she seems intelligent, and highly capable."

John agreed, though he knew from his experience of teaching alone that she was in for tough times. That night as he knelt by his bed, he offered special prayers for her.

With the end of the spring term in sight, John felt good about the institute. He had a new building and a dependable staff. Enrollment was up, and there could well be more pupils in the fall. A third teacher would be necessary. He was preparing a geography lesson late one afternoon and concentrating on the wall map when the sound of footsteps caused him to turn. Miss Williams had entered the room. In her hand she held the pointer so helpful when using the map.

"You'll need this. I mislaid it earlier today and just now remembered where I had placed it." She handed the long wooden rod to John.

He took it from her. "Thank you. I hadn't missed it yet, but certainly would have."

Miss Williams made no move to leave, standing with her hands clasped firmly together at her waist. "Mr. Ogilvie, I'm not certain I will be able to continue here for the new school term."

This unexpected statement jolted John. "I'm sorry to hear that. Is there a problem we can work out?"

She hesitated a moment before replying, staring out the window as though her thoughts had flown elsewhere. Returning her gaze to him, she sighed. "I simply need a change. The day to day work with very little break—sometimes it's just too much."

John was reminded of Sarah Barnes and the toll the school took on her health. Of course she'd had the additional stress of pushing for the new building and all the complications that entailed. Still, working daily with the students, plus the added burden of criticism from the general public, at times required an unreasonable endurance. This had nothing to do with John or an unfulfilled relationship. It was exhaustion—plain and simple. He had observed Miss Williams being sharp and impatient with the pupils lately, but women, he knew, were sometimes moody, and he had passed it off as simply that.

"Will the summer not give you enough rest and change?"

"Perhaps, but I can't say right now."

John suddenly had mixed feelings. The prospect of losing a staff member was unsettling. The Barnes Institute required at least the number of teachers it now had, and finding new recruits could be difficult. Yet, if Miss Williams' impatience with the pupils continued, that would not be good either. Maybe it would be just as well if she left.

Before the end of the week, an even greater blow struck when Louis announced his plans to leave Galveston. "It looks as though I'll be going to Austin to finish out my bureau responsibilities," he said. "I'll miss our invigorating talks, but we'll stay in touch."

Louis's departure would leave a huge void. Aside from the loss of their special companionship, without a roommate to share the cost, John would have to find a smaller rental.

As the close of the school year drew near, other concerns pressed on John. The constant flooding beneath the institute was already necessitating repairs. Also, with an enrollment of more than a hundred students and many of them very young, he felt it critical that a fence be installed around the school yard.

These problems drew a flurry of letters from Howard. As so often was the case, funds were running low in the coffers of the Missionary Association.

"We cannot pay for a fence," Howard wrote. As for the water damage, he suggested, *"If Maj. Stevenson can assist in repairing the building, endeavor to have it done before the rains have injured the foundations."*

Major Stevenson being the bureau, John mused, and about to leave Galveston.

Time was of the essence as far as financial help from the bureau was concerned. In one letter Howard stated:

> *I do not expect that we can receive any aid from the bureau after the end of June.*

John shook his head, tossed the letter aside, and sighed. *What about salary for my teachers? Surely they will be paid through the end of June.*

But when the doors finally closed for summer break, no bureau monies had been received for the staff at the Barnes Institute, a situation out of Louis' hands.

The teachers scattered for the summer. Whether Miss Williams would return or not remained a question. John wrote Howard and told him the need for a replacement. Now as he worked in the classrooms, cleaning up and laying plans for the new term, the empty building felt hollow. The hot summer air clung to him, and the echo of his footsteps as he walked about resurrected his gnawing sense of loneliness that never completely left—an ache merely dormant for the past eight months due to a compatible housemate and the daily camaraderie of other missionary teachers.

In need of diversion, John often strolled to the port early on Saturday mornings. The activity along the wharves as the steamers and tall-masted ships bobbed in the water awakened the day with an air of anticipation. The bellowing of dock workers loading and unloading merchandise, the rumble of wagon wheels on the planks, and the ever-present breeze filled with scents of the sea served to take the edge off John's loneliness. On one such morning early in July, he spent two hours strolling the waterfront before heading to The Strand. At that hour, the walkways began to fill with merchants and shoppers, and the July sun made its presence known, bringing heat to the moist air.

John paused to read a billboard tacked onto the side of a building;

CONCERT

Saturday, July 9th

8:00 pm

An evening of music

at the Masonic Hall

All welcome

He studied the words a few moments, his interest piqued. He committed the information to memory and was about to cross the street when a female voice drew his attention back to the poster.

"Look, Mama, there's a concert tonight. Oh, let's go."

John turned to see a young woman in a green summer frock reading the sign. The sun cast hints of red in brown hair curled in ringlets around her face. She stepped aside so the portly matron accompanying her could see the words and, in doing so, glanced in John's direction. His gaze met hers and an involuntary smile sprang to his lips. The young lady smiled in return before she blushed and lowered her eyes. John's pulse quickened.

As he sauntered toward home, those hazel eyes kept reappearing in his thoughts. By noon he had made up his mind. *I will go to the concert. It's ridiculous to spend the summer in solitude when I could get out, meet people, and become part of the community.*

At 7:45 that evening, dressed in his Sunday best, he joined a throng of concert goers parading to the Masonic Hall. As he entered the building, he kept alert for the young woman he had seen earlier in the day. He found a seat on an outside aisle toward the back near an open window and continued to scan the audience for her auburn curls. His heart jumped. There she sat with her mother several rows ahead, now dressed in a becoming yellow, a sprig of white flowers pinned to her hair. As the musicians took their places on stage, the young woman turned around and her gaze met John's for the second time that day. A warm smile sprang to her lips before she looked away. *She's interested.* The notion caused a joyful shiver.

The crowd hushed as the director raised his baton. All during the performance, fans fluttered constantly in the warm, humid air. John was thankful for the breeze through the window and also glad the young woman sat directly in his line of vision to the musicians.

An hour later an intermission was called, and the performers filed off the stage.

"Refreshments are served outside," a gentleman announced. "The second half of tonight's concert will commence in twenty minutes."

John found her standing some distance from the crowded refreshment table. She was alone, *Mama* nowhere in sight. He approached, hoping he appeared calm and self-assured, though he felt neither. She seemed younger than he had first thought, perhaps only eighteen. There was a sweet wholesomeness about her. The neckline of her dress was cut discretely, and its yellow color shown in her hazel eyes—now boldly focused on him as he drew near. He was trying to think of something clever to say when she spoke first.

"My, it is warm, isn't it?"

John almost melted at her soft southern drawl. "Aye, but the music counters the discomfort, don't you agree?" He immediately knew his answer was ridiculously stuffy and stilted.

She smiled, and dimples indented her cheeks. "Why certainly, but I don't believe we've met. My name is Clarice. Clarice Miller. And yours?"

"John Ogilvie. Perhaps something to drink would refresh you. May I get you some punch?"

"Oh, that would be most appreciated," her eyes shone, intelligent and flirtatious.

"I'll be right back," John said, and he wove his way through the throng to the refreshment table. A woman ladled punch into two cups from a huge glass bowl in which floated an extravagant chunk of ice. John returned with slow, steady steps so as not to spill the cold liquid. When he broke through the crowd he was dismayed to see Clarice's mother standing beside her and each woman sipping a cup of punch.

When Clarice spied John, her dimples reappeared. "There you are. Mama brought me some punch, too. Now I am certain to be cooled down. Mama, this is Mr. Ogilvie."

"Madam," John nodded a greeting, as he stood awkwardly holding the two cups.

The older woman eyed him with caution.

"You say your name is Ogilvie?"

"Aye, Madam. That is correct."

"You aren't by any chance the Mr. Ogilvie who teaches the coloreds, are you?"

"As a matter of fact, I am."

Her eyes darkened and she set her lips in a firm line, a verbal response seeming to escape her. Her attention was diverted to a gentleman in shirt sleeves walking by with a tray, collecting empty cups. Clarice's mother plopped her cup on the tray, grabbed the one from her daughter's hand, and deposited it next to her own.

"Come, Clarice. You have better company to keep elsewhere, and the concert is about to begin." She gave her daughter a firm guiding push in the direction of the hall. Clarice threw John a last glance, her eyes wide with embarrassment.

Still holding the punch cups, he watched the two women merge with other concert goers entering the building for the second half of the night's entertainment. When only the servers lingered outside busying themselves with cleanup, John downed a cup of punch in three gulps. Methodically swirling the pink liquid in the remaining cup, he sighed, then quenched his thirst a second time. Placing the empty cups on the refreshment table, he left the premises. Harmonic strains of "Jeanie with the Light Brown Hair" rendered by a male quartet followed his slow walk home, until distance and darkness swallowed the remnants of music and gaiety.

Chapter 39

Church services and his Sabbath school class kept John's emotions on track. He filled the weekdays tending to business demands from the AMA and the bureau, shoving from his mind as best he could the Clarice Millers of Galveston.

With major transitions occurring in the state, and the bureau being phased out, letters from the missionary association expressed an urgent need for the Barnes Institute to be deeded from the bureau to the AMA. Howard had signed the new deed and forwarded it to the New York office. He wanted John to reappoint the colored trustees, asking for the church connection of each.

> ...*Please name one for the African Methodist Episcopal Church if there is none. We need only one from each denomination & ought to have some white men there that we, also, can rely on...*

John gave these requests much thought, settling on Washington Green for the AME representative. This reliable pupil had grown in stature in the year since John's tenure began in Galveston. He'd be a good choice. As to a *"reliable friend"* of the AMA, he would ask William Sinclair, now a member of the House of Representatives.

Correspondence and issues regarding the deed popped up all summer, and John dealt with them the best he could. And there was still the problem of the teachers' pay. He wrote to the bureau's newly appointed superintendent of education, Carlos Bartholomew, in Austin, requesting the delinquent June pay for his staff. He also sought funds for necessary maintenance to the school.

"*It will be hazardous to open school in the fall without the requested repairs,*" he insisted.

It was mid-August before John received a short note regarding the pay checks. Bartholomew wrote:

> *Dear Sir:*
> *In reply to your letters ... I would say that the bureau had expended all of the school funds and hence the reason that a part of the "AMA" teachers received no pay for June. We used the funds as far as they would go.*

John tugged at his beard and said a silent prayer. He had done his best for the staff. If there were no funds, there was no point in pursuing the issue.

He picked up a second envelope received the same day, recognizing Sarah Skinner's delicate penmanship. She would be telling him when she expected to return to Galveston from her summer break and perhaps include a word or two about things in Wisconsin. He broke the seal and began to read:

> *Dear Mr. Ogilvie,*
> *It is with great sadness that I must inform you I will not be returning to Galveston in the fall...*

No. John's heart sank as he perused the rest of her words. Matters at home prevented her from meeting her obligations in Texas. She did not elaborate as to what those matters might be, but her words were decisive.

John closed his eyes a moment and took a deep breath. *Dear Jesus, I can't do it alone.*

He stood and paced, his thoughts spinning. Both members of his staff gone, with only a little more than a month until the opening of school! He turned and retraced his steps the length of the room, stopped and gazed out the window, wondering about the future of the Barnes Institute. A strong rap on the front door caused him to jump.

A familiar voice rang out. "Ho there. Anyone home?" Without waiting for a reply the door swung open and in strode Louis.

John's despondency pivoted one hundred and eighty degrees. "This is a grand surprise. What brings you all the way from Austin?"

"Business, of course. Bartholomew sent me to follow up on your multitude of requests for repairs to the institute. I need to check them out, substantiate the need, and estimate the cost."

"You couldn't possibly include June pay for the teachers in that, could you?" He handed Louis the letter just received from the superintendent.

Louis read the message and shrugged. "Wish I could help, but it sounds pretty final as far as pay is concerned. There seems to be money scraped up from somewhere for maintenance, but that's about it."

John sighed, "I suppose a wee bit is better than none."

They left for the schoolhouse immediately, and John gave Louis a tour of the facility, pointing out the problem areas. "These are important improvements, necessary for the safety of the pupils," he said. "I've checked with the local hardware store to get a feel for the cost. I can give you those figures." Louis made notes, and after discussion, they agreed upon the supplies required.

With the business at hand completed, they chose to eat supper on The Strand. The main business district bustled as always. The street was filled with the clamor of squealing carriage wheels, neighing horses, and people laughing and conversing. A red-capped monkey chattered away, holding out his miniature hand, begging for coins, while an organ grinder played an off-key tune. The air smelled of a mix of manure, sea, and a variety of foods being cooked. Louis and John wove through the crowd and chose a restaurant where they had eaten in the past.

"So, how are things in Galveston? Your summer been quiet?" Louis asked, as they settled at a table.

They sat next to a window looking out onto the busy street. While they waited for their orders, a group of finely dressed young women passed by. For a moment John thought he recognized the sweet voice of Clarice Miller. His gaze swept from face to face, but he was mistaken. He admonished himself for the stab of disappointment.

"Looking for someone in particular?" Louis asked, a flicker of a smile working at the corners of his mouth.

"Not really. Certainly not in that set. I've learned teachers of the freedmen don't mix with the society ladies of Galveston. It seems to me you said something about that once."

Louis shook his head. "You need to connect with one of the female varieties of your own calling."

It was John's turn for a wry smile. "It sounds like a fine idea. However, that match hasn't happened, and at the moment, I am fresh out of teachers in Galveston." He told Louis of the letter from Sarah Skinner. "I cannot handle one hundred and twenty students, ranging in age and abilities from five to twenty-five, alone." He tugged at his beard. "You have any ideas?"

"The bureau can't help you there. Do you hear anything from Howard regarding teachers?"

"He knows I'm in need of *one*. I'll write him tomorrow about this newest twist."

"Too bad you can't get someone like Julia Nelson." Louis unfolded his napkin and placed it on his lap.

John brightened. "What a triumph that would be. Do you think she would consider coming to Galveston?"

"Not a chance. She's been at Columbus less than a year and has done wonders. I understand she's also asking for an additional teacher."

Their discussion was interrupted by a waiter who brought plates laden with generous portions of shrimp, crab, and Spanish mackerel from the nearby waters.

Neither talked during the first few mouthfuls, then Louis changed the subject. "There's one more reason for my being here, John."

John raised his eyebrows and waited for what was coming next.

"Bartholomew wants someone to check out the possibility of building schoolhouses in some additional communities as a final effort by the bureau to meet its educational obligations. We need to determine what the freedmen are willing to do towards building the schools, what materials are required, and at what cost."

John swallowed a bite of crab. "It sounds interesting. Exactly where will you be traveling?"

"Mostly Brazoria County—Cedar Lake, Chance's Prairie, maybe more. The thing is, I won't be able to go because of other responsibilities. So... " He hesitated a moment, his gaze fixed on John. "I suggested you would be a good candidate to do this bit of exploring."

"Me?" Startled, John laid down his fork.

"Why not? You are as qualified as anyone. You can't start school here until repairs to the institute are made and Howard lines up some teachers for you. What do you say? Can I tell Bartholomew you'll do it?"

"Where does he want me to go? I have very little knowledge of Texas, other than Lavaca and Galveston. Estimating the cost of building a school, now that's a different matter."

"Good. You'll be paid, of course, and if you are careful you should be safe enough."

John grinned, unable to quench the excitement of the idea. "I'm willing as long as I receive detailed directions as to where I am to go and exactly what is expected of me."

"As good as done. I'll let Bartholomew know and you'll be hearing from him. You should prepare to leave in a couple of weeks."

Louis left Galveston the following morning. John immediately wrote to Sarah Skinner, acknowledging her decision with sincere regret. A second letter went to Howard requesting an additional teacher and telling him of the repairs about to take place at the Institute and about Bartholomew's request.

He walked the messages to the post office with new energy to his steps. The more he thought about Louis's proposal, the more eager he was to set out on the trip. It was a worthwhile venture and would counter the monotony of the summer.

A week later he received a long letter from Bartholomew giving specific instructions. The superintendent went into great detail on getting building supplies to the various locations once it was determined to go ahead with the projects, suggesting lumber could be shipped up either the Brazos or Bernard Rivers.

John suddenly had plenty to do to get things in order for school to start when he returned. Before he knew it, the two weeks had rushed by and it was time to leave. On his way to catch the train for Houston, the first leg of his journey, he stopped by the schoolhouse one last time.

Standing in front of the building, he squinted up at the morning sun where Washington Green knelt on the school roof affixing gutters to the eaves. "It's looking good, Washington."

"Yes, suh. The next squall what comes this way won't be running down our necks. Least ways not when we stands at the doorway." Washington wiped his sweaty palms on his trousers, descended a ladder and approached John.

"The lumber for the fence is come, too. Tomorrow I'll git to working on that." Washington glanced down at John's carpetbag and a look of alarm sprang to his eyes. "You ain't leavin' us, is you?"

"After all the work you've done to get things ship-shape? Not a chance. I'll be gone for a wee while on business before the fall term starts."

"When you git back, that fence will be all up." Washington grinned, rubbing beads of perspiration from his forehead with his shirt sleeve.

"The institute is much indebted to you, Washington. I'm on my way to find some men with your talent and willingness to build more schools in other parts of Texas. Wish me luck."

"Yes, suh."

John picked up his bag and marched the few blocks to the depot, whistling in time to his steps. His pocket held Bartholomew's precise instructions. He would also be seeking teachers for the Barnes Institute along the way. Howard had tossed that problem right back into his lap in his most recent letter:

> *...As to teachers we want you to get someone now in Texas—cannot well afford to send one. Suppose you take Miss Trussell, or if Miss Knapp or Nickerson at Houston are preferred perhaps you can get them. The colored man William A. Jones is also available if you want him. Use your best judgment and inform me.*

If John planned his trip right, he could find these prospective teachers and return with a full staff. The reference to Miss Trussell puzzled him. He didn't recall Howard mentioning her before, but the others were in towns he planned to visit. He'd see the two ladies in Houston first. As for William Jones, Bartholomew had set him up as a contact in Columbia.

Stepping up into the railroad car, he found a seat and settled back for the fifty mile ride to Houston. It was still early in the day. He should arrive in plenty of time to recruit a teacher or two.

Chapter 40

The three-week trip brought with it disappointment and frustration, but good moments too. John returned with no teachers, the ladies in Houston perplexed that General Howard would *"rob Peter to pay Paul,"* as Miss Nickerson had so adamantly put it.

As for Mr. Jones, he wasn't even at Columbia when John finally arrived. After conferring with a David Scott, another contact Bartholomew had set up, he left a message for Jones to get in touch with him.

On the brighter side, the possibility of the freedmen building schools for themselves in Hempstead, Brazoria, Chance's Prairie, and Matagorda was promising. Thus, as far as John's assigned purpose for the trip went, his report to Bartholomew was positive.

During his travels, John also took a sidetrack to visit Julia Nelson at her school in Columbus. They spent an afternoon sharing the joys and frustrations of teaching the freedmen, and she applauded the purpose of his travels.

"More schools. Excellent," she declared. "There can't be too many. These folks ache to learn, and it's the only way they can pull themselves out of the mire left by slavery."

She paced the small classroom as she continued with her passionate remarks. "If I were in charge of education in this state, there would be schools everywhere, and the educated coloreds would become teachers." Her voice rose and her steps thudded against the floor as though she were parading for a cause.

"And you know what else?" She stopped and looked at John, hands on her hips. "The coloreds and Anglos, and Mexicans, too, would all go to the same schools and learn together. That's how we would get beyond this...this tainted mentality of caste."

John stood and clapped as she concluded her fervent monologue. "Hooray! If you were running for superintendent of education, I would campaign for you."

"If I had the opportunity, I would do it," she said.

All the way home that particular conversation played in his mind. *She would make an excellent superintendent of education if given the chance.*

By the time John returned to Galveston, he had caught a cold and was running a fever. To be in his own bed seemed like heaven, and he was thankful he hadn't yet moved to new quarters. Twenty-four hours later, after a sound sleep, he felt well enough to venture out in the Galveston breeze and walk to the schoolhouse. Turning down Avenue M, he stopped short. A fence surrounded the brick building, giving it an entirely new look. Washington stood in front, brushing whitewash on an open gate.

"Washington, you were certainly true to your word."

"Yes, suh. Just like I tole you." He stood back to admire his work.

John scanned the completed project, smiling broadly. "I hardly recognized the place."

"That's what Miss Williams say, too." Washington dipped a ladle into a barrel of water, lifted it to his mouth and took a long swallow.

John gave him a puzzled look, wondering if he had heard right. "Miss Williams?"

"Yes, suh. She be in the schoolhouse fixing up for class."

"Miss Williams?" John repeated.

"That's right."

John took the front steps two at a time and pushed open the door. Sure enough at the far end of the room sorting through a box of books stood the familiar figure of Mary Williams. At the sound of the closing door she looked up and smiled.

"Good morning, Mr. Ogilvie. Are you surprised to see me?"

"Aye, that I am." His relief instantly mingled with a dozen questions. "I assume this means you plan to stay and teach. You may not know, but Miss Skinner won't be coming back."

"Yes, I do know. I heard from her. That was part of my decision to return. I wrote, but you were away."

John studied her a moment. She appeared to have gained some weight and the healthy color of her face encouraged him. "You look rested."

"I'm much better than at the end of the spring term. Mother spent the last three months pampering me, and I'm afraid I let her." She picked up a book and leafed through it. "So, when does school begin?"

"We were scheduled for October third—impossible now without more teachers. General Howard mentioned a Miss Trussell as a possibility. I need to locate her and see if she can come. I have asked Mr. Jones of Columbia, a colored man, to join the staff, too. Don't know that he will, but that would give us three good teachers."

A smile sprang to Miss William's face when he referred to *good teachers*, her pleasant demeanor a contrast to the impatient and tired woman she had become toward the end of the previous term.

That week John moved to a small, less expensive rental. It didn't seem like home, but he guessed the feeling would come eventually. The good news was Howard had already sent Miss Trussell on her way to Galveston. She arrived several days before classes were scheduled to begin. A short woman, younger than Miss Williams, she had taught for a time at a school in Victoria. John met her dockside after she disembarked from the Indianola steamer. She was overly dressed, wearing a bonnet and heavy cloak, and she brought with her what seemed to him too many boxes and trunks; but he couldn't complain; she was a teacher. "Madam, I am most happy to see you."

"The AMA must have thought you desperate," she said. "They did some reshuffling at Victoria and sent me on my way."

"Aye, we are in great need of teachers, and you will do nicely. Thank you for coming." He couldn't tell from her remarks and demeanor if she was happy to be here, but he certainly was pleased to have her.

By October 10th, only days before he now hoped to start classes, John had yet to hear from Mr. Jones. School opened just the same. John doubled his load, covering the advanced and night school scholars, while Miss Trussell and Miss Williams took the primary and intermediate pupils.

They were managing all right, but an unexpected article in the *Galveston Daily News* brought a new worry. The paper had a habit of editorializing and the freedmen's schools were often prime targets. This most recent commentary wondered aloud why the schools for the colored didn't employ colored teachers. John tore out the piece and enclosed it in a letter to Howard. *A restlessness is growing and I am still waiting to hear from Jones. Any suggestions?*

The newspaper story didn't escape the notice of those in the Negro community. The growing sense of a wrong that needed attention worked its way into John's evening class.

"Why ain't we got colored teachers?" one man asked.

"It seem only right," others echoed.

"You are correct, gentlemen, and we are working on it." The remarks cut John. He agreed with the concept of the coloreds teaching their own, yet he had built what he thought to be a strong relationship with these men. Now the mood generated by the news article seemed to be nibbling away at that camaraderie.

The rumble of discontent grew beyond the classroom. John was even stopped on the street one morning by two members of the Republican Association. "Is there truth in the story about you not wanting coloreds to teach at the school?"

"I've approached a Negro man who is very qualified for the job," John said, trying to keep his voice steady, "I'm waiting to hear."

"There is certainly more than one in the whole state of Texas. Perhaps you need some help recruiting."

"I appreciate your concern, but the matter is being handled by the proper authorities, and you need not worry about the quality of education for the freedmen at the Barnes Institute. Now if you will excuse me, gentlemen, I'm on my way to class." John tipped his hat and continued toward the school with a forceful pace, his jaw set.

On December 3rd, a message arrived from William A. Jones regretting he would be unable to come to teach at Galveston. No explanation accompanied it for the long delay in his response.

A few days later, six weeks into the 1870 fall term, a letter from General Howard contained the first encouraging words regarding staff vacancies at the institute. A prayer of thanksgiving formed on John's lips as he read:

> *...I wrote to Miss Stoneman yesterday, asking her to go to Galveston... she will be a popular teacher and can play the melodeon.*

Howard also referenced a Mrs. Smith as though John should know of her.

... she would be a good primary teacher and perhaps you had better try her for three months. We would not authorize more. Use your best judgment, you know we desire to shut the lips of all opponents and really wish to employ coloreds as far as it is wise.

John rejoiced at knowing a musical Miss Stoneman was on her way, regardless of her white skin. The reference to Mrs. Smith, however, piqued his interest and curiosity. She had obviously approached Howard, yet John sensed she was not affiliated with the AMA. Who was she? He thought back on his encounter with the members of the Republican Association. A feeling of unease circled in him. Perhaps Mrs. Smith was their pick.

He learned the answer in short order. It was mid-week and classes had adjourned for the day. John sat in his office at the Barnes Institute writing a letter to the sponsoring church in Muskegon, Michigan, when a knock sounded.

"Come."

The door opened and in stepped a Negro woman dressed in a fashionable gown. She held letters in a gloved hand and advanced toward John, her head held high. "Mr. Ogilvie?"

"Aye."

"I am Odelia Smith, an experienced teacher, and here for employment." She thrust the papers in her hand toward him.

John stood and smiled a welcome, though he felt a strange sense of ambivalence toward this woman who marched into his office with such an air of authority. "Good afternoon, Mrs. Smith. Mr. Howard of the American Missionary Association has mentioned your name. Please, have a seat." He motioned to a chair facing his desk. She obliged, removed her gloves and fussed with her hat while John sat and unfolded the letters handed to him. He began to read:

Sec. of the American Missionary Association
Sir,
I have the honor to enclose herewith testimonials of my capacity as a teacher from the M.E. Mission Association. I now ask from your association a situation as teacher in the Barnes Institute in this city.
I am respectfully,
O.D Smith

John raised his eyebrows at the reference which followed the introduction:

> *Mrs. Smith has taught for quite two years in this city and has I believe given earnest proofs of her fidelity and devotion as a teacher both capable and efficient.*
> G.Ruby
> State Senator 12th District

Below it, yet another testimonial appeared:

> *I do most fully concur in this statement of Senator Ruby*
> *James A. Shorter*
> *One of the Bishops of the A.M.E. Church*

John looked up. "Well, these are most impressive credentials, Mrs. Smith."

The woman sat stiff and straight, hands in her lap and her gaze intent on John. "Thank you. I'm a good teacher and ready to start immediately."

Here was the teacher all of Galveston seemed to think he should hire, and God only knew how much he needed her. Yet, he couldn't shake the feeling of apprehension.

"You've been teaching in Galveston?"

"Yes. The church has a school and I have been employed there."

"And what level have you taught?"

"Mostly primary, although I have had experience at intermediate, too." She held her chin high as she spoke.

John tugged at his beard and read again the letters of recommendation; Senator George Ruby and Bishop James Shorter were not persons to be taken lightly. Politics fairly leaped out of the written words. He swallowed hard in an attempt to quell his resentment.

"Unfortunately, Mrs. Smith, the primary and intermediate classes are already covered by teachers who plan to stay. Our vacancy is for the advanced scholars."

"Oh, that won't be a problem. I am a fast learner and can handle the older students. Why, I even know a few words in Latin."

"I'm not certain that will do. Many of these pupils are well into their second year of Latin. Furthermore, the missionary association has informed me someone is on her way here to fill that position."

"Is she colored?" The question flew out of the woman's mouth like a poisoned dart.

"No, I don't believe she is." He worked to keep the tone of his own voice level.

She glowered at him. "What do you have against colored teachers, Mr. Ogilvie." It was not a question, but a hard-edged comment.

He fought the bile rising in his throat. "Nothing at all, Mrs. Smith. In fact, I asked a Mr. William Jones of your same heritage to come teach and only recently learned he is not able to do so. It was a big disappointment."

"So it's black *women* teachers you find objectionable."

John sighed. "Madam, if you would like to take the class until Miss Stoneman arrives, I will be happy to have you."

"And how long will that be?"

"I can't say exactly. Perhaps two weeks—maybe more, maybe less."

She fingered her gloves, pondering the offer before speaking. "I certainly expect it to be longer than that. I shall be here at eight o'clock tomorrow morning to meet my students. I live just a few short blocks away."

"That will be fine." He knew his response had an edge to it, and he didn't care.

The woman put on her gloves, stood and smoothed her gown. "I will see you then." She left with the same determination she had entered.

John sat at his desk studying the closed door for several long minutes. The air in the room felt thin. He loosened his collar, picked up the letters to reread them, put them down, grabbed his coat and marched out of the building.

Chapter 41

John awoke often that night. He prayed each time, whispering words of repentance for his anger, and pleading for tolerance and insight, "Lord, can I be wrong about this? Surely you know I want a colored teacher for my pupils as much as Howard and the community want me to have one. You also know I can't compromise the education of these precious scholars."

The following morning he walked to the institute with a positive step. Mrs. Smith awaited him at the door. "Good morning, Mr. Ogilvie," She said, her jaw fixed as firmly as it had been the day before when she left his office.

"Good morning, Mrs. Smith." John tried his best to sound pleasant. *Surely she will smile at the pupils*, he thought, as he led her upstairs to the room for the advanced class.

She glanced around. "My, they's a lot of benches," she said.

"Yes," he said. "If all show up, we have seventy-eight scholars in this group. I have been teaching the class on a temporary basis and will assist you."

"That won't be necessary. Just show me the books they learn from and I can do it."

John felt a muscle twitch in his cheek as his own jaw became set. He walked to the far side of the room and pointed to a series of shelves. "History, Geography and Latin resources are here," he said. "These are the subjects currently being given our full concentration." He reached for a Geography text. "The assignment for yesterday was page fifty." He flipped the book open to the appropriate spot. "I usually write questions on the black board pertaining to the lesson and they either answer by hand or write on their slates."

"I will have them *tell* me what they learned," Mrs. Smith said, her dark eyes snapping.

John started to protest but caught himself before the words escaped. He pulled a Latin text from a shelf and turned to the chapter on conjugating verbs. "This is today's lesson."

The woman reached for the book, removed it from John's hands and studied the page, her brow furrowed. She set the book down without comment.

As John explained where they were in regard to history, Miss Williams appeared in the doorway. "Good morning, Mr. Ogilvie." A quizzical look crossed her face as she observed the unfamiliar woman.

"Good morning, Miss Williams. This is Mrs. Smith. She will be teaching the advanced scholars, at least until the AMA replacement arrives."

"A pleasure to meet you," Miss Williams nodded and smiled at the newcomer.

"The same, I'm sure," murmured Mrs. Smith. She attempted a fleeting smile before her glance swept beyond the younger teacher.

John turned to follow her gaze. Boys and girls were entering the classroom, the first to arrive being tall, muscular, sixteen-year-old Caleb. The new teacher immediately moved to the desk and busied herself with papers lying there.

Sensing anxiety in her actions, John trailed after her. "Are you sure you don't want an assistant for a few days?"

"I'm most sure." The crispness had returned to her voice.

John picked up one of the papers she had shuffled. "Here is a list of names of the pupils enrolled in the class. Not everyone shows up, but you can expect at least fifty. If there are any problems, I will be in my office." He left with great reluctance, yet hoping she would be less nervous with him out of the room. He whispered a prayer as he walked away, "Lord, please let this be right."

As the day progressed, he worked on lessons for the evening class in his office, straining his ears at all times for hints of what might be going on with the advanced scholars. The upstairs rooms seemed amazingly quiet—a good sign, he hoped. At the end of the school day, he deliberately watched for Mrs. Smith and approached her when he sensed she was leaving.

"Well, how did things go?" he asked with a smile accompanied by what he hoped was a cheerful voice.

"Very well, thank you. Those boys and girls are much happier with me teaching them than a white teacher who don't know their kind."

She tipped her head at John and whooshed by him toward the front door.

Miss Williams approached him, her arms laden with books. "Let's hope she is friendlier with her students than she is with the staff."

"She has the first day jitters," John said, remembering so well his early days teaching at both Lavaca and Galveston, "She'll come around."

With each day that week, the advanced pupils became less silent and by Friday the commotion was bothersome to the other classrooms.

"Are there problems I can help sort out?" John asked Mrs. Smith at lunch break.

"No, Sir. We are getting by just fine," she said in her no-nonsense tone.

An uneasiness about the situation consumed John. He pretended to ignore it Saturday, Sunday and into the second week. After school on Tuesday, while he sat in his office mulling through the situation, Caleb appeared at the door.

"Mistah Ogilvie, suh. Can I talk with you?"

"Aye, lad, please come in."

The boy stood before him, eyes down, biting his lip, hands thrust into his pockets. "It's about that new teacha." He hesitated, seeming reluctant to continue.

"Go on."

"Well, she ain't teaching us nothing. It's like she don't know what we don't know." Once Caleb got going, his words tumbled over one another as though he couldn't get them out fast enough. "It's like maybe we know more than she do. She nevah teaches no Latin and today she done whopped Nettie's hand with a ruler cuz she said Nettie spelled a word wrong, only Nettie did it right and the teacha didn't know it was right and that is not only not good that is bad." He stopped to gulp in a breath of air. "Cain't you come and teach us, Mistah Ogilvie, suh?"

Something inside John twisted up at hearing the boy's words. He fought to keep his composure. "Have a seat, lad. Let's talk this through."

Caleb slumped onto the chair, his eyes now focused on John, pleading. "What's they to talk about? I done said what I's going to say."

"And I appreciate you coming to me, but I need to say a few things, too. First of all, we need to give Mrs. Smith a chance."

Caleb opened his mouth to protest and John put up his hand. "Wait. Hear me out. She's only had a few days. This may be hard for you to understand, but it is very scary to be a new teacher in front of a large class. She needs time to get to know all of you and feel comfortable."

"But Nettie..."

"I'll talk to Mrs. Smith about the appropriate procedures to take in correcting a pupil," John said.

"But Nettie didn't need no correcting," Caleb shouted. His nostrils flared and he stood abruptly. "You don' understand."

"I think I do, Caleb, but it's my job to understand both sides, and we need to give her more time."

Breathing hard, the boy glowered at John for a full minute before he turned and stomped toward the door. John called after him. "I can promise you this, if things don't get better, she won't be staying."

The door closed behind the boy with a thud, and John shook his head in despair. He'd give Mrs. Smith her chance, but he wasn't going to sacrifice Caleb's education for the sake of politics.

John decided to confront Mrs. Smith first thing the next day before classes started. The proper way to approach her plagued him all evening and into the night, and he arrived at the institute the following morning wishing he were better rested. Climbing the stairs to the second level, he stepped into the room for the advanced students, looked around and saw no teacher. Hearing voices below, he retraced his steps to the primary classroom. Miss Trussell and Miss Williams were engaged in animated conversation, their backs to him.

"Good morning, ladies."

The two women immediately hushed and turned to face him.

"Good morning, Mr. Ogilvie," Miss Trussell said, a blush of embarrassment creeping into her cheeks.

John wondered about the subject of a discussion that had to be terminated so abruptly upon his arrival. "Is Mrs. Smith in the building?" he asked.

"No. We haven't seen her yet this morning," Miss Williams said. She turned to Miss Trussell. "Perhaps we should talk to him now of our concerns."

The other woman nodded her head and started to speak, just as footsteps sounded in the entry way. The three of them remained mute as two boys headed toward the upstairs classroom followed by Mrs. Smith. "It's about... her," Miss Williams said, her voice lowered to a whisper.

"Best come into my office for a few moments, then," John said. The two ladies joined him there, closing the door behind them.

Ten minutes later, the women left to tend to their classes, John having reassured them that things were under control, saying he would be talking to Mrs. Smith and, in any case, her employment was probably temporary. A replacement from the AMA was expected to arrive soon. He didn't add that he had heard no further word from Howard regarding the arrival of Miss Stoneman.

John's talk with Mrs. Smith took place after school dismissed for the day. By then he felt quite ready to deal with the situation and made certain he caught her before she left, positioning himself beside the classroom door. "Mrs. Smith, may I have a few words with you, please?"

She surprised him with an immediate "Yes, sir. We do need to talk," and she brusquely led the way to his office.

He had rehearsed a number of scenarios all day in preparation for this, and now she had tripped him up already. He closed the door and they both sat, ready for battle. He decided he would let her speak first. "And what did you need to talk to me about?" he asked, bracing himself.

"I told you when I came to teach here that I wanted primary or intermediate students, and you insisted on giving me advanced students and making me teach those horrible subjects and, and..." To John's amazement the woman broke into sobs. He had not counted on this. He groped in his pocket for a handkerchief, which he unfolded and handed to her. She waved it away, having retrieved one of her own from somewhere in her sleeve, continuing to weep, dabbing at her eyes and nose.

He could think of nothing to say to console her, quite the contrary, the only words that came to mind wouldn't help the situation at all. He remained silent while the woman cried herself out. She blew her nose a final time, then looked at John with what seemed to him an air of triumph, as though tears would solve her problems.

"I'm sorry the students and subjects perplex you," he said, "but it was understood from the beginning that the only need for a teacher was in the advanced class. There were no other options."

The woman's demeanor took an abrupt change and sparks seem to fly from her red, wet eyes. "Mr. Ogilvie, there certainly is another option. This school needs a colored teacher. No, it *must* have a colored teacher. If those white ladies can't teach the advanced students, then you can fire one of them and I will take her place."

"They are good, dedicated teachers. I won't do that."

Mrs. Smith stiffened. "Are you saying I am not a good teacher?"

Every muscle in John's body tensed while he strove to remain in control.

"No, I am not saying that. I agree we should have Negro teachers, but you lack experience and training where we need you most. I propose that you and I work with the advanced students together for the remainder of this week—longer if necessary. I am waiting for word on the AMA teacher and if she does not come it's important that you are ready to continue." He surprised himself at his own words and prayed he wouldn't regret them. However, they seemed to appease Mrs. Smith.

"Well, if that is the case, I guess I have no choice. Tomorrow you can join me in the classroom." With that she rose, nodded a goodbye, and walked out the door, leaving him amazed at how it always came across as though she were in charge.

The two worked together on Thursday and Friday and into the following week. John continually struggled to lead the class yet allow Mrs. Smith opportunities to teach. She failed miserably. Problems ranged from her lack of knowledge of the subjects to a complete inability to discipline. Scholars were ridiculed and rarely praised, though John set examples of positive reinforcements for lessons done well. The woman seemed blind to a kinder approach. By Thursday afternoon he knew he had a serious problem. Weary and worn down, he entered his office, sat at his desk, sighed and rested his head in his hands.

A soft rap snapped him to attention. In the open doorway stood a short, middle-aged woman. Strands of carrot-red hair escaped from braids circling her head, and her faded blue dress, wrinkled and travel-worn, bore mud stains along the hem. A well-used carpetbag thudded to the floor, along with what appeared to be a case for a musical instrument. The woman extended her hand toward him. With a large smile and cheery voice she said, "I am looking for Mr. Ogilvie, and I presume you are he? My name is Lizzy Stoneman. I'm sent here by Charles Howard to teach."

John's heart leapt for joy. In all his twenty-nine years, he had never known such a welcome sight. The fact that her pale skin was not the prerequisite color seemed of no consequence at the moment. She radiated warmth and self-assurance. Her handshake was firm and friendly. After their greeting, the woman plopped herself down in the chair opposite the desk, blowing a wisp of unruly hair away from her eyes. "I thought I would never get here," she sighed. "That is one long ride." She removed an envelope from a small, drawstring bag hanging on her wrist and handed it to John.

Reaching for it, he said, "I thought you would never get here either, and I'm sure you must be tired. Will you be rested enough to teach by Monday?"

"Oh, most certainly. That's what I came for."

Oh, glory! John swore he heard church bells ringing. Directing his attention to the envelope, he extracted a paper with the familiar letterhead of the AMA.

> *J.O. Ogilvie, Esq.*
> *December 13, 1870*
>
> *Dear Bro.— I send you Miss Stoneman, of whom I wrote. She will make you a good teacher for two months at least, and if you want her longer I presume she can stay another month. I hope you will also arrange to have one colored teacher employed—if not before at least after Miss Stoneman leaves. Or, if Miss Williams can have a school in the country and you do not need three teachers, you might substitute a colored teacher for her. I leave it to your discretion.*
>
> > *Fraternally yours,*
> > *C. H. Howard*

If only he knew, John thought shaking his head, *if only he knew.*

"Is something wrong?" Miss Stoneman asked, a note of concern in her voice.

Laying the letter on his desk, he looked at the travel-weary woman and smiled. "No, not at the moment. Not at least for two months. Right now we must get you settled. I believe Miss Williams and Miss Trussell are still here. I will introduce you to them and they can take you to the teachers' home. I'm sure you will find them agreeable housemates.

After the women left, John returned to his office to prepare for the evening class, yet he had trouble focusing on the assignments. His mind kept wandering to Mrs. Smith and her incompetence. The woman had obviously been deliberately hand-picked to fill a need seen by a colored contingency in the community, a group that went so far as to persuade two prestigious men to commend her. Unfortunately, someone had not bothered to check her qualifications. If John let her go, he could very well be forfeiting his own position. If he kept her, the scholars here would suffer. He weighed the pros and cons in his mind, though he knew from the start of the argument with himself what his decision had to be.

The following day, Friday, he allowed Mrs. Smith to work by herself one last time. At the end of the day he called her into his office.

"And what be the trouble now?" she huffed, refusing to take a seat.

"If you remember, I initially hired you to substitute until the promised AMA replacement arrived."

"The last we spoke, you wasn't certain she would come and so you said I could be the teacher. That's why you helped me."

John felt the hair on the nape of his neck prickle and he took a big calming breath before continuing. "Not exactly. I said I would work with you so you could be prepared in the event she *did not* come. She arrived last evening."

Mrs. Smith's eyes narrowed. "So now is this woman—this *white* woman—going to work with me instead of you?"

John took another deep breath. She still didn't understand, or simply refused to believe she was done.

"No. That was not the agreement. I'm afraid today was your last day. Miss Stoneman will begin on Monday. Thank you for helping out in the interim, Mrs. Smith, I greatly appreciate your assistance." *Surely, the Lord will forgive me one little fib for the purpose of sparing the woman's feelings,* he thought.

But her feelings weren't spared. "You lied to me!" she shouted. She pointed to the Bible on his desk, her finger trembling. "How can you pretend to be a follower of the Lord Jesus Christ and treat me like this?"

John stood so as to be on her level. "No, Madam. You may have misunderstood, but I do not lie."

"How dare the gov'ment and the missionary people send a prejudiced man to teach our children? Mind you, this is not the last you will hear of this. No sir-ree. You will be sorry you ever set foot in Texas. You'll see." There were no tears in her eyes this time, just burning anger that bore into John like augers.

"I'm sorry. I truly am," but his words, spoken to her back, went unheard as she ran from the room. He slumped to his chair, exhausted, not only because of the scene just played out, but from all the sleepless nights since the woman had first appeared in his office. Well, he had come full circle now, from accused of being a "nigger" lover and having his life threatened because of loyalty to his scholars, to this accusation of being prejudiced against the very people he had learned to love. As to her threat? With her prestigious backing, his job could be as good as gone.

Chapter 42

John sorely missed the companionship of Louis that long weekend. Writing the particulars to Charles Howard had to compensate for the actual presence of someone to discuss the events with. In many ways, a great weight had been lifted from his shoulders, but he couldn't shake the feeling that his decision to fire Mrs. Smith would come back to haunt him.

Nonetheless, Lizzie Stoneman's arrival in mid-December could not have been more timely. John noted how the students took immediately to her. She had a motherly quality about her, and the fact that she played the melodeon sweetened the atmosphere even more. The Christmas pageantry was upon them and her musical prowess added to the festivities.

"Do you play carols?" John asked

"I play anything you want," she said with good cheer and not a hint of arrogance.

"Kin you play 'Oh, Chullun, Christ is Come'?" Violette asked, her dark eyes dancing.

"Can you show me how it goes?"

The girl's clear voice began singing what John had learned was a song once chanted long ago by colonial slave women.

Oh, chullun, Christ is come to heal you of yo' danger.

Other students joined in. *Pray that you may be reconciled to the Child that lays in the manger.*

Miss Stoneman squeezed the bellows of the melodeon, choosing the appropriate chords and picking up the last few phrases, then the entire song was repeated by everyone, including John. Each day for the remainder of the school year, he ordered a grand assembly in the largest room for the singing of carols. The walls still seemed to hum from the goodness of it well into the evenings. Christmas break, 1870, at the Barnes Institute began on a strong note.

Still, the matter of Mrs. Smith's dismissal hung heavy in John's mind. Letters from Howard, though always supportive of his decision, continued to encourage the hiring of a colored teacher when a vacancy occurred. John thought of his able assistants in Lavaca, Samuel and Mrs. Wallace. There must be more out there like them; however even they would not be capable of teaching the advanced classes. There simply hadn't been time for many of the Negroes to master those subjects. Miss Williams and Miss Trussell themselves would be hard pressed to do so. More than that, John sensed the problem was not going to be solved by simply finding another colored teacher.

On February 16, a Wednesday, John hiked to the post office to pick up mail. The wind blew colder than usual, accompanied by a foggy dampness, the kind of weather that always made him think of Scotland and bring with it a stab of homesickness. As he entered the building the wind pulled the door from his fingers, slamming it shut behind him.

"More blustery than usual, eh Mr. Ogilvie," the postmaster said.

"Reminds me of my boyhood. You don't happen to have a letter for me from Scotland, do you?"

"No, but you have a registered letter from your friend in Chicago. Looks important. Gotta sign for this one." He dipped a pen in ink and handed it to John along with a printed form.

John scratched his signature and took the bulky envelope, puzzled. Never before had Howard sent correspondence by registered mail. For one horrible moment he wondered if he had been relieved of his job. Ever since early December, that possibility had been hovering over him. Yet nothing from the AMA had even so much as hinted at it. Tucking the envelope securely under his coat, he leaned into the wind and hurried home.

Once inside, the door secured against the wind, John extracted the envelope from the safety of his coat, pulled out a chair and sat at the table. He carefully opened the seal revealing two pieces of paper. The first, legal-sized and official looking, baffled him. The heading read Galveston, January 8, 1871—originating from here more than a month ago and returned to him by way of Chicago.

He read on:

At a meeting of the Republican Association held in this city on the 23rd November 1870, the following resolutions were offered by Judge Nelson, and unanimously adopted.

"Whereas the Barnes Institute is a public pay school, largely patronized by the colored citizens of this county, and partly built by said citizens,

And whereas during the entire administration of said school for a period of years past, colored teachers have been especially ignored in said Institute,

And whereas there are at this time living in this county competent teachers in every way qualified for duty in said Barnes Institute, who because of the invidiousness of the managers of said institute (said managers being understood to be the American Missionary Association) are debarred from the exercise of their vocation in said institute,

Therefore—resolved that the Republican Association of Galveston, ever mindful of the rights and privileges of a large portion of its members, do reprobate the actions of said managers of Barnes Institute aforesaid and recommend to the former patrons of said institute an entire avoidance of the same until justice be done, honorably and fully towards teachers herein mentioned.

On motion they were unanimously adopted.

To the Secretary of the American Missionary Association.

I beg to transmit with these resolutions an application from Mrs. Smith for a position as teacher in Barnes Institute. Compliance with her request for an appointment will go far toward removing a disagreeable impression resting on the minds of the colored citizens of Galveston, which the resolutions accompanying this indicate.

Your very obedient servant,
Frank Webb, Editor, Galveston Republican

A chill crawled into every part of John's body. In his hand lay the reason for the entire debacle with Mrs. Smith—beginning way back in November. He read through the resolution once again, shaking his head at the inclusion of such negative words as *invidiousness, debarred, reprobate* and *disagreeable*. The way this had been handled, without so much as approaching him in person for a discussion on the issue, left a bad taste in his mouth. Laying the first document aside, he scanned the second. Covered with writing on both sides, he quickly surmised it contained four separate messages, each with its own date, and written by four individuals: Frank Webb, O.O. Howard, George Whipple, and Charles Howard. This paper had been making the rounds for weeks and had only now caught up with him.

The first three notes simply passed the resolution from one hand to the next. The fourth, and longest, was from Charles Howard. As John read the words, his tension eased. Here was the standard response from the man, trusting John's decisions as always. Though Howard reiterated the need for a colored teacher, he left it up to John's discretion. He once again recommended W.A. Jones, whom Howard still seemed to think was willing to teach at the institute, then added "*but you doubtless have other candidates in view...*"

John's attention turned once more to the resolution from the Republican Association. He had met Frank Webb, a colored man, at a Union League meeting and he seemed most congenial. John learned he was originally from Jamaica and worked for the federal government in some capacity before coming to Texas. He now edited a weekly paper, the *Republican*. Educated and articulate, he was very good at drawing up these resolutions which appeared often in his publication.

John paced the room in circles until he felt lightheaded. If he had seen this document earlier would it have influenced his decision whether or not to hire Mrs. Smith permanently? Pausing before a window he stared out at the community of Galveston. *No, it would not have mattered. I would have done the same under any circumstances.* It was, in fact, a relief to know where and how the attempt to place Mrs. Smith had come about.

He resumed pacing while he sorted through the tangle of thoughts on the subject. There was more at stake here than the good name of the Barnes Institute. The best teachers and education for the freedmen was the highest priority, of course, but the AMA had been tarnished in the process, John's name in particular. Grabbing his coat, he marched out into the wind toward the office of the *Galveston Republican*.

Rain added to the blustery weather, and by the time John reached his destination his outerwear was soaked through. Upon entering the building, he was assailed by the smell of ink and the clank and hum of a printing press. A man sat on a high stool hunkered over a counter, concentrating on setting type, while another worker stood behind the press, methodically feeding newsprint to the mechanical monster.

"I'm looking for Mr. Webb," John shouted over the din. "My name is John Ogilvie."

The man on the stool looked up and motioned with his head toward a door in the back. John approached and knocked firmly.

"Come," a voice bellowed.

John turned the knob and entered the small, stuffy room, his stride as confident and businesslike as he could muster. This had to go well. He closed the door to shut out the noise. A short, balding black man rose from behind a desk to greet him, pulling an unlit cigar from his mouth, he motioned John to sit. "What's your business, mister..."

"Ogilvie. John Ogilvie of the Barnes Institute."

"Ah, yes, of course. And how may I help you?" Mr. Webb stuck the cigar back between his teeth and returned to his chair.

John sensed the query was merely a formality. Surely the man knew exactly why he was here. Truthfully, he was surprised that, after Mrs. Smith had been let go, Mr. Webb hadn't initiated contact with him, demanding an explanation as to why the woman had been fired. *Well, I am ready to give my side of the story*, he thought.

Amazed at his inner calm, John pulled the papers received in the day's mail from his waistcoat pocket. "I only today received this resolution regarding the hiring of a colored teacher for the institute. I feel there is a misunderstanding about our intent that needs to be discussed."

The man removed the cigar from his mouth once again, reached for the paper, studied it and then handed it back to John. "Ah, yes. Didn't Mrs. Smith approach you about a position?"

The question took John aback. "Aye, she did. The only vacancy we had at the time was for the advanced pupils, and though she said she preferred the primary grades, she insisted she could teach the older scholars. I allowed her to work with them for a couple of weeks, but unfortunately, she lacked the training required and I had to let her go. It had nothing to do with her race. It had to do with what was best for our scholars."

Mr. Webb sucked on the cigar and studied John for a moment. He removed the brown stub from his mouth and cleared his throat. "I was not aware of that," he said, frowning. "And did you hire someone else for the position? A colored person? This is a big issue, you know. Your school should be required to have colored teachers."

Mrs. Smith hadn't told them after all. He couldn't believe it. Yet as he thought about it, the dismissal was undoubtedly a big embarrassment. After she cooled down from her threats, she obviously couldn't admit to those who had sent her that she couldn't handle the job. For a split-second, John felt sorry for her. He leaned forward in his chair.

"Yes and no. A very capable teacher from the north, white, was already on her way to Galveston, sent by the AMA before Mrs. Smith appeared. She is now teaching at the institute, but only temporarily. The Missionary Association is assisting me in finding a colored teacher to take her place. We believe as strongly as you do that we should have Negro teachers." He paused, watching Mr. Webb closely for any reaction to his comments, waiting for an accusation of racial prejudice in the firing of Mrs. Smith. None came. The man continued to chew on the cigar, his inner thoughts unrevealed.

"You should also be aware," John said, "that before Mrs. Smith approached us, and before your resolution was drawn up, I might add, we had attempted to hire a colored teacher, a Mr. Jones. Unfortunately, he declined."

Mr. Webb, removed his cigar, coughed, cleared his throat and studied the object in his fingers. "Well, it sounds as though you and the AMA have taken our concerns to heart. The Republican Association will be very pleased." He rose and extended his hand to John, the cigar back between his teeth.

John stood and shook the offered hand. Obviously the meeting was over, but he had one more thing to say. "I hope you and your Association understand that the well-being of the freedmen is our main objective."

"Of course," he said, "The Barnes School is a fine institution."

John headed into the storm, amused by the contradiction of Mr. Webb's parting remark and the language in the resolution by the Republican Association. He nevertheless felt the rough waters had been smoothed and his own reputation restored. A cheer poised on his lips at the relief and excitement of the successful meeting. He could now move ahead with an idea that had been building in his mind for several weeks.

Chapter 43

The inspiration had taken root at a luncheon a few weeks earlier where John was the guest of George Honey of the Texas Treasury Department. Visiting from Austin, the man had been encouraged by Louis to look John up. John gladly agreed to meet Honey for dinner, eager to hear any news of Louis and the goings on at the state capital. Once their meals had been ordered, the discussion naturally turned to education. Honey, formerly a representative of the AMA, had at one time supervised the organizing of schools for the freed slaves in Texas.

"Things should start getting interesting for education in the state," Honey had remarked, between bites of his meal.

John looked at him quizzically. "How is that?"

"The legislature is in the process of establishing a state-wide public school system."

"So I've heard. And how do they propose for it to be funded?" John asked, thinking of the difficulty of maintaining the bureau schools with no money.

"Taxation, though there's a lot to be worked out yet."

A spark of enthusiasm spurred more questions from John. "Will the schools be mixed? Racially, I mean."

Honey shook his head. "That's highly unlikely. A separate system for each, perhaps."

John put down his fork. "A separate system? Isn't that a violation of the constitutional rights of the freedmen?"

"It will be challenged, of course. However, Governor Davis will be appointing a superintendent of public instruction sometime late spring. We can only hope the right man gets the job."

The remark shook loose the memory of Julia Nelson's passionate monologue on what she would do if in charge of the school for Texas. "Does it have to be a man?" John asked.

Honey raised his eyebrows at the question. "What are you driving at?"

"I know a woman who could do the job admirably."

Honey almost choked on a swallow of coffee. "Surely you are jesting."

"Not at all. Julia Nelson, who heads the freedmen's school in Columbus, has excellent credentials. I'm certain she could get substantial backing from those who know her and would accept the appointment should the governor select her."

"You cannot mean that, nor could Mrs. Nelson with her good sense desire to take on such a responsibility."

It annoyed John that the man was not taking him seriously. He shifted in his chair and leaned closer to his visitor. "If you knew her as I do, you would not think it so absurd. The woman is highly intelligent and certainly capable."

"Actually, I do know her, and I agree with you on her excellent credentials. I would gladly assist Sister Nelson in any way, but the work is beyond the physical power of a woman to do. It would subject her to thousands of miles of travel, and expose her to slander at which her sensitive nature would revolt." He shook his head and took another sip of coffee before continuing. "To approach Governor Davis with this suggestion would be impudent. He could never be persuaded to entertain the idea for one moment."

John sighed and settled back in his chair. Honey was right, of course, though a woman's physical stamina really had nothing to do with it. Julia Nelson's record proved she had plenty of strength. Texas, the nation for that matter, simply wasn't ready for a woman to hold such a position.

As John lay in bed later that night the entire conversation with George Honey repeated itself in his thoughts. Finally he became stuck on one sentence: *"We can only hope the right man gets the job."* So, if not a woman, then what man would be the right man? By morning the seed had been planted and taken root. All during the day and into the week the idea fermented. John would strive for the appointment himself.

The more he dwelled on it, the more keyed up he became, and the more certain he was that he wanted the position. *Think what I could do to help alleviate racial injustice in the state.* He believed he had a chance, and prayed on the matter many times over. He had started a very successful school from scratch in Lavaca, and not only did he now hold the prestigious job of principal at the

Barnes Institute, he had assisted Eugene Bartholomew in establishing schools in other parts of the state. To be sure, if this were a position elected by the people of the state, a teacher of the freedmen might not stand a chance, but the superintendent of education was to be appointed by the governor. John had supported Davis for governor and had campaigned for him.

The only problem John could foresee at the time was the unpleasant episode with Mrs. Smith. Now, after the meeting with Webb, and with the eventual placement of a colored teacher at the institute, that would become a non-issue. *I'll write Congressman Sinclair and Senator Ruby*, he thought. *If I can get these two men on my side, half the battle is won.* Once his decision was made, John's pen couldn't write fast enough.

Sinclair wasted no time in replying to his query, writing, *I shall most willingly do anything in my power to assist you.*

The response from Senator Ruby gave John pause. Ruby wrote:

> *I do not know what name the governor will submit for Supt. of Education but am told that the position has been assigned or will be so to an old friend of His Excellency—I will however submit your claim and no doubt Col. Sinclair will assist ...*

John carefully folded Ruby's letter and placed it next to Sinclair's in a special file labeled *Application for Superintendent Of Schools*. Perhaps Ruby's comment about the position being assigned to an old friend was only a rumor.

Sinclair had suggested he put together a petition for signatures as proof to the governor of his qualifications and broad base of support. John found a professional printer who prepared the petition to his specifications, ready to present to his first backers, the staff of the Barnes Institute.

The morning of the day he was to make his announcement at school officially and begin his campaign, Miss Stoneman approached him in his office.

"Mr. Ogilvie, may I have a word with you please?"

"Aye, of course. Is there a problem?"

"Well, not with me, but you seem terribly preoccupied lately. If I may be so bold as to mention it, you seem to be suffering from absentmindedness."

"Absentmindedness?"

"Well, yes. That and the humming. Not that there is anything wrong with humming, it's just that you aren't quite yourself, and to tell you the truth, I've been a little worried." Her gray eyes held a look of concern as she scanned his face.

"Humming?" The remark caused him to chuckle. He wasn't even aware he'd been humming. "As a matter of fact, I do have something unusual on my mind. Something very important that will affect us all. Would you do me the favor of asking the other teachers to meet me here after school to discuss the matter?"

"Why, yes, of course." She cast him a peculiar look he couldn't quite decipher and eased out of the room.

Now and then during the day, John caught himself humming, and each time he had to laugh. He couldn't remember being so energized about anything as this venture. *Superintendent of public instruction for the entire state of Texas. Think of the possibilities. With everyone working together, as Mrs. Nelson had expounded, the state will have the best educational system in America.* He paced his office, humming and pondering all the while. He could hardly wait for the eager reaction of his teachers and scholars. It was time the word got out and his crusade begun.

They crowded into the tight space of John's little office at the stroke of three, Miss Williams, Miss Stoneman, and Miss Trussell, their faces grave. *Do they think I'm going to fire the whole lot of them? Well, the mood will change to an air of jubilation in a few moments.* He had donned his coat for the meeting so as to look appropriately worthy of the announcement he was to make.

He leaned forward, hands on his desk. "I want you to be the first to know that I plan to apply to Governor Davis for the office of superintendent of public instruction for the state of Texas." He smiled broadly at the conclusion of his statement, waiting for the whoops of joy and support from his staff.

It didn't come. The women looked at each other in disbelief and for a full anguish-laden minute, said nothing. Finally, Miss Williams spoke up, "You can't be serious."

It felt like a slap in the face. The walls in the humid little room suddenly seemed a vise slowly closing against him. "I can do the job, ladies. Surely, you of all people should know that." His response came out raspy as he tried to swallow against a growing knot in his throat.

With that remark, they all started talking, and the tension melted like a snow bank in sunshine, exposing what lay underneath.

"You can do it, Mr. Ogilvie, better than anyone, only what about the institute? What will we do with you gone?" Tears gleamed in Miss Williams's eyes as she spoke.

"Surely, you wouldn't abandon the students here—and us," Miss Trussell added.

"Hush, ladies. I think we need to let Mr. Ogilvie tell us more before we jump to conclusions." Miss Stoneman pushed back her ever-errant lock of hair. "The way I see it, helping out the state is not abandoning us. Let us hear his plans."

John breathed a little easier, mentally embracing this newest member of his staff—always so willing to speak her mind. He spent the next half hour sharing his excitement and thoughts of a Texas with equal education for students of all colors and backgrounds. "I know it will be difficult and there will certainly be opposition to some of my plans should I get the appointment, but with determination good things can happen."

By the end of the session, all three ladies signed his petition. As they went their separate ways, Miss Stoneman hung back. "Well, now I understand the humming. I would sign my name for you twenty times if I could. I just hope you aren't being naïve, Mr. Ogilvie. This is a mighty big bite to chew."

"Perhaps, but reality is built on dreams, Miss Stoneman. Nothing good happens without dreams and the pursuit of those dreams."

She nodded and smiled. "Of course you are right."

After the teachers left, John took time to write Julia Nelson of his plans. She would certainly understand what he was about. He grabbed his coat, tucked the letter into a pocket, and strode out the door for the post office.

Everywhere John went for the entire week he carried the petition. As the list of names grew, so did his confidence. He garnered as many notable signatures as he could. The pastor for the Baptist church, where he held Sabbath school classes, signed it, as did William Townsend and Reverend Norton. The latter seemed most enthusiastic.

"If you get this position it will be a fine day for education in our state," he said. "We need a champion of the Negroes to head our schools. Is Senator Ruby planning on signing? That's what you need. It would certainly make the governor stand up and take notice."

"I've already approached him," John said. He thought back on the letter from the senator. The man hadn't really said he would sign a petition, but he didn't say he wouldn't either.

Scarcely a moment passed when his future as state superintendent didn't occupy some portion of John's thinking. In the evening when his lesson assignments were completed, he drafted outlines for following through on his plans should he receive the appointment. He dug through his memory for every meaningful personal connection he had made since arriving in Texas. He knew many former bureau employees who now held government positions. He needed those signatures. However, many of them resided at the state capital—Louis, of course, Sinclair and Ruby and others. He studied the petition and decided it was time to circulate it in Austin. On February 15, he sealed the envelope containing the document, along with instructions, and mailed it to Sinclair, feeling light-headed and jittery.

As if he didn't have enough on his mind, in the middle of all this Miss Trussell handed in her resignation, leaving John short-staffed once again. He immediately wrote Howard of this newest dilemma, stating:

> *Miss Williams is now handling both primary and intermediate classes, and though she is not complaining, I know it is too big a load for her. I would appreciate any help you can offer; however, I do have a replacement in mind locally. I will advise you on my success...*

Of course he hated to see Miss Trussell leave, yet John recognized that her absence now propelled him to fulfill his promise to Mr. Webb. During Sabbath school classes, he had been observing a colored woman who worked well with the younger children.

The Sunday following Miss Trussell's hurried departure, he approached Miss Bates after church. Removing his hat, he cleared his throat. "I can tell you enjoy those little children, Miss Bates. Have you ever taught school?"

"You mean real school?"

"Aye, that's what I mean."

She cast him a cautious glance before replying. "Well... a few years back I done stood in now and again at a freedman's school when the teacher got sick."

John's fingers tightened on the brim of his hat. "Would you consider a position at the Barnes Institute teaching the primary grades?"

The woman's eyes widened. "Well... I don't know about being a real teacher every single day."

"There is pay," John said, "and I will assist you with the lessons until you feel confident on your own." He could almost see the thought processes going on in her head by the expressions on her face.

"Would I be teaching the *little* chilluns?" she asked.

"Yes, mostly, though some of the primary students are older."

"And I would get paid to do that?"

"Yes." John held his breath as he awaited the answer. Her wide smile told him what he wanted to know before the words came out of her mouth.

"Then I believe I will say yes."

They agreed to meet at the school the next morning at seven o'clock. He donned his hat at a jaunty angle and hummed all the way home.

Miss Bates arrived promptly as planned. She looked very much like a school marm, dressed in a crisp but modest tan-colored dress with a row of ivory buttons from her waist to the tip of the collar high on her neck. Before they began working on lesson plans, John showed her the room for the primary class. A shaft of morning sun beamed in from the window, highlighting the rows of empty benches. On the blackboard at the front of the room someone had written two columns of names.

Miss Bates eyed the list. "How many chilluns?"

John sensed apprehension in her voice. "Sixty-five if they all show, but rarely does that happen. And they aren't all little children, Miss Bates. This is where any freed slave who wants an education begins with the basics."

She nodded her head in understanding and took one more sweeping glance at the room before John escorted her to his office.

"We will spend as much time as you need reviewing lesson plans and textbooks," he said. "Miss Williams and Violette Green, one of the advanced students, have been covering the primary class and will continue to do so until you are ready to step in."

As the morning progressed, John was pleased to observe Miss Bates's excellent reading skills. "Where did you get your schooling?"

"I lived on a cotton plantation during slavery times and worked in the big house. My mistress taught me when she taught her own chillun."

"Do you know arithmetic, too?"

"Some. I can add and do take-away. Don't know much about them fractions or dividing."

"You needn't worry about that for the primary grades."

They sat side by side, leafing through text books and working sample arithmetic problems. John also talked about classroom procedure, discipline and other issues that might arise. At eleven o'clock, he set the primer and study papers aside, stood and stretched. "I'm sure you are ready for a break. Do you want to meet the pupils?"

"Yes, suh. I may as well get started. Meetin' the chilluns is what I want most."

The eagerness in her voice pleased John. Their time in review seemed to have eased the hesitation she had displayed earlier. He led the way down the short hall to the large primary room. A hodgepodge of boys and girls now crowded the benches. Attentive gazes focused on Miss Williams who sounded out words at the blackboard. Upon seeing the visitors, she put down the pointer and stepped to one side.

John approached the front, and all heads turned to the young woman behind him. "This is Miss Bates," John said. "She will be your new teacher. Some of you may already know her."

Little Hattie Cook squealed and clapped her hands, "From Sabbath school!" Others took her cue. A murmur of voices rose, and a chorus of claps followed.

Miss Bates's face beamed. When the applause subsided, she offered a friendly, though soft, "Hello."

The plan had been for her to observe Miss Williams conduct the class for the remainder of the morning, but John could see time might be better spent in an informal get-acquainted session. He left the room sensing this was going to work out just fine.

At lunch break and recess, he observed Miss Bates chatting with Miss Williams and Miss Stoneman, the three smiling and laughing in animated conversation. In mid-afternoon, he stepped into the primary class to see how things were going. Miss Williams had returned to her own room, and Miss Bates sat on a stool facing the students. She read from the primer with great intonation. On the blackboard behind her were words from the text lesson, chalk letters printed in a precise penmanship. John smiled and quietly eased away. *She's a natural.* Knowledge of her hiring was sure to warm the hearts of all those who had strong convictions that a colored teacher should be on staff at the Barnes Institute.

The entire week went well, and for the first time in months, classes settled into a comfortable routine. During lunch break the following Monday, John once again marched through the puddles of a blustery storm to the office of Frank Webb. This time the rain refreshed him instead of feeling like a soggy veil of gloom.

Upon entering the building, the typesetter recognized him. "He's in. Just pound on the door."

Moments later John stood in front of Webb's desk, the aroma of cigar smoke invading his nostrils as he reached out a hand in greeting. "Good morning, Mr. Webb."

"Good morning to you, Ogilvie. How are things at the Barnes Institute these days?"

"Fine, sir, just fine."

John left a half hour later with a promise from Webb to approach the Galveston Republican Association about supporting him for the office of superintendent of public instruction. Webb's parting words, "I think you would do a splendid job," rang in his ears and lightened his step. He doubted such a commendation would have come forth had he not confirmed the hiring of a colored teacher at the institute. Though he had no assurance the Republican group would endorse him for the state position, he prayed Webb could persuade the association to go along with the idea.

Ignoring the wet weather, John returned to school by way of the post office to pick up mail. He always looked for a letter from his father, though one rarely came, and none appeared this day either. However, Howard had written, and another envelope bore the return address of the House of Representatives, Austin, Texas. That would be from William Sinclair—undoubtedly a response to the petition. John tore open the envelope while still at the post office, his heartbeats accelerated. The note, in sweeping penmanship, was short and to the point:

Austin, Texas, Feb. 22, 1871

Dear Ogilvie,
  Yours of the 15th, instructions with enclosure, is received and shall have prompt attention.
          Yours Truly,
          Wm. N. Sinclair

Surely this meant that Sinclair was going to circulate the document. John knew he would breathe more easily when he had proof the signatures he wanted were actually affixed to the petition.

The reading of the other letter, from General Howard, waited until he returned to his office. John guessed at its contents and he was correct. The General spent two pages naming possible candidates for Miss Trussell's spot. Including, once again, Jones. The man wouldn't give up. John shook his head, stuffed the letter back in its envelope and laid it to one side.

A knock sounded at the open door to his office, and he looked up to see Miss Williams. "Come in," he said, and motioned to a vacant chair. Ignoring his gesture, she approached the desk.

"I'll only be a minute. I just want to return this book and say how pleased I am with Miss Bates. She has a little learning to do, but has good control of the children." She handed John his copy of *Poems and Songs of Robert Burns.* "Thank you for the loan. Though I must say the students had trouble understanding the Scottish words. They'll be happy we are on to something else."

Glancing down, her eyes caught sight of the envelope face up on the desk. "I see you have heard from Howard. What does he say about your application for state superintendent of schools?"

Annoyed and uncomfortable at her intrusion into his private correspondence, John answered quickly, feigning nonchalance. "I haven't actually written him that bit of news yet. That's on my agenda for today, along with telling him about Miss Bates."

"Well, he should be pleased when he hears both reports."

After she had gone, John sat in thought for a few moments, tapping his fingers on the book of poems while he contemplated her parting remark. He was not all that certain Howard would be pleased to learn of his desire to head the education of the state. *Maybe I wasn't totally truthful when I said I planned to write that news today. A letter, yes, and I will certainly include the hiring of Miss Bates, but perhaps I won't mention my political ambitions, at least not yet.*

The letter regarding Miss Bates was sent the following day, and Howard replied in short order, congratulating John on her hiring and requesting additional information so he could forward her commission. Then he plunged again into suggestions for yet another teacher, reminding John that Miss Stoneman was there only on loan.

...I will send you down one good teacher as soon as possible. Will transfer Miss Keen from Tangaloo to Galveston if she will answer. She is a lady of excellent education but of no great force—a graduate of Rockford Seminar, and of a devoted Christian spirit. She offered to go to Texas or to California having determined to spend her life as a missionary—Would she be expected to govern the large school? I judge that Miss Stoneman does in your absence. Perhaps Miss Bates can govern in your absence if Miss Keen shrinks from that duty.

This paragraph bothered John for several reasons, and he tugged at his beard as he reread it. The teacher he sought for Miss Stoneman's replacement had to be of a sturdy character and able to handle the more advanced students. It sounded doubtful Miss Keen was the right choice. He sighed and shook his head. Maybe with luck, this woman would not respond to Howard's request.

That evening, as he stepped out the school door at the close of the late class, he heard someone call. "Ogilvie. Wait up!"

Through the shadows of the night, a portly figure merged, rushing toward John waving a paper. It was Frank Webb. The man stopped to catch his breath and thrust the paper at him. "I'm so glad I caught you. I know it's late, but I thought you might want this. I just came from the Republican meeting, and everyone supports you. Here is a partial copy of the resolution drawn up this evening—that part which involves you. I will see that you get a complete copy later."

John scanned the document, though he couldn't make the words out in the dark. "Thank you, sir. I am much obliged. I will send the association a letter of gratitude. This means a great deal to me." He hoped his voice didn't sound too childlike with excitement.

They parted company, and John hurried home where he burst through the door. With trembling hands he lit a lamp. In its glow he read:

Whereas, the Republican Association of Galveston County was called together tonight...

He followed the words down the page until he came to that certain paragraph he sought:

Resolved, that we respectfully request his Excellency, E. J. Davis, to appoint J. Ogilvie to the Superintendency of Public Instruction for the State of Texas.

Chapter 44

John's elation at his growing support for the state appointment didn't remove his teacher dilemma. A letter from Howard dated March 6th ordinarily would have brought rejoicing, but when he read the words, he rubbed his forehead and sighed.

> *Miss Anna M. Keen will leave Tangaloo for Galveston, within a week probably after you get this. Please write to her and give her the number and street of the home and a word of welcome, as she goes alone.*

So, the Barnes Institute would be harboring Miss Keen, after all. An incompetent teacher could throw the institute back into a turmoil again. There had to be a solution. The only one that came to mind was probably a lost cause, but John had to try. When school was out for the day, he snagged Miss Stoneman. "Can I see you a moment please?"

She followed him to his office, eyeing him quizzically as he shut the door behind them. "Don't tell me you've heard from the governor about your appointment already?"

"No. Not yet." He smiled at her question. "I'm afraid the process, whatever the outcome, will take a while longer."

Her face clouded over. "Well, then, if this is about Caleb, I believe we have the discipline under control, and it shouldn't be a problem in the future."

"This has nothing to do with Caleb. It's about you. I'm hoping to talk you into staying for the remainder of this school year."

"Oh, that." She plopped down on the nearest chair. "Well, Mr. Ogilvie, I came as a favor to Mr. Howard, and as much as I would like to stay, I just can't. I'm on loan, and my school at Huntsville is expecting me back by the end of March."

"What if we sent someone else to teach there in your place?"

Charcoal and Chalk

"I'm afraid that just wouldn't do. I made a promise, and a promise is a promise." She released a huge sigh. "I just can't be in two places at once."

He shook his head and leaned back in his chair. "Aye, you are right, but I needed to make certain. We'll miss your cheerful spirit and your talent on the melodeon."

"Well, it's not as though I were leaving tomorrow." She shifted in her chair and eyed him with an uneasy look. "Is it?"

"I have word that your replacement is on the way here."

"Oh, my. Shall I be packing?" She batted at a wisp of hair in her eyes.

"No, not yet. Let's wait until Miss Keen is standing on the doorstep. That may be a couple of weeks or more away."

John watched with a heavy heart as Miss Stoneman left his office. He hated to lose this exceptional teacher. Yet he should give Miss Keen a chance before judging her on a few remarks from Howard. After all, he did say she was an excellent scholar. Pulling out paper and pen, he scribbled a few lines of welcome to the "meek" Miss Keen, providing her with the address of her destination in Galveston.

The following day, John received a sobering letter from Sinclair.

March 13, 1871

Dear Ogilvie,

I suppose you have been wondering why you did not hear from me and what progress I was making. I am sorry to say that I have not been able to get the petition signed by our senator as yet and have not presented it to Major P. for signature for the reason that he spoke of you in such a way one day as to lead me to think it would be useless. Col. Patten signed it.... Mr. Ruby did not decline to sign it, but postponed the matter. You can draw your own inferences...

Please let me hear your wishes,
Yours Truly and Fraternally,
Sinclair

John was not surprised at the Major's reaction; after all, they did not know each other well. But he was piqued at Ruby's postponement to sign the petition, and even more irritated at Sinclair for delaying the whole thing. He paced the small office space and on one turn jammed his hip painfully against the corner

312

of his desk. Limping to his chair, he sat and studied a spot on the ceiling until it blurred out of focus. Even though a letter from Ruby had indicated the governor might have someone in mind for the position, that didn't mean the senator couldn't throw his support in John's direction. *Confound it.* Opening a desk drawer, he pulled out the envelope containing the resolution presented to him by Frank Webb the day before, along with a blank sheet of paper. Dipping a pen into ink he began writing:

> *Dear Sinclair,*
>
> *Herewith I send a copy of the resolution unanimously passed by the Republican Association. I wish you would present this and the petition itself to Mr. Ruby and Maj. Plumbly and either get their signatures or refusal, then ask Senator Tendick. If he refuses hand it in to the governor as it is. If Davis refuses to recommend my appointment, good and well. Whatever the result I will not forget those who befriended me. I am very much obliged to you for the interest you have taken in my welfare. I only wish that you had gone ahead without delay.*

John signed the letter, placed it into an envelope with the resolution and melted a seal on the flap. Time was wasting. He needed to push this forward.

A letter from the Missionary Association a few days later once more shifted his attention to the teacher issue at the institute. To his surprise, he learned that not one, but two teachers were on their way to Galveston. Miss Keen was due to arrive on March 20, and a Miss Mary Nichols would also be joining the staff, arriving by the end of the month. He would certainly accept them, and hopefully the AMA had funds to pay these ladies.

***

A warm wind rustled the oleander bushes across the island the morning Miss Keen's ship was due in. In spite of his lack of enthusiasm, John would not allow her to find her own way in a strange city. He hired Alphonse and his carriage to drive to the harbor, and sat up front with this favorite pupil. The horse clopped forward, its head held sideways against the stiff breeze. John had opted not to wear a hat for fear of it being blown away.

"So you is getting more teachers," Alphonse said, as they rolled along. "Not for us night scholars, I hope. We needs you, Mr. Ogilvie."

"No. These ladies are to teach the day classes. Miss Stoneman will be leaving, and the others could do with more help."

A worried look crossed the man's face. "You still goin' to teach us when you is principal for all of Texas?"

John chuckled. "Alphonse, that is not a sure thing, but if it does happen, I will do everything in my power to continue as your teacher."

"I sure do hope so, suh. I sure do hope so."

Alphonse pulled the horse to a halt overlooking the bay where the ship, just in from New Orleans, swayed against its moorings. Smoke trailed from the tall stacks, shifting direction at the whim of the wind.

"Wait here." John bounded onto the splintered boards of the dock and pushed his way through the throng waiting for passengers to disembark. Stevedores rushed about hollering to each other, hefting trunks and boxes unloaded from the Morgan steamer. A string of travelers thumped down the gang plank, waving at friends or family members who had come to greet them. A petite lady, dressed in a dark skirt and white blouse draped by a shawl, followed behind. Gripping the handles of a carpetbag with both hands, she glanced around expectantly.

This must be she. John stepped forward. "Miss Keen?"

She looked up at him, smiled, and held out a gloved hand. "Yes. I'm Anna Keen." He took her hand and returned her smile, surprised at the firmness of her grasp.

"I'm John Ogilvie, principal of the Barnes Institute. Welcome to Galveston."

"Thank you. I am so glad to finally be here. It's been a rather rocky ride."

"Are you well?" He wondered if her face, framed by a ring of light brown braids, was always such a delicate color.

"Yes, I'm fine. Only glad my feet are on earth again." She looked down at the wharf on which she stood, comprised of weathered boards, under which the waves rippled and slapped, and laughed. "Well, almost."

John laughed too, then realized he still held Miss Keen's hand in his. He felt a rush of warmth to his cheeks as he released his grip and reached for the bag she had dropped during the welcome.

"A carriage is waiting for us. Is there more luggage?"

"Yes, I have one trunk. Oh, there it is," she exclaimed, pointing to a medium-sized chest. A label affixed to the side read BARNES INSTITUTE, GALVESTON, TEXAS. John found a dockworker who hefted it onto his shoulder and followed them to the waiting Alphonse. The two men positioned the trunk on top of the coach while John assisted Miss Keen inside. Abandoning his earlier place beside the driver, he took the seat opposite her.

Alphonse clicked to the horse, and the carriage slowly moved through the busy harbor street. Miss Keen adjusted her shawl, which had blown loose during the short walk to the carriage. "Is it always this windy?"

"Always a breeze of some sort," John said. "Not necessarily this strong, though I must be honest and say it is sometimes much stronger."

"I suppose I shall get used to it." She gazed out the window for a few moments then added, "I'm amazed at how warm it is, and only the end of March."

John couldn't help but notice an eager shine in her eyes as she spoke. She caught him looking at her, blushed and lowered her gaze. Embarrassed at making her uncomfortable, he felt the color return to his own face. He raised his hand to his mouth and feigned a slight cough.

"We'll go to the teachers' home first, and you can meet Miss Williams. Our other teacher, Miss Bates, lives at home. You will meet her later. We'll give you a tour of the school when you are rested."

"How far is it to the school?" She kept her eyes focused on the passing scenery while she spoke.

"Only a few blocks," he answered. "Galveston Island can easily be walked across."

"It's not quite what I expected." Her gaze seemed not to miss a thing as the carriage made its way through the commercial district and onto the residential streets. "Here it is at the very bottom of America, and so up-to-date."

"Aye, it is indeed," John said. "I think you will like it here."

Alphonse pulled up in front of the unassuming house and helped his passengers down from the carriage. He and John unloaded the trunk, and they each took a handle. Miss Keen followed behind, her carpetbag in hand, as they approached the front door where Miss Williams stood to greet them.

Though reserved, Miss Keen's smile revealed a pleased acceptance of her new housemate, and John watched the friendly exchange between the women with satisfaction. When he felt everything was under control, he excused himself to head on foot for the institute.

"I'll bring Miss Keen over later," Miss Williams promised.

"I'll be there." He had papers to correct for his evening class and Sabbath school lessons to prepare. As he walked, he began to hum. Though waiting for word from Sinclair on the status of his petition created a constant anxiety, a peculiar buoyancy now filled him—something he couldn't quite explain—an unexpected anticipation totally apart from his political aspirations. One thing he did know, his worries about Miss Keen had been unfounded. Clearly she was a dedicated, intelligent woman, and though shy, she didn't seem meek at all to him. She would do just fine.

Chapter 45

On Friday, a week into April, John received an envelope from Julia Nelson in Columbus. She had obviously been doing some campaigning for him on her own. A short note from her was attached to a letter.

Not having time to write you a letter, I send one I have just received:

From Senator R. P. Tendick:

Dear Madam:
...Mr Ogilvie's application has been referred to the governor sometime ago. I wrote a strong endorsement on the same upon your representations. Col. Sinclair (my roommate) and Maj. Stevenson, who is here at present, also recommended the appointment. There are many applicants among others; Col. DeGress late Capt. U.S. Army. Col. Sinclair tells me that Ogilvie's appointment is very doubtful. The gov. will take a man who has not only a clear record but who at the same time yields a powerful political influence.

The new school bill passed...and provides for the appointment of an Assistant Superintendent for each district. In case Ogilvie should fail to be appointed Superintendent, I propose for him to come in as Assistant Superintendent...

John tugged at his beard, an uneasiness forming in the pit of his stomach. Though he meant to be grading class papers, he kept returning to the letter. The hour was late, the night dark, and shadows danced about the walls from the flame in the lamp on his desk. Familiar names rose from this most recent correspondence regarding his application for state superintendent of public education: Senator Tendick, Colonel Sinclair, and, of course, Louis. John was gratified that these prestigious men had all endorsed him, but for the first time since the application process began his spirits sagged. The outcome didn't look promising, at least not for the top position. *But what about assistant superintendent? If I were to garner that position for the Galveston district, I might still make a difference.*

A knock on the door startled him. Returning the letter to its envelope, he shoved it into the desk drawer.

"Yes?"

"Mr. Ogilvie. We have good news." The voice was that of Miss Nichols, the newest recruit to the teaching staff.

Well, he could certainly use good news. "Come in."

The door swung open, revealing not only Miss Nichols, but Miss Williams, Miss Bates and Miss Keen as well. John stood. "Come in, ladies. And what are you about at this hour?"

"We knew you were here working and voted to come and tell you that we just received word we have permission to hold the May Day picnic at the McKinny place."

The four women crowded inside the office, and in spite of the shadowy light, John could tell they were beaming. It seemed like such a trivial matter compared to the news in the letter he had hidden away, yet he knew a big effort had been made by his staff to get this special venue for the May Day celebration.

"Well done, ladies. Well done."

He scanned their faces, his gaze lingering on Miss Keen's a fraction longer than the others. Both she and Miss Nichols had settled into their teaching roles at the institute in an admirable fashion, already endearing themselves to the pupils. Dark-haired Miss Nichols, tall and lithe, possessed a buoyant spirit and talked with zeal about almost anything, quite the opposite of Miss Keen. Still, the latter's quiet manner and ever positive attitude held an alluring quality that attracted John. He was happy with both women, and now his school and staff were to be showcased at the estate of the McKinny pioneers of Galveston.

"It looks like we have a bit of planning on our hands."

"Yes, but I think you will be pleased." Miss Williams, the veteran of the group, took the lead, adding, "We have many ideas."

And so they did. The following days brimmed with plans for the May Day celebration. It was decided to make the big occasion a joint effort of the Barnes Institute and the children from the Baptist Sunday school and the Methodist Episcopal Church. Meetings were held every afternoon to organize the event.

"We must involve all the children," Miss Keen said. "No one should be left out."

"A May Queen and court from the Institute and each Sabbath school," Miss Williams offered.

"And a parade and picnic," added Miss Nichols.

Even Miss Bates, who usually sat quietly back agreeing with whatever the other teachers suggested, was enthusiastic in her contributions. The extra hours of planning provided a welcome diversion for John as he waited for the governor's decision. He monitored the May Day planning meetings, but found he needn't add much.

Sunday afternoon, April 30th, a day normally reserved for rest and Bible reading, found them all at the McKinny place. John had recruited some of his night students to help construct a stage under a natural arch between two trees in the center of the grounds. The women arrived with armloads of flowers and greens, which they arranged in pots of water around the stage. Vases of multicolored blooms lavished the tables set up in anticipation of the abundance of food that would appear for the picnic the following day.

When at last the grounds had been transformed into a scene befitting three May queens and their attendants, John stood back to admire the results. Even though summer was yet to arrive, any physical exertion produced beads of perspiration. Pulling a handkerchief from his pocket, he wiped his forehead. He hadn't bothered with his jacket after church, and early into the preparation of the grounds had loosened his collar and rolled up his sleeves to ward off the heat. Even so, his shirt now clung to him. His hair, usually combed in place, felt disheveled. Normally this wouldn't bother him, especially after a busy afternoon's work, but he spied Miss Keen making her way across the lawn toward him. She had been working steadily along side everyone else; nevertheless she appeared calm and tidy, making John even more self-conscious.

He noticed she carried two tall glasses of water, and smiled as she approached. "You look like you could use some refreshment," she said, handing him one of the glasses.

He reached for it and inadvertently touched her hand, creating a tingling sensation in his own fingers. They stood side by side, sipping the water.

"Do you think we are ready?" Miss Keen asked. "It really has been a big undertaking, and the children are terribly excited. The banners are all completed, and did you know that Miss Williams found a brass band to lead the parade?" Her pale blue eyes shone with delight.

In her few short weeks at the Institute, John had never known her to say so much in one breath. He smiled broadly. "Aye, it will be a grand day."

The First of May dawned sunny and bright. Even the ever-present wind remained a calm breeze. The celebration was indeed grand, from the procession along the streets of Galveston to the McKinny place, to the very last speech by the Honorable Judge DeBruhl. Each Queen of May, beautifully costumed, recited original poetry, concluding with the dramatic words, "Love God and man, and when we leave life's short and fleeting day, we'll all meet in that happy land, we'll all be Queens of May."

The affair ended at four p.m., after which adults had only sufficient time to wash up and change before an evening event by the Daughters of Zion Society at the Saint Charles Hall. The teachers attended, and John purposely found a seat next to Miss Keen. His first impression of her had been that she was rather plain; but tonight, seeing her dressed in a soft blue gown that matched her eyes and smelling of honeysuckle, he found her exceptionally lovely.

They walked home together as a group, two by two, John next to Miss Keen. "Have you grown accustomed to Galveston?" he asked her.

"Living next to the gulf is a new experience," she said, "but I'm learning to like it."

At one point, he took her elbow and guided her around a large puddle. She smiled a radiant *Thank you* that burrowed into his heart.

Later, in the afterglow of the day's events, John wrote and submitted a long piece to the newspaper:

>...*It was a place flowing with mead, lemonade, and soda water... The children jumped ropes and flew high in swings, and ring games and music from the band filled the intervals...Could the enjoyment last, we would wish all months were May, and every day the first one.*

The event had been so successful and heady, that John's anxious wait for word from the governor was temporarily forgotten.

Chapter 46

A late storm blew in on Thursday, bringing thunder, lightning, and heavy rain.

"I can't believe it," Miss Nichols said. "What if this had happened on May First after all that preparation? The children would have been absolutely devastated with disappointment. God was surely smiling down on us, offering thanks for all our work and dedication, saving his torrents for later."

John listened and chuckled. He couldn't help but wonder if God cared that much about May Day celebrations. "Aye, tis good that we had agreeable weather. Now let's hope this storm goes away as quickly as it has come." But the storm intensified with each hour and during the evening class the wind blew so hard the windows shook. Only half the class showed up. Water puddled under desks from rain-drenched clothing, and each flash of lightning and thunder clap interrupted lessons.

Finally, Washington expressed what they were thinking, following one nerve-rattling rumble.

"If this keeps up I ain't goin' nowhere. I'll sleep on this here floor if I has to."

Just as he spoke a brilliant flash sizzled through the building followed immediately by a horrendous roar of thunder. The two young women in the class screamed.

"It's all right," John said, tension tightening his shoulders. "We're safe in this sturdy building." Though he had been jarred himself, he knew his statement to be true. In fact, his pupils were better off here in the brick schoolhouse than in their modest homes, except perhaps for the few who lived as domestics in some of the city's finer residences.

Lightning lit the sky and thunder boomed. The intensity of the storm frayed nerves until lessons were forgotten. They all stayed an extra hour, and when the rain finally diminished to an occasional spray whipped about by wind gusts, John and the scholars gathered up their things and hurried out the door to reach their homes before dark.

The following morning dawned bright and sunny, like a naughty child attempting to hide mischievous deeds, but the evidence lingered in dripping eaves and small lakes about the roads. On the schoolhouse steps, John scraped mud from his shoes before unlocking the door. Why he happened to look up, why he didn't know, but when he did, the very real danger of the previous night shook him. A corner of the roof hung charred and loose—a victim of a direct hit from the lightning. If it hadn't been for the sheets of rain, the fire started by the strike might have spread and consumed the schoolhouse. Alarmed, John's first order of business was to scribble a note to Howard requesting money for repairs—and for a lightning rod.

Later that day, he climbed a ladder to inspect the problem first hand. A ragged black hole yawned on the front corner of the building where fire had obviously worked its way along the eaves before being dowsed by the rain. A singed board fell apart in his hand when he tugged at it to determine exactly what would be required for a repair.

"Hello up there!" A familiar voice hollered from below. "I see you are striving for loftier heights one way or another."

John looked down into the smiling face of Louis Stevenson. "Hello to you, too!" Taking one more quick appraisal of the damage, he descended the ladder. "Good to see you, Louis. Sorry I can't greet you properly." He held up his soot-smudged hands.

Louis gave a low whistle. "Last night's storm?"

"Aye, it was a bad one. Had the scholars scared out of their wits. Me too, I might add, though we didn't know we'd been hit until this morning. I've already requested a lightning rod from Howard." He studied his former roommate as he spoke. Louis wore a new suit, looking as dapper as John had ever seen him. "So, what brings you to Galveston?"

"Several business matters. Can you join me for a quick meal before your evening class?"

John's immediate thought was Governor Davis had sent Louis with a message regarding the appointment. *But no, surely I will receive word in an official letter.*

"That will be fine," he said. "Give me time to clean up. We can eat at my place. I have enough for the two of us." Either way, he didn't want to receive the news in public.

In his tiny kitchen, John made gravy for biscuits that he had baked the day before and poured two cups of coffee. He and Louis talked of when they roomed together, how things were in Austin, and yesterday's storm until he thought he would burst from tension. Finally, he couldn't stand the idle chit-chat a minute longer. "You didn't come all the way from Austin to talk about the weather. What's on your mind, Louis?"

Through the window, the late afternoon sun illuminated Louis's face, accentuating his expression for the quick moment of hesitation before he spoke. John knew what was coming. "You have word about the appointment, don't you?"

Louis nodded. "This is not official, but I wanted to tell you in person. Colonel DeGress got the position. It's not a surprise, John. Even if the governor had given you the nod, your appointment probably wouldn't have passed the senate." He paused to take a swallow of coffee then continued. "In case you didn't know, there was a nominee before DeGress who was rejected partly because he favored mixed schools. We supported you as a friend, knowing all along what the outcome would be. Not that you wouldn't have done a fine job. You simply weren't the political choice. But take heart, there is a good chance you will be appointed to a supervisory position."

After all the weeks of not knowing, John experienced no particular emotion at the news. He had dealt with disappointment after reading Tendick's letter forwarded by Julia Nelson. This simply confirmed that message. At times the waiting had been intolerable. Now, if anything, relief at the certainty eased that constant angst.

"I have one more piece of news," Louis said.

Mystified, John studied his friend's face, unable this time to read any overt message there. He waited.

"I've tossed my hat into the ring for Congress."

John's pent-up emotions broke loose, and throwing his head back, he released a huge guffaw. "I see you haven't learned from my experience."

Louis smiled but didn't join in the laughter. "I'm serious, John. I would expect you, of all people, to understand and to lend me support."

"Sorry, old friend, I didn't mean to make light of your desires. I've learned it's not easy waiting out a decision—though you are cut of tougher cloth than I. But running against Clark? Why?"

"Clark *and* Giddings."

John shook his head, wondering at his friend's decision. "Giddings, a Democrat, I can understand, but Clark as the incumbent Republican is mighty stiff competition."

"You've undoubtedly heard there is a movement afoot to dismantle the Union League. Some Republicans, Clark among them, feel white voters are leaving the party because of its association with the league—meaning the freedmen. I helped create that organization, and I believe in what it stands for and all its accomplishments." Now Louis was up and pacing—pounding the clenched fist of one hand into the palm of the other. "We can't let Clark water down all that we have striven to achieve. There has to be an alternate choice for Republicans."

John felt a swell of pride for his friend. "You *are* serious."

Louis nodded, his eyes blazing. "You weren't afraid to go up against the odds for the very same reasons, John. I believe you and I *are* cut from the same cloth, in spite of what you say, and I need your help."

"I'll do what I can for you, Louis, though obviously I carry little political clout in this great state." He held out a hand and grasped Louis's in his. "And best of luck."

"Thanks. I knew I could count on you. And one more thing."

John raised his eyebrows. What now?

"I'll be moving back to Galveston, seeing how this is the district I'll be representing—if I win the election. Have you room for me?" Louis glanced around the cramped quarters.

"Of course," John said without hesitation. This was the best news yet.

John never heard from the governor regarding the appointment for superintendent of instruction, the assumption, he guessed, being once the word spread, the runners-up could figure out the obvious. Immediately following a public announcement in the papers regarding the appointment of DeGress, John's staff and other acquaintances offered awkward comments of condolence, some going so far as to say the governor's nearsightedness in his selection was a huge loss for the state.

***

On a day in late May when he was having trouble refocusing his drive, he closed the books on his desk, organized scattered papers in a neat pile, grabbed his coat and headed for the front door. As he passed Miss Keen's classroom, she stepped into the hall.

John nodded. "Good afternoon, Miss Keen." He slowed his pace but continued toward the exit. She fell in step beside him. "If you are walking, I'll join you as far as the teachers' home."

"It will be my pleasure." He opened the front door for her. They continued down the schoolhouse steps and strode along the walkway, side by side.

At first, neither spoke, then Miss Keen suddenly blurted, "I know you must be disappointed, Mr. Ogilvie, about not getting the state appointment, I mean."

She stopped and faced him, a look of compassion filling her eyes.

"I had hoped to make a difference, Miss Keen. That is the disappointment."

"Why, you *are* making a difference. I see it in the faces of the students at the institute every day. You have changed many lives right here."

At her sincerity and quiet words, a soothing warmth settled in him. "Thank you. That is very kind of you to say. I hope you are right."

They continued their walk in silence. All that needed to be said for the moment had been spoken. Her encouraging comment had meant more than she could ever know. He bid her goodbye at the teachers' home and continued on his way, his step lighter. Miss Keen was right. He didn't need a bigger piece of the educational pie to make a difference. He would carry on at the institute and do what he had always done—his best for the freedmen under his tutelage.

Then in June another letter arrived:

May 31st, 1871, from the office of Superintendent of Public Instruction, State of Texas.

To J. Ogilvie, Galveston, Tex.
I have the honor to transmit herewith your appointment as Supervisor of the 5th Judicial District in the Educational Department.
If you accept the appointment, you will subscribe the enclosed oath, have it acknowledged by competent authority, and return it to this office, with a letter of

transmittal, stating your age, color, sex, and post office address.

   Should you decline the appointment, return the commission and other papers.

I am, very respectfully,
Your obedient servant
J.C. DeGress
Sup't of Public Instruction

It was a printed form letter with blank spaces filled in, a personal contact of sorts, from the new superintendent, and it began an immediate healing of his wounded self-respect. Questions poured into his mind.

   If I accept, will I continue as principal of the Barnes Institute? What areas does the 5th Judicial District serve? What about my salary?

Pulling a sheet of paper from a drawer, John wrote down each query. That done, he leaned back in his chair, tapping his pen against the armrest, formulating a plan. First, a letter should go to DeGress, asking for details, also a telegram to Howard in Chicago. He couldn't make a decision until he heard from both men. As for his staff, they need not know about the appointment until he had decided yes or no. Following a light supper, he set to the task of writing DeGress; the clock struck twelve midnight before a satisfactory letter lay on his desk. First thing tomorrow he'd mail it and then telegraph Howard, asking where he stood with the AMA if he accepted the supervisory position.

When John arrived at the institute the next morning he was surprised to find a clutch of pupils gathered in front of the building looking skyward. Miss Williams stood behind the group as he approached.

"What's going on?" he asked.

She pointed to the newly repaired roof where a workman was in the process of securing a long metal pole in an upright position.

"The lightning rod, Mr. Ogilvie. I assumed it was all right to let them go ahead. The children are all excited, and it seemed like a good chance for a science lesson."

"Excellent," John said. He watched in fascination right along with the pupils A second workman hammered U-shaped nails to hold a thick copper wire along the slope of the roof and down the side of the school building where it connected to a stake. When the project was completed, the men explained how the entire assembly

326

diverted lightning from the building by carrying the electrical current to the ground.

"That keeps it from jumping around and causing fires," one of the men said.

As the pupils moved into the classrooms they chattered to each other in high-pitched voices, the outdoor science session staying with them. Storm clouds developing throughout the day intensified the restless mood.

"If they is thunder and lightning, we is safe now," a smug Adeline said.

"Does that contraption really work?" Willis wrinkled his brow.

"Of course it does," Violette said, hands on her hips. "You heard the man."

As the sky darkened, John sensed an unease among the scholars, in spite of the new *contraption* mounted to the building.

"Maybe we got that up just in time," Miss Bates said.

Her premonition proved to be right. Another storm rolled in that night and all day Saturday, causing havoc throughout the island. The pupils and staff spent Monday recess cleaning up debris from the wind and rain.

In the classrooms preparation for public exams began. An air of expectancy breezed through the institute, overriding the oppressive June air, the better scholars eager to do well, others anticipating the close of school in a few short weeks.

By Thursday, John began to be anxious himself. He had not yet received answers to his questions from DeGress or Howard. Friday morning, long before dawn, he tossed about on tangled sheets. The sticky heat pressed down on him like a giant hand until breathing became a chore. Somewhere a shutter banged every few seconds as yet a third storm approached. This one tore through Galveston with a vengeance, closing school and most businesses for the remainder of the week.

Chapter 47

On Saturday morning, John quickly dressed, stuffing his feet into an old pair of boots for the muddy trek to the business district. Rumors of boats washing ashore piqued his curiosity, and he needed to get out of the house and let loose a passel of energy. Even before the harbor came into view, he spied a mast where it shouldn't be. Crossing over to 19th, he skirted objects mired in muck, tripping over a half-buried crate as he stared down the street. A schooner and several sloops lay askew in the road, a surreal scene like a fairytale gone mad. Crowds of onlookers, mostly men, plodded about, their hands on hips, heads shaking.

A man beside John gave a low whistle. "Sure is somethin'. Ain't never seen nothin' like it."

A second man joined them. "I hear two bodies have been uncovered. Could be more yet. You should see what's left of St. Patrick's Church. It got blown to shambles."

The first man gave another whistle of disbelief. John stood silent. With no interest in exploring the damage further, he trudged back home. Shucking his muddy boots on the stoop, he entered the house and, seeking solace in his Bible, offered prayers for all those who had lost property and lives.

On Monday, most scholars returned. Difficult as it was to get back to a normal routine, the teachers continued studies for the upcoming exams. The following day John received the much anticipated reply from DeGress. His heart sank as he read the superintendent's words, for the 5th Judicial district covered the southernmost part of Texas. He couldn't possibly continue as principal of the Barnes Institute and supervise schools so distant. That would surely influence General Howard's feelings also.

Then there was DeGress's response to John's question regarding salary:

...The legislature made no appropriation to pay the traveling expenses of Supervisors. This office will furnish them with the necessary books and stationery for the transaction of the business of their office. There is no appropriation for office rent. The salary of all officers is paid out of the available school fund in the treasury.

This triggered more doubts as to whether a supervisory position was his calling. John hurriedly wrote Howard of the particulars, asking for guidance. He also sent a note to DeGress stating he preferred to be supervisor in his own district.

I know this area so well and could easily continue as principal at the institute here.

It was difficult to twist his thoughts away from the supervisory dilemma, but the end of school was at hand. On Thursday afternoon John met with the staff to evaluate the progress of the scholars, and to plan for examinations and other activities related to the close of the term.

"I will take it upon myself to contact the dignitaries we expect to attend the recital," he told the teachers. "And one more thing: I'd like to know your summer plans as soon as possible. There are schools elsewhere in Texas that continue throughout the summer and need teachers, if you are so inclined. Also, please advise me before the end of the term if you intend to return here next fall."

The meeting concluded, and the women left the room talking among themselves until only Miss Williams remained. She faced John. "May I speak with you a moment?"

He immediately sensed what she was about to say.

"I'm sorry, Mr. Ogilvie, but I won't be returning next fall."

He expressed his regrets and praised her for her support during the last two years. He could almost see a burden lift from her shoulders as she hurried out the door.

When Miss Bates approached him later with the same message, however, he felt a sense of loss. She represented a victory on his part and served a vital role at the institute.

"Is there a problem I can help with? Some adjustment that we might make to keep you here?" He held his breath waiting for the answer he wanted to hear—hoping there was a way to change her mind.

Miss Bates blushed and fingered the lace on a handkerchief she held tightly in her hands. "No, suh. My leavin's got nothin' to do with you or the school. You see, I's gittin' married and leavin'

Galveston all together." Happiness spread across her face, and John smiled with her. He couldn't argue with such a reason.

"Well, if that's the case, I wish you the very best, and if you ever need a reference for a teaching position, please contact me."

Miss Nichols told him in passing the following day of her intent to return in the fall, after a summer break, of course. That left Miss Keen—Anna. At the end of the school day, she stood at his office door. "Mr. Ogilvie?"

His pulse quickened and he stood. "Come in."

"It's about summer. I know the right thing to do is to volunteer at one of the other schools, but I want to go home to Wisconsin and visit my parents. The vacation will make me a better teacher next fall when I return here." She hesitated a moment, then added, "Assuming you want me."

He responded with an immediate smile. *Want her? Aye, more than she knows.* He managed a professional tone as he replied, "Of course you should go home. And I'm certainly hoping you will return. The institute needs teachers with your excellent qualifications."

"Thank you very much." She hesitated a moment than added, "I enjoy working with you, Mr. Ogilvie." She turned to leave.

"Wait." He had not yet mentioned to any of the teachers his possible supervisory position away from Galveston. He had to tell Anna.

She turned back to face him, a quizzical look in her eyes.

John stepped toward her and cleared his throat. What blurted from his mouth was not what he had planned. "The new opera house, have you attended yet?"

"No." Miss Keen still looked puzzled.

"Would you care to accompany me tomorrow night?"

Her face lit up. "Why, Mr. Ogilvie, I would be honored, but..." A blush crept up her cheeks. "Do you think, well, is it appropriate for a teacher to be seen in public with the principal? Socially, I mean?" She fidgeted with the hem of her sleeve.

John reached for her hand, and she did not resist. "I think it is most fitting," he said. "Shall I come by for you at seven?"

Miss Keen nodded, slipped her hand from his and eased out the schoolroom door.

He watched her leave, glad for his impulsiveness. There was still the matter of revealing to her the possibility of his leaving

Galveston as supervisor for another district, but perhaps while they were together tomorrow evening...

For the next twenty-four hours, education in Texas took second place to thoughts of Miss Keen. John spent Saturday polishing his shoes, airing his best suit, and rushing to town to buy a small bouquet of violets. At a quarter to seven, Alphonse brought his carriage around, for which John paid him extra.

When John approached the front door of the teachers' home, a schoolboy's jitters took hold of him and he whispered a small prayer. "Please, Lord, let everything go right."

And it did, from the time she took his arm and he escorted her to the carriage until he returned her home after the performance. The only flaw was his inability to mention the supervisory job. He promised himself he'd tell her after church the next day, but the opportunity didn't present itself then, either.

***

Monday, Juneteenth, the freedmen celebrated their emancipation. Organized by the colored people themselves, it was a grand affair with a parade, food, and music. John, along with the other teachers, attended. He marveled, as he had the very first time he witnessed this event on a much smaller scale in Lavaca, at the jubilation so apparent in the dancing, speeches and bountiful food. He observed Miss Nichols and Miss Keen shedding a few tears as they experienced for the first time the powerful feelings exhibited by the Negroes commemorating their release from bondage.

John and Miss Keen stood together as the festivities wound down, and he at last took a few moments to tell her of the pending supervisory appointment.

"I haven't mentioned it to the others, and won't until I make a decision," he said, as he explained his tentative situation. "I'm waiting to hear from Howard." There had been no official word from DeGress about changing his assignment to Galveston, and John feared it was not going to happen.

At first Miss Keen said nothing, and he wondered if she didn't understand what he was telling her. Then she said, "Of course, I would rather you stay in Galveston, but if you think by supervising other schools under the leadership of Colonel DeGress you can make a greater difference, then perhaps that is what you should do."

Her eyes were lowered, and he could still see no evidence of her interest, other than what would normally be expected from a conversation between two educators.

But as the evening grew late, he sensed that she wanted him to stay. Her eyes had told him so, but he mustn't let her feelings override the bigger picture—his reason for being in Texas in the first place.

His immediate future coalesced the very next day upon receipt of a letter from Howard.

June 15, 1871

Dear Bro. I prefer that you should remain as principal of a school. If you can get the position of school director I think you will be of service to the AMA...

Here was the direction he had waited for, clear and simple. The first sentence was all he needed to hear. John picked up a pen, dipped it in ink, and began a note to DeGress declining the appointment. At the conclusion of his brief reply, he breathed a sigh of relief and knelt in prayer.

The remaining days of the term kept the institute staff busy from dawn until late in the evening. The public exams commencing on June 26 continued for most of the week, and as John reported to the newspaper:

"The scholars acquitted themselves worthily and creditably to themselves and their Institute. Thus closed the second session of Barnes Institute, and we know we would not lose much by comparison with schools and pupils of longer standing and better advantages."

Honored guests at the closing ceremony included Senator Ruby, Judges Nelson and Debruhl, Johnson Reed, Esq., Frank Webb, Esq., and Elder J.S. Campbell. It was a satisfying conclusion to the school year.

Chapter 48

In mid-July, a firm rap resounded on John's office door. He marked the page he was reading and closed the book. *Who would be out in this oppressive heat?*

"Come in."

The door swung open and in marched a man he did not remember ever seeing about Galveston. Of medium build and slightly overweight, the stranger presented himself with a pompous air of great importance.

"Mr. Ogilvie?"

"Yes." John rose and extended a hand for a formal greeting. "How may I help you?"

"I am Captain William Walker, school supervisor of the 18th Judicial District. I am here to look over the Barnes Institute and make plans for the staff and curriculum for the coming school year." He cast an eye about the room, ignoring John's outstretched hand. "Hummm. Appears a little cramped. Perhaps a wall could be moved to allow more space."

Anger pulsed in John's veins. He withdrew his hand. *Who does this man think he is, storming into this institute as though he owns it?* "Have a seat," John said, any tone of congeniality gone from his voice.

Captain Walker promptly sat in the waiting chair, plucked an invisible speck of lint from his brown tweed suit, and met John's gaze from across the desk. "Of course, you know the state plans to take over the institute as part of its program for educating the coloreds."

John stared at the intruder, not certain he heard correctly. "I understand the state would like to include our building as part of the public school system. My staff and I are willing to work with the state, but I don't agree that you are to take it over." He waited a moment to control his words before continuing. "My contact with the missionary association tells me DeGress has offered to rent the facility. I am happy to discuss those terms with you."

The man shifted his weight and cleared his throat. "No need to get testy, Mr. Ogilvie. It's my job to handle all the technicalities so the schools can open by September fourth. There is a lot to be done. I need to find competent teachers, too."

"That is not an issue here. We have two excellent teachers returning. A staff of three is ideal, and with the help of the missionary association, we will fill that vacancy."

"Mr. Ogilvie, apparently you don't understand. That is no longer your responsibility."

"Captain Walker, as principal of the institute it *is* my responsibility."

"Actually, that will be the responsibility of the directors, who will also determine who shall be principal. I am still working on appointing directors for the schools in my district."

Now John was on his feet. "Captain Walker, this school was paid for and built by funds raised by sponsoring churches and the freedmen themselves. It is governed by a board of trustees of which I am a member, and I have been given authority by the board and the American Missionary Association to use my discretion as to the terms of rental of the building to the state. Colonel DeGress is aware of this, and he also said he will favor the appointment of our teachers. I suggest you confer with him on these matters." He gripped the edge of his desk. "Good day, sir."

The man rose. "Well, I'm sorry this was not a more amicable meeting. I will speak with the superintendent and get back to you." He turned and left the room with the same arrogant stride as he had entered.

John slumped into his chair, a heavy lump settling in his stomach. He would fight for his teachers, regardless of what became of him.

No, by God, more than that. I will keep my position as principal of this institute. There is obviously some sort of misunderstanding. It simply needs to be straightened out.

But a dark cloud of doubt hovered in his mind.

I asked for the supervisory position now held by this Captain Walker, a fact of which this man must certainly be aware. A misunderstanding can be dealt with, but politics is something else.

Howard had expressed the hope John would be appointed one of the directors. It now looked doubtful that would happen. He wiped the perspiration trickling down his face as the little office closed in on him. Striding out the door, he headed for the gulf shore. For an hour he hiked along the sand, the breeze and salt air slowly clearing his thoughts. He needed support, not only to secure his own position, but that of the teachers to whom he had promised jobs for the coming school year. *And the scholars, what of them?* They trusted him. This worried John more than anything.

He returned home, hoping his housemate would be there—someone to talk to. Louis had moved in a month before, but it wasn't like old times. He was usually off somewhere campaigning, and tonight was no exception. John spent the evening prayerfully reading his Bible, then worked late into the night on letters to DeGress, Howard, and, almost as an after thought, to Senator Ruby, telling of the visit from Walker and the *misunderstanding* regarding rental of the schoolhouse and hiring of the existing staff.

***

That Ruby responded first came as a surprise, but the content of his letter stunned John even more. In his role as Deputy Collector of Customs for Galveston, Ruby offered John the position of Marine Clerk in the Custom House and named a salary much more lucrative than anything he had received in the years he worked for the bureau and the missionary association. John's first reaction was about preserving his school job. Yet, year-end salaries had not come forth, and with the state now in the business of public education, who knew what the future held? In the meantime he must have a salary, not only for his daily needs, but to continually feed the cache for his own advanced education, a dream he still intended to realize.

The day after receiving Ruby's offer, John paced the length of the classrooms at least fifty times. Excitement grew with each step as he thought through the possibilities.

Aye, I'll accept the offer, at least until the decision of the Institute is resolved.

He wrote Howard immediately, telling of his decision.

> *I will not let this interfere with my responsibilities to the AMA and the institute. The pay will help me through the remainder of the summer. And while I am on the*

subject of money, may I remind you the teachers are still waiting on their salaries for June.

John arose early each morning and walked the few blocks to the Custom House on 20th Street where he clerked for eight hours. The job was easy enough, shuffling papers and working with numbers and the public; but he missed the challenge and rewards of teaching. As September neared, confusion and disagreements with the state regarding the institute continued. The problem didn't seem to be with DeGress but with Walker, who had been given full responsibility for negotiating the rental of the schoolhouse and hiring of the teachers. The man kept dragging his feet as to the terms for rent, and insisted the teachers apply to the state for their former positions and pass an examination before being accepted.

Howard's letters to John grew more intense:

We must have our teachers adopted by the state— Col. DeGress has proposed it and I must trust you to work it out amicably with subordinates. Would not Maj. L.W. Stevenson aid us in this thing and in getting them to rent our building? We have done it in every other state, thus enabling us to increase our work greatly, why not in Texas?

Louis was off campaigning, and even were he in Galveston, John wasn't certain his friend and former bureau assistant school superintendent currently wielded that must influence.

One evening, as John walked home from work, he encountered Washington Green and his daughter Violette returning from a shopping trip.

"Papa bought me a new dress for the first day of school. I'm going to be the very best student this year, I promise," Violette beamed.

"That wouldn't surprise me one bit," John said. "You have always been among the best." He refrained from giving her braid a gentle pull of affection. How he loved this bright youngster.

Washington fidgeted with the hat held in his hands. "There is gonna be school, ain't there, Mr. Ogilvie? I hear a meetin' of the trustees' been called cuz you got another job an' the state might get us different teachers. That ain't true, is it?"

John placed his hand on the man's shoulder. "There are some things that need to be worked out, Washington. School may start a little late, but don't you worry, the teachers and I will be there. You will learn more about it at the meeting."

"Yes, suh, Mr. Ogivlie." He looked at his daughter. "Now we got to get along home and show your mama that new dress."

John watched the two continue up the street. Washington was such a faithful trustee. The man would be at the meeting. John had no doubt about that. However, like his other night pupils, Washington believed John could do no wrong, a conviction he found both a blessing and a curse.

Upon entering his home, John felt a rush of joy. Louis sat at the table busily writing.

"Ahoy, mate," John pulled out a chair. "Good to see you. How goes the vote gathering?"

"Hard to tell. How are things at the Custom House?"

"Rather hum-drum."

"And the school situation?"

"Still the same." He wasn't going to pounce on the man for help the minute he walked in the door.

Louis tossed John a folded paper. "Well, here's something else to chew on. This was tacked to the door when I arrived. It's from your landlord."

John quickly read the short note:

A family member will be moving into the house at the end of the month. Please pay up your rent and vacate the premises no later than two weeks hence. Thank you for being such a reliable occupant.

John shook his head. "Sometimes lately I get the feeling I'm being kicked clear out of Texas. Do you have any thoughts on where we can move?"

"Not off hand, but it had better be cheap. I don't have a job at the moment. Guess we both had better look."

John sat at his desk at the Customs House the following morning, the August heat already promising an uncomfortable day. He tugged at his beard and wiped at beads of perspiration on his forehead, ignoring a sheaf of paper before him, his mind muddled with how to deal with Walker and now the worrisome prospect of finding a place to live. The bell on the door jingled, distracting his thoughts, and in walked Miss Nichols.

"You're back early." John leaped up from his chair and crossed the room to greet her. He had kept the teachers advised of the complications with the state by way of letters during their summer break, but he knew they still assumed things would be ironed out in their favor by September, including their delinquent pay. And now with Miss Nichols standing before him, he almost believed it himself.

"Yes, here I am," she said. "Ready to take Captain Walker's exam and show him he has nothing to worry about."

"Walker creates his own worries," John said. "I'm about to finish up here for the day. How about joining me for supper, somewhere we can talk. Louis is back, maybe he can come, too, though I never know about his evening plans."

"Frances, our new help, is preparing a meal at the teachers' home," Miss Nichols said. "Please join me there, say in about an hour? The Major is certainly welcome, too, if he is available."

Louis was not at the house, so John left him a note and headed for the teachers' home—humming—something he hadn't done for a while. When he stepped into the parlor he was suddenly aware of how lonely his summer had been.

Miss Nichols spoke up as she greeted him. "I had a letter from Anna quite recently, saying she planned to leave for Galveston soon. It shouldn't be too many days before she arrives."

John and Anna exchanged letters often, but having this news reinforced made it all the better. Over the meal, he filled Miss Nichols in on more details regarding the stalemate between the state and the AMA. "Howard is becoming impatient. He's having Colonel Sinclair as a member of the board of trustees draw up a contract. We're asking seventy dollars per month for use of the property along with maps, globes, and charts. In return they are to hire all our teachers, including me as principal. If they do not agree to these terms, the contract will become null and void. But enough of this. Tell me about your summer."

He stayed for an hour after dessert. "I do appreciate the meal and the company, but I must get a good night's sleep. Tomorrow I have to spend the day searching for new living arrangements." He told her of the note from the landlord.

"Goodness, you certainly don't need that problem right now." She seemed to ponder the situation a moment, then her face lit up.

"Why don't you and Louis move in here? Frances lives at her own home, unlike our former help, so there is an extra bedroom."

"I don't think—"

"It would save the AMA money and we all know that is a good thing, plus there have been times when we wished we had the protection of a man. We women have spent some fearful nights here."

The idea both jolted and intrigued John. Miss Nichols' arguments made sense, plus meals would no longer be a problem. Yet he wasn't sure it would be proper for men to live here with the women. Then he recalled his overnight stay on the way to Minnesota. "Aye, perhaps we could. Let me talk to Louis about it."

When the clock struck midnight and Louis had not yet returned, John blew out the lamp and crawled into bed. During the wait he had mulled over Miss Nichol's offer enough to conclude the reasons to move into the teachers' home outnumbered the reasons not too, regardless of what Louis might decide. In the morning he banged around in the kitchen making breakfast while the sleeping Louis snored a few feet away on the sofa.

"Hey, can't a man sleep in on a Saturday morning?" A crotchety voice sputtered from under a pillow.

"If you'd get in at a decent hour, it wouldn't be a problem. Besides, I have a tempting proposal to discuss with you."

He explained Miss Nichol's suggestion.

"That's a grand idea. Why would we even hesitate? Living with the teachers means good meals and comfortable beds. I, for one, am tired of sleeping on the sofa. There *are* separate beds, aren't there?"

John laughed, thinking back on his days at the Wallaces' when Jacob was in town. "Aye, two beds. If there was only one, you'd have to find your own place."

John telegrammed Howard to make certain it didn't cause any problems with the AMA, carefully numbering the positive points for the move. Howard was quick to agree. John and Louis would contribute toward the food and rent, of course, saving the ladies some of their precious income, and saving the missionary association even more.

The move was made well within the allotted time requested by the landlord.

Miss Nichols turned in her application to teach at the institute the Monday after she returned. "To expedite things and promote a show of cooperation," she told John.

In the meantime, Supervisor Walker communicated with Howard, but not with John. In fact, anytime John attempted to contribute information to Walker regarding the opening of the school, his efforts were squelched. He was definitely out of the loop.

At the Custom House Friday morning, September 1st, John tried concentrating on the documents before him, fighting a deep urge to walk out the door and head for the institute. Three more days and school was scheduled to begin under the auspices of the state. But would it?

"Hey, Ogilvie, here's a message for you, and from the looks of it, I'd say it's from a lady." Robert Thomas, a co-worker, thrust an envelope at him, then stood by, curiosity scrawled across his face.

John's heart somersaulted as he recognized the handwriting. He snatched the envelope from Robert's fingers. Tearing open the seal, the familiar script brought a flush of warmth:

> *Dear Mr. Ogilvie,*
> *I am finally in Galveston, having encountered unexpected travel problems along the way. I am anxious to see you and to learn details of the opening of the school. Can you join us for supper at the teachers' home this evening at 7:00?*
>
> > *Regards,*
> > *Anna Keen*

She had left for Galveston before John had a chance to write her of his move to the home, and today Miss Nichols was at the school preparing lessons, so there was no one to tell her of the new arrangement. He smiled to himself. *Yes, Anna, I will be there.*

Robert chuckled and broke into a grin. "Your ears are turning red. It Must be good news."

"Aye, that it is. Is the courier still here?"

"Yep. He's waiting for an answer. What shall I tell him?"

"Tell him to wait." John picked up pen and paper and wrote:

Dear Miss Keen,
   So glad you have arrived. I will be there promptly at seven.

   Yours Truly,
   John Ogilvie

He inserted the message into an envelope, affixed a seal on the flap, and strode to the waiting courier. "Thank you, sir. Now if you will deliver this to the lady, I will be much obliged." He dug into a pocket for a coin, which he handed to the boy.

Returning to his desk, he studied the stack of papers with disinterest.

A second note, this one from Sinclair, arrived at two p.m. He was in Galveston and requested they meet at the schoolhouse at five thirty that evening. John felt a rush of joy and relief. *Surely this means all parties have agreed to the terms of the contract and school will begin on time.*

He hummed through his work for the remainder of the afternoon, feeling as though the hand of God had reached down and pulled him upright once more. He came close to handing in his resignation as marine clerk before leaving, but decided against it until he knew all the details.

As soon as he walked into his office at the institute, the somber look on Sinclair's face altered his mood. "So, the contract still isn't signed."

"No, but you need to be aware I am permitting classes to begin here on Monday because Colonel DeGress is anxious to open as many schools as possible on that day under the new system." Sinclair hesitated, seeming to study John's face for a reaction before continuing. "Are you aware that only one of our teachers has applied to Walker for examination?"

"Aye. That would be Miss Nichols. Miss Keen arrived only just today. But you know as well as I that taking this exam should not be an issue. The contract says our teachers shall be hired, including me, and that does not mean we have to apply or go through the absurdity of an exam."

Sinclair did not respond. There was more here than John was being told. "What seems to be the problem? I don't understand this delay. The school and its staff have an outstanding reputation. It's almost as though Captain Walker has something personal against me." The impact his words had on Sinclair's expression sent a shudder through John. He had found the answer. "That's it, isn't it?" His words came soft and slow.

"I'm afraid so."

"Why?"

"Jealousy, maybe. Who knows? I suspect there are some politics involved. Basically, if Howard insists you must be hired along with the teachers, the contract won't be signed. I'll still work at it and in the meantime advise Howard as to what's going on."

John rose from his chair, walked to the window and gazed out at the neighborhood. Everything looked exactly as always, the rest of Galveston unaware that his progression of work in Texas had just been shattered. He slowly exhaled. "That man doesn't know what he's doing."

Chapter 49

John trudged home in near despair. He had been so eager to see Miss Keen, expecting to sweep into the house bearing the great news that all issues had been resolved. Now he had to tell the ladies the trouble existed because of him and, what was most maddening, he wasn't sure why.

He stood on the front porch, breathing deeply to calm his rapid heartbeat and regain his composure. He knocked out of habit, and a smiling Anna Keen opened the door. "Welcome, Mr. Ogilvie. Please come in. I understand this is your home now, too. What a practical plan."

John couldn't control the wide smile that sprang to his lips. It felt so right to have Anna here. "I'm glad you approve, Miss Keen, and it is good to see you." He shrugged out of his coat, happy to be rid of it in the muggy September weather.

Anna took it from him and hung it on the rack beside the door. "We are eager to hear your news regarding the school." She spoke with more animation than usual and her face appeared slightly flushed.

She is as happy to see me as I am her. The thought raced through John. *I wish I'd brought flowers, but that was the furthest thing from my mind after the devastating meeting with Sinclair.*

"I have much to say about the school, but first I want to hear about your trip. You ran into problems?"

Miss Nichols emerged from the kitchen carrying a platter of fried chicken. "Can we talk over supper? Everything is ready and hot. Will Major Stevenson be joining us?"

"No, he is off campaigning for a few days. You might as well get used to that."

They took their seats at the table.

"Mr. Ogilvie, will you please say grace?" Miss Nichols asked.

Both women looked at him expectantly. He smiled and bowed his head. A moment of silence centered his thoughts. "Dear Lord, bless this bountiful table and the hands that prepared it. Bless these women who give of themselves so unselfishly in your service. May we all be ever mindful that we are here to do thy will no matter how that might manifest itself. Help us to understand those things that confound us and let us not forget to trust in you. Humble us in your presence and in the presence of others. In your holy name, we pray. Amen."

As he prayed, his anguish since learning of Griffin's pointed dislike for him slowly unraveled, and a peaceful quiet lingered in the room.

Miss Nichols broke the stillness. "Well, what will you have, Mr. Ogilvie, a drumstick?"

As the food was passed, conversation resumed, first with Miss Keen's account of a delayed train due to a derailment and a myriad of minor mishaps along the way. Over dessert, she turned to John. "Enough about me. We must hear about the school. Will we be starting on Monday? And do we have a third teacher?"

"I just came from a meeting with Sinclair. The state, mostly Walker, is still balking at signing the contract, but because Superintendent DeGress wants the schools to open on Monday, our board of trustees is allowing it. The two of you will have to do the best you can until more teachers are hired. Miss Eastman, who was expected to join us, has health problems, and probably won't come."

"And what about you? Will you help with the day classes as you have done in the past?" Miss Keen's eyes sought his.

John took a deep breath. "Not for now. Not until this is resolved." He hesitated a moment before continuing, amazed at how composed he felt. "It seems I'm the problem. Walker is agreeable to hiring all the staff except for me. He doesn't like me and wants me out."

Miss Nichols jumped to her feet. "I don't believe it. With all you have done for the school and the students? What is wrong with that man?" She flung her napkin down, stacked empty plates together with a clank and marched into the kitchen.

Miss Keen sat still, all color drained from her face. "I don't understand it. You are the finest man I have ever known." She blushed and lowered her gaze.

He reached for her hand. "Thank you for your confidence, Anna. It means a lot. Somehow it will work out for the best." Her fingers tightened on his, a reassurance like no other.

Miss Nichols swept back into the room and dropped into her chair with a huge sigh. "Well, what are we going to do about it?"

John released Anna's hand, their intimate moment ended. "Sinclair and Howard are trying to work something out, but if Walker refuses to hire me, there will be no contract. The state won't get any of us, including the schoolhouse which they desperately need."

"Then what?" Anna asked.

"Howard suggests we reopen under the auspices of the AMA."

Miss Nichols folded her arms across her chest. "Where will the money come from? We have yet to be paid for last June."

"We'll have to raise tuition."

A look of concern sprang across Anna's face. "But can the scholars afford it?"

"Some can. Some can't," John said. "That is better than no school at all. However, there is an alternative."

"And what might that be?" Miss Nichols asked.

"I can leave the institute. I think Walker will sign the contract if I am out of the picture."

"No," Miss Nichols was adamant.

"But where would you go?" Alarm resonated in Anna's voice.

"There are schools still hiring missionary association teachers. Howard has recently alluded to several where he could send me. Either way, I won't show up Monday for the opening of school. You ladies will have to brave it on your own. In the meantime, we'll see what Sinclair can do for us."

This final suggestion numbed further conversation, and an awkward silence stilled the room. Miss Nichols stood. "I'm worn out from setting up at school all day, and Miss Keen, you must be exhausted after your travels. We should go to bed." She reached for Anna's hand. "Good night, Mr. Ogilvie."

Anna cast an anxious glance in John's direction before she and Miss Nichols closed the door behind them.

In his own room, John turned down the lamp wick and sat in the dark, once more going over his conversation with Sinclair earlier that evening. Again despair swamped him. *Dear God, help me with this.* After long moments of thought and prayer he reached the only logical conclusion. If the standoff persisted much longer, for the sake of harmony, he would step down from his position as principal of the institute.

All day Monday, September 4th, during his hours at the Custom House, John's thoughts focused on the Barnes Institute, the teachers, and the scholars. Leaving work promptly at five o'clock p.m., he hurried home, anxious to hear about the first day of school. As he reached the door, his tension eased. The thought of Anna being there made him smile. Throughout the summer there had been a hollowness inside him, and in spite of all the turbulence in the past weeks, knowing she was back in town had sweetly filled that void.

He entered the house without knocking—still a strange sensation—almost as though he were committing a social blunder. Hearing voices in the kitchen he followed the sound. Anna and Miss Nichols stood at the dry sink assisting Frances.

"Hello, ladies. How did the day go?"

All three turned to look at him. Miss Nichols spoke first. "Good evening, Mr. Ogilvie. All right, I guess." She sighed. "Mr. Walker showed up first thing this morning, strutting through the classrooms as though he owned them." Her voice sounded tired.

"There were very few students," Anna added.

"I expected as much," John said. "Information to the public has been confusing and tenuous." He couldn't help but notice a troubled look in Anna's eyes. "Is there more? Something you're not telling me?"

The conversation was awkward in the presence of Frances. Anna glanced over at Miss Nichols and an understanding seemed to pass between them. She slipped off her apron. "I need some fresh air. Would you care to go for a walk, Mr. Ogilvie?"

"Aye." John smiled, though he sensed conversation during their stroll might not be light and pleasurable.

Anna's expression remained solemn as they left the house. A light fog swirled about them and neither spoke for an entire block before Anna stopped and turned to look at him. "One thing you need to know: Sinclair stayed over in Galveston for the beginning of school. This afternoon he came by and talked to us about the low attendance, saying Walker feels it was deliberate. Oh, Mr. Ogilvie, he thinks it's due to secret work you have been doing among the colored people."

John's temple began to throb. "Where in God's name does he get these ideas?"

"Miss Nichols and I told Sinclair that was absolutely not the case. He and the rest of the trustees know it, but convincing Walker is another matter. He is angry at me, too, for not filling out the application or taking his exam."

John shook his head, his own anger rising again. The ladies shouldn't have to suffer on his account. "We'll have to wait and see what the week brings." He took Anna's arm and tucked it under his, determined to catch a few moments of pleasure during their time together.

On Friday they learned the answer. Walker formally rejected all the AMA teachers. John telegraphed Howard immediately, who followed up by letter, laying the way for the next step.

> *September 12, 1871*
>
> *Dear Bro,*
>
> *I have today written to Col. Sinclair that I desire him to confer with the other trustees and if they agree with my views, to refuse the house to the authorities unless they will reestablish our teachers. Then the question is whether to offer our own school with tuition as before or to withdraw altogether from Galveston at present. Little good comes from something bad.*
>
> *I am willing to abide by a decision of the trustees. But on the other hand if there is a disposition to concessions by the school authorities and supervisor through the influence of Col. Sinclair and Col. DeGress, I am willing to send a man to relieve you at Galveston and send you to Columbus, Miss. or to some other place in Texas if you prefer. But in that case you ought to be put in to organize I think and keep the school operating until a new principal shall arrive. However, I much prefer you should remain at that school if practicable.*
>
> *I shall be anxious to get the views of the trustees. I telegraphed DeGress of your rejection and teachers, asking, "Will you correct this wrong?" I have no answer as yet from him.*

John's hands shook, his heart heavy. Even though Howard said he preferred John stay, he suspected those were simply words. Nothing seemed to be leading up to his staying—quite the opposite. And for the AMA to withdraw from Galveston altogether was out of the question. The school fought for by Sarah Barnes, a

dream that almost destroyed her health, must not close down
because of political squabbles. He read the letter once again and
released a heavy sigh. He had put it off as long as possible, hoping
against hope that things would change. Now he knew what he had
to do.

The women were out shopping. John sat alone in the parlor,
head bowed. The door opened and Anna walked in carrying a
basket of groceries. He stood, her presence instantly gratifying.

Anna set the basket down and pulled a scarf from her head.
Her glance caught hold of the letter in John's hand. Studying his
face, her smile paled. "Is something wrong?"

"It's from Howard, containing more of his thoughts on the
school situation."

"You're troubled."

The worry in her eyes both touched and pained him. "You
might as well know, Anna. I plan to resign. I'll have a letter to that
affect prepared for the next trustee meeting."

Shock clouded her eyes. "But Howard wants to you to stay."

"No, under the circumstances, he does not. He is proposing I
go to Columbus, Mississippi, and he will send another man here to
appease the state's authorities." As he spoke the words, the truth
cut even deeper.

"No. Surely things can be worked out."

"I have given it much thought. Howard is right. For me to step
down is the best solution."

She moved swiftly to him. He reached out and drew her close,
the letter dropping to the floor. Her arms went around him and
they held each other tight. John buried his face in her soft, sweet-
smelling hair, savoring the sensation of her heartbeats mingled
with his.

"John," she murmured, "Please don't leave. We need you. The
students need you."

He couldn't speak. Never before had she called him by his
given name. The sound of it, the intimacy of it, and the feel of her
in his arms brought a new joy. The fervor with which she clung to
him made him dizzy as the realization dawned that this woman
might actually care for him as deeply as he had hoped. When he
finally found his voice, it was only to murmur, "Anna, Anna," his
lips pressed against her hair.

She pulled away first, her eyes moist. "There must be another
way."

John wiped her cheek with his thumb to catch an escaping tear. "I'll still be in Galveston for a while. At least until Howard finds a place for me, and in the meantime I have a job at the Custom House. It's you and Miss Nichols I'm concerned about, with little income and waiting for the state to make up its mind."

Anna reached up and smoothed her hair, her fingers trembling, her cheeks pink. Taking a deep breath to regain her composure, she said, "We will be all right. It just seems so terribly unfair. The institute belongs to the freedmen, and the state should respect that fact; but more than anything, you should remain as its principal."

John couldn't take his gaze off her and had to smile at the anger displayed on her face, so uncharacteristic of this gentle woman. The fact that her resentment grew from what she saw as an injustice to him touched him deeply. More than that, Anna knew without being told how hurt he was that Howard would let him go to appease the state.

***

John kept on at the Custom House. He would quit only when his new orders came from Howard. Being busy all day, every day, kept money coming in and his mind occupied. At first he worried the ladies wouldn't have anything to do while negotiations with the state continued, but he learned in a hurry that wasn't so. In the evenings they talked about their days—catching up with sewing, letter writing, and reading, and according to them, hardly enough time for that. Though it was all women talk, John was thankful he had a lively place to call home.

Louis returned from his road trip a week later. His first evening there he contributed little toward the supper conversation and excused himself early for bed. When John later joined him, he found his roommate still awake and reading in the dim lamplight.

John sat on the one chair in the room and pulled off a boot. "Are things not going well?" he asked.

Louis sighed, laid the book down and rubbed his eyes. "It's an uphill battle. There's a lot of support for Clark out there, and depending on where I am, even more for Giddings. In the beginning, Sinclair thought my prospects were good unless the wire-pullers and tricksters gerrymandered me out of it. Looks like that might be the case. Just the same, I'm as stubborn as you, my Scottish friend, and I refuse to quit."

John didn't respond.

"You seem a little down yourself," Louis said. "Has school started?"

"Aye, classes met for one week then shut down. If and when it reopens, it appears I'll not be a part of it."

Louis sat up straight and swung his legs to the side of the bed, his book falling to the floor with a thud, a look of disbelief on his face. "Surely you aren't leaving."

"I have a lot to tell you, old friend."

They talked for an hour, John filling Louis in on the impasse with the state and Howard's recent reactions.

"This isn't like you, John, to give in so easily." Louis was now wide awake and pacing.

"It seems I'm the problem," John said, "and though Walker is being unreasonable, it's unfair to the scholars and the teachers for me to stand in the way when they could be back at school."

"Is there anything I can do? I'm acquainted with DeGress from bureau days. Maybe I could talk to him, though it may not help. I hear he is a strong supporter of Clark. Blasted politics."

"I'm much obliged for your offer. I suppose you could try, but I doubt it would help." John ran a hand through his hair and sighed. "We both know I should be out there stumping for you right now. Unfortunately, my support might work against you at the moment."

Louis lay back on the bed, propping his head up on the pillow with his arm. "Are you still working at the Custom Office?"

"Aye. It brings in money and helps control my anger."

"That's where you need to be—not following me around. Just throw my name out now and then as the best candidate. Every vote helps."

John changed into his nightclothes, turned the lamp wick down and found his own bed. He stared into the darkness. Along with everything else, he had let Louis down. The room filled with silence like cotton stuffed into a hole. Election day was less than two weeks away. His friend had every right to be angry and hurt that he hadn't done more to support him.

Soft snoring from the other bed brought a smile to John's face. This was not the sound of anguish over a disloyal companion.

Chapter 50

On September 26, with no other place to convene, the trustees crowded into the teachers' home for a meeting. All were present except for Sinclair, who had returned to Austin, and each man in the small group wore a solemn face. Anger and frustration could almost be grabbed like something tangible. But John sensed hope hung in the air also. The newly elected president, Washington Green, stood tall, proud, and nervous at his unaccustomed position of importance.

"I call this here meetin' to order," he said with great authority, "Now we needs to figure what to do about our school."

John read part of the latest letter from Howard:

> I see there is no chance that the state board will take our teachers. I therefore cannot consent to their occupying the schoolhouse. Please request our trustees to take possession of the house to the exclusion of everybody until Oct. 2, when you and the ladies there may open.

"General Howard has written to DeGress and Walker refusing the lease." John said. "He also mentions if the state won't turn over the school, we may have to use force of law."

"I vote we open school like it was before," Alfred Perkins said. Clapping and cheers broke out and unanimous "ayes" circled the room.

"The only problem with that is the pupils will have to pay a higher tuition," John said. "Can they do that?" He watched the faces of the colored men in particular. They were the ones who would know the answer to this question.

Washington shook his head. "Well, I dunno about that. What with my new job and all, maybe Violette and I can keep on going, but there'll be some folks won't come."

More discussion followed, and it was decided school for some was better than no school at all. Washington and Perkins agreed to approach Supervisor Walker the following day with their decision and ask for the key.

"There's one more thing," John said. From his inner coat pocket he pulled out an envelope, handing it to Washington. The man read it to himself first, disbelief crawling across his face as the meaning of the words sunk in.

"This here says Mr. Ogilvie won't keep on at the school." His voice broke at the announcement.

A chorus of loud, startled "No!"s rang out.

"But if we run the institute on our own, there is no reason for you to leave," one man protested.

John simply shook his head. "It is partly the money," he said. "We needed that monthly rent from the state. Howard wants me to go to Mississippi, where some of my salary can be paid from a fund."

More objections from the trustees poured forth. John held up his hand. "For now, that is the way it is. If I could change it I would. I think you all know how much the school and the scholars mean to me." He tried to ignore the ache in his chest. Yet he mustn't appear defeated in front of these men. He promised the trustees he would stay to organize and begin classes as Howard had suggested. When the meeting adjourned, John shook the hand of each member, then watched from the window as they trooped up the street and out of sight.

To John's gratification, hope still prevailed with the teachers. "We will write Howard on our own," Anna said. "Everything will turn out fine. You'll see."

The next evening as they were sitting down for a meal, a knock sounded at the door. Miss Nichols hurried to answer it with John close at her heels. Washington stood on the porch, his clothing damp from a light rain. "Mr. Green, please come in," Miss Nichols said. "Won't you join us for supper?"

The trustee removed his hat and stepped inside, his dark face grim. "No, thank you, Ma'am. I need to speak to Mr. Ogilvie."

John tensed. "What is it, Washington?"

"Suh, they won't give us the key." Washington's eyes narrowed. "I helped pay for that building, Mr. Ogilvie. It belongs to me and my little girl and the other freedmen. That was the promise of Miss Barnes, and the state's got no say so about that."

John laid his hand on the man's shoulder, feeling the heat of his anger. "I know, Washington. We aren't giving up."

When Washington left, John joined the ladies at the supper table, announcing the reason for the man's visit. The ladies were at a loss for words. John offered grace—a few, unoriginal words. Dishes were passed in silence. As a plate of rolls went around for a second time, Miss Nichols found her voice. "So, does this mean we need to get a lawyer?"

"That costs money," Anna said, a crestfallen look on her face.

John swallowed a sip of coffee before answering. "I hope we don't have to resort to that. We may have pushed things a little soon. Perhaps Walker had not yet received Howard's letter refusing the lease and asking for possession of the building. We'll wait a bit then I will visit him myself and demand the key."

Three days later, John sat in Walker's office listening to the man's words.

"You want your job back, Ogilvie? All it takes is a guarantee you will vote for Clark and do a little campaigning for him."

John stood, his chair scraping the floor with a grating screech. "Sir, your tactics are deplorable. Who I vote for has nothing whatsoever to do with the Barnes Institute. Now, about the key..."

The man shrugged, and continued tapping a pencil against the desk.

John found his way out and marched directly to the office of a local lawyer. He would not pray forgiveness for his wrath as he had sometimes done in the past. The Bible held all sorts of examples of legitimate anger. His father had once said, "anger in a righteous cause is a virtue."

As he entered the lawyer's office, John reflected on a letter from Howard, received only the day before. It had countered his original suggestion of using force of law. *"Nothing is gained by religious or benevolent associations entering into law-suits and quarrels,"* Howard had written. However, he also said, *"Please make certain that every colored man in Galveston understands about the underhanded and dishonest way in which those officials have conducted themselves."*

After his visit with the attorney John retraced his steps and headed for home. *Well,* he thought, *wait until Howard hears about Walker's latest comment.*

That afternoon, September 30th, John composed a letter to Howard telling of Walker's refusal a second time to turn over the key:

You were correct in that politics are at the heart of the matter, so in light of this newest development, I have consulted a lawyer about our rights. There was no charge for the consultation, and I will keep you posted.

As John wrote, sitting alone at the dinner table in the teachers' home, the wind outside distracted him. It had been blowing all morning, stronger than usual, and each glance through the window showed more dark clouds piling up over the gulf. The women were out visiting the homes of some of the scholars, and Louis had been gone since early morning. John waited for their return, his anxiety rising. Rain began to spatter the window panes. Branches screeched against the house, and then a loud crash outside caused him to jump. *Where in heaven's name are Anna and Miss Nichols?*

He stood for the umpteenth time and walked to a window. No one in his right mind should be out in this relentless gale. With a surge of relief, he spotted the two women struggling against the wind and rain. A short distance behind them another figure pushed forward. Anna and Miss Nichols entered the house, looking as though they had been thrown into the gulf. They had scarcely removed their soggy outerwear and shoes when Louis burst through the door.

"Whoo-eee. I almost got blown right by the house and out to sea." He pulled off his coat, hung it on the rack by the door, and started to walk across the parlor to the kitchen.

"Oh, no you don't," Miss Nichols exclaimed. "You take off those shoes and carry them to the back porch. You are not tramping mud through this house."

John watched with amusement as Louis, normally a very much in-charge person, meekly obliged.

As the day progressed, the fury outside grew in intensity. They sat around the dinner table, sipping hot soup, the flame in the lamp dancing in its chimney. John told of his visit to Walker but didn't mention the man's insistence that he support Clark for Congress. He did, however, say he came away without the key to the institute. "So, I have contacted a lawyer."

Before anyone had a chance to respond, something floating on the current of wind outside slammed against the house. Miss Nichols gave a shriek. Then, obviously embarrassed at her involuntary response, she composed herself and said, "This is getting too common-place. Next teaching assignment I ask for will be far inland."

"We lived through the June storms," Anna said, "I expect by morning this will have passed over too."

John admired her attempt at bravery. The angry roar from the gulf made conversation difficult. Yet there was one difference—this time they were all together. John abandoned any talk of his frustrating day and suggested singing rousing hymns.

At ten, Anna said, "I don't know about the rest of you, but, God willing, I plan on going to church in the morning, and I need some sleep."

They took her cue and retired to their respective rooms. John slept in fragments. The storm running rampant through Galveston seemed to parallel the tempest in his own life—acts of aggression over which he had no control. *Dear God,* he prayed, *help the people of Galveston brave the wind and water, and help the scholars, Miss Nichols, Miss Keen, and myself survive our own struggles.*

In the morning everyone appeared bleary-eyed, and no one ventured outside to attend church, as rain and wind were still on a rampage.

"We can have our own service here," John said. "I think the Lord will forgive us for not killing ourselves to get to church."

They sang and prayed, and John dug into his memory for one of his better sermons from his Lavaca days. Some of his words disappeared beneath the howling of the storm, but most were heard.

Later that day, as he stood at a window looking out, Anna appeared beside him. "Your sermon this morning was so meaningful, Mr. Ogilvie. You *will* have your own church someday. Of that I am certain."

He smiled. "Thank you, Anna. With the Lord's help, that is my goal, though I'm learning His plans are not always what I have in mind."

Louis joined them as they stood observing the storm. "Maybe this will keep all voters away on Tuesday except the able-bodied and strong-willed, who of course will be my followers. Birds of a feather, you know."

"We'll pray for your success," Anna said, and she excused herself to join Miss Nichols in the kitchen to prepare supper. Frances would not be braving the storm to get from her house to theirs today.

On Monday, October 2nd, the power of the hurricane diminished. Water from the storm filled the streets, the gulf and bay mingling throughout the island as though it resented the intrusion of land in its midst. By October 3rd, election day, the sun rose golden against a blue sky. John and Louis ventured to the polls, sloshing through the sludge and rivulets. Unlike the election two years previous, John was now a citizen and registered to vote. He would have stuffed the ballot box for his friend if he could—especially after Walker's ultimatum. A surprising number of voters showed up, the sunshine obviously a strong factor, even though the stench of dead fish and sewage permeated the air.

Hurricane damage lay strewn about the city and after John and Louis cast their ballots; they walked about to have a look. Again, as in June, small boats floated inland, circling aimlessly on the water-logged streets, or slammed askew against buildings and flotsam. On 20th Street they encountered John's co-worker, Robert Thomas.

"I guess it could be worse," Robert said, shaking his head. "We could all be drowned. The *S.S. Hull* sank off the coast during the height of the storm. All hands were lost."

John rubbed his temple and whispered a prayer for the poor souls onboard the steamer, the unpredictability of death shifting his own problems into perspective.

The polls recessed at noon. The early votes would be counted and posted during the day, so John and Louis returned to the courthouse to see. Louis marched into the building, seeking the bulletin board while John hung back. Louis returned with a wide grin, and John felt his own stomach somersault. *Could he possibly have won?* Of course these were just early numbers and for Galvston only, But still...

"Good news?"

"I'll say. I got five more votes than Clark."

John stepped up to scan the names and numbers, and chuckled. Stevenson 19; Clark 14. He clapped Louis on the back. "Well done, my friend, well done."

They headed for home, neither mentioning the 293 votes for Giddings, Democrat, whom the *Daily News* had endorsed.

In the end, the total count for the district left Louis in the dust and the results for Clark and Giddings so close that accusations of fraud were flying. "I'm glad not to be a part of that," Louis said. "Like you, John, I thought I could make a difference, but it was not to be."

With the storm and elections over, John refocused on the Barnes Institute. Charging tuition still troubled him, but perhaps with a strong plea to sponsoring churches the amount could be set low enough for all scholars to attend. He pictured the indomitable Sarah Barnes and her dream. He mustn't let the result of her hard work die.

As requested by the AMA, Sinclair annulled the contract that allowed the state to rent the schoolhouse, and in spite of General Howard's hesitation to take legal action, John returned to the lawyer's office. If the missionary association expected to open the school and run it as a private institution, they had to get possession of the building. For now, he would sacrifice some of his own pay as marine clerk to get things rolling. The lawyer issued a writ notifying the state directors to give up possession of the building before October 10th or proceedings would begin against them.

Chapter 57

On October 6th, John resigned his position as marine clerk. It was time to forge ahead and prepare to open the school, whether he would be staying or not. *Surely, the building will be ours any day now.*

He arose early the following morning, Saturday, in high spirits over the goals he had set for himself and the institute. The rest of the household still slept, and he quietly made coffee, gulping down a cup while he munched on a slice of buttered bread. Leaving a note on the dining room table, he let himself out the door and headed for the schoolhouse. No one had checked there yet for storm damage. Though they still waited for a key to the building, he could at least determine what repairs, if any, would be required for the exterior.

The evening before, he had told Anna and Miss Nichols of his resignation at the Custom House and his decision to stay long enough to reopen the institute as a private AMA school. Both women beamed with obvious relief.

"Howard must keep you here under those circumstances," Anna said.

In his heart, John felt she was right, but couldn't make promises. "We shall see. There are still things to be worked out."

After a cursory look, John determined the sturdy brick building appeared to have weathered the wind and rain well. A few shingles lay about the grounds and a window pane had shattered when a shutter came loose. The remaining windows, boarded up due to the closure, were still secure, and because of the building's elevated foundation, he doubted any water had seeped into the interior. A prayer of thanks sprang to his lips.

When John returned home, the ladies had eaten breakfast and were cleaning up in the kitchen. Louis sat at the table sipping coffee and reading a paper he had walked to town and back to get.

Since the election, he was restless, and John suspected he would be leaving soon.

"So, how's the school look?" Louis asked.

"It's in good shape. A few shingles gone and a window needs replacing. That's about it."

"Good. It's a well-built structure."

On hearing their voices, the ladies came from the kitchen. "Well?" Anna asked.

When John reported minimal damage, a radiant smile stretched across her face. "Wonderful. Do you think we can start school on Monday?"

"I doubt it will be that soon. We need to hear from Howard first. I telegraphed him of the writ and our intentions to open the school," John said. "He should be contacting the directors, also Walker and DeGress, to inform them. I'll notify the trustees. As soon as we have a key then we'll spread the word to the pupils and get started."

"That might take days," Anna said, disappointment coloring her voice.

"Maybe, maybe not."

Louis folded the newspaper and laid it on the table. "I hate to throw water on the flames, but there is always the possibility the state will counter the writ."

John nodded. "They might. But perhaps when they see how serious we are, it will reopen negotiations." He was determined to be positive about the future.

On Sunday morning, vehicles were able to make their way through most of the streets without getting mired in the muck. Alphonse swung by with his carriage to take them to church so the ladies wouldn't get their shoes and hems muddy. As they alighted from the coach, John took Anna's hand, tucking it under his arm to assist her in avoiding a particularly deep puddle. She continued to hang onto him as they walked up the church steps and entered the sanctuary. It felt so right, the two of them together.

The Reverend ranted on about God sending violent storms to strengthen the weak and punish the sinners. John didn't particularly agree.

I would have given a quite different message. His thoughts wandered. *Fall classes must start as soon as possible. There are freed coloreds waiting for an education. That is why we're here, in this town, at this time.*

His own future could wait. For now, he must be true to the likes of Washington and Violette Green, and to the others.

By Wednesday nothing had been heard from the lawyer or Griffin regarding service of the writ, and surprisingly, Howard had not telegraphed a response. Agitated over the delay, John scratched follow-up letters to Howard and Sinclair. He pulled on his boots and coat and stepped outside. Sunlight waltzed with shadows as he hiked toward town. Passing by Adeline's home, he waved at the girl's mother who was sweeping leaves off the porch.

Mrs. Westley returned the greeting with a bright smile. "Mornin', Mr. Ogilvie. Better day today."

"Yes, Ma'am, it truly is." He stopped and removed his hat. "And how is Adeline?"

"She's waitin' for school to start up. When that goin' be?"

"Should be soon. We'll get the word out when we know the exact date."

The woman stopped sweeping and leaned on the broom handle, a frown wrinkling her forehead. "I hear tell school's goin' to cost us more money from now on. That ain't true, is it?"

John cleared his throat to rid it of a pinched feeling. "If students can pay a little more, it will keep the school going, Mrs. Westley."

The frown stayed in place and she tugged at a knitted shawl slipping off one shoulder. "Might make it so's Adeline can't go. Her daddy be outa work right now. It's all we can do to keep food on the table."

A picture flashed in John's mind of a grinning Adeline awarded best reader in the intermediate classes after the public examinations. This girl absolutely had to continue her schooling. Along with Violette Green, John pegged her to be a teacher in a few years. "Don't you worry, Mrs. Westley, Adeline will be accepted no matter what. I'll see to that."

"Don't look good if some pay and some don't."

John thought quickly so as not to offend the woman. "We have scholarships—special money sent from churches up north for excellent students like your daughter. She still pays, only with God's help, and someday she returns the favor by teaching other students."

Mrs. Westley eyed John steadily, tugging at her shawl again as though trying to take hold of what he just said. A smile began to work at the corners of her mouth. "Adeline a teacher? Do you really expect so?"

Charcoal and Chalk

"I do, Mrs. Westley. She is a very bright girl."

"That would be somethin'. Really somethin'. You be sure and let us know when school starts." She began sweeping again, this time with renewed vigor, not even noticing her shawl had slipped completely off her shoulders and onto the porch.

John tipped his hat to her and continued on his way, her alto voice following him on the breeze. *"Ride on, King Jesus, No man can a hinder me, Ride on, King Jesus."*

As he walked, John thought through what he had said in his impromptu explanation to Mrs. Westley.

The money from the churches isn't exactly scholarships, but it was sent to keep the schools functioning and that's what matters. One thing for certain, the institute is not going to turn any pupil away. The money will come from somewhere. Suddenly he could hardly wait for the doors to open. *As soon as possible I'll write a dozen churches.*

Striding into the post office, he deposited his mail, then asked if there was anything for him in return. "Nothing, Mr. Ogilvie," the postmaster said. "And don't expect to hear from Chicago for awhile. Have you seen today's paper?"

"No, something important?" He didn't like the tone of the man's voice.

"According to the story, that whole city burned to the ground Sunday night."

John's mind raced. "Impossible. It's a big place. I've been there. The whole town couldn't burn."

"Find a paper and read for yourself."

John pushed open the door and bolted up the street. A young boy stood on the corner of Market and 20th, waving the *Galveston Daily News*. John reached for a copy and the boy pulled it back. "That'll cost you, mister. It ain't for free."

John fished a coin from his pocket and handed it to the boy. "Keep the change," he said, not wasting time to check the amount.

"A half-dollar. Thanks, mister."

John scarcely heard him as he stared at the headlines:

Wednesday, October 11, 1871,
THE DREADFUL CALAMITY AT CHICAGO.
The fearful conflagration that has just laid a large portion of Chicago in ruins must awaken feelings of commiseration in every bosom.... The dispatches tell us that

the great city of Chicago is destroyed; that hundreds of millions of active capital have vanished; that already one-third of the inhabitants are homeless and dependent on others.

John revised his plan for the day and headed for the telegraph office where he sent a message to Howard: *Just learned of the fire. I pray you are safe.*

The telegraph operator looked at the destination and gave a low whistle. "I'll get it there if I can. From what I hear, most places burned to the ground and there ain't much left of that city. Heard say it started in a cow barn, of all places."

"Let me know when I get a reply," John said.

"Certainly will. That's my business." The man began tapping the message before John was out the door.

He hurried home to tell Miss Nichols and Anna of this latest development. As he marked the distance in long strides, he wondered how this catastrophe would affect not only the Barnes Institute, but the other missionary schools under the direction of the Chicago office.

Anna sat quietly. Miss Nichols wrung her hands and paced. "Sometimes I wonder if the Lord wants us to continue school here at all. We just get one blow after another."

"The Lord has nothing to do with it," John said. "Right now we need to be praying for Brother Howard and the others at the missionary office in Chicago."

Days passed and no word came from Howard. John checked often at the telegraph office until the clerk grew irritated at his constant appearance. "Nothing's coming in from Chicago," he said. "I will let you know if you get a message."

One morning John left home early, marched to Walker's office and knocked firmly on the door. With the election over and done with, perhaps politics was no longer an issue.

The supervisor seemed happy to see John. "I hope you are here to tell me you have heard from Howard about a settlement. I've received no correspondence from him since the fire. We need to start classes." He motioned John to sit. "I have a deal to offer your teachers."

John's heart leaped. "I'm glad to hear that, but I haven't yet received word from Howard either, and am terribly concerned." He sat in the proffered chair. "What is your plan?"

"There are several schools outside of Galveston waiting for teachers. It would behoove your ladies to take these positions. They can start immediately."

John about strangled on the words working their way up his throat. He had promised the Lord he would handle the conflict in a Christian manner, but if he said what he was thinking he'd roast in Hell for sure. He stood. "I will tell the ladies what you have suggested. However, I don't think that is a viable option. Our desire is to reopen as a missionary school—apart from the state." He kept his voice even, trying to hide any hint of frustration and anger. "I would appreciate it if you would turn over the key to me now so we can get on with what this is about—teaching the freedmen here in Galveston."

Walker stood also, his face red. "Ogilvie, you are impossible to work with, that is why I have done all my negotiating with Howard and Sinclair. I will not agree to anything until I have heard directly from them. Good day."

***

The trustees convened again in the parlor at the teachers' home on October 17. Anna and Miss Nichols asked if they could sit in. "We have comments to offer," Miss Nichols said. John agreed. They were as much a part of this as he.

After Washington called the group to order, John announced he had not heard from the AMA since the fire. He told of his meeting with Walker. "He won't hand over the key until he hears from Howard. He has places for our teachers in other schools, if they are willing."

Washington looked at the women. "Is that what y'all want? It would give you work."

Miss Nichols sat up straight, bristling. "I think that man is very anxious to get us away from the people here because he is almost certain he will be obliged to give up the schoolhouse and wants to have revenge in some way."

Anna spoke next, her voice strong, "I agree. I haven't stayed in Galveston all this time to turn around and leave. I plan to see it out."

"That settles it then," Washington said. "We is goin' to wait until we hear more from General Howard. We all know he is on our side."

"Is he even alive?" another trustee asked. His words brought a hush to the room, and every face looked at John expectantly—as though he had the answer.

"He must be," John said. "We would have heard if—if any personnel in the missionary office hadn't survived. It is strictly a communication problem caused by the fire." But a fear had been voiced that had been eating away at John a little more each day when no letter or telegram came.

By the adjournment it was agreed they would strive to open the institute by the first Monday in November, whether they had heard from the AMA or not.

Before dawn the following morning, John sensed movement in the room, and when he forced his eyes open he caught the glare of the kerosene lamp on the table between the beds. Louis was fully dressed, folding clothes and tucking them into his traveling bag.

"What are you doing?"

"Leaving. I'm simply treading water here, and I have business to attend to in New York and Washington." He dropped a shirt into the open bag, turned toward John and sat on the bed. "I'm thinking I'll go by way of Chicago and see if 38 Lombard Block still exists."

Suddenly, John was wide awake. He pushed the covers back and sat up. "You would do that?"

"It's as logical a reason to leave now as any."

"Aye, that would be good. It is terrible not knowing."

Chapter 52

Two days following Louis' departure, and eleven days after the Chicago fire, the postmaster handed John a letter. The return address on the plain, white envelope read 204 N. Madison Street, Chicago, not Lombard Block, but above it in a precise, unfamiliar hand was written the words American Missionary Association. John's heart skipped a beat. Tearing open the seal, he quickly scanned the contents. The first reference was to the receipt of his correspondence on October 4, sent before the fire. The real news followed:

> *The fire has engulfed us with the rest of Chicago business. Our safe still lies in the ruins, unopened. As yet we cannot know the state of its contents. The Galveston deeds were in it. But they were on record at Galveston. Will not a transcript of the record meet your wants?*
>
> *All our materials for annual report are destroyed. Will you not send us at once the status of school for last year?*
>
> *Names of teachers*
> 1. *Whole no. of pupils in school*
> 2. *Whole no. in S. School*
> 3. *List of Trustees*
>
> > *Yours truly, C. H. Howard Sec.*
> > *per M. Phelps.*

The name Phelps was new, but surely General Howard had dictated the letter and thus had survived. John would have liked more personal details about the fire itself, yet typical of Howard, the correspondence was all business.

John prayed the deeds in the safe at Lombard Block remained intact and with a sinking feeling wondered what other documents related to the institute might be gone. *There was no mention of my telegram or my follow-up letter regarding the continued standoff with the state. Those messages were probably lost in the confusion in Chicago, especially if the AMA has moved its offices.* He sighed and stuffed the letter back in its envelope. Louis was still on his way, so Howard and his staff had no knowledge of the latest goings-on with Walker.

At home, John read the letter to the ladies. Anna broke into a smile at the news. "Our prayers have been answered." Then her expression grew somber. "Think of the horrors of that night—everything going up in flames."

Miss Nichols shook her head in solemn agreement. "And all our papers in their safe. Surely they'll be protected."

"I wouldn't be too certain," John said.

"I'll help you gather the information requested by Howard," Anna said. "It shouldn't be too difficult to pull it together."

Miss Nichols moved around the parlor with a feather duster as they talked, filled with nervous energy. She dusted a heavy vase and set it down with a hard thump. "I do hope Louis writes when he gets there. We have got to move forward here." She sighed, and John couldn't help but note the firm set of her jaw. The weeks of waiting were eating away at all of them.

With Anna's help, the report was not a huge chore, and John posted it the following day. It amounted to a thick envelope that contained statistics from the previous year and three pages bringing Howard up to date regarding the impasse with the state.

Three days later John sat in the parlor at the teacher's home reading another letter he had just received from Chicago. Howard did acknowledge John's letter of October 10th, and his follow-up telegram regarding the writ. But the news was not good:

> *The fire has swallowed up our office with all records, and the safe is yet unopened. The state of its contents is unknown. We cannot verify the remittance of $30. The banks are not in working order and our deposits with one of them are doubtful. We cannot get at any money for the present....*

The thirty dollars referenced Miss Nichol's missing pay—something that should have been resolved long before the fire. But it was the statement regarding the banks that caused John more distress. His earnings as marine clerk were dwindling and soon there would be no cash left for him and the ladies to live on. He continued to read:

> *If another man should be put into your post and you employed elsewhere, would the substitute be able to get state pay?*

This was too much. Howard obviously still had in mind to send him away, regardless whether the issue with the state was resolved or if the school remained a private AMA facility.

John crumpled the message and tossed it onto the table. Sighing, he walked to the window, his will sapped by frustration and disappointment. He couldn't fight anymore. With a fingernail, he chipped away at the paint on the ledge, staring through the pane at nothing in particular.

A gasp caused him to turn. Anna had entered the room and she was standing by the table, a look of dismay on her face. He saw that she held the letter in her hand. She immediately dropped it.

"I'm so sorry," she said. "It was just lying there and—well, like it had been thrown away. I couldn't help but—you have every right to be angry at me." She laid the wrinkled sheet back onto the table."

"I'm not angry, Anna, not at you, maybe not at anyone. I think the anger is drained out of me."

"It will be all right. You will see."

He smiled. This had become her favorite phrase, but each time she spoke it, the words held less conviction.

He walked to the table, picked up the letter and stuffed it into a pocket. "I'm going for a walk."

He had no particular destination, simply a need to get away from the house. For the first time since moving in with the teachers, John wished he lived alone. The inquiring looks of the women when he brought home mail—or didn't bring it—was getting to him, and their attempts at being cheerful were wearing thin. He headed toward the docks where he could get lost in the commotion of loading and unloading ships.

Taking the most familiar route, John passed the Custom Office, and as he did so Robert stepped out the door. "Hello, Ogilvie. It's good to see you. Has your school opened yet?"

"Afraid not. The Chicago Fire destroyed the missionary headquarters, you know, and communication between the parties has come to a halt."

"Hmmm. I suspected as much. You in need of work?"

John raised an eyebrow. "I thought my position here was filled the moment I left."

"You're right, but I know of something else. How about a job with the Internal Revenue collecting taxes? A great opportunity. Gets you off this sand bar onto the mainland to check out the countryside and meet new folks. The government even provides the horse."

"I don't think that's a job for me. But thanks, anyway."

"I'm just trying to help you out. I heard they had an opening. Sounded like a good chance for a frustrated school teacher to take off, unwind, and get paid for it."

John thanked him again and continued toward the harbor. Making his way through the hustle of stevedores, he gazed across the water to the land beyond. He hadn't been over there since his schoolhouse trek for Bartholomew. Now it seemed to crook a finger at him. He leaned against a railing and watched a locomotive chug along the bridge crossing the channel, smoke rising in puffs from its stack.

Earlier that morning he had checked the tin under his bed in which he kept his spare cash. Sixteen dollars and twenty cents. Aside from the few coins in his pocket, that paltry amount equaled the sum total of his funds on hand. It wouldn't last long and he knew Miss Nichols and Anna were in the same fix.

Robert's words teased him, playing tag in his mind between logic and fancy. Perhaps he would stop at the IRS office and inquire about the job. The plan for school to open the first of November now seemed doubtful. *I'll go mad with nothing to do if I'm put off again for another month, and no matter where I'm eventually sent, Howard still expects me to start things up here. What would it be like, collecting taxes, riding a horse...the peace and solitude...*

John turned back toward town, his feet leading him to a door emblazoned with gold lettering that read United States Internal Revenue, Assessor's Office. He stood there a moment tugging at his beard, rereading the sign and feeling a little foolish. No harm in asking a few questions. Before he could talk himself out of it, he entered the building.

The man behind the counter looked up through rimless spectacles. "May I help you?"

"Perhaps. I'm inquiring about a possible opening for tax collector."

When John left the Internal Revenue office, the forms he had been given lay carefully folded against his chest in an inside coat pocket. The man said if he returned his application and it was approved, the entire process would only take a week before he could begin collecting taxes.

When John arrived home, the place was abuzz. Two young women from Minnesota had arrived to spend the night. Friends of Julia Nelson, they planned to leave for Columbus in the morning. The supper table conversation was constant chatter and a pleasant change. At least it took John's mind off more pressing matters. For sleeping arrangements, Anna and Miss Nichols doubled up in one bedroom leaving the other free for the guests. John heard whispers and giggles into the night. The diversion was good.

***

Several days passed before John made up his mind about the IRS job. On Thursday morning, October 26th, he again tucked the application into his pocket, with the blanks filled in. He left the house after breakfast, taking long strides against the wind until he stood once more at the door with the gold lettering. Inhaling deeply, he turned the knob and marched inside.

The man at the desk received the papers with a broad smile. "Glad you decided to apply. If everything checks out, you can begin work on Tuesday."

The tax job filled John's thoughts as he left the building. It sounded like a sure thing, and Tuesday, October 31st was only five days away. He headed for the Custom Office to seek out Robert. "Thanks for the tip, friend. It looks like I may be collecting taxes by next week."

Robert grinned. "Glad you took my advice. Let me know how it works out." He stood and shook John's hand. "Good luck to you."

Exiting his former work place, John rounded the corner to the adjacent door and entered the post office. The postal clerk handed over an envelope bearing the now familiar Madison Street address in Chicago. John had hoped for something from Louis, but perhaps this was just as good. Choosing to stay out of the wind to read the letter, he stood to one side and opened it while still in the

373

building. He unfolded the single page, again in the neat hand of Phelps on behalf of Howard, and read:

> *Dear Sir,*
> *Enclosed please find draft on account for $150. Please take the trouble to send us a receipt. We have no blanks to forward.*

John stared at the draft. The banks in Chicago were obviously up and running again. But one hundred fifty dollars? An amazing sum. Was this for him alone—some sort of apology or vote of confidence? He was getting so many mixed signals from Howard. He ran his fingers through his hair and though puzzled, smiled broadly with relief. Whatever Howard's intent, John would share. It was not only fair but necessary. He hurried to the bank to cash the check and fill his empty pockets.

When he arrived home, he found Anna on her hands and knees mopping the kitchen floor. Strands of her brown hair escaped from a bandana tied around her head. A muslin apron covered her dress, and a smudge of dirt colored one cheek. During these days of tight finances and extra time on their hands, they had let Frances go, the ladies sharing the housework themselves.

Upon seeing John, Anna immediately stood, wiping her hands on the apron. "Mr. Ogilvie, I thought you would be gone all morning. Forgive my appearance," she said. And then, as though he needed further explanation, she added, "It's cleaning day."

"Obviously," John said. Grinning, he removed his hat and coat. He was usually gone when the women did heavy chores. In the early mornings and evenings they made every effort to look their best. However, he found Anna as charming as ever in her dowdy attire, and for the moment any concern about her appearance came second to his news. "I have something to tell you and Miss Nichols."

Anna's eyes grew wide with excitement. "Good news about the school, I hope?"

Of course, she would think that. "Sorry, I didn't mean to give you false hope. No word yet related to the opening of school, but what I have runs a close second." He glanced around. "Is Miss Nichols here?"

"No. She went out for a few supplies. She should be back in an hour or so."

His pulse quickened. An hour alone with Anna. The letter in his pocket made a crinkly noise as he reached for her arm and led her to the table in the dining room. "No need to wait until she returns. We have to talk."

He pulled out a chair for her and sat in one next to it. "Two things," he said, reaching for the envelope in his inner pocket. "First is this." Opening the flap he extracted three bills and laid them on the table. "Howard sent a draft. Here is fifty dollars for each of us."

Anna's hands flew to her cheeks. "Oh, my. Surely this is meant just for you. Howard usually sends pay to each of us directly."

"One hundred and fifty dollars, Anna. Fifty apiece. I'm certain that's what he had in mind. We're in this together. We all have to eat, and there must be other things you need as well."

"Well, we could certainly use it. Miss Nichols is right now spending the last of our funds on groceries. You know she is still waiting for her missing check. I'm expecting a little cash from my father in the mail any day now. I can pay you back when that comes." She let the bills lie with no further argument. "You had something else to tell me?"

John took a deep breath. "I'm applying for another job."

Alarm spread across Anna's face. "I don't understand? Why are you doing this?"

He pushed back his chair, stood and walked to a window, staring out at the street to avoid the bewilderment in her eyes.

"There are many reasons," he said. "First, we need the money and I can't stand not doing something—anything—day after day. We don't know if this school situation is ever going to be resolved, and even if it is I sense from the tone of Howard's letters that I'm not wanted here." He hesitated a moment before adding, "That, actually, I am in the way."

There, he had said it, all those feelings he had kept pent up for weeks, and as the words spilled out of his mouth the pain of rejection came with it—raw and real.

"No, John. You are wrong." Anna sprang from her chair and in an instant came to him. "That is not it at all, and oh, don't you see? The students need you." She placed a hand on his arm, forcing him to look at her. "I have told you this before. Why can't you believe me?"

"It's more than that." He didn't know how else to explain it to her. They stood there, inches apart searching each other's face for unspoken thoughts. The room seemed to whirl around him as

John reached out, touched the scarf tied around her head, and slipped it off. When he laced his fingers through her hair, he half-expected her to resist his bold, impulsive move. Instead she lifted her face to his, welcoming the anticipated kiss. Their lips had scarcely touched, when the front door flung open and Miss Nichols rushed in.

"Anna, I'm back and wait until you see the bargain I found."

Anna immediately stepped away from John, breaking their embrace. She knelt down and picked up the scarf lying at her feet. John turned and faced the doorway, attempting to appear casual through his frustration at the incomplete kiss.

"Oh," Miss Nichols said, stopping to stare, her arms wrapped tightly around a bag bulging with groceries. "Oh," she said again. "Mr. Ogilvie. I didn't realize you were back." Her cheeks turned crimson. Obviously, the quick maneuvers to conceal their embrace weren't fast enough.

"Mr. Ogilvie brought some cash from General Howard," Anna stammered. She walked toward the dining room to point out the bills. "Fifty dollars for each of us."

"For each of us? Why, that's wonderful!" Miss Nichols deposited her bundle on a chair and hurried to the table. She picked up one of the bills, pressing it to her chest. "Thank-you, General Howard. I like you better today than I did yesterday."

"And there's more," Anna said, eyeing John.

"More money?" Miss Nichols stared in disbelief.

"No," John said, "more news."

Chapter 53

The roan quivered as John brought her to a halt. He leaned forward and smooth-talked in the horse's ear. "Time to rest, Jessie." Blowing air out her nostrils, the mare flicked an ear and stood still while John scanned the horizon. The country lay flat between him and the Trinity, the wild grasses bending in a cool breeze. Beyond the river, golden sprays of sunlight fanned through the woods, a visual reward after a day's work. Unfolding the map provided by the Internal Revenue office, he studied the lines representing trails, roads, and rivers, then looked up again, squinting in the late afternoon light. He had been traveling along the Trinity and nearby communities for five days. Tomorrow he should reach the little community of Clark, but today he planned to stop early and take care of some correspondence.

The stretches of travel between appointments had given John much time to think. He at least owed Howard an explanation as to what he was about. Dismounting, he tied Jessie to a tree, and took from the saddlebag a small wooden box containing ink, pen, and several sheets of folded paper. In no hurry, he settled on the grass, laid the box beside him, and drank in his surroundings. The breeze stirred leaves in the tree above, while the setting sun cast a glimmering sheen across the river. *Molasses glass,* John thought, and reveled in the glory of it. Sometimes he questioned why God dared put people, with all their flaws, on earth to detract from the holiness of nature. But then, there'd be no one to enjoy the wonder.

Turning his attention to writing before dark settled in, he began putting on paper words composed over and over in his mind as he and Jessie had cantered through the countryside:

Nov. 7, 1871, to C. H. Howard,

Dear Sir,

Since I last wrote, I was offered the office of Dept. Collector of Internal Revenue. I accepted for two reasons. 1st at that time I doubted whether the trustees would get the building or not. 2nd the tone of your last letter led me to think that I was rather in the way. I felt somewhat hurt, but said nothing. If you wish me to remain, let me know and on what terms....

Fraternally yours,
J. Ogilvie

John suspected letters from Howard were accumulating for him at the Galveston post office. This one, which he planned to mail tomorrow, would bring yet another response. What that might be, he could only guess.

But enough of serious matters. His thoughts turned to Anna Keen. Her essence rode with him continually. The evening before he set out to start collections he and Anna had shared a few moments alone in the parlor.

"I wish you weren't going," she had whispered, her eyes dark with concern. "I'll pray for your safe return every moment of every day."

"It's not forever," John had said, "and you know the reasons for it. I'll be fine. It's a good thing, Anna, to be gone from here for awhile." He caressed her cheek, then leaned forward and kissed her gently on the lips.

Anna had returned the kiss, and murmured, "Oh, John, I will miss you so."

He heard her words again now, as he often had since leaving Galveston, plain and clear as though she were beside him—each time spreading a welcome shiver of delight clear to his toes.

His sincerest hope, though, was that Anna would not have much time to sit around and worry about him. He left instructions that if the building was obtained, she was to start classes and take charge until he returned. He had learned during the past months that Howard had misinterpreted quiet for meek. Anna, in fact, was strong and capable.

The actual collecting of taxes had so far been quite an education. John carried a list containing names and addresses of folks who lived on ranches or in villages along the Trinity. His encounters ran the gamut of absolute refusal to pay the taxes owed, accompanied by cursing, to being treated as a welcome guest and sharing of meals. One family even allowed him to sleep on his bedroll in their hallway during a rainy night.

The end of this particular day settled in cool and clear. John lay beneath the stars listening to night creatures hoot and howl, feeling a contented part of their world.

He awoke moments before dawn to Jessie's neigh as she grazed at her tether. A mist lay low across the prairie grass scattering the light of the morning sun into a thousand effervescent droplets. Coaxing embers from his fire of the night before, he was able to heat enough coffee for a cup of warmth, washing down two biscuits before he packed up and headed out.

That morning he mailed the letters as he passed through Clark. Traveling north for another two days, he met reasonable success with his collections, then turned to retrace his steps, hoping to catch some of his earlier clients in a more solicitous mood. On November 10th, he stayed the night in a rooming house in Liberty, paying for the luxury of a hot bath. Before sleep, he wrote another note to Anna, telling her of his adventures and saying he missed her, words on paper that seemed flat—not at all representative of his true feelings. He sighed. Scribbles of ink would have to do for now.

The following morning, one other guest joined him at the breakfast table, standing awkwardly aside while John bowed his head and whispered grace. When the praying was obviously over, the man pulled out a chair and sat.

"Good morning," John offered.

The man nodded, but said nothing. The innkeeper placed a plate piled with flapjacks in the center of the table and John helped himself. His table companion stacked several on his own plate, drenched them in honey, and took a hefty bite. Still chewing, he mumbled, "You a preacher man, mister?"

John shook his head no. "Collecting taxes for the Internal Revenue."

His table partner quit chewing, swallowed hard, then said, "Well, I had you figured as a preacher for sure, all dressed up and saying prayers and such." He took another bite, chewed and swallowed. "Internal Revenue, you say? Folks don't much like the gov'ment coming after their money, you know."

"So it seems," John said, swirling a bite of flapjack in honey pooled on his plate. "And what might be your line of work?"

The man had conveniently stuffed another huge bite into his mouth and muttered something unintelligible, but a couple of moments later, before adding more to his gullet, he announced, "I'm not from around these parts, just passing through. I'll be clean out of Texas by nightfall."

John smiled and shook his head, "You can relax. I've contacted everyone on my list." He suspected if he had admitted to being a preacher, the man most likely would have left in a hurry, too— afraid he might pass a collection plate. He'd grown accustomed to folks not always agreeing with his choices in life.

Refreshed from a good night's sleep, John continued on his way. Once on the trail, he sang. Jessie's cadence seemed to match the rhythm of his tunes and she twitched her ears as they trotted along. Most often he lifted favorite hymns to the countryside, but now and again he found himself belting some gospel tune learned from his colored friends. Today, *"Ride on King Jesus, Ride on,"* sprang from his lips, echoing Adeline's mother in her joyous state upon entertaining the thought that her daughter might actually be a teacher someday.

Being gone from his pupils made John acutely aware of how deeply they had touched him. As he rode, he acknowledged these days traveling alone in the wilderness had worked wonders. His anger at Walker and DeGress, his feeling of being betrayed by Howard, plus his frustrations had abated. The sense of conclusion stayed with him throughout the day, rolling around and around in his mind until it became finely polished, like pebbles in a flowing stream.

He made two successful collections during the day. Though dark clouds had gathered by nightfall, John's spirits remained high. Finding an abandoned shack, he cleared away the rubble under a section of roof large enough to protect both him and Jessie. "We'll be safe and dry here, girl." The horse nuzzled him, as though she understood. John fastened her lead to a solid plank, removed the saddle, and offered her a handful of oats. After a light snack of his own, he settled in for the night, sleeping amazingly well.

Sheets of falling rain accompanied by wild and frequent flashes of lightning and peals of thunder, awoke him in the morning. Rather than venture out, he stayed holed up in the makeshift shelter, reading the best he could in the dim light and munching on persimmons—a gift from a congenial household he had visited the day before. He also commenced to thinking about the Barnes Institute and its purpose, a much less perplexing study miles from the turmoil and in his now calmer frame of mind. *Perhaps I am part of the problem, my pride having been wounded at not being offered the supervisory position held by Walker.*

He tugged his beard at the thought. Politics had definitely played a part in it, but maybe he couldn't see the picture as clearly as he should. In a letter from Sinclair, late in September, the Colonel had written,

> *Isn't it possible for you and Walker to come to some amicable arrangement? It is to the interest of the AMA as well as for the good of the school system.*

In the ramshackle hut, with wind and rain pounding on the scant piece of roof, John knelt in prayer. "Dear Lord, Forgive me my trespasses as I forgive those who have trespassed against me." That simple, familiar phrase acted as a cleansing agent for his soul and conscience, and it stayed with him during the remainder of the day and throughout the night.

On Monday, November 14th, John left the Trinity for the last two days of his journey. Refreshed and eager to be back, he felt on course, his mind settled. Upon his arrival home, if Anna and Miss Nichols weren't already conducting classes, the freedmen would be taught—no matter what arrangements and agreements it required.

Chapter 54

An evening breeze had blown away the last traces of rain and a quarter moon lit the fading sky when John arrived in Galveston. He found things the same as he had left them—the school still closed and the ladies at home. And though they seemed joyous and relieved at his return, he sensed an underlying current in the air, a feeling of anxiety. After unpacking and cleaning up, he joined the women in the parlor, where, rather than sitting and attending to her sewing, Anna paced, casting him nervous glances.

"I hope you aren't angry with me, Mr. Ogilvie."

"Angry?" He looked at her in surprise. "I've never had reason to be angry with you." He wished they were alone, but Miss Nichols stood by, making no effort to leave the room. Whatever had occurred was no secret between them, and Anna apparently needed the other woman's support during this confession.

"I'm afraid I may have overstepped my boundary and meddled in your affairs, but I felt it important."

John raised his eyebrows, his curiosity mounting. He tried his best to control the smile working at the corners of his mouth. He couldn't imagine any transgression this fine Christian lady could have committed.

"And what might those boundaries be?"

"I wrote to General Howard." She looked away from John as she spoke, purposely avoiding his gaze as the words tumbled from her. "I told him you were deeply hurt when he suggested you go elsewhere to teach, and even though he may have heard otherwise, the students were not dissatisfied with you, in fact, quite the contrary. I also suggested perhaps we had been thoughtlessly abandoned by the missionary association." Now she turned to face him, her cheeks flushed.

"And have you heard back?" he asked, his voice caught as he spoke. He could never be cross at her for defending him.

"No, but it's been long enough since I wrote," she said, fidgeting with the crocheted trim on her sleeve. "I expect a response any day."

"Well, Miss Keen," John said, not taking his gaze off her, and aching to hold her close, "I wrote him also, expressing some of the same sentiments. We should both be hearing soon. Howard is usually quite prompt with his replies. In the meantime, ladies, I plan to sit down with Walker and have an amicable talk with him. Whatever the outcome, the conflict must stop and school begun as soon as possible."

Anna was still fixated on John's reaction to her letter. "You're not angry with me?"

"Far from it." He felt dizzy with the knowledge that she had been so bold as to send such a letter on his behalf.

First thing the following morning, John strode to the office of the Internal Revenue Service and turned in the money he had collected. The clerk seemed satisfied with his efforts and not surprised at his resignation. John left with his pay in a pocket and a prayer in his heart as he headed for a discussion with the supervisor of schools, district eighteen.

"Have a seat, Ogilvie." Walker indicated the only chair opposite his desk. "I hear you've been out of town."

"Yes, sir, and doing a lot of thinking while I was gone. I want to apologize for any problems I may have caused regarding the school." The words came easier than he had imagined.

"Your apology is a little late, but that's neither here nor there since you are going to get your way as it is. I've heard from Sinclair, Howard, and a lawyer during your absence, and I'm through fighting this battle." He pulled open a drawer, took out an envelope on which was written *Barnes Institute—Keys*, and slid it across the desk. "The building is yours."

The action stunned John. It was as though the Lord, with his gentle, benevolent magic, was sitting right there beside him placating Walker.

"Thank you," John said. He picked up the envelope and stood, holding out his hand. To his surprise Walker also stood, and reaching out he grasped John's hand. A smile, ever so slight, played at the man's lips.

Then as John turned to leave, Walker tossed out a parting remark, "But don't expect any favors from the state."

John hummed all the way to the post office. The postal clerk saw him coming, reached into a cubicle and handed him two letters. "These have been waiting here a couple of weeks. I thought maybe you had left for good."

"Not yet," John said.

He glanced at the return addresses—one from Howard, and finally, one from Louis. John added them to the cache of treasures in his pockets and hurried home to tell the ladies the splendid news.

When he laid the keys on the table, John not only received a warm hug from Anna, but Miss Nichols, too, and both women cried. *I wish all their problems were solved,* he thought as he held an arm about each lady's waist. *Howard may still have in mind to replace me, but for now this is one of the best moments of my life.*

Anna eyed the two unopened envelopes lying on the table. "What does Louis say in his letter?"

"Let's find out." John tore open the seal and scanned the page, then laughed. "A man of few words, as always." He read it aloud:

> *Dear Ogilvie,*
> *I found Howard alive and well. I know you have heard from him. I am on my way to New York. Will write more later.*
> *Regards, Louis*

Howard's letter was dated November 7th, the very day John had scribbled his own message while sitting by the glassy Trinity. It would not be a response to either his or Anna's heartfelt notes. The words began, *"Nothing in our safe was saved."* Disappointing, but not a surprise. The letter continued to say Howard would write to the New York office for an official copy of the transfer of the institute to the AMA by the Bureau, confirming ownership of the building and grounds, so as to collect rent from the state.

"It sounds as though he still thinks the state will take over the school," Anna said. The astonishment in her voice matched the look on her face.

"I'll send a letter right off," John said. "We have the keys and the school is ours. Surely Howard will be pleased. But for now, we need to get the rooms ready and word to the scholars that classes start on Monday."

Miss Nichols jumped up. "Oh joy, it is really going to happen." She grabbed Anna's hands and the two circled around, laughing and singing like primary children at recess.

After a midday meal, John and the teachers walked to the schoolhouse. Once doors were unlocked and windows opened, they settled down to the project at hand. The notices to be distributed took some thought. Parents and scholars must know the institute was to open as a private missionary school and a tuition of one dollar a month was expected. However, no pupil was to be turned away, and if the money was not available, sponsoring churches would help. Once the wording was agreed upon, the two women set to writing. John took out pen and paper himself to inform Howard they now had possession of the building and the institute would open on Monday, November 20th, to continue as a private AMA school. Biting the end of his pen, he thought a moment before he boldly added the terms he requested should he stay as principal for the school year.

A small group of scholars convened on that Monday morning, most appearing with the dollar tuition in hand. Miss Nichols covered the primary and intermediate grades, Anna the advanced, and John the high school and evening classes.

For the entire first day, pandemonium reigned, not because of disorganization, but due to the excitement of those in attendance. John looked on with pleasure as little girls in new dresses hugged their teachers, and boys arrived freshly scrubbed wearing clean shirts.

"I is so glad to be back learning," Adeline said, unable to control her wide smile. John took special note, that in spite of her mother's concern regarding the money, this prize scholar promptly turned in her dollar the very first day.

By Tuesday, things had settled down. Books were open, slates out, and brows furrowed in deep thought. The familiarity of the routine felt right. Yet one more hurdle had to be jumped before the week ended. As soon as classes let out, John holed up in his office, a trace of anxiety simmering deep inside him while he prepared an agenda. At four o'clock the trustees would gather for the first time since the opening. This meeting would be true proof as far as his independent actions were concerned. Concentrating on a list before him, pen in hand he didn't see the figure tread quietly to his open door.

"Mr. Ogilvie?"

Anna's unexpected voice caused his heart to lurch. He immediately stood.

"Miss Keen, come in."

"I have it," she said, and walked swiftly toward him holding out an envelope, a wide smile lighting her face.

"And what might '*it*' be?" he asked, puzzled.

"Howard's reply to my letter. And look." She opened the flap and extracted two drafts holding them out for John to see. "Thirty dollars owed Miss Nichols and the fifty-seven dollars long due me. And listen to what he says."

She unfolded a sheet of paper and began to read:

> *Dear Friend,*
> *We are very glad to get your letter and the information it contains. You must hold on in Galveston until the matter about possession of the schoolhouse is settled. We do not cast off teachers in trouble and should not discharge you without notice.*

Anna stopped reading. Her hands shook and John noticed tears forming in her eyes. She handed him the letter.

"Here, you read the next part."

John took it from her, scanning the words silently:

> *We have no other than the highest opinion of Mr. Ogilvie and proposed the change to relieve him from embarrassment. We were not dissatisfied with him, and knew the colored people were not. But we also knew that he suffered embarrassment from the attitude of some in political power, and might see relief in a change.*
> *Remember to assure him of our confidence which is shared also by his self-denying lady assistants at Barnes Institute.*

A lump formed in John's throat as he read. On finishing the last sentence, he looked up at Anna. Though tears streaked her cheeks, the smile on her face sparkled.

"See?" she said. "General Howard acted only out of concern for you and he truly values your work."

The uneasiness John had experienced in anticipation of the board meeting was gone. "Well, my dear," the affectionate term escaped his lips without a thought, "I certainly can't scold you for meddling in my affairs with this kind of response, now can I?" He gazed at her, thinking his heart might burst apart any moment from the love he felt for this special woman. "Thank you, Anna, for prompting these words of reassurance."

"It's none of my doing," she said, "It's because of who you are."
Her smile never faltered as she dabbed at her wet cheeks with a
small, embroidered handkerchief.

John read the words once again, folded the letter and handed
it back to her from across the desk. "You are a remarkable
woman."

A male voice in the doorway broke the spell. "Mr. Ogilvie, suh,
may I have a word with you before the trustees meet?"
Washington Green, dressed in a suit and looking very official,
entered the room.

"Good evening, Mr. Green," Anna said, fully composed. "I was
just leaving."

"'Evenin', Miss Keen. Violette surely do like her lessons."

"She's an excellent student." Anna turned to John. "I'll see you
later, Mr. Ogilvie," and holding Howard's letter to her bosom, she
seemed to glide from the room.

The board meeting went well, with all members agreeing
school should continue under the current terms. No one had a
problem with John taking it upon himself to open the school
without consulting the trustees even though Howard still
considered negotiating with the state.

"Ain't this what he suggested hisself if the state didn't want our
teachers?" Washington asked. "An we said we was going to open
up school ourselves once't we got the key."

Adjournment ended on an upbeat note, and John entered his
evening class an hour later, stimulated and confident.

His own personal vote of confidence came from Howard, via
Phelps, a few days later, this in response to his letter of November
17, wherein he announced he would reopen the school and
suggested the terms of his employment be the same as the
previous year. In spite of the reassuring words in the letter to
Anna, John held his breath as he unsealed this newest note from
the missionary association:

> *Dear Bro,*
> *...Gen. Howard regards you, Mr. Ogilvie, as one of the
> best of men and would not hurt your feelings intentionally
> for the world. We are glad that you have started the
> Barnes Inst. under the auspices of AMA. Howard accedes
> to your request of $500 salary ... and is very glad to
> retain your valuable services for the association on your
> own terms.*

Chapter 55

As hard won as the preservation of the Barnes Institute had been, to say nothing of his own position as principal, John knew when June arrived his days of working with the freedmen would be at an end. He had come to teach, to raise the former slaves out of ignorance and set them on a path of independence. In return he had learned from each of them. Visions of Sam Canfield, Lucinda and Patsy Harper, the Wallaces, Washington and Violette Green, and oh so many more often paraded through his head. They would always be there, and a part of him. Leaving would be bittersweet, but lately John dared allow himself to think toward his own future, beyond Texas, beyond the South and its reconstruction, which was drawing to an end.

On a Friday evening during Christmas break, he dipped his pen in ink and began a letter, one waiting to be written since even before he left Scotland. With careful deliberation, he scratched out his message and signed it with a flourish. Rereading his words, he whispered a short prayer, then placed the page in an envelope pre-addressed to Yale Theological Seminary, New Haven, Connecticut. Drawing a stick of wax over the flame of the lamp beside him he allowed several drops to cover the closure flap then sealed it with an O. This was the beginning of his tomorrow.

**

The year 1872 arrived in a rush, and the next few months flew by. Anna proudly wore a ring on her left hand; they planned to marry after he completed his studies. "I'll wait for you," she said. "No matter how long it takes."

Though eager to get on with his future, there were moments when John wanted to slow the calendar, times when he stood at the front of class and watched dark, curly heads bent over books and slates. He wondered what would become of them.

In early March, he wrote to Samuel Canfield. It had been a long while since they had corresponded, and he mustn't lose track of this pupil who had been such a vital part of his first days in Texas. Samuel responded post haste, and upon opening the envelope John noted the neatly penned script. A warmth rippled through him. One would scarcely guess this came from a man freed from slavery, uneducated until only a few short years ago. John began to read:

> *Dear Brother,*
> *Yours of recent date has come to hand. I am very glad to hear you are yet alive and well.... All of your old acquaintances join me in sending love to you.*

Samuel went on to tell of the classes at Lavaca and how he continued to teach advanced studies. He referred to the levels of arithmetic and grammar he had accomplished, saying he had also learned a great deal in elocution. But it was the last paragraph that spun like gold around John's heart.

> *Sunday after next being the 1st Sunday in April, I am to be regularly ordained. I would be glad for you to be here, as I was one of your scholars. You ought to come, any how, to see one of your children shoulder the cross, for I have learned much of what I know from you.*
> *I am your brother in Christ.*
> *Sam H. Canfield.*

Here was John's greatest reward—a gift for all the heartaches, challenges, and frustrations of the past five and a half years—the reason why he had been called to this vast and often harsh territory. In the very words of one of his students, with the Lord's help, he *had* made a difference. He bowed his head.

The Texas sunset cast the last golden rays of daylight through the office window of the Barnes Institute, promising a clear and cool night.

John tucked Samuel's letter into a drawer for safekeeping, then strode down the hall, singing with loud exuberance:

"*Let the church roll on, my Lord, Let the church roll on,*" and entered the classroom to teach his evening scholars.

Afterword

Staff members who had worked with John Ogilvie Stevenson, including a Miss Lane, finished out the school term, leaving Texas in June of 1872. The American Missionary Association continued to run the Barnes Institute the following year, though John's replacement was not well received and attendance dropped. A letter from General Howard to John, dated May 21, 1873, stated:

> *I regret to say the Galveston school has not been a success and we have closed it (May 1st). I am looking now for someone to take that. Perhaps a lady will do for next year...*

Anna returned home to spend time with her parents. Wedding bells rang three and a half years later on August 24, 1875, following John's graduation from Yale, with a B. D. degree.

John served as minister in Congregational churches in Ellsworth, Connecticut, as well as Shenandoah and Waterloo, Iowa. He later received a B. A. degree from Oberlin College and, in 1892, was honored with a D.D. degree from Tabor College. He and Anna had seven children, four of whom lived to adulthood. Anna Keen Ogilvie Stevenson died May 21, 1888, eight months after the death of her infant son, Louis. She was forty-three years old.

John subsequently married Ella McDonald. They had no children. After years of preaching, he lost his voice, but continued communicating his thoughts through writing. He edited the *Woman's Standard*, a newspaper published on behalf of women's suffrage, and wrote editorials for the *Waterloo Courier* expressing his views on a multitude of subjects, from politics to religion. He died in 1912 of asthma "complicated by heart disease" at seventy-one years of age. Many heartfelt tributes were printed following his death. An editorial from the *Waterloo Courier* summarized how he had lived his life:

> *Dr. Stevenson had a soul of justice, conviction, charity and democracy. His beliefs were notable above all things for their championship of the underdog. He loved the right. He loved the weak, the poor, the helpless and abused. Waterloo has lost a man whose counterpart is not known to us anywhere. And humanity has lost a friend, a friend who spent his last years in humble circumstances but who now takes his place in eternity among the elect of great minds and souls.*

Flora Beach Burlingame

Author's Notes

The Bureau of Refugees, Freedmen and Abandoned Lands was established by the federal government to transition the former slaves to their new status as "freedmen." Promises of forty acres of land, an education, legal aid, and military protection either never became reality or were services often mishandled by bureau agents. As a result, the Freemen's Bureau was dissolved by 1869—except for its one success, education, which continued for another year and a half. Working with benevolent societies, the bureau recruited teachers from the north to establish schools and teach the freedmen throughout the southern states.

John Ogilvie Stevenson was my great grandfather, and this book was inspired by the letters written to him by his contacts in the Freedmen's Bureau and the American Missionary Association during his tenure as a teacher of the freed slaves in Texas. Most of the incidents written here are real, and were based on these letters, plus stories, editorials and sermons written by John in his later years. I have embellished on them, adding dialogue, description, and minor characters, to bring this marvelous story to life for the benefit of the reader.

I used Ogilvie as his surname, partly to avoid confusion between him and Louis Stevenson, and because he wrote several short stories about his tenure in Texas referring to himself in the third person as Ogilvie. After much research I learned that he took a few liberties with fact in his own stories. I considered this his permission that I might do the same.

The personnel of the Freedmen's Bureau and the American Missionary Association, and their letters quoted in this book, are authentic. The only exception is Lt. Mitchel—a made-up name for an actual bureau agent who apparently "absconded" with the bureau money intended for the Lavaca school. Captain Walker, the school supervisor caught up in politics and importance of his job in Galveston, was real, but his name in my book is fictitious.

The farmer, Carl Cranston, was real, though his name was Sam C. Cranston. I took liberties with the C. and made it Carl to avoid confusion with Samuel Canfield, another important and genuine character. John O. Stevenson mentioned the Cranston farm in several of his later writings and editorials. With the help of the Dodge County Historical Society in Minnesota, I was able to obtain Cranston's obituary which also referenced his daughter, Lucy, and her medical career. I found several other references to Lucy in John's sermons.

The name Neal Wright is fictitious, though John tells of befriending a soldier who settled in Lavaca and who subsequently died of yellow fever. The poignant letter written to Wheelock following the burial of the soldier, and just prior to his own illness, is one of the few John copied for his own records before sending.

The yellow fever epidemic of 1867 along the gulf coast was real and deadly. John Ogilvie Stevenson, one of the few teachers of the freedmen who stayed in Texas for the summer, came close to death after falling ill with the terrifying disease. It wasn't until 1900, when the Reed Commission set upon finding the cause, that it was determined yellow fever is contracted by the bite of the *Aedes aegypti* mosquito. Prior to that, it was thought the disease was spread by direct contact with infected people or contaminated objects.

I visited both communities where John Stevenson taught. There is documentation of the Barnes Institute in a file at the Rosenberg Library in Galveston, and the location where the school once stood is easily found. In Port Lavaca there was no knowledge by local historians as to where the school may have been, but John wrote about the school he started in the warehouse "under the bluff." There are no deeds on record for the acquisition of the lot where the new school was constructed. His benefactor, George Ware, was an actual person, but whether he was involved in the purchase of the property, I do not know. In a note to himself, John wrote, "...lot bought, deed shown to SAC Vic."

John's summary of his Texas tenure tells how he first lived with a French family (no name given) in Lavaca, but, in his own words, due to "the Ku Klux excitement and the odium that was visited on all who boarded teachers of Freedmen," he was convinced he must build himself a "dwelling place." Many of the pupil's names I gleaned from his written sketches, including that of Mrs. Wallace, his oldest day time "scholar." I gave her a husband, Joe, and made them the Negro couple with whom he boarded while he constructed a house on a lot they owned.

The K.K.K notices are real, copies of which were in a scrapbook put together by John. In a later sermon, he referenced keeping a gun in the pulpit when he preached in Lavaca, and a letter to her parents from Anna Keen told how he slept with a gun under his pillow for protection during his tenure in Lavaca. His encounters with Klan members—including the kidnapping—are fiction.

The story of Uncle Booker came from one of many editorials written by John for the *Waterloo Courier* following the loss of his voice after years of preaching and public speaking.

I do not know for a fact that Samuel Canfield and Mrs. Wallace took over the Lavaca school after John left, but Professor Barbara Hayward, who wrote a thesis on the freedmen schools in Texas, came across a letter from Louis Stevenson referencing a letter from John O. Stevenson saying he (John) was organizing the school at Port Lavaca under two of his "most advanced pupils."

Though there are references to John's correspondence with Sarah Barnes in the AMA letters, her notes to John are created in my mind and based on his later stories plus comments from Sarah's great grandson, James William Hosking, with whom I communicated during the writing of this book.

With the exception of Mrs. Smith and Miss Bates, the names of teachers in this story are real. (Those two represent actual teachers. I changed the names.) Dialogue and incidents involving the arrivals and departures of all teachers are fictitious, though most of the circumstances stem from fact—such as delinquent pay. The controversy surrounding that of "Mrs. Smith" was told in a narrative written by Stevenson in later life.

George Ruby and Frank Webb were actual people. Clippings from Webb's *Galveston Republican* appeared in John's scrapbook, including the two resolutions regarding the institute's need to hire Negro teachers, and the one recommending John for State Superintendent of Schools.

John's trip away from Galveston to determine if the freedmen would build their own schoolhouses is well chronicled through the lengthy letters of then superintendent of bureau schools, Eugene Carlos Bartholomew. However, it is unclear as to which schools were eventually constructed after the bureau folded.

Louis W. Stevenson of the bureau and John O. Stevenson actually roomed together in Galveston and both sought political careers in Texas as indicated in my book. Their personal relationship lasted well beyond their Texas years. A newspaper account in John's scrapbook, dated August 27, 1887, tells of the death of Louis Stevenson. John and Anna Keen Stevenson named their son, born that same month, Louis. (The baby, their seventh child, died several months later and Anna's death followed in May of 1888.)

Before applying for the position of superintendent of public instruction himself, John did indeed suggest to George Honey of the Texas Treasury Department that Julia Nelson would make a good candidate for the job. Honey's response: *The work is beyond the physical power of a woman to do*, is an exact quote from a letter he wrote to John regarding that appointment.

Letters from Anna Keen to her parents during her tenure in Galveston tell of Louis and John eventually living in the teachers' home. These letters give additional insight into the difficulties during the time the state wanted to take over the institute, and showed the development of the romance between Anna and John.

According to an article clipped from the *Commercial,* Dec. 4th, 1869, Samuel Canfield (colored) of Lavaca, did apply for the office of Justice of the Peace, then withdrew—obviously under pressure. He stayed in contact with John and the touching quote at the end of the book is an actual excerpt from one of his letters.

All storms mentioned in my story are documented in letters, newspaper accounts, and or history books.

Any quotes from newspapers are from clippings found in my great grandfather's scrapbook or obtained from researchers with whom I corresponded in Texas.

The names of preachers in Galveston are genuine, as is that of the Methodist minister in Lavaca who lost his life to yellow fever. J. D. Braman & Co. was the owner of the warehouse in Lavaca; however I made up the name, Oswald, for its agent. All other characters are fictitious and any semblance to actual people is purely coincidental.

During the two weeks that John collected taxes along the Trinity River, he kept a small note book, making observances as he went. I used several of his descriptions in that particular chapter of the book.

The letters to John written by the American Missionary Association personnel and those of the Freedmen's Bureau, plus other documents including Anna Keen's letters that I held in my possession I donated to the archives of the Rosenberg Library in Galveston, Texas, May, 2010.

About the Author: Flora Beach Burlingame

Flora Beach Burlingame was born in Palo Alto, California, but moved to Washington State as a teen. Her love of history was inherited from her father who delighted in sharing his historical knowledge with her.

She later attended Washington State College (now WSU) where she met and married her husband. They relocated to Southern California and three children later, she obtained a degree in Legal Assisting from Pasadena City College and studied Journalism at California State at Los Angeles.

When her husband retired, they moved to the Central California Foothills where Flora pursued her lifelong dream of writing.

She was commissioned by *The Fresno Bee*, a major California newspaper, to write a hundred years of history on three counties for a Centennial edition, and was a contributing editor for the quarterly newsletter of the Museum and History Center in the historic gold rush town of Mariposa, California. In addition, she wrote features and a regular column for the foothill section of the *Fresno Bee*.

In June, 2011, National Public Radio's Central California Valley station featured *Charcoal and Chalk* during their program *Valley Writers Read*, which received wide acclaim.

Flora is a member of the Texas State Historical Association and the South Texas State Historical Association. After completing *Charcoal and Chalk*, she donated the original letters and documents of John Ogilvie Stevenson to the Rosenberg Research Library in Galveston, Texas.

Bibliography

Personal Papers and References:

Original letters and documents from the American Missionary Association to John Ogilvie Stevenson: 1867 to 1873 (John O. Stevenson papers, Rosenberg Library Galveston, Texas)

Original letters received by American Missionary Association from John Ogilvie Stevenson: 1867 to 1873 (Amistad Research Library)

Original letters and documents from The Bureau of Refugees, Freedmen, and Abandoned Lands to John Ogilvie Stevenson: 1867 – 1870 (John O. Stevenson papers, Rosenberg Library, Galveston, Texas)

Original letters from George W. Ware and Samuel Canfield (John O. Stevenson papers, Rosenberg Library, Galveston, Texas)

Stories written by the Reverend John Ogilvie Stevenson (Stevenson Family documents in possession of Author)

Editorials by the Reverend John Ogilvie Stevenson *Waterloo Courier*, Waterloo, Iowa (Yale Divinity School Library, New Haven, Connecticut)

Sermons by the Reverend John Ogilvie Stevenson (Yale Divinity School Library, Record Group No. 30, New Haven, Connecticut)

Letters from Anna Keen to her parents (John O. Stevenson papers, Rosenberg Library, Galveston, Texas. Also, Stevenson family documents in possession of Author)

Keen and Stevenson Family Bibles (Stevenson family documents in possession of Author)

Notes of Sarah Barnes in Barnes Institute file at Rosenberg Library, Galveston, Texas

National Archives 105.3.9 Microfilm publications: M803

Letters and email messages from James W. Hosking, great grandson of Sarah Barnes

Books:

Time of Hope, Time of Despair, by James E. Smallwood

The Freedmen's Bureau and Black Texans by Barry A. Crouch

Overreached on All Sides, The Freedmen's Bureau Administrators in Texas, 1865-1868 by William L. Richter

Christian Reconstruction, The American Missionary Association and Southern Blacks, 1861-1890, by Joe M. Richardson

Texas after the Civil War, The Struggle of Reconstruction, by Carl H. Moneyhon

Yankee Stepfather General O.O. Howard and the Freedmen, by William S. McFeely

Indianola, The Mother of Western Texas, by Brownson Malsch

Indianola and Matagorda Island 1937-1887 by Linda Wolff

All the Days of My Life, by Amelia E. Barr

Galveston, a Different Place, a History & Guide, by Virginia Eisenhour

Galveston, A History, by David G. McComb

Galveston, A History of the Island, by Gary Cartwright

The Galveston That Was, by Howard Barnstone, photographs by Henri Cartier-Bresson and Ezra Stoller

Slaves Without Masters by Ira Berlin

Days of Jublilee, the End of Slavery in the United States, by Patricia C & Frederick L. McKissack

To Be A Slave by Julius Lester

Go Down Moses, Celebrating the African-American Spiritual by Richard Newman

History of American Congregationalism by Atkins and Fagley

White Terror, The Ku Klux Klan Conspiracy and Southern Reconstruction by Allen W. Trelease

Flora Beach Burlingame

The Souls of Black Folk, by W.E.B. DuBois

Been in the Storm so Long, The Aftermath of Slavery by Leon Litwack

Reading, 'Riting, and Reconstruction, by Robert C. Morris

Narrative of the Life of Frederick Douglass, an American Slave, Written by Himself

Everyday Life in the 1880s by March McClutcheon

Chicago, a Pictorial History, by Herman Kogan and Lloyd Wendt, Bonanza Books, New York

Others:

Winning the race: education of Texas freedmen immediately after the civil war, a Thesis –University of Houston, 2003, by Barbara J. Hayward

The Freedmen's Bureau Schools in Texas, 1865-1870, Alton Hornsby, *Southwestern Historical Quarterly 76 (April 1973): 414*

Historical Sketch of Dodge County, Minnesota by W. J. Mitchell and U. Curtis

Dodge County Historical Society, photocopies and information regarding Rice Lake, Minnesota

Handbook of Texas Online

Indianola Bulletin

Flakes Bulletin—Galveston, various dates 1870-1872

Galveston Daily News, various dates 1870-1872

Early Maps of Texas CD

Migration and the Migratory Birds of Texas, By Clifford E. Shackelford, Edward R. Rozenburg, W. Chuck Hunter and Mark W. Lockwood

**If you enjoy
Great stories about the
History of Texas You'll love...**

The TexasNavy
By Alex Dienst

A Cactus Navy?

Everyone has heard of the *USS Constitution* and the *USS Constelle tion*. They were among the first ships commissioned into the United States Navy. But fewer have ever heard of the *Liberty* and the *Invinci* They were the first two ships commissioned into the Navy of the Repu lic of Texas.

Between 1835 and 1845 the Republic of Texas had their own fleet. between court martialing each other, suppressing mutinies, legalizing piracy and getting stone drunk in New Orleans, they found the time to soundly beat the British- and Spanish-trained Mexican navy.

In 1906, Alex Dienst made an exhaustive study of the Texas Navy. I ing original source documents and newspaper accounts of the day— now, in many cases, long lost—he put together this intriguing book.

It's a little known story of chaos and confusion, mixed with unparalle heroism; and it deserves to be told again.

**A fascinating and neglected part of our
nation's nautical history.**

WWW.FIRESHIPPRESS.COM

All Fireship Press books are available
directly through www.FireshipPress.com, Amazon.com
and via leading wholesalers and bookstores throughout
the U.S., Canada, Europe, and Australia.

Lone Star Rising
Voyage of the Wasp

by

Jason Vail

Beware the Wasp!

For fans of Alternative History, *Lone Star Rising* is essential reading. Jason Vail joins the company of   Robert Conroy, Harry Turtledove, and Eric Flint.

George Washington is dead. The American rebellion has failed. The few surviving revolutionaries, lead by Andrew Jackson, have fled to Spanish territories and the wasteland called Texas.

But Jackson is not content to be a Spanish subject. He dreams large. Texas must be free and independent from the corrupt old empires of Europe. But with no army other than the Texas Rangers, and no navy, Texas has no hope of opposing the mighty forces of Spain.

No hope, that is, until David Crockett meets an unemployed, sardonic naval officer named John Paul Jones II on the wharves at Baltimore.

Together they buy and refit a broken down warship to become the first ship of the Texas Navy.

With a handful of Crockett's men, the blessing of a witch, and a dubious crew of French pirates, they set sail to seize Spanish treasure and remake history in a ship called ... TS *Wasp*.

Fireship Press
www.FireshipPress.com

Sales@ Fireshippress.com
Found in all leading Booksellers and on line
eBook distributers

**For the Finest in
Nautical and Historical
Fiction and Nonfiction**

WWW.FIRESHIPPRESS.COM

Interesting • Informative • Authoritative

All Fireship Press books are now available
directly through www.FireshipPress.com, Amazon.com
and via leading bookstores and wholesalers from coast-to-coast